KILL THE KING

A KNIGHT'S REVENGE ~ BOOK 3

ELIZABETH DEAR

Copyright © 2023 by Elizabeth Dear Publishing LLC

Editing by McKinley & Jamee at Hot Tree Editing

Cover by Cherie Foxley

Formatting by Elizabeth Dear and Stephanie Osu, PA

All Rights Reserved.

No Part of this book may be reproduced in any form or by any electronic or mechanical means, including information storage and retrieval systems, without written permission from the author, except for brief quotations in a book review.

To Sarah. Thanks for joining me on this crazy journey and not thinking I'm an absolute weirdo. Your support means so much.

SYNOPSIS

In Saint Gabriel City, the rule of the Four Families ends *now*.

They're bottom-feeding criminals pretending to be the model of the American dream.

They suck the City dry to serve themselves and the elite class that licks their boots day in and day out.

They murdered my parents out of sheer, unbridled greed.

And now, they've dared to take Zach from me.

With my boys, my family, and the Shadows by my side, I'll finish this fight. No more dancing around the corporate boardroom—we've come to destroy the Families, and we'll give it everything we've got.

And we'll continue to run the halls of Holywell Academy while we do it.

Peter Hargraves, Andrea Ferrero, and James Spencer—I'm fucking coming for you, and your sons will be by my side to the bitter end.

*This is a New Adult, college-age dark academy romance. It is the third and final book in the trilogy and ends with a HEA. It is also a Why Choose romance, which means our heroine has multiple love interests, and she will not have to choose between them. As always, this series is for readers age **18+** and contains a ton of foul language, <u>very</u> steamy scenes, and violent themes. If you've read Storm the Gates (A Knight's Revenge Book 1) and Seize the Castle (A Knight's Revenge Book 2) and want to see how Jolie and the boys get to their happy ending, jump in!*

A NOTE FROM THE AUTHOR

Hey team! Nothing new to report here. If you've read Storm the Gates (Book 1) and Seize the Castle (Book 2), you're in the right place.

Same content warnings apply as the previous books—gun violence, murder, mayhem, and some gore. There is a brief depiction of an *attempted* sexual assault of a side character. We also have spicy group sex stuff (!!), and many, many uses of the F-bomb and other swears.

We're doing it, guys. We're taking down the Families and riding off into the sunset. A little pain, a lot of love, and a big dose of adventure lie between us and our happily ever after.

Thanks for coming on this journey with me, Jolie, and her boys.

- *Elizabeth*

PS: I know I haven't given you guys a new playlist since Book 1, but if you need an emo theme song for this one, just throw on "A Love Like War" by All Time Low on repeat.

PROLOGUE
ZACH - AGE 12

I wasn't sure how long I'd been in the basement of Ferrero Tower, but it felt like several days had passed.

I ran my gaze around the dull cement walls of my surroundings for the millionth time since I'd been shoved into this little room. I hadn't known Ferrero Tower had a dungeon in its basement, but I wasn't surprised.

I was learning a whole lot of terrible stuff about my Family since I'd been forced to watch my mom commit murder while my best friend lay bleeding and dying on the floor in front of us.

With nothing else to do but wait, I counted the cracks in the wall again and then the metal bars of the door. I was bored, but being bored was better than being beaten. I was sure Ramon and his Enforcer buddies had run off to tell my mom I hadn't learned my lesson yet, but they would definitely be back.

Or maybe they were still pissed I'd bitten Rogers' finger off, but screw that guy. He'd deserved it for letting a twelve-year-old kid get the drop on him.

Probably because I'd been thinking about my visitors

right then, the clank of the lock sounded, and the hinges creaked as the door began to open, announcing the arrival of whomever had come down here to torment me now.

Expecting Ramon or his team of assholes, I got a little jolt of surprise as my mom waltzed through the door, her shiny black high heels clacking loudly against the smooth, bare floor.

"Oh, my sweet baby," she said with a little scandalized gasp. She hustled over to where I sat on the floor, my back propped against the cold wall because I'd refused to take even a little comfort in that joke of a cot they kept in here. "What have they done to you, Zachary?"

"What you ordered them to do, Mom," I said dully.

She crouched in front of me, the slit in her skirt only just allowing her the movement. I gave her a blank stare as she caressed my face, taking in my puffy, swollen eye and the cut on my forehead. My face throbbed, my body ached, and I was pretty sure I had a cracked rib. I hurt, and I was pissed, but nothing they'd done to me was serious or life-threatening.

Nothing that would permanently scar the beloved Ferrero Heir.

Not physically, anyway.

"Baby, you know I don't want any of this," she cooed at me, forcing a concerned look onto her pale, flawless face. "But we have rules in this Family, first and foremost of which is that my commands are to be followed without question. I only want what's best for you. For *us*, Zachary."

"Sure, Mom."

She stroked my shaggy, dark hair, greasy from sweat and going a few days without a shower—not that skipping a shower was unusual for me. I smelled ripe, and I hoped my mom was really offended by my stench.

"Now, I think it's time for this nonsense to end," she said, standing up. "I've taken the liberty of confiscating all of your possessions from the Knight girl. The pictures on your cell phone have been deleted as well."

Despair consumed me. I shut my eyes and threw my head back against the wall.

That was all I had left of her.

Mom went on, unmoved by my distress. "The Knights were traitors, Zachary. You need to accept this now and purge them from your life. You will not hang onto any childish fantasies that pretend otherwise. That is why I had Ramon's team search your room. It is not okay for you to stab my Enforcers in the leg with kitchen knives when they are carrying out my orders."

I said nothing.

She reached for my wrist and jerked me to standing. I let her because I didn't care anymore.

"Let's go home," she said, her voice light and breezy like she'd suggested we go get ice cream. "I know you'll be a good boy for me from now on, won't you?"

Fat chance.

I'd have to try harder not to get caught, though.

"Yes, Mom."

"That's my baby! I know you'll always do what's best for our Family in the end. That's how I raised you, after all."

She clutched my arm as I limped out of my little cell, following her through the bowels of the basement and to the elevator.

My mom could have her Enforcers smack me around all she wanted. I was never going to forget my best friend. I was never, *ever* going to call her a traitor.

And I was never going to be Mom's perfect little soldier.

I'd play the part, but I looked after myself, Bennett, and Noah now.

Screw Ferrero. Screw the Families.

They broke my *real* family, and someday, they would face the consequences.

CHAPTER ONE
ZACH - PRESENT DAY

Ramon's hard, emotionless face took up my entire field of vision as he knelt in front of me. To anyone who didn't know him, he looked as blank as he always did when he worked—directing Ferrero Enforcers, hovering around my mom, carrying out orders—but I could make out the excited glint in his eyes.

He fucking loved giving me what he thought I deserved, and he hadn't been given this chance in years.

"Your mother has done nothing but give you everything you could have ever wanted, and this is how you repay her?"

I spat a wad of bloody saliva in his face, and he buried his fist in my gut. "You ungrateful little shit."

I coughed. It hurt, but honestly, I'd had worse. Max Miller had hit me harder, and I'd enjoyed that shit. Ramon was getting soft in his old age.

"Is that the best you've got, motherfucker?" I rasped. "My girlfriend can throw a better punch than that. You better get it all out now, because I'm going to break every bone in your fucking body before this is over."

He scoffed at me before standing to launch a hard kick to my side, and I coughed again as I bit off a groan. He spat, "You'll be lucky if your mother lets you out of Ferrero Tower after this, boy. I suggest you think long and hard about how you're going to grovel for her forgiveness."

I snorted out a laugh. Mom was still delusional after all these years.

She still thought these tricks could break me. That they could keep me in line and force my loyalty to Ferrero.

That I didn't have any power beyond what she allowed me to have.

I tracked Ramon's path back to the middle of the empty warehouse where I was being held under the watchful eyes of at least ten Ferrero Enforcers. They'd smartened up over the years, apparently, because they'd locked my arms securely behind my back with good old-fashioned chains since I'd long ago learned to break zip ties. The chains looped around my wrists, securing me to the cold metal pole I'd been reclining against for the past twenty-four hours or so.

I'd also gotten a bit better at figuring out how much time had passed during these little episodes, tracking the comings and goings of what was left of Ferrero's highest-level Enforcers as they'd entered and exited in shifts during my confinement.

So far only Ramon had the privilege of beating on me. I guessed he was pretty pissed that I'd killed five of the eight guys Mom had sent after me before they'd managed to take me.

Ramon approached again, kneeling to offer me a drink from a new bottle of water. They'd also allowed me a few energy bars during my stay, and I'd eaten them. I was no longer the dumb kid who threw a tantrum and went on a hunger strike when I was being punished like this.

I needed my strength because I was going to end everyone in this fucking room for making my Princess worry.

And I knew when I didn't show up to her bed last night or answer any calls today, she was going to go off. My baby girl loved me, even if we hadn't said those words yet, and she was not to be fucked with when she was angry.

"If you think your little girlfriend is going to come save your ass," Ramon said, yanking the water bottle from my lips after I'd drunk half of it, "I have bad news for you. We have a small army set up on the bridge. No one's getting through."

That confirmed what I'd suspected—I was in some nondescript, off-the-books warehouse in Industrial City. I'd been in and out of almost every Ferrero cell and torture space over the years, and I knew this wasn't one of our properties in the City. Instead, we were in the rundown, uninhabited area to the east of the river, made up mostly of shipping containers and dilapidated warehouses. It was accessible from the City by a single narrow bridge or by the occasional container ship that parked at the docks to the north.

I hadn't known that Ferrero held any property over here, but I knew for a fact that Hargraves had storage facilities somewhere in Industrial City where it kept some of its less-than-legal *medicinal* products.

I eyed Ramon, giving him my most unaffected stare. "Tell Mom she's really fucked up this time. I'm not a kid anymore—she can't have you beat loyalty into me. And if one hair is harmed on my girl's head because of this stupidity, I will burn Ferrero Tower to the fucking ground with all of you in it."

Ramon shook his head like he was my disappointed dad. "She'll be so ashamed. You can kiss all the freedom she's so graciously given you all these years goodbye."

I snorted. *Freedom—is that what we're calling it?*

"Let me have a shot at him, boss!" Anderson yelled from the group guarding the entrance. "He killed our fucking team lead."

I sent a savage grin in his direction. "He washed out, Anderson. If you let your mark steal your gun and get your head blown off in an eight-versus-one fight, then you clearly can't hack it as a Ferrero Enforcer."

Ramon slammed a fist into my side. "Shut the fuck up. I've had enough of your mouth and your attitude to last a hundred goddamn years."

I stifled a pained groan. He'd already nailed me on that side once, and if I didn't already have a broken rib, I probably did now.

As Ramon stalked off again, I felt the chill of the night seep into the stark warehouse floor. I was thankful I'd managed to get my long-sleeved T-shirt and sweatpants onto my body after my shower and before Ramon's team of assholes had burst into my room in our penthouse, but I definitely wasn't wearing shoes. I was not looking forward to another sleepless night chained to this fucking pole with icy feet and a numb ass.

I'd only dropped by the tower in the first place to appease my mom, deciding to swing by for a brief visit when she'd summoned me during my evening workout. I grabbed a shower in my room before I was supposed to meet her in her home office, intent on also packing a bag with the few things I had left in my room that meant anything to me in case it was the last time I returned there.

I'd barely pulled my pants on when I was ambushed, and I fucked up by not putting my Rolex back on my wrist first thing. It, along with the internal panic button the three of us all had hidden in our watches, sat uselessly on my nightstand, right next to my fucking gun, so I had to improvise.

They won, and I lost, but five Ferrero Enforcers had to die before they managed to knock me out and drag me all the way out here.

And while my Princess will have missed me at bedtime, it was a stroke of luck that Frankie would have missed me even earlier—we'd been set to have a drink together in a basement dive bar near the Academy about an hour after I was nabbed.

If anyone could possibly be more hacked off about me disappearing without a word than my brothers or my girlfriend, it would be Frankie.

One of them would hunt us down eventually, and I could only hope it would be before my mom ordered me moved to another location or Ramon slipped and inflicted more lasting damage than usual.

Just as I was steeling myself for another cold, uncomfortable night, the heavy door slid open, and the telltale click-clack of high heels announced the inevitable.

My mom had arrived.

Without a word, she stalked through the team guarding me, her long wool coat swaying as she moved. She pushed her oversized sunglasses to the top of her head, revealing her cold, dark gaze as she took in my battered form sprawled on the floor and chained to a pole. She frowned, as if seeing the violence she wrought up close and personal was surprising to her. Then she pulled her two-thousand-dollar scarf tighter around her neck, like she was bracing against the cold that she no doubt found reflected back at her in my stare.

"Oh, Zachary."

She knelt in front of me, stretching her tight skirt to its limit, and she reached up to caress the side of my face. Fortunately, I still had use of both of my eyes, but I had a gash in the side of my head, and the blood that had oozed from it was now dried on the side of my face and my neck.

"Mom," I said, smiling like my usual charming self. "Come to join the party? We haven't done this in a while—I was starting to think you were getting soft."

Her concerned frown morphed into the anger I was certain she really felt. "I see you're not taking this seriously. I shouldn't be surprised—these little *corrections* never did seem to make a permanent impact on you."

"Wouldn't be in the best interest of Ferrero to permanently scar this pretty face, Mom," I quipped, still forcing a smile through the throbbing pain in my ribs.

She pulled her hand from my cheek and stood up to peer down at me with her nose in the air. "Do you know why you're here, Zachary?"

I let my shitty smile fall away, a blank look then settling over my face. "Because Jolie Knight got one over on you, and you're taking it out on me."

She began to pace in front of me, the loud clicking of her heels against the cold cement floor grating on my ears. "No, baby. You're here because I suspect you've actually *fallen* for that little tramp. And that calls your loyalty to our Family into serious question, because by the end of this little fight she's started, she will be dead, and Ferrero will have everything she stole from us and then some." She paused to look down at me. "And it would just *gut* me, Zachary, if you were standing in my way."

"It *would* be pretty inconvenient for you to have to find a new Heir."

She rolled her eyes at me before resuming her pacing. "I gave you and your little friends access to the most coveted, beautiful women in the City who were at your beck and call any time of the day or night, and still you let yourself be pulled away from your own Family by that girl. Why? Because you have some fond childhood memories?"

I glared at her. "Because she belongs with us. Whatever bullshit reason you and the others concocted for murdering the Knights didn't change that."

"She's trying to destroy us, Zachary," she snapped. "What we did that night, we did for the Families. I did it for Ferrero. For *you*."

I barked out a laugh. "Sure, Mom. Just like you have your bodyguard beat on me for *me*."

She sighed, that look of faux concern back on her plastic face. "I'd always assumed you had more of me in you, Zachary, despite the fact that you look just like your poor father. But maybe I was wrong. He always was just a beautiful idiot."

I scowled, feeling protective of my dad even though I had only vague memories of him. He'd died in his sleep of a brain aneurysm when I was five, but I did remember him as a happier, blonder version of me. In hindsight, I had no idea what the fuck he saw in my mom besides what was in her bank account.

"So," Mom continued, "I think I'll leave you here with Ramon and his team a little longer, baby. I need you to really think about what's important to this Family."

I didn't need to look across the room to know that

Ramon would be giving me his version of an evil smile, which was just slightly less of a grimace than he normally wore.

"And," she went on, "once Ramon is satisfied with your... course of treatment, you'll be coming home with me. I'm certain the Academy will allow you to finish the semester via correspondence, and that will allow me to keep a *close* eye on you until I'm confident you've chosen the right path." She knelt in front of me one last time, her dark eyes boring into mine with the vicious ferocity she normally directed at everyone but me. "And that will also give us time to put that obnoxious little Knight skank in an unmarked grave next to her parents. I suspect that once she's removed from the board, you'll remember who you are, Zachary."

I tried to smother the shiver that wracked my body. I knew Jojo was ready for her war with the Families to turn violent, but it didn't stop the brutal wave of panic and despair at the thought of losing her again.

Through that terror, I forced one last smile for my mother. "Game on, Mom. I can't wait until you realize just how badly you've fucked up."

She shook her head, standing once again and turning on her heel. She stalked back across the room, motioning to Ramon as she approached the door.

"Fix this," she barked, and then she was gone with a loud slam of the door behind her.

Ramon watched her go, like the sick, devoted puppy he was, before he returned his dead eyes to me.

He advanced, and I braced myself for a long night.

CHAPTER TWO
NOAH

I stood on the dock of the Boathouse, a rowing club in Olde Town and apparently the place where our Jojo had been fished from the Obsidian River on the worst night of our lives. Bennett and I looked on as a horde of men and women dressed in black and armed to the hilt swarmed the dock, each of them focused on their assigned task of preparing our boats to cross the river and land on the shores of Industrial City.

"Seriously, Martinez?" Bennett snapped at a familiar man who skirted by us, carrying what appeared to be a flamethrower. "Was being my personal guard so terrible?"

Martinez grinned at Bennett. "It wasn't, actually, but you know my time with Spencer was also spent doing other things I found a lot less... palatable. The mission of the Shadows is more in line with my values." He winked at us both as he sauntered away, tossing the flamethrower into one of the boats.

"Unbelievable," Bennett muttered. "I'd thought he *died*."

"Yeah," I said lamely. I remembered how bummed fourteen-year-old Bennett had been when his favorite bodyguard disappeared, and twenty-year-old Bennett was not impressed to find him here, very much alive and apparently part of a secret resistance organization that had been lurking in the City all these years, lying in wait for the right time to move against the Families. "Kara's over there," I added, motioning toward the Boathouse's doorway. "Remember she was my mom's guard before Mom bailed on us?"

Bennett just grunted as he eyed the still-very-buff woman in her forties where she was engaged in a serious conversation with Dom, our de facto leader for this little raid to extract the wayward Ferrero Heir.

Our heads snapped to the other side of the dock as Jolie emerged from around the side of the building. She still wore the emotionless mask that had descended over her face the second Frankie had reported Zach's disappearance. She'd shut down immediately, becoming singularly focused on saving Zach while shoving aside all the soul-shattering shit that she'd just gone through at the hands of her uncle.

She'd pulled the trigger on something called "Phase Three," and Bennett and I were now getting a crash course on the true extent of the power behind our girl.

"I don't know if I'm more worried about Zach or Jojo," I said, adjusting my weapons belt. "I know Andrea won't have Zach hurt in any life-threatening way, but that doesn't mean he's not suffering. And Jojo is... not taking this well."

"Recall she made an entire Tier One company disappear and had the CEO put in prison because I came to school with a shiner," Bennett said as his consuming gaze followed her every move. I hadn't thought the way he looked at her could get more obsessive, but now that they'd had sex and apparently also swapped *the L-word*—because

Bennett didn't do anything half-assed, the bastard—his intensity when it came to Jolie was at an entirely new level. "I'm surprised Ferrero Tower is still standing, honestly."

A gruff voice sounded behind us. "You boys all caught up yet?"

The owner of the Boathouse, an older guy named Bruce who was sporting a gray ponytail, white stubble, and track pants from the eighties, stepped up beside us. He glanced in Jojo's direction with a knowing grimace before turning his attention back to us. "She'll snap out of it eventually. I was worried, but when she looks at you two, she does soften up a bit. She's still in there."

"She's been through a lot in the past twenty-four hours," I replied. "It's understandable."

"She's a survivor," he agreed. "I knew it the moment I pulled her from the water all those years ago."

Bennett and I both jerked our heads in his direction. "You're the one that found her?" Bennett asked.

"Who else? I own the place."

"And you handed her over to this... Shadows organization, trusting they'd do right by her?" I asked. I shuddered to think of all the ways that night could have gone even *more* wrong.

He grunted in irritation. "I took her to Dominic, trusting *he* would do right by her. Her later involvement with the Shadows was her decision."

I watched as Jolie and Max stood huddled together on one of the boats, both of them muttering into the speaker of Jolie's phone, probably talking to Zepp. I knew I'd get my update from Silver, as she was now squarely in Zepp's business and enjoying poking at him on a regular basis.

Bennett looked at Bruce again. "So, the Shadows are a secret army of people who have a problem with the Families? People who've defected or otherwise been harmed by us?" He paused, swallowing hard. "*Them*. Harmed by them."

"Yes," Bruce replied. "It's a network of those in the City actively opposed to the rule of the Four Families. Every member has their own personal reasons for joining. There are certainly many who have a history of working within the Families."

Bennett pondered this for two seconds before stating what we were both thinking. "There are Shadows undercover within the Families today."

Bruce cracked an amused smile. "Yep."

"Damn," I said. Our parents had *no* fucking clue this existed right under their noses.

Bruce went on. "Some of us have had loved ones get on the wrong side of the Families. Many have had an injustice done to them personally. We have people from all walks of life with all kinds of skills, from the hackers and the muscle you see here, right down to the kitchen worker at the Euphoria Club who left the door open for your girl one night last fall."

We both tensed at the reminder of what *Joanna Miller* had been up to last semester—the *danger* she'd put herself in—before I dared to ask Bruce the obvious question. "What pushed you to join?"

He was quiet for a beat. "My wife passed away ten years ago of a cancer that would have been treatable had she been allowed into the program at City Center Hospital. But we didn't have the right last name or the funds."

A Hargraves hospital. Shame curdled in my gut, and I vowed to fix it.

"And now that you—*we* have Jolie's fortune," Bennett

said, swiftly changing the subject, "the Shadows have decided to come out into the open?"

"Yes, though we became a pretty well-funded organization about fifteen years ago when we had some... people of means join up," Bruce replied. "But things have moved quickly over the past few years. What happened to Jolie was a rallying cry—not even the innocent children of the Families were safe in this City, for Christ's sake."

"And her mission to avenge her parents and destroy the Families aligns with the reason for the Shadows' existence," I finished.

"Indeed." He motioned to the flurry of activity on the dock. "And here we are, throwing some of our best men and women into a battle with Ferrero to rescue the Ferrero Heir because Jojo loves him."

Bennett bristled. "And because he's a valuable asset to the organization."

"And that, sure," he replied, chuckling.

All three of us watched as Jolie abandoned her position in her boat and made her way toward us. She was dressed in the same black tactical gear we were all wearing, and I took a moment to appreciate how sexy my girl looked in cargo pants.

She came to a stop next to us and gave Bruce a squinty-eyed stare. "Is that a crossbow?"

Bruce nodded, motioning to the weapon he had strapped to his back. "Did you think I only knew how to bark orders at middle schoolers learning to row?"

She almost cracked a smile at that. "Pretty much, yeah."

"Angel," Bennett said, using his new pet name for her that made even *my* insides gooey. "Are you doing okay?"

"I'm fine, Bennett," she said, and her hard expression relaxed just enough when she looked at him to appease us both. "We're going to get Zach back, and we're going to make anyone who's laid a hand on him pay with their life."

I reached for her, and she let me pull her into my side. I felt her sag against me, releasing a little bit of the tension she was carrying, and I pressed a kiss to her temple. Bennett moved in front of us, and he was bold enough to grasp her chin with his big hand, forcing her to look him in the eyes.

"We will get him back," he agreed before he took her mouth in a demanding kiss. He was the only one around here not treating her like she was a bomb about to go off. After a few seconds, he pulled back to stare her down again. "Do not do anything reckless tonight, or I'll have Noah put you over his knee."

She shivered, and I grinned. "Look at Spencer being a team player already," I whispered into her ear.

She let out a breathy sigh, then she snapped out of it and shook us off. "Focus, both of you. Have you heard anything else from Frankie?"

"No," I replied. "He's still got eyes on the team they have blocking the bridge, but he hasn't texted again since he reported Andrea crossing back into the City."

"That bitch is dead," she spat.

Maybe, but not tonight, it seemed. "Zach's used to this, sweetheart. He's tough and won't let her get to him."

"I don't give a fuck. No one touches him and gets to live."

Bennett and I exchanged a loaded look. Jolie in overprotective-beast-mode about one of us was such a turn on, but we had to lock it up until Zach was safe and we'd all had a nap.

The minute Frankie had informed us that Zach had gone missing, we'd thrown ourselves completely into finding him. Jolie, Bennett, and I had taken fifteen minutes to retrieve Jolie's belongings from the Knight penthouse —*her* penthouse now, truly and completely—showered, changed clothes, then spent the night camped twenty floors below in Silver's command center, coordinating with Zepp and the Shadows to scour the City for Zach's whereabouts.

Frankie had come through by ten o'clock this morning, having located the one Ferrero Enforcer who was in on the plans for Zach's kidnapping and not also either hidden at the location with Zach or dead on his bedroom floor in Ferrero Tower. Frankie had made quick work of that unfortunate soul, and an hour later, Silver and Zepp had identified a piece of property owned by a Ferrero shell in Industrial City.

The blockade of the bridge happened soon after, so we knew we'd found our target. And since there was a small army on the one car route into Industrial City, we would be going by sea.

Bennett's phone buzzed, and he ignored yet another call from his father. I'd ignored three from my own father since last night, both of them likely growing very annoyed that we'd disappeared from the Academy and were nowhere to be found in the City.

Fuck them. I was already done with my dad and the decaying corpse that was Hargraves, but after Bennett told me what he'd learned listening to Anders wax poetic about selling his own flesh and blood to the Families for power and money, and I'd given him the final piece of the puzzle— the world-changing contents of Jolie's dad's flash drive— we both knew it was really and truly over for us.

Fuck our parents. Fuck the Four Families. They'd pay for what they did to our girl and then lied to our faces about for seven goddamned years. If she wanted to slit their throats, I'd help her do it and then pop the champagne afterward.

A whistle sounded. "Yo, Nathan! Spencer! Load up—we're moving out."

I scowled at Max while Bennett had the audacity to snicker.

"Don't fucking encourage him," I griped as we followed Jolie and Bruce to our assigned boat.

Jolie smirked at me over her shoulder—a welcome sight. "Don't worry, Noah. He'll run out of *N* names eventually, then he'll have to get a new bit. I doubt he'll ever stop hitting on Bennett."

It was Bennett's turn to scowl as we climbed into the speedboat. Max barked out a laugh. "Fuck no. And since everyone's so good at sharing around here, Jojo will share Big Man with me, won't you?"

"In your dreams, Max," she replied, but that smile was threatening to break through her hard mask.

Max winked at us, and I decided I hated him slightly less.

"Everyone ready?" Dom called out. He and Kara had boarded one of the other four boats carrying our group of two dozen. "You all have your marching orders. In and out. Shoot to kill. Let's bring Zach home."

He cast a fond look over at Jolie, who returned it with a curt nod. She'd blanked again.

We fired up the boats, Bruce at the helm of ours, and we were off to save Zach before we lost him forever to the dark side of Ferrero.

CHAPTER THREE
JOLIE

As Bruce maneuvered our boat along the western shore of Industrial City, I pulled my balaclava over my face and tightened the straps of my helmet. The clock was ticking, and I'd have Zach in my arms again within the hour if everything went according to plan.

Zepp's voice sounded in our earpieces. "Our drone picked up twelve heat signatures at the target. Ten scattered around the front of the warehouse with at least six guarding the main door. There's one guard on the small back door, and our boy is likely being held back wall, center."

Fresh rage thrummed through my veins.

"Thanks, Zepp," Dom's voice responded. "Shadow Team, get ready to disembark. Boat drivers, prepare to head south after we unload."

There was no dock on the west bank of Industrial City, and Andrea had made sure the docks to the north under the bridge into the City were blocked by a large container ship idling on the water. So, we were doing a drive-by to unload before we trekked the half mile inland to our target.

Bennett appeared next to me. "Ready, Angel?" He pulled his own face covering up over his mouth and nose, his mossy green eyes scanning the shore with a focused intensity that settled something in my bones. "They're not prepared for this. The Families have no fucking idea who stands against them."

"Damn right," Noah said from my other side, slinging his sniper rifle onto his back.

"I'm ready," I replied. "I have a lot of anger to burn off right now."

"Strap in, lovebirds," Max called to us as he straddled the side of the boat. "It's go time."

And with that, we were off. The shoreline, shrouded in darkness under the cloudy night sky, blended right into the black waters of the river. As our boats skirted along the crumbling retaining wall, we hopped over the side one by one, taking care to land lightly in our heavy boots on the dusty gravel.

Dom signaled to me, and he peeled away with the larger group, headed to attack the warehouse from the front in the most distracting way possible.

"Be safe, sweetheart," Noah whispered to me, squeezing my hand before he melted into Dom's group.

As Team Shock and Awe disappeared through the narrow pathway leading into the first cluster of shipping containers near the shore, my little team snaked southeast, intent on attacking the inadequately guarded back of the building.

"Bennett, I'm leading," I griped as he strode ahead of me, his big body moving through the shadows like a slippery ghost.

"Nah, I like this better," Max said from behind me. "We can stare at that fantastic ass."

"Max, your eyes better be on your *surroundings*," I hissed over my shoulder.

Bennett remained silent, refusing to give up the lead, and the three of us wound our way through the rusty warehouses and crooked, flickering streetlamps until we'd worked our way inland and the shoreline disappeared from view.

Kara's hushed voice came through our earpieces. "Team Shock and Awe is in position."

"Team White Knight is fifty yards south of target, ready to approach," Bennett replied.

"*Bennett*," I snapped. "Stop doing my job."

"Shh, Angel," he murmured. "We're about to get Zach back."

I blew out a breath. Fuck yes, we were.

Max snickered from behind me. "That was too easy, Jojo."

"Shut up, Max."

We moved another twenty yards forward, and Zach's prison came into view. The warehouse was a large cube of faded brown brick, its few narrow windows dark and covered by steel bars. In the dim yellow light of the sidewalk lamp, we could just make out the drab green door that allowed entry to the back, our only obstacle a small, rusty padlock hanging above the brass doorknob.

Suddenly, an explosion sounded from the front. The loud clatter of someone ripping open the large rolling steel door of the main entrance followed, and then—

Chaos.

Shouting, rapid gun shots, the bright orange flare that lit up the sky—Martinez and his flamethrower at work—and that was our signal.

We rushed the back door, and Max made quick work of

the shitty padlock with one precise bullet. Bennett lifted his heavy-booted foot and kicked the door in, and within two seconds, the lone, confused guard was down, the victim of my semi-automatic pistol and my rage.

"Zach!" I shouted as I hurdled the Enforcer's body and ran for the center of the back wall.

He was there, splayed out on the cold floor, his back against a steel pole and his arms behind him, wrapped in fucking *chains*.

Bennett and Max covered me, firing shots toward the front of the warehouse where the few Enforcers who hadn't run outside into the commotion were engaged in a fight with Kara's team.

"Princess!" Zach's tired face lit up like Christmas morning as I sprinted his way. "You missed me."

"Shut up, you ridiculous, sexy asshole," I breathed as I fell to my knees in front of him. "Of course I missed you. Don't do this shit to me again." I ran my gloved hands all over his body, feeling for injuries. There was blood all over his fucking clothes and his face, and everyone in this goddamn warehouse was going to *die*.

"I'm okay, baby girl, I promise," he said. "Just see if you can get me out of these chains, yeah?"

Bennett had positioned himself in front of us, pistol held aloft, and he was firing the occasional shot into the fray in the front.

"Here!" Max yelled, pulling something from the pocket of one of the fallen Enforcers. He launched it at Bennett, who snatched it out of the air.

"Key," he said, turning to toss it my way.

"Fuck yes," I hissed as I caught it, then I scrambled around the back of the pole and jammed the key into the lock on the chains. It clicked, and the chains fell away from Zach's arms and pooled on the floor in front of me.

Zach was on his feet in an instant, looking no worse for wear as he bolted for the front of the warehouse.

"Zach!" I shouted, suddenly terrified. He wasn't wearing Kevlar like the rest of us—what the fuck was he thinking?

Bennett tossed him a gun, which Zach caught in one hand without so much as a glance at it as he streaked past Bennett, and I watched in equal parts awe and horror as he launched himself over the back of the metal table that had been flipped on its side—where a lone Enforcer had taken cover while continuing to fire shots at Kara and her team.

Just as one of those shots hit Kara in her shoulder, Zach tackled the Enforcer to the ground behind the table.

"Shit," Bennett swore as the sounds of struggle ensued. He pulled me to my feet, and we both dashed to the front of the huge room. The occasional popping of gunshots continued outside, though the shouting and general sounds of mayhem had abated.

Zach jumped up from behind the table, a second gun in hand and new bloody gash on his forehead. He tucked his extra pistol into his sweatpants—a model of gun safety—and aimed the other at his captive as he proceeded to drag him out from behind the table by his leg while wearing a feral smile.

Ramon.

"Inside is clear," Kara announced into our earpieces as she nursed her wounded shoulder, aided by a concerned Julie—her second-in-command and her wife.

"What did I say, Ramon?" Zach said as he dropped him in the middle of the floor, his gun still pointed at Ramon's head. "I told you that before this was over, I was going to break every bone in your body."

"You don't have the balls, boy," Ramon bit out through clenched teeth. He was clearly in pain, so Zach must have already done a number on him.

"You don't think so?" Zach asked lightly. He tossed a look over at Bennett and me. "Make sure he doesn't go anywhere."

We both drew our weapons and aimed them at Ramon while Zach padded on his bare feet to the corner of the warehouse. He proceeded to dig in a black duffle bag he found there.

"Aha!" he exclaimed, pulling a set of brass knuckles from the bag. "Did you think I didn't remember the times in the past when you'd gotten these babies out for my punishments, Ramon? You warned me we were about to take a trip down memory lane before you were so rudely interrupted by my Princess and her...." He cast a curious look around the warehouse at the few members of our Shadow team that weren't dealing with whatever was going on outside. "Personal commandos."

I glared at Ramon over the barrel of my gun. "You've tortured Zach before?"

Bennett gave my hand a comforting squeeze. "Andrea started punishing Zach this way right after they took you from us."

I squeezed the trigger, burying a bullet right in Ramon's kneecap. He screamed in pain, so I went ahead and shot the other knee out, too, because I liked the symmetry of it all.

"Oh fuck, baby girl," Zach cooed at me as he returned to my side to lord over Ramon as he convulsed on the floor. "That was hot, but you gotta leave some for me, okay?" He pulled me in for a lingering kiss to my forehead, and then he got to work.

After sliding the brass knuckles onto his right hand, Zach proceeded to brutally and painstakingly break as many bones in Ramon's body as possible while the rest of us looked on with both respect and grim satisfaction. After Zach finally ended it all with a clean shot to the head, I pulled him into my arms. He sagged against me, still breathing hard, and I vowed to never let him go again.

"I'm fine, Princess," he said, wrapping an arm around me and sandwiching me between his big body and Bennett's. "Just need a decent night's sleep, and I'll be good as new."

We'd just see about that, but before I could argue with Zach about the need for our doctor to go over him with a fine-tooth comb, the rest of our team finally began to stream through the open bay door.

"Outside is clear," Dom announced in our ears about ten seconds before he walked through the door. "We had a few of the runners get away, but they won't be showing their faces in the City again after that kind of cowardly shit."

Noah walked next to him, and he pulled his face covering down to reveal a wide smile. Dom, on the other hand, looked... pouty?

"What crawled up your ass?" I asked Dom as he came to a stop near us and cast a detached, clinical stare over what was left of Ramon.

He huffed. "I challenged Hargraves to a little competition, and I lost."

Noah pulled Zach into a bro hug before sliding in front of me to do his obligatory check over my whole body for injuries. I swatted him away, muttering about how I was a big girl and completely unharmed, *obviously*, and he just chuckled at me before he turned to Dom. "It was pretty even, Dom. The team took a few of your easy kills with that grenade. My side of the roof just had more bodies to choose from."

"Still," he griped, and I stifled a smile. My dad had gotten into a sniper competition with my boyfriend, and if that wasn't a good summation of the state of my life right now, I didn't know what was.

It was Bennett's turn to step in front of me where I stood, still clinging to Zach, and he pulled his balaclava down before tugging mine off as well. He wrapped his big hand gently around the back of my neck as he searched my face, those powerful green eyes threatening to pull me into a trance. "You back with us now, Angel?"

I sighed. "Yes. Despite our... current surroundings, I feel more at peace than I ever have now that I have all three of you with me again."

"Good," he rumbled before stealing a raw, possessive kiss from me. I moaned into his mouth, and I felt Zach suck in a startled breath next to me.

When Bennett pulled away, Zach was grinning from ear to ear. He motioned between the two of us. "Sooo, when did *this* happen?"

I shrugged. "After Bennett beat Anders to death with his bare hands for drugging and kidnapping me and also for selling my dad's priceless research to the Families who murdered my parents for it."

Zach was silent for a beat, his eyes bouncing between us, before he said, "I've missed some things."

"You've missed some things," Noah agreed.

I snuggled into Zach's side as I gave Bennett a dreamy smile. "We fucked and he also *L-worded* me."

Bennett returned my smile with a smug grin of his own while Zach pouted next to me. "Seriously, man? You're the world's most stubborn fucking asshole about her all this time, and suddenly you're jumping ahead of the rest of us with the *L-word*? Unreal. Fuck you."

"That's what I said," Noah told him, but they were both grinning—clearly as happy as I was that the four of us were a solid unit once again.

Zach's dark gaze snagged on something across the room. "Wait, is that... Martinez?" His narrow-eyed stare tracked Martinez's tall, muscular form as he breezed through the bay doors, tossed a salute our way, then moseyed over to check in with Kara.

"Another thing you missed," Bennett grumbled, sounding bitter. I'd known that Martinez had worked deep within the high levels of Spencer years ago, but I hadn't known until earlier tonight that he'd also been Bennett's bodyguard for a stint. "Our girlfriend is the leader of a powerful underground network of Family defectors. Keep up."

"I'm not sure I'd say I'm *the* leader—" I began, but then another of our team ambled by.

"Hey, boss lady," Rocky said to me before he looked at Zach. "Good to see you in one piece, Ferrero."

Zach gaped at him. "*Et tu*, Rocky?"

Rocky, who had been a head bouncer at the Club in his previous life, just shot Zach a saucy wink before joining the huddle with the rest of the team.

Zach shook his head. "He was one of the best guys we had at the Club before he up and disappeared two years ago. What an asshole."

I grinned sheepishly at all three of my boyfriends. "We

have collected some interesting people in the Shadows. But now that includes you guys, right?"

"Of course it does, sweetheart," Noah replied.

"In the what now?" Zach asked, confused.

Before I could launch into my explanation of who the fuck all these people were, the loud screeching of tires sounded outside the bay door.

Every single one of us drew our weapons as one of the armored SUVs that had been blocking the bridge from the City slid to a grinding halt right in front of the warehouse entrance. The driver's door opened, and Frankie hopped out.

"Aw, damn, did I miss all the fun?" he asked, unbothered that he had twenty guns pointed at him. He slammed the door, and a black-clad body that had apparently taken a ride on the hood of the vehicle slid to the ground with an unimpressive thud. He stuck out his lower lip and said with a dramatic whine, "You guys said I could play with the flamethrower."

He strolled inside, and even the most seasoned members of our team watched him warily. Frankie's ratty baby-pink tank top was soaked with blood, the spatter crawling up his neck and onto his face. He'd slung his AK-47 haphazardly across his back, and I didn't even want to know what other sharp objects he had strapped to his body.

The only person not gaping at him was Max, whose hungry gaze tracked Frankie's every movement as Frankie approached where I stood with my boys.

"Goddamn it," I swore under my breath. "I think Max fucked Frankie. Or if he hasn't, he definitely wants to."

Zach snorted. "In his dreams. Frankie doesn't fuck outside the Club, Princess."

I wasn't so sure about that, given that I'd just watched

Frankie's caramel eyes slide toward Max and then bounce away like he didn't want to get caught looking.

Ugh, Max.

"Nephew!" Frankie crowed as he neared us. "Glad to see you looking well and in the arms of your beloved." He stopped to examine Ramon. "Ah, I see someone got what was coming to him. Want me to have that delivered to my dear sister's doorstep?"

"Definitely," Zach replied. "Pin a note to his chest that says she should consider this my resignation from Ferrero."

"Done," Frankie said, grinning. "I should probably tender my resignation as well. I think I've burned all the bridges—literally and figuratively." He waggled his pierced eyebrows, then he looked at me. "Got a place for me in the Shadows, Little Knight?"

The hum of shocked whispers and muttering sounded around us. The infamous Frankie Fingers wanted to join the Shadows?

And I wasn't even going to ask how he'd known what the Shadows were in the first place.

"Um, fuck yes, we do," I replied. "And at Knight, if you want it."

He beamed at me before performing a little bow. "I am at your service, my lady."

"Alright, team," Dom called out, waking everyone from their slack-jawed stupor at watching Frankie Fingers swear fealty to the Knight Heir. "Clear out. Martinez is going to torch the place. We meet the boats in ten."

"Fuck, I need a nap," Zach moaned. "And... some shoes."

We'd get him both of those things, and I'd make sure he didn't leave my side for the rest of the night.

CHAPTER FOUR
JOLIE

I woke the next morning in my bunk at home, my entire body pressed against Zach as if I'd tried to crawl inside his skin while we slept. I'd buried my face in the soft sleep shirt he'd borrowed from Max, and he smelled like my shampoo, awakening that possessive animal in me as I breathed him in.

She was content and very smug this morning.

Muffled voices outside the bedroom door told me that the others were awake and puttering around our little kitchen/living room. Noah had slept on the couch and Bennett on an air mattress next to him, the latter having not-so-politely declined Max's offer to snuggle in his bunk below mine.

"Morning, baby girl," Zach rasped, arching against me with a languid stretch. "Sleep okay?"

"Yes," I muttered into his chest. "After our doctor assured me you would live."

Zach had staples in his head, a broken rib, and a few other swollen body parts, and he'd promised me it was nothing he hadn't dealt with on a regular basis, given how much time he spent using his fists in the cage.

"Don't worry about me, please, Jojo," he whispered into my hair. "All things considered, I think you've had a much worse past forty-eight hours than I have."

Zach had received the full debrief as we all ate Chinese takeout around our little kitchen table late last night, so he was now up to speed on my traitorous uncle, my dad's research, and the lurking, silent monster that was the Shadows.

"I don't know," I mused, pulling my face from his T-shirt and looking into those gorgeous dark eyes. "Anders died a brutal, painful death for what he did. I have the answers I've been seeking for seven and a half years. I have all three of you back with me. Max, Dom, and Laura are safe and healthy. And the notorious Frankie Fingers is now a Shadow and full-fledged member of Knight." I raised my brows, giving him a little grin. "Things are actually looking pretty great for me."

He returned my smile, dipping in for a kiss that quickly turned filthy. I moaned against his lips, and I felt him harden against my stomach. "Let me have you, baby girl," he whispered against my lips, his deep rasp turning urgent. "I need you."

"Zach," I moaned. "My *family* is outside the door."

"I can be quiet," he replied with a sexy grin. "Can you?"

I fell into that hungry stare, and I could only nod. He made quick work of my sleep shorts, inching them down my thighs just enough for me to pull one leg out, and I tossed that leg over his trim hips as he pulled his dick from his pajama pants and slid home.

I whimpered as he buried his groan in my neck, and he

began to move inside me, slow and steady, while he dipped his hand between us, a rough finger finding my clit. He brought me quickly to a toe-curling climax, and he smothered my pained whine with a hungry kiss. He came with me, and afterward we held each other again for a few quiet, blissful minutes.

"You know I'm in love with you, Princess?" he murmured in my ear.

I sucked in a breath. "Yeah?"

"Of course I am." He righted my shorts and ran his fingers through my messy hair before pulling away just enough to stare into my eyes. "First, I loved you the way a twelve-year-old loves his best friend. Then I loved you as I mourned you, our lost angel. And now? I've never met such an incredible, sexy, *powerful* woman, and the fact that this woman is *my* Jojo? I was a goner from day one, baby girl. I'm so fucking in love with you, it's not even funny."

A tear leaked from my eye, because apparently Bennett had broken the dam, and I was a crier now. "I love you too," I whispered. "Always have, always will."

"That's good, Princess," he replied with a blinding smile. "Because you're never getting rid of me."

Just as he rolled me onto my back and climbed on top of me, someone pounded on the bedroom door.

"Keep it in your pants, Ferrero!" Max barked through the closed door. "Breakfast is almost ready, and then we all have shit to do."

"Ugh," Zach groaned, rolling off me. "Sounds like he needs me to kick his ass again."

I smacked a quick kiss against his lips, then I shimmied down the little ladder attached to the bunks. When I hit the floor, I peered up at where Zach flopped over the edge of the bed, watching me, and I gave him my sternest glare. "I'm going to need you to give yourself at least two weeks before you even think about getting back in that cage, or I'll beat your ass myself."

He just shot me a sexy smirk, his eyes heating like he'd really enjoy that. I returned it with an exasperated look and went hunting for some clothes.

I emerged from the bathroom sometime later, dressed in leggings and an oversized sweatshirt, mercifully free of the mess Zach left between my thighs. When I arrived in the living room, I found all three of my boyfriends—the Heirs of the Four Families of Saint Gabriel City—looking contrite as they sat in a neat row on the couch. Dom loomed over them with his arms crossed.

Max was seated on a stool at the kitchen bar, shoveling cereal in his mouth with an eager smile as he looked on. Laura busied herself in the kitchen, very obviously pretending to ignore the situation in the living room.

"—and you won't be fighting over her like dogs with a bone, do you understand me?" Dom was saying.

"Yes, sir," Bennett replied.

"Of course not," Noah added.

"She'd cut our balls off," Zach finished.

"Dom," I said, my tone saccharin sweet and very threatening. "What's this about?"

"Hey, honey," he replied, smiling warmly and impervious to the daggers I glared at him. He motioned me over, and I padded across the hardwood floor and onto the threadbare carpet in our tiny living room, coming to a stop next to him. "I was just having a little chat with your boys, here. I am completely convinced of their feelings for you as well as their loyalty, but I just wanted to make sure everyone was confident they could handle the dynamics of a polyamorous relationship."

"Oh my God, Dom," I groaned, feeling my face heat.

"It's okay, sweetheart," Noah said with a soft smile. "We get that our relationship isn't the norm and has come together under... interesting circumstances. Dom's just asking questions because he loves you."

Zach coughed into his fist. "Kiss ass."

I eyed Bennett with raised brows. He was the newest member of this... situation, after all, and I wasn't exactly sure how confident he was in the whole thing. That thought flew out of my head, however, as I took in his sleep-rumpled brown hair, his tight gray sweatpants, and his thin white sleep shirt that failed to hide the outline of the gorgeous angel wings tattooed across his broad chest.

He caught me staring at him like a lusty bitch, and a cocky little smirk played across his handsome face before he wiped it away and said, "We had eleven years of being as close as friends could be, and even death couldn't break that bond. We'll figure it out together, Angel."

Laura let out a little squeal from the kitchen. "He calls her 'Angel'? Oh my God, I'm going to cry."

"Keep it together, Mom," Max muttered around a mouthful of cereal.

Dom nodded, seemingly satisfied, and he looped an arm around my shoulder to give me an affectionate squeeze. "You deserve so much love, honey. I'm glad you have them back again."

I sniffed. Goddamn it, the waterworks *had* to stop. "Thanks, Dom. So am I."

He meandered away, heading for the kitchen, and I gave in to my baser instincts and crawled right into Bennett's lap.

"Morning, Angel," he rumbled, wrapping his arms around me and pressing a lingering kiss behind my ear that sent tingles down to my toes.

"Hi, Bennett." I sighed, snuggling into him as I reached out for Noah, who reclined next to him on the middle couch cushion, looking similarly sleep-disheveled and delicious.

Noah threaded his long fingers through mine. "Hey, sweetheart. How are you feeling?"

"I'm good," I replied. "I'll be ready to rejoin the real world soon, I think."

"Good, because Bennett was only able to buy us one more day excused from class before the dean started making noise about getting our parents involved. So, we have a lot to do today if we're going back to school tomorrow."

Zach returned from the kitchen with two hot mugs of coffee and settled himself on the sofa table, facing us. He handed me one of the mugs like the king he was, and the sexual moan that escaped me after that first delightful sip had all three of them squirming.

"Easy there, Princess," Zach purred. "I don't like thinking that your coffee got you hotter than I did earlier."

Noah snorted. "I knew that was your 'I just got laid' face, Ferrero. I can't believe you sat here and looked Dom in the eye after that."

"Dom and Laura know I'm a grown woman with healthy sexual needs," I declared from my perch in Bennett's lap. "They're cool—they have to be, since Max is basically a walking hard-on."

"I heard that!" Max shouted from the kitchen.

"You were meant to!" I yelled back.

"We're too young to be grandparents!" Laura announced to the room, because apparently things weren't already awkward enough.

"Ugh," I groaned, and my boys all chuckled at my flushed cheeks. "Let's eat so we can get to work. I want to get things rolling before Ramon is even cold on Andrea's doorstep."

By late afternoon, we'd made a lot of progress.

"So, the patents have been filed, and we're going to be able to run everything out of the Foundation?" I asked Zepp through the speakers of my laptop currently propped on my lap where I was seated on the floor of the living room. I had my back against the couch, and Noah was sprawled out on the cushions above me, one hand fiddling with his phone while he ran the other lazily through my hair. He'd just returned from Laura's office down in the bookstore, which he'd commandeered for several hours to conduct his own business.

"Yes, we will be funding your charitable work with the profits from the greatest tech breakthrough of the decade, since apparently you've decided you do not want to be the richest person on the planet," Zepp grumbled.

"I'm plenty rich."

"That's the spirit," Noah chimed in.

Zepp took an audible sip of his energy drink. "Fine, I get it. I won't fight you about it, since you gave me a massive raise, allowing me to keep myself in the finery to which I have become accustomed."

"How long ago was it that you washed the hoodie I know you're wearing?" I asked as I scrolled through the various documents Zepp had posted to our secure server.

We heard him sniff. "If I had to guess... at least a month."

Noah leaned over my shoulder, giving my ear a little nibble before he said into my speakers, "Silver told me she sent you a set of brand-new Knight Technologies polo shirts so you'd have some clean laundry."

Zepp huffed, turning sulky. "That was unnecessary, and I'm still pissed she found my address."

Entertaining as the ongoing war between Zepp and Silver was, I was tired, and we still had to get ourselves back to campus later. "I'll get everything signed and back to the team tonight. I just want my dad's work to be in good hands."

"It will be, Jojo. This was a good move."

He signed off, and I shut my laptop, relaxing my head against the couch and basking in Noah's continued ministrations.

After a few quiet minutes, I asked him, "When are Zach and Bennett coming home?"

"On their way now," he replied. "Be proud of Zach—Bennett says he stayed out of the cage even after Max called him a 'pampered pretty boy prince.'"

"Ugh, Max," I growled, which turned into a tiny moan as Noah fisted my hair with a gentle tug.

"Relax, sweet girl," he murmured. "Zach behaved, and they'll both be home in one piece any minute now."

Zach and Bennett had spent the day working on their own projects before they'd fucked off to Dom's gym to blow off steam. Zach promised me that he would stick to light weights and bag work because I'd discovered that the key to his obedience was not threatening him with violence—that only turned him on—but instead issuing a firm warning that the muffin shop would close if I found even one new bruise on his perfect body.

His eyes had widened in genuine horror, and he'd sworn to me that he'd be good.

Bennett, on the other hand, went to fight. He'd decided he was going to prove himself to the numerous members of the Shadows that frequented Dom's gym that he was not, in fact, a *pampered pretty boy prince*, but a fucking force to be reckoned with.

I wept inside over missing what was likely Bennett in his tiny gym shorts dominating in the cage while I met with Zepp, finishing my tasks for the day.

The sacrifices I made so that I could crush my enemies.

I dropped my laptop to the floor next to me before I twisted in my spot and climbed onto the couch, draping my body across Noah's like I was his blanket. I tucked my face into the crook of his neck, and he wrapped his arms around me in a snug, safe hug that I never wanted to leave.

"Back to the real world tomorrow," I mumbled into his neck.

He sighed, squeezing me tighter.

We'd head back to the Academy tonight and be back in class tomorrow morning like nothing at all had happened over the last three days.

Like we hadn't discovered the Families had murdered my parents just to *steal* from them.

Like Bennett hadn't killed my uncle right in front of me for what he'd done to us.

Like Zach hadn't been kidnapped by his own mother

before we decimated the entire Ferrero Enforcer team and stole the most valuable asset from their ranks.

But we knew it was only a matter of time before the Families caught up, and then we'd see what they had in store for us.

CHAPTER FIVE
BENNETT

I'd once thought that the day I publicly rebuked the Spencer Family—if it ever came at all—would be accompanied by feelings of terror, apprehension, and guilt. I assumed that if I ever decided to stand against my father, I'd still have doubts lurking in the back of my mind like a disease, telling me that I wasn't doing the right thing—that Spencer was still my future if I would just be patient and hold on for better days.

I felt none of those things as I strode into the dining hall on Friday morning with Jolie's smaller hand tucked into mine. As soon as we'd begun our walk from her dorm apartment to Holywell Hall, I laced my fingers firmly through hers in a way that dared her to argue with me. She'd raised an eyebrow at me, but the smile that tugged at the corner of her mouth told me all I needed to know. Zach and Noah had fallen in behind us after tossing identical understanding looks my way.

This was my first open declaration of "fuck you" to my father, and I was so damn proud to be doing it with Jolie Knight's hand in mine.

The best friend he'd taken from me just so he could steal her Family's legacy while he pretended they'd done something to deserve it.

The innocent little girl he'd tried to murder while he acted like Spencer stood for anything other than unchecked corruption and greed.

The now grown woman who was back to take everything from him.

"*Holy shit, they're back,*" someone whispered loudly from one of the long banquet tables stationed closest to the door. Every eye in the room hit the four of us, and the loud hum of chatter cut off instantly as we made our way down the long aisle toward the front of the hall.

It didn't take long for our nosy classmates to spot Jolie's hand in mine, and the furious whispers began.

"Looks like we're caught," Jolie murmured as we walked, her head held high and her gorgeous eyes scanning the room with cool intensity like the queen she was. "I suggest you warn your groupies that I have a knife in my boot and am feeling extra stabby today."

"Behave yourself, Angel," I chided her, stifling a smile and the beginnings of an erection while Zach and Noah both chuckled behind us. "Everyone here will understand that you're mine in short order."

"Ours," Zach said.

"Ours," I agreed.

Jolie squeezed my hand affectionately, and I felt like I could fly.

I'd never been more content in my entire life than I had been when I woke this morning to find my Angel sleeping peacefully in my arms, her white-blonde hair fanned across the tattoo on my bare chest that I wore in her honor. Noah had wrapped himself around her back, their legs intertwined, while Zach had starfished out in the rest of the open mattress space of Jolie's giant bed, all of us too tired after the events of the past two days to do anything but pass out in a pile after we'd gotten back to campus last night.

I was relieved to discover that not only was I unbothered by the presence of other men in bed with *my* girl, but that it felt *right*. Because it was us—the Heirs, my brothers and me and the love of our lives—all together again.

This was my Family.

I led the group up to our familiar table on the raised dais, and Jolie shot me a questioning glance.

"I threatened the dining manager within an inch of his life," I replied casually. "I want them all to see you up here with us."

As we ascended the stairs, the whispering around us intensified. I pulled a chair from the head of the table for Jolie, and she smirked at my chivalry, patting my suited chest as she pranced past me, her hips swaying in her tight jeans in a way that had all three of us staring at her ass in front of the entire school.

Before she could sit down, I grabbed her chin and brought her lips to mine, and I drank in her little moan like it was the finest wine.

The ear-splitting shriek that sounded from the front tables was as predictable as it was obnoxious.

"Bennett!" Harper screeched as she marched toward the dais. "What do you think you're doing? We are *engaged*!" She waved her ringed hand around like we all needed the reminder, while her right hand hung limp at her side, her broken wrist encased in a white cast.

Jolie blew out a frustrated breath, and I kept my possessive grip on her chin as I smiled down at her. "I apologize,

Angel." I made sure my voice carried to the front tables. "Let me take care of this. I'll just be a minute."

The pleased flush that hit her pale, freckled cheeks made everything worth it.

I spun on my heel and stepped to the edge of the dais, ensuring that Harper remained on the floor below me and did not have the chance to start marching up the short stairs.

"Bennett, we have a *contract*!" she squawked, coming to an abrupt halt at my feet. "You cannot seriously be taking up with that vulgar bitch! I won't allow it. My *father* won't allow it!"

"*Quiet*," I barked, and the entire hall went eerily silent.

"Bennett—"

"I said, *quiet*." I peered down my nose at her, channeling my father whenever he wanted to make someone feel particularly small. "You dare insult an Heir of the Four Families of Saint Gabriel City?"

She gaped at me for a fraction of a second before she stood taller, her usual self-important air returning. "I would never insult you, Bennett. You're my future husband. I was talking about that skank—"

"Do not finish that sentence," I said, keeping a deceptively even tone. "You do not insult the Knight Heir. You do not even look at her. She is so far above you that you're lucky—*all* of you are lucky—to even be allowed to breathe the same air as her."

"Man, he always has to one-up us," Zach muttered behind me.

"Shh," Jolie whispered. "I love *all* my presents from you guys, and this one has been a long time coming."

It sure had, and I was such a stubborn fucking idiot for taking this long.

"Bennett, I don't know what's gotten into you," Harper seethed below me. "But I think you've forgotten we have a legal, binding contract. We're getting married, and we're going to rule this City *together*."

"I have some news about that, actually, Harper," I replied. "The marriage contract in question was between you and the Spencer Heir. As of this morning, I've resigned from Spencer and am no longer the Heir. My father has been notified, and our contract is now null and void."

"He did *what*?" Jolie hissed behind me.

"His father was going to find out soon enough, sweetheart," Noah murmured.

And I was only sorry I hadn't been a fly on the wall when Elise undoubtedly delivered my terse message over my father's morning coffee.

I let an amused smile play across my lips as I said to Harper, "Unless, of course, my father finds a new Heir. I suspect he'll be in the market for one, and you're more than welcome to chase whoever that unfortunate soul is for the status bump you're so pathetically desperate for."

Snickers sounded from the crowd, and Harper was back to fish-mouthed gaping at me, like what I was saying to her just didn't compute. I was sure it didn't—she was the type of highest Tier heir who'd never been told no with respect to anything ever in her life, and I was thrilled to be the first person to toss that bucket of ice water on her head.

I hoped it was as cold as the Obsidian River in December.

I regarded her coolly. "Was there anything else you needed, Harper? My breakfast is getting cold, and I'd like to spend some time with my girlfriend before class."

Her stunned silence continued. The color had drained

from her face that was at first flushed with rage and now pale with shock. I gave her my back, ready to move on from this bullshit forever, when she finally sputtered, "You can't just *resign* as an Heir! That's ridiculous, Bennett. You're a *Spencer*."

I glanced at Jolie where she leaned casually against the front of our table, watching, with Zach and Noah pressed in tight on either side of her, and the warm smile full of love she beamed my way was like nothing I'd ever felt in my entire life.

My Angel was here with me—with *us*—and we were going to face this cruel fucking City together.

I tossed a careless look over my shoulder at Harper. "No. I'm a Knight."

It only took until the end of the lunch hour for the other shoe to drop.

The four of us had exited the dining hall to the usual stares and whispers, Jolie and I heading to crew practice, Zach to the gym, and Noah to his Friday afternoon office hours, when Dean Jansen stepped into our path.

"Your parents are here," she said, her words brisk and peevish. "I have taken the liberty of clearing the library and reserving the largest conference room there for your meeting." She paused, her pursed lips contorting as her gaze landed on Jolie. "You are not invited, Miss Knight."

I wrapped an arm around Jolie's waist, and she leaned into my body as she stared down the Dean of Holywell Academy like she was nothing. Zach chuckled from her other side, lifting the hand that held hers to place a delicate kiss to her wrist. Noah sighed from my left, lifting his phone to his face to check the time like this whole thing was an annoying inconvenience.

"I think we both know I'll be going wherever I'd like, whenever I'd like, Dean Jansen," Jolie said lightly. "Unless you'd like to see what kind of challenge campus security wants to give me? Might be fun, but it would make a pretty nasty mess, and the boys here would be late to their meeting. They're just as bloodthirsty as I am, and we've all had a rough few days."

"Miss Knight, such threats are uncalled for," the dean snapped. "This is a Family matter, not a Holywell matter, and it is not *campus* security you should be concerned about."

Zach snickered. "Should we tell the good dean here what you did to the best Enforcers in Ferrero two nights ago, Princess?"

Jolie gave him an indulgent smile. "None of it was as beautifully brutal as what you did to your mom's bodyguard, Zach. I still have a picture of his mutilated corpse on my phone. Should we show the dean?"

I coughed, but then I remembered I didn't give a fuck about decorum anymore.

Dean Jansen's face turned whiter than her daughter's had when I'd dismissed her in front of the entire school this morning. "That... q-quite enough," she sputtered. "I suggest you do not keep the heads of the Families waiting."

We watched as she stalked away, her cream pantsuit swishing with her hurried steps. I sighed, still clinging to Jolie, and I looked each member of my Family in the eyes.

"It's time," I said. "We'll give them the meeting they want, and then there's no going back."

They each nodded, smirks and bored looks wiped away. Only steely determination remained.

We made the ten-minute trek across the quad in silence, and the bright sun of the warm spring afternoon failed to burn away the dark cloud that descended over me as we neared the library.

I would face my father for the first time since I'd found out the depraved reason he murdered the Knights and took my Angel from me, and it would take all of my strength not to end him where he stood.

The Holywell Academy library was once a cathedral that held Catholic mass nightly before money became the one true religion of Saint Gabriel City. We entered the arched wooden doors and processed single file down the aisle, Jolie leading despite the dark look I gave her when my instincts screamed that she do otherwise—which she ignored.

The rows of long study tables had been deserted, the dimly lit chandeliers that hung from the vaulted ceiling above them glinting in the bright light that streamed through the stained-glass windows. At the back of the library, what once had been the altar was now closed off with a wooden door that led to study rooms and the largest conference room on campus.

Four Enforcers stood sentry there, and I recognized one of them as part of my father's detail.

As we neared, the Enforcer stationed in front of the door barked, "This is a closed meeting, Heirs only—"

Without breaking stride, Jolie reached behind her to pull two daggers from the pockets of her little black backpack and launched them at the Enforcer who'd spoken, pinning him to the door by his shoulders like a butterfly to a board.

"Fuck me, I'm so turned on," Zach muttered. Noah and I grunted in agreement as we hurried after her.

Our sweet little best friend had risen from the grave deadly as a viper and sexy as fucking sin. It was a miracle the three of us could ever manage to focus on anything else while in her presence.

The impaled Enforcer shouted in panic as the other three shook themselves from their shock and reached for their weapons. Zach, Noah, and I drew our own pistols before they could, and they froze, wide-eyed and inexplicably confused by our hostility.

It seemed our parents hadn't been truthful even with the people tasked to keep them safe.

"Release those magazines, boys," Jolie commanded. "This isn't a friendly meeting."

They did as they were told, but only after Noah buried a bullet in the wood an inch from butterfly-guy's ear.

Once they'd disarmed their own weapons, Zach and I made quick work of the four of them, leaving them huddled on the floor, pissed off, with their hands cuffed behind their backs.

"It's been a pleasure, Sanders," I said to the man I recognized from my father's team as I stood from my crouch next to him. "Don't get any ideas."

"So, it really is true, then?" He wrinkled his nose in disgust as he shook his head. "You've turned on Spencer."

I stared down at him, blank mask in place. "It turned on me first."

He scoffed before muttering under his breath, "Must be *some* pussy."

"Uh-oh," Noah said while Zach let out a snort, the two of them flanking Jolie by the door.

I pulled my pistol from my suit jacket and fired a single

bullet into Sanders' kneecap, shattering it instantly. He let out a pained roar, and the rest of the group began shouting in alarm, struggling with their restraints.

"Anyone else have anything smart to say?" I asked them in a bored voice.

They quieted, and I tucked my gun away. I joined my Family by the door, taking a second to steal a scorching kiss from my Angel.

"God, you're fucking hot," she murmured against my lips.

I smirked. "And you're fucking mine. Let's go inform my father."

CHAPTER SIX
JOLIE

We entered the library's conference room to find Peter Hargraves, Andrea Ferrero, and James Spencer alone and not so patiently waiting for their sons.

All three sets of eyes snapped to me as I entered one step ahead of my boys, still twirling the bloody knives through my fingers that I'd unceremoniously yanked from the shoulders of the Ferrero flunky I'd stuck to the door.

Peter and Andrea both sat behind the table. Peter lazed with his legs crossed, while Andrea sat ramrod straight, her dark eyes hard and her normally pale cheeks flushed.

James Spencer lingered behind them, standing tall under the high windows of the back wall, his hands fisted at his sides. The look of loathing he aimed my way would've made a lesser woman cower in the corner, but I was not a lesser woman.

I was his worst fucking nightmare, and now I had his son.

"Oh, goodness, Jolie, that is really not necessary," Peter said, eyeing my knives and giving me a patronizing smile.

"We aren't here to hurt anyone." He ran a nervous hand through his wavy, barely graying blond hair as he shifted uncomfortably in his seat. The gesture reminded me so much of my Noah, and it made me despise Peter even more.

"History says otherwise, Mr. Hargraves," I replied as the guys spread out beside me so that we stood in a line, a united front against the Families.

"Yes, well," Peter began in a smooth voice, still hanging onto that smile. "I think—"

"Shut up, Dad," Noah snapped, and the way the smile dropped from Peter's face was a thing of beauty. "You don't speak to Jolie. Not after what you've done to her."

Peter sighed. "Noah, if you would have just taken my calls, we could have *discussed* all of this. Obviously, I did not know you were at the Hargraves Tech offices when I sent the team in—"

"Dad." Noah gave my hand a quick squeeze before he stepped forward and took up a power stance right in front of his father, towering over him with his arms crossed over his hard chest and glaring down at Peter with disgust. "I said, shut *the fuck* up. You're done here. You know it, and I know it. Hargraves is mine now, and as of yesterday, the last of your major investors have dumped you and joined me under the Knight umbrella. Say your goodbyes to this City and fuck back off to the Maldives or wherever the hell you've been wasting your days."

I squeezed my thighs together and took a calming breath. Noah was using his dominant voice, and it was turning me the fuck on.

Not the time.

"Peter, get some fucking control, *now*," James barked.

Peter tossed him an irritated glance over his shoulder before turning back to his son, trying once more to force a smile. "Noah, I am so proud of how you've handled things while I've been away. I am certainly ready to let you step into a leadership role, but this nonsense with Knight has to stop. We do not let people steal from us."

I snorted, and Noah's cold smile was so vicious that even Andrea looked alarmed. "You're right, Dad," he said, leaning down to place his palms on the table, his navy suit stretching across his broad shoulders with the movement. "When stealing from a member of the Four Families, we make sure to kill them first, including their innocent children, isn't that right?"

James and Andrea's heads both snapped to Noah then, and all three of them watched him warily. This was the first indication any of us had given that we might know the truth about my parents' murders.

Peter gawked at Noah like he didn't recognize him at all. "Son, I don't know what's gotten into you. I'm offering you the helm of Hargraves, but you need to reverse course, and quickly."

"You're still not listening, Dad," Noah growled, and I stifled a moan. "I already have the *helm*. It's all mine. I even bought out the entirety of Hargraves Tower yesterday and awarded a contract to an up-and-coming builder from the Southside. She's going to help me turn the first ten floors into a state-of-the-art healthcare center for low-income citizens. Isn't that great?"

Peter gasped in alarm. "Noah!"

"Enough, Peter," James snarled. "You've been outplayed by your own son because you're never fucking *here*."

Noah stood again, giving his dad his back and rejoining our line. He paused in front of me to press a lingering kiss to my temple while I grinned savagely at his father.

"And if you think you'll still be sitting pretty on top of

all your dirty drug money, Mr. Hargraves," I said, "Knight's new head of security is taking out all of your stash houses in Industrial City as we speak. I think you're about to have some unhappy customers."

He paled while Zach barked out a laugh. "Oh shit, did you guys let Frankie play with the flamethrower after all?"

My grin widened. "We sure did."

"Zachary!" Andrea snapped, the mention of Frankie and Industrial City likely reigniting her fury. "That... *mess* you made a few days ago was ridiculous and unnecessary. You are continuing to let that *bitch* cloud your judgment."

Zach shrugged, eyeing his mother with amusement. "You fuck with the bull and you get the horns, Mom. I told you, and I *definitely* told Ramon, repeatedly—for years—not to fuck with me. Then I warned you both not to fuck with my Princess. How's the hunt for a new security team treating you?"

She bristled. "Where is your uncle?"

"Weren't you listening?" Now Zach's smile had vanished, and he was every bit as cold as I'd ever seen Bennett at his stoniest moment. "He's out lighting up every last bit of Peter's drug inventory. He works for Jolie now because she treats him like a fucking human being."

Andrea swallowed, the thought of being on the wrong side of Frankie unsettling to just about anyone, before she let the rage descend. "You do not want to oppose me, Zachary. I will crush you into dust and remold you into something I can actually be proud of, and I'll make sure you're watching as I slit your girlfriend's throat right in front of you."

Zach's guns flew from their shoulder holsters under his suit jacket. Andrea's eyes widened as he aimed them both right at her head. "Say that again, Mom. Threaten the woman I love one more time."

She sagged a bit in her chair, waving a dismissive hand in his direction. "Honestly, Zachary. I am your *mother*. You're not going to shoot me, for crying out loud."

"Try me," he growled. "And try rebuilding Ferrero's security team after Jolie Knight destroyed the best you had and stole Frankie Fingers from you. Try to keep your gun-running operation going after I purchased every open mercenary contract on the market yesterday. Knight Tower is now a fucking fortress, and Ferrero is a festering open wound. I'm done, Mom. Fuck you, and fuck Ferrero."

My heart warmed even as my stomach dipped under a burst of nerves. Zach had worked his ass off after his rescue to hit his mom at her most vulnerable—and to keep her that way—all while making sure we had the most secure tower in the City. I loved him so much for it, but I worried for him nonetheless.

Andrea sniffed, her cold, dark glare sliding straight to me.

I knew, as the guys did, that their parents were going to hold out hope that their Heirs would return to them—that if they could get me out of the way, I'd no longer be there to lure them away from the Families with my wild fantasies and magical pussy.

I returned her stare. "Enjoy that sinking ship, Andrea. When I'm through with you, you'll be on your knees, begging me for mercy—mercy that you didn't show my mother when you laughed in her face as you shot her."

"Enough of this!" James thundered. He strode forward, now standing at the table between a seething Andrea and a shell-shocked Peter. His menacing stare shifted from me over to Bennett, like he'd been about to unload on me before he remembered he had his own Family issues to address. "What the hell is wrong with you, Bennett? Your friends being hypnotized by a cunt is one thing, but *you*? I thought you were better than this, and now you're about to irreparably fuck things up with the Jansens."

Bennett returned his father's fury with a cold, bored stare. "I've resigned as the Spencer Heir, Father. Or did Elise forget to inform you of that during a moment when your dick wasn't down her throat?"

Zach and Noah both snorted, and I discreetly picked my jaw up off the floor. Bennett had never dared even *look* at his father wrong in all the time we'd been friends. I knew he'd grown into his own man over the years, and I trusted his deep devotion to me now, but to say it was a shock to see him not only oppose his father but sling an insult at him in the flesh was a gross understatement.

"That's nonsense, *son*," he spat, seething. "I knew you weren't nearly ready to step into a leadership role at Spencer, but I never thought you were this stupid."

I tensed, my dagger hand feeling twitchy. Bennett ran a soothing palm down my back from his spot next to me. "Ah, well, I always was such a disappointment," he replied casually. "I would think you're glad to be rid of me, Father."

James slammed his hand down on the table, and only Peter flinched. "Stop saying that shit." He stepped away from the table, pulling his phone from his pocket to glare at it, then shoved it back into his pants before looking at Bennett again. "Where is your mother?"

Bennett shrugged. "She's a grown woman, and last time I checked, she wasn't a prisoner in Spencer Tower. Maybe she got tired of hearing her husband fucking the help right down the hall."

Jesus Christ, Bennett wasn't here to play.

And he also wasn't going to tell his dad that Bridgette Spencer was safely ensconced in an adorable condo Bennett had purchased with his Alastia money a few blocks from my family's home in Olde Town. I actually knew for a fact that as of half an hour ago, she was drinking tea with Laura in her store while they discussed their favorite books—with Martinez in tow. Bennett had threatened him with a very painful death should one blonde hair on either of their heads be harmed on his watch.

"She hasn't been home in three days, and there's been no activity on her card," James said, his eyes narrowing with suspicion. "Or yours. Are you so desperate to rebel against me that you're borrowing money from Knight?"

Bennett cracked a smile. "Jealous, Father? Hargraves is dead, Ferrero is dying, and Spencer is right behind them both. Knight is already more powerful than it ever was, and Jolie isn't even finished with you yet."

Peter scoffed. "You boys are delusional if you think Knight is more powerful than the Families."

"In that little bitch's dreams," Andrea sneered.

James blew out a frustrated breath, shooting them both some menacing side-eye before he ran his enraged gaze over the boys. "We will give the three of you one last chance to do the right thing and return to the Families. I'm confident that when your little girlfriend is six feet under for daring to challenge us, you'll remember that you can have literally any piece of pussy in this City, and you'll *thank* us for setting you back on the path you were born to walk. Nothing is worth giving up your place as Heirs of the Four Families of Saint Gabriel City. Do you hear me? *Nothing*."

I felt the boys tense next to me. As impervious as they were to their parents' insults and threats against them, they were a lot more sensitive when those insults and threats were directed at me.

Bennett squeezed my hand, and I knew he was about to turn this meeting over to me. He looked at his father one last time. "Jolie Knight is the love of my life, and you took her from me. You slaughtered her parents right in front of her and ordered the same for her—an eleven-year-old *child*—and then you lied to me about it for *years*. You claimed they'd broken the code of the Families—that Jeffrey Knight and his entire Family deserved to be dragged into that conference room and executed. We know now what a crock of shit that was, and we're *never* coming back to the Families. You three made your bed, now you have to fucking *lie in it*."

James paled, while Andrea's face had grown redder, if that was even possible. Peter appeared puzzled, like he just couldn't comprehend that we'd somehow discovered the truth and that his son could really be finished with him forever.

I stepped forward, feeling so much strength in the wake of Bennett's impassioned declaration. With my boys standing behind me, I was unstoppable.

I was *loved*.

"I was just wondering, Mr. Spencer," I said, examining my dagger as I twirled it lazily through my fingers. "Have you heard from Anders lately?"

It took him a moment to tear his wide-eyed stare from Bennett, but those evil brown eyes finally slid over to me. "Your uncle appears to be missing," he said through gritted teeth. "And I suspect you're about to tell me that you know where he is."

I chuckled, all of my energy focused on keeping a light, unaffected air in front of the man who'd killed my dad when I really just wanted to rage and tear his still-beating heart from his body. "I actually don't know where he ended up." I tossed a look over my shoulder at Zach. "Does your cleanup crew have a favorite dumping ground?"

He smirked at me. "They have a few, Princess. Want me to get an exact location so we can head out there and piss on his grave?"

I blew him a kiss. "Next date night, babe."

"*Enough*," James spat. "Congratulations, Miss Knight. You've apparently murdered your own uncle. And here I thought the deaths of your family members were why we're all here in the first place."

"No," I snapped. "I did not kill my uncle—though I would have loved to have had the pleasure. Your *son* killed my uncle with his bare fucking fists. Do you want to hazard a guess as to why?"

All three of them glared at me in silence. They knew what was coming.

"That's right. Anders confessed to everything because he thought I was going to hand him the keys to the kingdom he's been desperate for all these years. Bennett did not take kindly to hearing how my uncle sold his own flesh and blood to you three criminals for the false promise of money, power, and apparently that reprehensible cunt, Elise Proctor."

"Preach," Zach muttered.

James Spencer finally took a seat at the table, feigning calm, but I knew he was seeing the hope they'd all held onto of finally getting their hands on my father's discovery dissolving right in front of his eyes. He steepled his fingers under his chin and gave me an assessing once-over.

"I assume you've unlocked your father's flash drive."

"Yes."

"And I assume you've ascertained the value of what was contained there."

"Yes."

"So, you understand that your father would have had the power to ruin all of us. To destroy the institution of the Four Families because he found it so... *distasteful*. To upend the way things are done in this City. To bury Hargraves, Ferrero, and Spencer if he so chose." He leaned back, crossing his arms over his chest, and his hard stare once again darted to Bennett, almost *imploring*. "We made a calculated decision to defend the Families. You would have done the same in our shoes."

"Keep telling yourself that, Father," Bennett replied, bored. "How does it feel to sit there today and know that it was all for nothing?"

Noah chimed in, staring at his own dad like he was a bug under his shoe. "How does it feel, Dad, to know that by murdering two innocent people and attempting to murder a child just to steal the tech breakthrough of the decade, you've now lost your Heir and all of Hargraves?"

"And how does it feel, Mom," Zach added with his own maniacal grin, "to know that I hate you so much for what you did to my girl that I broke every bone in the body of the one man left on the planet who could stand your presence for more than ten minutes? That I'm going to enjoy every second of watching the love of my life tear down what's left of Ferrero brick by brick?"

"And how does it feel to know, illustrious leaders of the Four Families of Saint Gabriel City," I went on, because we hadn't even gotten to the real kicker. "That the one thing you wanted—the thing that set all of this in motion—is so far out of your reach now that you will never, ever have it? Miraculene is now the property of the Knight Foundation, and we've gifted all of my dad's research to universities around the globe. The money made from this revolutionary technology will be going into scholarships and grants for low-income students. *Nobody* is going to become obscenely rich from my dad's work, and the world is going to be a better fucking place because of it."

"Are you out of your fucking mind?" James shouted.

"Noah, I think we should talk about this—" Peter began.

"Zachary, you will speak to me this instant—" Andrea barked.

"We're done here," I announced. "It's over for you three. I'm coming for what's left of the Families. The Shadows are coming for you, too, and your sons will be with us every step of the way."

The silence stretched for what felt like hours as we all stared at one another, resignation finally seeping into each of their addled minds.

Eventually, James spoke, his words low and dark. "We will not hold back. We will end you, little girl, and our sons will watch it happen as punishment for their terrible decisions. There are no rules in this game, but you will *not* create a mess like the one you made in Industrial City at this Academy."

Oh, God forbid the Families' crown jewel be tainted by the war they started seven and a half years ago. They wanted things to seem like business as usual, and a big part of that was having the Heirs they hoped would return to them continue to go to class like nothing was amiss.

"Fine," I said. It benefited us to have the Academy as a neutral zone, anyway.

"Let's go, Angel," Bennett said, and James blanched at

the beautiful name his son had given me. "I'm tired of my father's eyes being on you."

I clasped his hand in mine, and Noah threaded his fingers through my other one. We gave their parents our backs.

"Noah!" Peter's voice was desperate.

"Zachary!" Andrea shrieked.

"Bennett." A last low, threatening growl from James.

We slammed the conference room doors in their faces, marched past their still-bound guards, and my boys left the Four Families behind for good.

CHAPTER SEVEN
JOLIE

We'd just stepped across the threshold of my dorm apartment when I was lifted off my feet and thrown over a broad shoulder.

"Bennett!" I screeched as my chest hit his suited back. "What the fuck are you doing?"

He didn't answer, instead just tightening his grip around my legs as he strode toward my bedroom.

"Oh, fuck yeah," Zach said from behind us as he closed the front door. "I like where this is going."

I lifted my head to glare at him, my body bouncing around Bennett's back as he walked. Noah shot me a wink as he and Zach hurried along behind us.

Then I watched their eager smiles disappear as Bennett slammed my bedroom door in their faces.

As he turned the deadbolt, a fist pounded on the door. "Come on, man!" Zach shouted. "No fair!"

"Sharing is caring, Bennett," Noah added.

Bennett finally dropped me to my feet only to smash me up against the door, his big body covering mine as he ran his hands over my jean-clad ass and began to drag his lips up my neck, ending any protest I'd been about to make regarding the locked door between me and my other boyfriends.

"Do you two assholes think I've forgotten what you made me watch after that god-fucking-awful engagement party?" he growled at Zach and Noah through the door.

A beat of silence, then they both snickered. "You deserved that," Noah said.

"You did," I agreed as I dug my hands under Bennett's suit jacket to explore his muscular back. "And no one *made* you stay."

He yanked me away from the door, lifting me by my butt so that my legs looped around his waist as he walked, then he dumped me unceremoniously onto my bed.

"Don't worry, Angel," he said with a wicked grin that had my panties wet in an instant. He threw his jacket off and began loosening his tie. "I'll still let them watch."

He pulled his phone from his pocket and typed something onto the screen. He yanked his tie from his neck and tossed it to the floor next to his jacket before striding over to my dresser and standing his phone against my jewelry box. I could just make out the live feed of me sprawled out on my bed playing on its screen.

I heard the muffled sound of both Zach and Noah's phones vibrating out in the hallway. "Oh, well played, Spencer," Noah said with a laugh. "Sweetheart, he's sent us a link to a livestream."

"Dude, just let us in. If I'm gonna watch, I want the real deal," Zach griped.

"Fuck off and take what you're given," Bennett barked at the door as he prowled toward me, slowly unbuttoning his dress shirt while he raked his hot gaze over my entire body.

I lay still, utterly captivated by him and mind-meltingly turned on by the fact that Zach and Noah were going to watch as Bennett did unspeakable things to me in this room.

His shirt fell to the floor, revealing his broad, sculpted chest decorated with *my* wings, then his pants followed. By the time he reached the foot of my bed, he was clad only in his tight black boxer briefs and sporting a monster bulge that made my mouth water and my pussy clench with need.

He jerked me toward him by my ankles, then he set about unbuttoning the silky purple blouse I'd picked to wear with my dark jeans and boots today. "Do you know, Angel," he said as he lost patience and ripped my shirt apart, the last few buttons flying onto the comforter. "How many times I fucked my fist before I could fucking think straight after I watched you come on Zach's face?"

Zach made a pained noise out in the hall, and I gasped as Bennett slid my pants and panties down to my ankles in one smooth pull. "Tell me," I demanded, my voice slipping into a moan as he cupped my lace-clad breasts in his big hands, now laser-focused on them.

"Three," he replied, unclasping my bra at the front with one deft flick of his fingers. "Three times. And it wasn't fucking enough. It was never going to be enough. You were under my skin and in my soul and I never hated and loved something so much all at once in my entire life."

He ducked down to suck my nipple into his mouth while he tweaked the other with his fingers. Then he switched, sinking his teeth into my other nipple, and I hissed at the twinge of pain. "Careful, Spencer. I have teeth too."

"Yeah, bite him, Princess," Zach said.

Bennett, calling my bluff, released my nipple with an audible pop before slamming his lips onto mine. He pinned my hands to the bed as our tongues tangled in a dance for dominance before I caught his lower lip between my teeth and bit down hard.

"Fuck," he swore, releasing one of my hands so he could grip my chin, holding me still as he claimed another brutal, possessive kiss. "Behave, Angel. I am going to do so many filthy fucking things to you, and you're going to enjoy every last second of it."

I bared my teeth at him. "Not if I do filthy fucking things to you first."

"You tell him, sweetheart," Noah called out.

Bennett arched a brow at my challenge, delicious fire behind those mossy eyes, before he yanked my boots off my feet, followed by my pants, then I was completely naked and back in his arms again, my legs wrapped around his hips as his hands gripped my ass. I pulled his face to mine and shoved my tongue down his throat as he walked us to the wall opposite my dresser, and he groaned, opening for me like a good boy.

I was pleased with myself until my back was slammed against the wall and my naked body suddenly hefted high. Before I could register what was happening, my legs had been thrown over Bennett's shoulders and his face was buried in my pussy.

"Oh fuck," Zach swore from behind the door. "Seriously? Now he's just showing off."

I moaned, weaving my fingers into Bennett's hair as they scrambled for purchase, but he had me pinned tight to the wall as he ran his tongue from my ass to my clit again and again.

"Does that feel good, sweetheart?" Noah asked, his

voice dropping into that gruff, dominant register that made me fucking gush. "Do you like Bennett's tongue in your pussy? You look so pretty up on that wall."

"Yes!" I cried as Bennett wrapped his lips around my clit with a possessive growl. "Oh my God, yes. It's so fucking good."

"Then come on his face, Princess," Zach rasped with need. "Noah and I want to see you fall apart up there."

Bennett picked up the pace, sucking and licking and devouring me like a man possessed until I tipped over the edge, screaming and gripping his hair as a wave of ecstasy shot from my core through my entire body.

I heard Zach groan before Noah said, "Good girl," with a little moan of his own.

Bennett gave me a few more slow licks, like he was savoring my taste, before he carefully let me slide down the wall and back into his arms.

"Fucking perfect, Angel," he rumbled, capturing my mouth again.

"Mmm, I love you," I mumbled against his lips like a smitten fool, and I felt him grin.

He carried me back to my bed, this time laying me gently down on the mattress before crawling on top of my body. He loomed over me, his hands on either side of my head as he studied my face with his familiar intensity. "I love you, too, Angel. You are the light of my fucking life and my reason for getting out of bed every morning. I will give you everything you've ever wanted, including my father's head on a silver fucking platter." He dipped a hand down to slide two thick fingers inside of me, and I gasped, both at the intrusion and at his impassioned words as they soaked into my body.

"Bennett," I moaned.

"Now we're going to show Zach and Noah how well you take my cock. Would you like that, Angel?"

I *would* like that, but he'd had the upper hand too long.

Using all of my strength, I rolled us just like I would have if we'd been grappling in the cage. The move took him by surprise, and he grunted as I straddled his ripped torso, the wet heat of my core now planted solidly over his dick—still inexplicably encased in his boxers.

"How about I take your cock how *I* want it, Bennett?" I taunted him, reaching between us to free that beast from its cage. It was solid steel and heavy in my hand as I stroked him lightly, and I dove in to take his mouth again.

He groaned, wrapping one big hand around my throat while the other shot to my breast, and he accepted my hungry kiss while I worked his dick faster with my hand.

"Way to put him in his place, Princess," Zach called out.

"It's not going to last," Noah muttered before he said, louder, "Sweetheart, better put that dick where you want it before he does it himself."

Bennett tore his mouth from mine, moving to nip at my earlobe before he shouted, "Shut the fuck up out there!"

I went to slide down his body, ready to *own* him by fitting as much of that big dick into my mouth as possible, but he grabbed me by the biceps and halted my progress. Then he flipped us, rolling me onto my stomach before pinning me to the bed.

"Fuck you," I hissed as I bucked against him. "Let me put your cock in my mouth, asshole."

"Later, Angel," he replied before plunging his finger into my wetness again. "It's cute that you think you're in charge when we're fucking." He removed his finger from my pussy, and I had two seconds of warning as he circled that slick finger around the tight ring of my ass.

"Bennett," I growled.

"Tell me no," he demanded, increasing the pressure.

I did not tell him no. Instead, I pressed my ass back against him, taking the tip of his finger into my body all on my own.

"Fuck," he bit out, then he slid his finger all the way into my ass.

I whimpered at the intoxicating mix of pain and pleasure, fisting the comforter next to my head as Bennett shifted behind me, arching over my back and pressing kisses down my spine as he slowly and carefully pumped his finger in and out of my tight hole.

"Aw, sweetheart, where's Bennett's finger right now?" Noah purred.

"It's in my ass," I moaned.

Zach let out a pleased rumble. "Does that feel good, baby girl?"

"Yes," I sighed before tossing Bennett a serious look over my shoulder. "You're not putting your monster cock in my ass."

"Hmm," he said, now kneeling behind me and studying his finger as it moved in and out of my body. "No, not today, Angel. But I know you can take *anything* I give you because you were made for me."

"Stop fucking around and put your dick in my pussy," I snapped. "Give it to me, Bennett."

"You heard the lady, Spencer!" Noah yelled.

Zach chimed in, "Better fuck her right, man, or I'm breaking this door down and doing it myself."

Bennett gently removed his finger from my ass and rolled me onto my back. He bent down to steal a filthy kiss before he said, "Fine. Let's make sure those two fully comprehend what I'm about to do to you."

He stood, finally peeling his boxers all the way off, and he marched over to my dresser and grabbed his phone, returning to stand between my open legs, his huge dick jutting proudly from his carved body. He dragged my ass to the edge of the bed and lined himself up with my dripping wet core.

He held the phone up. "You want me to show them how I stretch you so fucking wide, Angel?"

I shivered. "Yes. Show them."

He aimed the camera down at where we were joined, and he pushed into me so painstakingly slowly that my eyes rolled back into my head.

"Oh *fuck*, Princess," Zach swore as he watched what must have been an obscene picture of my pussy enveloping Bennett's substantial girth. "Goddamn, look at you take that thing."

"He wasn't kidding, was he?" Noah mused. "Sweetheart, tell us how it feels."

Bennett finally bottomed out, both of us letting out a low groan, and then his hooded eyes met mine and held them captive as he began to pump his hips, one hand still pointing the camera downward and the other wrapped around my thigh.

"It feels fucking amazing," I replied, rocking my hips in time with Bennett's thrusts. "I'm so full, and Bennett makes me come so *hard*."

He growled, picking up the pace and pounding into me as I cried out for more, more, more, all while Zach and Noah shouted encouragement from the hallway, desperate to see me fall apart on their best friend's dick.

Bennett finally abandoned the camera, tossing his phone against the pillow above me and giving Zach and Noah a prime shot of us over the top of my head. He surged forward, his big body covering mine, then he threw my legs over his shoulders and bent me in half.

"Oh, shit, oh my God, Bennett!" I wailed as he ground down on me, his big dick buried deep and his pelvis working my clit with every rock of his hips.

"Fuck *yes*," he hissed as I contracted around him. "Come for me, Angel."

"Come with me!" I cried, digging my nails into his shoulders as my climax crested, slamming into me like a tidal wave. "All of you. *Come with me*."

As Bennett let out a hoarse cry and shuddered above me, I heard low, satisfied groans out in the hallway.

I wrapped my arms around Bennett, the two of us melting together in a pile of satiated goo, and I whispered in his ear, "Thank you for coming back to me."

He cupped my cheek and brought me in for an uncharacteristically sweet, gentle kiss. "I never left you, Jolie. Not really—it just took me a little while to be brave enough to show you that."

After a minute, he rolled off me and sauntered into the bathroom, and I ogled his round, tight ass and meaty thighs as he went. He emerged with a washcloth, diverting to the door to flick the lock before returning to the bed to clean me up.

Zach and Noah filed in, both of them clad only in their disheveled dress shirts and pants and grinning from ear to ear.

"Keep your dicks out of her," Bennett commanded as they crawled onto the bed to cuddle me while he finished tidying up the mess between my thighs. "She needs to rest."

"So *bossy*," I lamented. "Not much has changed, has it?"

Bennett just shot me a warning look before he strode back toward the bathroom.

Noah chuckled as he pushed my hair off of my sweaty forehead and dropped a kiss there. "You were beautiful, sweetheart. So fucking gorgeous."

Zach, meanwhile, ran his tongue languidly over my nipple before rolling onto his side to grin at me. "We definitely just jacked off in the hallway together watching that, Princess. You know, like bros do."

My beast was satisfied with that. I snuggled deeper into Noah's side, reaching for Zach's hand to pull him in tight. Bennett returned, now wearing his boxers, and he made himself at home between my legs, laying his head on my belly.

"Let's stay like this until dinner, then we can figure out what to do next," I whispered, running my fingers through Bennett's damp hair. Anything to cling to this quiet moment in the arms of all three of them before we had to face our new reality.

"Sounds good, sweetheart," Noah murmured, his lips brushing against my shoulder, and the others hummed in agreement.

I knew I would burn the whole world down to keep these boys with me.

CHAPTER EIGHT
JOLIE

It was a familiar scene, except this time, I was also sitting stiffly on the couch next to the boys while we accepted the tongue lashing we probably deserved from a loved one.

Mari paced in front of us, her heeled boots clunking against the hardwood floor of our dorm apartment, her arms crossed and a serious look on her face as she mulled over the flood of information she'd gathered since her plane had touched down in the City this morning.

"I have been gone for one week," she said, her tone deceptively light. "*One. Week.*"

I'd known I was in trouble as soon as our door had flown open half an hour ago, and my best friend and roommate had stalked angrily inside, wheeling her Gucci carry-on beside her, her oversized sunglasses still on her face and her soft sweaterdress not even a little bit wrinkled from her transatlantic flight.

We'd been having a quiet Saturday morning, my three gorgeous boyfriends and I. Zach had made everyone breakfast—testing me by wearing only an apron and his underwear—and we'd eaten together while we talked about anything that *wasn't* the impending war we'd just declared together against the Families.

I'd been curled up in Noah's lap on the couch, lazily making out with him while Bennett and Zach cleaned up the kitchen, when Mari had arrived. I felt terrible for not even remembering her flight back from Madrid, where she had spent the week with Carmen, was today.

But, to her point, a lot had happened while she was away.

"Imagine my surprise," she went on, still pacing, "that when I'm making my way through the atrium downstairs, I have no less than *five* different people ambush me to confirm some very *wild* rumors."

"Mari—" I began, but she held up a hand, cutting me off with an accusing look.

"And then I arrive home to have my alleged *best friend* not only confirm those rumors but calmly inform me that, actually, so much other crazy shit has happened?"

Zach chuckled next to me on the couch. Noah held my hand, his thumb rubbing soothing circles on my palm, though he also appeared amused. Bennett lounged in our oversized armchair, his long legs crossed as he scrolled through his phone, unperturbed by Mari's ire.

She went on. "So, let's recap, shall we? While I was in Spain, you discovered your dad's revolutionary research, then you were drugged and kidnapped by your uncle, who was apparently a secret villain and the major reason your parents were murdered. He was then brutally killed by Bennett Spencer, who has now joined your harem of devoted boyfriends despite being a stubborn, broody bastard to you all these months—"

"To be fair, he's still a stubborn, broody bastard," I said, only to receive a dark, threatening look from Bennett over the top of his phone—a thing that used to rile me up but now only made my panties wet.

Mari ignored me, now counting on her fingers. "Then your other boyfriend was kidnapped, you rescued him with the help of a powerful, secret organization that no one in the City knew about that apparently you are *the leader of*, you decimated the Ferrero Enforcers, then you declared open warfare on the Families—*again*—on Academy grounds. Oh, and your newest boyfriend dumped his fiancée in front of the entire school. And not once, through any of this, did I receive even a text message, not to mention a *phone call*, apprising me of the situation. Do I have that right?"

I winced. "I didn't want to... worry you."

"Uh-huh." She was unimpressed, and she held my apologetic stare with a look that dared me to make another excuse as she whipped her phone from her purse. She scrolled and tapped the screen to make a call, and we all sat silently as the call rang on speakerphone.

"Hey, babe," Max's voice purred through the phone. "You back on City soil?"

"Max, mi amor," Mari cooed right back, and it scared the shit out of me. "¿Qué pasa? How was *your* week, hmm?"

Max caught on that he was in danger. "Um, it was... alright."

Mari still glared at the four of us as she spoke into her phone. "Was it, now?"

"Babe...," Max began, but it was over for him as she decided to unload in colorful Spanish, rolling her eyes at me one last time before stomping off to her room, her suitcase rolling smoothly next to her as she barked into the phone.

She slammed her door a little harder than necessary, then I sagged back into my couch cushion.

"Fuck, I'm the worst friend," I muttered.

Noah wrapped his hand around my thigh and gave me a reassuring squeeze while Zach tossed a muscled arm around my shoulders and pulled me in close.

"She's just worried about you," Noah said. "I think she knows that this week was... difficult for you and that the life you lead is dangerous."

Bennett locked his phone and slid it into the pocket of his sweatpants before his eyes met mine, a soft and understanding look lurking there. "Angel, I think you should let Mari decide how deep into this she wants to go with us. It's understandable that you want to protect her, but she's a big girl. And I think Zach may be able to help you make it up to her."

I beamed an appreciative smile at Bennett and received a heart-stopping, genuine smile from him in return. I sucked in a shaky breath, ignoring the knowing chuckles from the other two, before I shifted under Zach's arm to look at him. "What's he talking about?"

"Well," Zach said, pulling his own phone from its perch on the end table. "As you know, Anzaldua, as the City's Tier One hotel giant, is affiliated with Ferrero. But my mother's woes are becoming public knowledge, as is my defection to Knight, so we've had a few of Ferrero's remaining allies see the writing on the wall and come crawling. Mari's parents are one of them."

I perked up. "When?"

He dropped a quick kiss on my lips before putting his phone to his ear. "Hey.... Oh, fuck you, Marcus. You can earn your giant paycheck and quit bitching.... I happen to think

Silver is a *very* fair boss.... No.... Yes. Give me the latest from Anzaldua."

As Zach listened to whatever this Marcus person was telling him, I shot a questioning look at Noah.

He grinned. "Marcus used to frequent the underground fighting rings unofficially sponsored by Ferrero. He was also a thorn in the side of the Families as a gray hat hacker that somehow hadn't been snatched up by the Shadows. Zach talked him into joining us and put him on Silver's team, and I think they... butt heads. He's now Zach's guy like Zepp is yours."

"Oh," I replied, feeling pleased by my boyfriend's initiative. "Does Bennett have a guy too?" I swung my inquisitive stare in his direction.

"No one I trust," Bennett replied. "Silver's in charge of the Spencer side of the Shadows."

Zach finished up his call. "Thanks, man.... Oh, fuck off. I'll kick your ass anytime. Come down to the Southside—that's where I train now.... Yeah, later, dude."

Then he filled me in.

When Mari emerged from her room an hour later, now wearing the finest silk palazzo pants and a matching crop top—her Saturday loungewear—I was ready to present our proposal to her.

Noah made her a cup of coffee, and Bennett abandoned his spot in the armchair and offered it to her before taking over the corner of the couch. He tucked me neatly into his side and clasped my hand in his.

Mari appeared relaxed and at least willing to hang out in our presence—score one for me—and she eyed Bennett's and my intertwined hands with great interest.

"That," she said before taking a delicate sip of her coffee, "is going to take some getting used to."

"It was... quite a development," I hedged. Mari knew the story now, though I'd left out the frenzied-fucking-in-my-prisoner-chair part of it all.

Zach, who was still shirtless but had put on some flannel pants since Mari's return, cleared his throat from his spot where he was casually leaning up against our living room wall.

"Mari, Jojo and her harem of devoted boyfriends would like to have a chat with you, if that's cool," he said, deploying his sexy smirk.

Mari, unaffected by that move, narrowed her eyes at him before dragging that suspicious stare to me.

I pasted on my contrite face. "First of all, I'm sorry for the radio silence during everything that went down the past week. I'm sure I don't have to tell you it was intense and draining and scary, but that's not an excuse for my failure to check in."

She hummed. "It's not, but despite everything I said, I do understand. You're used to holding everything close to the vest, and I know what you're doing is dangerous. But I do want to be... involved." She swallowed, now looking nervous. "I talked to Carmen and did a lot of thinking this week. I think I do want to... join Knight. But I don't really have much to offer."

"Untrue," I replied with a huff. "But also, on that note, Zach just informed me that your parents have... reached out. They've requested a meeting with Knight, given the uncertainty surrounding Ferrero at the moment."

Mari's jaw dropped. "They did *not*," she hissed, indignant. "And they know the *Knight Heir* is my best friend! They've done nothing but bitch about your enabling my 'rebellion.' *Joder*, I cannot believe those two-faced opportunists!"

Her coffee abandoned on the end table, she hopped to her feet and began pacing again, her incensed muttering alternating between Spanish and English.

"Mari," I said gently. "This is your first order of business as a member of Knight. You decide the fate of Anzaldua. Welcome your parents into the Knight fold if they promise to quit their bigoted bullshit. Toss them out to survive on the dregs of Ferrero if they don't. Take the meeting. Don't take the meeting. This is *your* decision."

She paused, looking first at me, then at each of the guys. "Really?"

"Really," Zach replied. "Anzaldua would be a huge get for Knight, but not at the expense of our values." He glanced at me, his smile widening. "Fuck, it feels awesome to have values."

"Sure does," Noah agreed from his spot on the other end of the couch.

"I...," Mari began before she shut her eyes with a pained expression. "I haven't seen them since the holiday break. They've only been getting worse about my relationship with Carmen. And yet, I *still* can't believe they went around me to get to my best friend. Through *Zach*. Ugh." Her eyes popped open, and the fierce girl I knew as my best friend was back. "We'll set the meeting, but let's make them sweat for a while. I can't wait to see their faces when they figure out who holds their fate in her expertly manicured hands."

I let out a sigh of relief, and Bennett squeezed me affectionately.

The road to "good friend" status was going to be a long and bumpy one, but I hoped this was a start.

Our Saturday afternoon was spent in the library, huddled at the end of one of the long study tables. Someone had cleaned the blood off the door to the conference room and the carpet below it, and now students were spread across the cavernous room, whispering, working, and oblivious to the gauntlet that we'd thrown down in here twenty-four hours ago.

I was sitting next to Zach, and Bennett worked on my other side at the head of the table. Mari and Noah took up the seats across from us, and we'd all managed to make headway on the homework we were very behind on after the events of the week.

We were also far enough away from the nearest of our classmates to speak freely while still being out in the open and *seen* by half the student body—because while none of us trusted James Spencer as far as Mari could throw him, we knew the Families' desire to make a giant mess by attacking us around other Academy students was low.

"That's close," Noah said to Mari as he looked over her Chem homework. "But you missed number four and number fifteen."

"*You* try spending most of the semester with Annie as your lab partner," Mari huffed at him. "I know she's not dumb, but that professor-banging skank was not a team player."

I snorted, and even Bennett had lightened up enough these days to crack a smile.

Might've had something to do with the fact that I was currently playing footsie with him under the table, but who could say?

I grinned at Mari. "Did you thank Noah for ridding you of Annie forever?"

She pursed her lips and waved a dismissive hand at me.

"Um, no, because he did that for *you*, chica. And I'm certain you've already thanked him in ways he *really* appreciates."

"*Mari.*"

Noah's beautiful smile was only the slightest bit smug. "She's not wrong."

"Angel," Bennett rumbled, and Mari visibly swooned just as she had the first time she'd heard Bennett's name for me. He hooked his foot around my ankle, inviting me to tear my heart-eyes away from Noah. Zach was still engrossed in his tablet, but he continued to absently trace patterns on my thigh with his fingertips as he read.

I looked at Bennett. "Hmm?"

"I think we all need to acknowledge that our parents are dropping the pretense of being unwilling to kill you," Bennett said, almost keeping the distress from clouding his face. "You've moved against the Families publicly multiple times, and you've hit them hard enough that even their strongest allies are about to jump ship. They're desperate enough to risk their image now."

Zach grunted in agreement. "Especially because you have us. They made it extremely clear that they think we'll run right back to them if they can just get rid of you."

None of this was news to me, but I hated to see the strain of worry that had crept onto all three of my boys' faces, not to mention the near panic on Mari's. "I know," I said with a wry grin. "But history shows I'm pretty hard to kill. I'm like a cockroach."

No one found that amusing.

I sighed. "We're prepared for this, guys. I know it's all new to you, but I've known I was going to be in this position for seven long years. We're full steam ahead, and we're going to end it as soon as possible."

"So, what's next, then?" Mari asked tentatively, like she wasn't sure she really wanted to know.

"Well," I began. "Noah's already taken everything worth having from Peter." I beamed a loving smile his way, and he preened. "And Andrea's scrambling. Ferrero makes a lot of its money with guns and muscle, and Zach's cut her off from just about any capable assistance she could hope to procure after we blew a hole in the Ferrero Enforcers."

"Amazing what you can do with a little money and the connections you make being forced to do the Family's dirty work for years," Zach mused, now tucking his hand in between my legs like a deviant.

"But Spencer still stands," Bennett said. "They've lost their major tech VCs to Knight, but my father's empire is still mostly intact. He's plotting."

I twirled my pen between my fingers, wishing it were my knife. "I know. Zepp and Silver are working on something, but I think we need a shot across the bow, like, soon."

"Spencer cares the most about the Family image," Bennett said, leaning back in his chair and folding his arms across his chest. He'd dressed down today in his crew shirt and team joggers, and his corded forearms flexed with the movement—something I could now ogle to my heart's content without a shred of guilt. He clocked where my eyes went, and while his reproachful face said, "Behave," his heated eyes definitely said, "I'm going to fuck your brains out later." I smirked at him, but he forged on. "As the white-collar powerhouse, Spencer has a higher proportion of investors and partners who find the violence, murder, and underhanded shit... distasteful. They know it exists, but they don't actually want to be publicly associated with it. It may be time to make another huge statement in the press."

"I can help with that," a deep voice purred, and Raiford

Montgomery sauntered out of the stacks, raking his hand through his blond coif and flexing a bicep in his polo shirt as he moved.

He grabbed a chair from the table next to us and pulled up a seat at the corner of ours, right smack dab in between Bennett and me. He gave me a lascivious smile, and if my boys' looks could kill, Raif would be dust in the cracks of the hardwood floor right now.

"Is that so?" Mari asked, lightly elbowing Noah as I smothered a snicker.

"Sure," he said, oblivious to how close to death he was walking as he continued to give me his flirty eyes. "I have a proposal for the lovely Knight Heir, if she'll hear me out."

CHAPTER NINE
ZACH

This motherfucker was about to die.

He eyed my Princess up and down like he was imagining her hot, tight body naked, and his cocky fucking smirk said he thought he had an actual shot at making that a reality.

"Let's hear it then, Raif," Jojo replied, reaching between her legs where my grip on her thigh had tightened possessively to give my hand a little squeeze.

I did not loosen my grip.

"Well," he drawled. "First off, I was hoping you were still taking applications for your roster of hot, rich boyfriends? As the City's most powerful Heir, not to mention its most beautiful woman, I really don't think you should be limited."

Nope.

Before I could swipe Jojo's knife from her boot with every intention of climbing over her to stick it right in that asshole's abdomen, Bennett had jumped from his chair, grabbed Raif by the collar of his stupid fucking baby blue polo shirt, and slammed him up against the wall behind our table.

Jojo squirmed in her seat, squeezing her thighs together around my hand. I let out an amused hum, leaning in to whisper in her ear, "Something got you hot, baby girl?"

"Shh," she hissed, laser-focused on where Bennett was now snarling in Raif's face.

"Oh, come on, man," Raif was saying as Bennett wrapped his large hand around Raif's throat. "The violence is unnecessary, especially in the *library*."

Noah and I both chuckled at that. Little did he know.

Bennett was unmoved. "You will keep your filthy fucking eyes off her," he growled. "She is not open for business. She is not some exclusive fucking club you can buy or charm your way into. She's mine, she's Noah's, and she's Zach's. It has been the four of us since the day she was fucking born, and it will *only* be the four of us until the day we all stop breathing. If I catch you staring at her like she's your last fucking meal ever again, I will end you. Do you understand me, Montgomery?"

The low moan that Jojo smothered in her throat had my dick twitching in my pants. I met Noah's amused stare with one of my own.

Finally having Bennett fully *in* this thing with us was both a massive relief and unexpectedly entertaining.

Mari fanned herself dramatically. "Okay, I understand now, chica. Even *I* felt that in my lady parts."

Jojo let out a pleased sigh. "Right?"

"Okay! Okay! I got it," Raif muttered, raising his hands in surrender. "I actually do have something to propose that might help Jolie in her... current adversarial position against the Families."

Bennett glared at him, not moving a muscle, until Jojo

finally called him off. "Let him down, Bennett. People are staring, and I think we all know Montgomery Star Media could be useful to us, if that's where this is going."

With one last threatening look, Bennett released Raif, who sagged in relief against the wall while Bennett strode back to his seat like nothing at all had happened.

Raif, who'd apparently decided to stop being a dumbfuck, took the open chair next to Noah. He now sat a comfortable distance from our Princess, who just eyed him with a look that said he'd better impress her with whatever he'd come to say.

"Right, well," he said, swallowing nervously, all that idiotic bravado from earlier vanished. "As you all are aware, my family has kept a very loose affiliation with Ferrero, but we've operated as independently as is possible in this City. Obviously, the current state of... unrest within the Families is starting to become public knowledge, and we're ready to break completely."

Interesting, and not unexpected. It wouldn't be a huge loss for my mom because Montgomery hadn't been that useful to Ferrero to begin with, but every little thing helped in this fight. With a dubious look, I asked, "And what do your parents want in return for Knight's support in this break from my mom?"

He shrugged. "Honestly? To be left alone. They don't want to be taken over by Knight or owned in any way, despite the potential... monetary incentives."

Jolie stared at him in silence. I knew she gave zero fucks about Knight taking over a media company unless it would cause a direct and devastating hit to the Families, but I could see her mind whirling nonetheless. "Knight isn't interested in owning the whole City, Raif. Tell your parents they're clear to bail on Andrea, and we'll back them. But I suspect you have something else you're offering for this alliance?"

He nodded. "You want to wage war in the press? Every one of our media properties is available to you. Sit for an interview with my mom. Have the Heirs with you, and we'll run it on every platform we've got. The Saint Gabriel Star Today news and culture blog is the most trafficked website on the entire East Coast. My mom has ten million followers on social media. We can help you tell the world anything you want about the Families."

I looked around the table at my brothers, my girl, and Mari—savvy in her own right in the City's culture circles—and all of them looked as encouraged as I felt. Given the new information we had about exactly what our parents had been trying to do when they murdered the Knights and the very real evidence Jolie now had her hands on in the form of her dad's research, this actually had the potential to ruin the Families in the eyes of not just the City, but the entire world.

"Schedule it for tomorrow," Jolie commanded, not fucking around now. "My people will be in touch."

Then she stood up, effectively dismissing Raiford—that useful little weasel—and she grabbed her backpack, ready to work.

"Let's go, team. We have a lot to do before tomorrow."

I yanked at my collar for the twentieth time since I'd donned my suit earlier this morning.

"I hate playing Heir," I griped to the room.

"You look sexy, Zach," Jojo said from her spot in Montgomery Star Media's hair-and-makeup chair. She dragged her eyes across all three of us where we stood, stiff and on high alert, along the wall of her dressing room. "You all do," she added with a sultry smile.

"Seconded," Max quipped from his spot on the opposite wall. Unlike Bennett, Noah, and me, who were all dressed in our finest suits, he got to be here in his tactical gear. "I do love me some rich pretty boys. Big Man fills out that Tom Ford so *deliciously*."

Bennett sighed irritably, and Noah pouted next to me. "Does he really need to be back here, sweetheart? The three of us are packing, and I know you have your gun strapped to your thigh under that dress."

She uncrossed and recrossed her legs, and my eyes darted like a heat-seeking missile to the sexy-as-fuck thigh holster she wore under her deep purple dress, her gun just visible through the slit in the fabric. She tutted at us. "I know you guys are plenty deadly. Max is just here for a visible show of muscle. Get along, please."

"You heard her, Nikko," Max added with a shit-eating grin.

Noah sighed and banged the back of his head on the wall.

The quiet woman putting the finishing touches on Jojo's makeup had been fastidiously ignoring all of us like a pro, and it was only her presence that had prevented me from booting Max out into the hall and bending my Princess over the dresser while I showed her other boyfriends how to make our girl scream.

A knock sounded at the door before a polite voice called, "Sound check in five minutes, please."

The makeup artist released Jojo from her ministrations, and our gorgeous girl unfolded from her chair, smoothing her dress and standing tall on her designer heels. She grinned at us. "Let's go ruin the Families, shall we?"

Bennett eyed her with that obsessed look of his before he shoved away from the wall, grasped her chin in his hand, and stole a raw, possessive kiss. "You look beautiful, Angel. Don't hold back out there."

"Stop it, I'm *swooning*," Max crooned, and all four of us rolled our eyes at him.

We made our way into the quiet hallway and headed to the spacious, brightly lit studio where Montgomery Star Media conducted its interviews with City VIPs. The Tier One company owned the bottom ten floors in a modern high-rise that sat along the river several blocks to the northeast of Knight Tower. It was quiet today, with only a skeleton crew working on this Sunday for the hastily scheduled interview with the resurrected Knight Heir who was shaking up the City.

I laced my fingers through Jojo's as we walked, and she hummed happily when I brought her wrist to my lips for a soft kiss. I whispered, "I love you, Princess. I'm so fucking proud of you."

I was so taken in by that adorable blush that hit her cheeks—the one that only Bennett, Noah, and I could elicit from the stone-cold, badass bitch that was our girl—that I almost missed the weird fucking look the passing janitor had fixed on Jojo.

Just as he made a sudden, jerky move to grab something from the front of his cart of cleaning supplies, I moved.

"Get down!" I shouted, tackling Jojo to the ground just as the janitor ripped a pistol from the cart and fired.

The bullet hit the wall above our heads, and Max and Noah had both already pulled their own weapons and fired in the "janitor's" direction. He dove behind his cart, wheeling it back down the hall toward the stairwell and shielding his body as he returned fire.

Max, the only one of us wearing a Kevlar vest and a helmet, ran after him. "Go! Get Jojo out of this hallway!"

"Fuck that, I'm going to kill that cowardly little bitch," Jojo seethed as we rolled to our feet, keeping low.

"Princess, if this was a Family hit, there'll be more coming," I said, pushing her along the wall. "Spencer still has quality Enforcers at its disposal."

"And this gutless bullshit reeks of my father," Bennett spat as we ran for the studio.

"Incoming!" Max shouted, his heavy boots now pounding behind us. "Hargraves, help me out here."

Noah whirled, pulling both of his pistols from where he wore them under his suit. A quick glance over my shoulder revealed that the janitor bitch had unlocked the emergency stairwell door, and half a dozen more non-disguised Enforcers had entered the hall.

"Kill the girl. We need the Heirs alive!" one of them shouted as they began to rush forward, weapons raised.

Max laid down cover fire as Noah squared up, taking out two of the invaders with clean headshots right off the bat. The others scattered, and we used the lull to sprint out into the large circular television studio.

We found Lucinda Montgomery, Raif's mom and legacy Tier One heir to the Montgomery Star Media Empire, cowering behind the plush sofa where she interviewed her guests, her two camera men with her.

"What is going on?" she cried. "Are those gunshots?"

No one answered her, the five of us fanning out into the wide room and readying ourselves for battle.

"Stay down!" Bennett ordered as he flipped the long metal table sitting along the wall onto its side, spilling coffee service and pastries across the floor. "And roll the cameras!"

Bennett ducked behind the table, and Jojo and I were quick to join him. Noah had taken up a post behind the couch opposite Lucinda, and he now had the best sight line to the door. Max was shouting into his earpiece, which meant the fun was really about to start.

I shot my own message to my team, darting a quick look out of the floor-to-ceiling windows of the studio, the midmorning sun giving us a technicolor view of the City streets four floors below. "We've got eyes on the building's entrance," I announced. "In case there's a second wave."

"There will be," Bennett replied, grim, and Jojo just nodded like that was a given.

"Someone fucking leaked," she muttered as she checked her magazine and shoved it back into her gun. "The Montgomerys have a mole."

"A dead one," I grunted.

Just as the Enforcers streamed out of the hall and into the studio, guns blazing, a loud crack sounded, and the glass window behind the couches shattered in an explosion of glass.

Martinez and Rocky flew into the room, abandoning their perch on the window-washing platform outside.

"They really tried it, huh?" Rocky shouted as Martinez and Max managed to tackle two of the Enforcers to the ground. Rocky popped off a shot at another guy who dove out of the way, sliding across the floor and coming to a stop in front of our table.

I kissed my girl's cheek before I said, "I'm taking this one, Princess. Be safe."

Then I vaulted over the table and pounced on the guy as he scrambled for his gun.

Chaos ensued. I made quick work of my captive, and it didn't take much longer for the others to do the same. Jojo dropped the last guy, who'd turned to take aim at me where I crouched over the body of his buddy, with a perfect shot to the head.

"Is that all of them?" she asked as we all stood dusting ourselves off.

"In here, yes," Bennett replied, tucking his firearm away as he made his way over to check on Lucinda and her crew.

Shots rang out from the streets outside, and we realized Noah had disappeared out onto Martinez and Rocky's platform.

I jogged over to stick my head out of the shattered window. "How many are in the second wave?" I shouted at him.

He fired down at the street below. "I got three, and I'm pretty sure Dom got at least five from the patio of the restaurant across the street."

Jolie appeared next to me, surveying the street with a critical eye. She had blood spattered up her arm that was not hers, and her once perfectly curled hair was wild around her gorgeous face. "And Dom thought he was going to get to eat brunch over there undisturbed."

An ear-splitting scream rang out, and a black-clad body fell from the floor above us, dropping right in front of our window and heading for a very painful end on the pavement below.

"What the—" Jolie began, when another body sailed past us, meeting a similar fate.

I snorted. "Yeah, I figured Frankie might be here somewhere. He's both always around and never around, somehow."

She just nodded sagely. "Right."

Max stuck his head out of the adjacent shattered window. "Got the all-clear. Mrs. Montgomery is freaking out, so you should probably let her know if you still want to do the interview."

Jojo snorted. "Fuck yeah, I do. The Families sent the cavalry in here to stop me from doing that exact thing. They don't get to win this one."

Noah climbed back in through the window, and as his feet hit the studio floor, I turned to press my girl right up against him, her back hitting his chest. He held her tight as I smashed my lips to hers, my adrenaline still pumping and making me horny as fuck. "Go get 'em, Princess. I'll try not to mount you on that couch in front of everyone, but it's going to be a fucking test of self-control."

She moaned as Noah dragged his lips up the column of her pale, delicate neck. "It is such a shame," he said softly. "You're so sexy when you're in warrior mode, and it's never convenient for us to fuck you afterward like we're dying to."

"Ugh, stop it, you two," she whined, all the while fisting my dress shirt in her wandering little hand and leaning into where Noah nuzzled at her neck. "I have to get my game face on."

"She's right. Let her go, you horny fucks," Bennett groused as he approached. He yanked Jojo away, grasped her face in both hands to lay a greedy kiss on her lips like a hypocritical dick, then led her to the couch.

Then we sat on that couch, all four of us still dirty and bloody from the brazen attack on our girl by the Families, as Jojo told her story to Lucinda while the cameras rolled.

She reminded the world of what she'd witnessed when she was eleven years old, and this time, the three of us were there to confirm, on the record, that we saw it too.

She described the discovery of her dad's miraculene

breakthrough and Anders' confession of the true motive behind the Knights' murder. The wide-eyed, confused look she'd given Lucinda when she asked if Jojo knew the whereabouts of her uncle now was a very nice touch.

Finally, she laid out what she'd done with her dad's research by taking the biggest tech discovery of the decade and essentially giving it away for free to research universities while also starting the largest scholarship program for low-income students in the world.

Bennett, Noah, and I took turns describing the decaying state of our Families, our love for Jolie, and the "horrific attack" we'd suffered only minutes prior to the interview, which Lucinda promised would be spliced together with the footage of Spencer lackeys invading the studio like locusts.

By the end of the hour, the Families looked like despicable, desperate pretenders, while Jolie looked like the righteous angel not to be fucked with that she was.

"Thank you, Miss Knight," Lucinda gushed as we wrapped. "This is going to be a look at the Families that no one has ever been privy to before."

Jolie eyed her coolly, her congenial interview persona now nowhere to be found. "Lucinda, you have a rat in your house. No one outside of my team or yours knew I would be here today and for what reason. However, the Families not only knew, but they were also able to get past your paltry security with a weak disguise. It's unacceptable."

Lucinda gulped. "I.... It couldn't have been one of ours."

"It certainly wasn't one of ours," Bennett replied, and she wilted under his stony glare.

When her eyes darted my way, I gave her my chilliest smirk. "I suggest you find the rat and have him or her delivered to Knight Tower in short order, or we'll let Frankie Fingers comb through the entire company himself."

She paled, nodding mutely.

"Excellent," Noah said with his bright smile. "It's been a pleasure, Lucinda. We'll have our cleanup crew invoice you once they're finished here."

With that, we left the studio. I drove us back to the Academy in my Ferrari, Noah and Bennett both declining to ride shotgun so they could wrap themselves around Jojo in my tiny backseat.

No one spoke, and I cast glances in my rearview mirror the entire drive, drawing comfort from the image of them huddled together, my brothers and my girl, as the events of the day finally settled over all of us like the crushing weight they were.

Reality sank into my skin, hardening me from the inside out.

When this whole thing was over, my mom would be dead.

It was the only way I wouldn't lose my girl again—this time, for good.

CHAPTER TEN
JOLIE

"We are indeed troubled by the allegations made by Miss Knight, especially given that she has been able to produce the evidence regarding the astounding miraculene research left to her by her father. We are also sickened by the violence perpetrated against her that Montgomery Star Media was able to record. As such, we will be ending our partnership with Spencer, effective immediately."

I leaned closer to Noah, looking over his shoulder to watch the end of the press conference being held by the largest global investment bank in New York City as it played on his phone. We sat in the back row of our Monday morning Finance class, waiting for the professor to begin his lecture while also pretending we didn't feel the wary stares of almost every student at Holywell on us at all times.

A text popped up on Noah's screen.

Bennett: Spencer stock is tanking

I pulled my phone from my bag to respond in our group chat.

Jojo: good thing I had Zepp invest your trust fund entirely in Knight last week

Noah snorted next to me. "He was ready to refuse every last dime from that trust. He'll thank you later, I hope."

I waggled my eyebrows at him. "Or spank me later, probably."

Noah hummed happily under his breath. "He wishes. You only let me do that, right, sweetheart?"

I felt the flush tinge my cheeks, but I kept it together, leaning in to brush my lips against his ear. "That's right. I'm only a *good girl* for you, Noah."

He shut his eyes and let out a low, pained groan.

Zach snickered from my other side. "That wasn't nice, Princess. It's been all work and no play around here lately, so the blue balls are really setting in."

I turned to look at him, arching a brow. "The faster we break the Families down into the tiny, little pieces of garbage they are, the sooner we'll have unlimited time for you three to just fuck me to your hearts' content."

Zach just smirked, those dark eyes full of a *lot* of promising things, before he turned back to his phone and his new partner in crime—Mari, who sat on his other side. They'd been plotting the fates of the various Ferrero cast-offs knocking at Knight's door, and their blossoming friendship made my heart squeeze a little.

He tossed his phone onto his desktop as he got to chatting with Mari, and it was then that I noticed Zach had set the lock screen to a still shot of me from the attack at Montgomery Star Media. I was standing tall behind the flipped craft services table, my dress torn and my hair askew as I held my Glock high to take out the last remaining Spencer goon. The reminder made me feel powerful while also scaring the shit out of me, because that Enforcer had been about to take a shot at Zach when I'd ended him.

While no one had sustained any major or lasting injuries—including Lucinda, her employees, and the few members of our Shadow team that had been on hand just in case things had gone exactly as they had—it had still been too fucking close.

The low thrum of dread that now beat through my veins was a new development. When I'd started this journey in earnest—the day I'd shoved my grief aside and told Dom that I was going to destroy the Families for what they'd done—I'd numbed myself to anything that wasn't the mission. I knew the risks, and I accepted them.

But now I had three of the biggest pieces of my heart back, and the thought of losing any of them in this war filled me with pure, unbridled terror.

I shook those thoughts away, refusing to collapse into an emotional puddle in the middle of Finance class. James Spencer was paying for endangering my boys, and he was about to pay some more.

The class passed quickly when I finally let myself become absorbed in the lecture. When the professor dismissed us at the end of the hour, we packed our shit, unhurried, Mari and Zach still giggling together like schoolgirls and Noah continuing to shoot me heated glances that said he would bend me over his desk at the first available opportunity.

Hell yes.

"Ugh, what?" Mari suddenly spat at a group of students lingering a few rows below us, several of them shooting hateful glares in our direction. "If any of you have a grievance you want to address with the Heirs, I suggest you do it quickly or move along."

Of course, Chad was at the center of this little group, with Dane Jefferson hanging awkwardly off to the side, and the small flock of Tier Two ass-kissers who ran around with Harper and probably fucked Chad on the regular were there to sneer at us too.

Chad's beady eyes were hard, and he spoke through gritted teeth. "We don't have anything to say to *pretenders*."

Zach's lazy smile was his most dangerous one. "Careful, Hendrickson. I don't give a fuck if you insult me, but one word against my girl or Mari and you'll find yourself having a really bad night tomorrow at Fight Night."

The girls tittered, and Chad's eyes widened just a fraction before he scoffed. "Whatever, Ferrero. Once that cunt is put down, all the cowards who fled the Families will end up right back where they were. This little war your bitch started because she's a hysterical drama queen is only going to end one way."

I felt Zach vibrating next to me, and Noah had just blown a hard, calming breath through his nostrils.

I knew the feeling—it had taken a mountain of self-control to stop myself from beating the life out of Chad Hendrickson every single day since I'd first stepped foot in Holywell Hall.

Forcing an unaffected smile, I ran a soothing palm down Zach's back while squeezing Noah's hand with my other. "It's okay, guys. Chad's a little sore the feds just came knocking at the Hendrickson manor, aren't you, buddy?"

Chad's square face flushed red all over. "The feds don't fucking scare my father. You should've stayed dead, bitch, because now it's open season." He jerked his head at his groupies, and they trotted after him as he stalked off.

Zach cracked his knuckles. "Tomorrow night's gonna be a fucking bloodbath."

That threatening growl reverberated in my panties. "Can't wait."

"You're calling it 'Operation Perv Sweep'?" Mari asked around a bite of her salad. "Did Zepp name that one?"

"Silver, actually," Noah replied, taking a sip of his second coffee of the day.

Hannah Langford gaped at us. We'd dispensed with the raised table and were back in our usual seats at lunch, so Hannah, John Tyler, Raif, Devin, and a few of Devin's very chill Tier Two buddies had joined us. "You sent the feds after a dozen Spencer-connected families?" Hannah asked, incredulous. "I can't believe the feds finally grew enough balls to even set foot in this City."

I shrugged. "They're feeling braver since Knight invited them here."

Mari's shrewd gaze cut across the aisle to where Chad sat with Harper and their dwindling but vocal group of students loyal to the Families. Harper was comforting Chad, running her one good hand up and down his meaty arm and whispering to him. "No wonder Chad was running his mouth earlier," Mari said. "His daddy might *actually* end up in jail."

Bennett squeezed my thigh under the table, and I grabbed his hand, cradling it in my lap. This little project had been in the works for a while as our first real shot at Spencer, and Bennett had been all too happy to help bring it home last week after he'd abandoned his Family once and for all.

Over the years, the Shadows had collected information on a group of the City's Spencer-connected elite whose special *predilection* was pornography featuring underage girls and boys. We had a good batch of evidence on Benedict Hendrickson (and by association, Chad) and a few others, and then my venture into James Spencer's safe had yielded his stash of blackmail material on several more Tier One Spencer allies. Once Zepp had downloaded all of this information to Bennett last week, he'd been able to add the rest of the names.

"I wish I'd paid better attention to this shit, Angel," Bennett mused, brooding next to me at the head of the table per his usual. "My father used to bitch about Hendrickson and his little circle of deviants like they were risking the Spencer empire's fake perfect image, but I hadn't known he was talking about a fucking child porn ring."

I began rubbing little soothing circles on his palm with my thumb. "I know, Bennett. There's nothing you could have done, anyway, but you remembered all the names your father has ever complained about in connection with Hendrickson. They're all getting what they deserve because you *were* paying attention."

"Yeah, man," Zach chimed in from his spot on Bennett's other side. "These pedos are about to get ass-fucked by the feds, and Spencer is going to be hard-pressed to stop the bleeding. Not even the most cynical of the greedy Tier Twos is going to want to touch any of these companies now, and your ability to collect and retain your father's bullshit over the years was a huge part in making that happen."

Bennett huffed, but I caught the corners of his lips threatening to turn up in a smile. After years of constantly being called a failure by his father, it would take some time before Bennett would truly believe he was anything but.

I'd remind him at every turn, and so would Zach and Noah.

I floated through the rest of the day on autopilot, still trying to get back into the grind of school after everything that had happened in the past week. I took grim satisfaction in the constant updates from our team on the downfall of the Spencer white-collar pedophile club, and, despite the rising tensions of this war that we all carried with us now day in and day out, I managed to sleep soundly that night with my boys curled around me.

The next evening, after throwing myself wholeheartedly into crew practice and inhaling my dinner sandwich of choice, Zach diverted me from the walk back to our dorm, pulling me instead toward the gymnasium.

I'd almost forgotten it was Fight Night once again.

"Oh shit, are you fighting tonight?" I asked him as he tugged me through the gym doors and into the basketball arena that was dimly lit and smelled of sweat and Clorox. "Warn a girl, Ferrero. I would've brought a change of panties."

He smirked at me over his shoulder. "You'll see, Princess."

The festivities were well underway. The usual ring of gross, sweaty boys hovering around the thick tumbling mat created the makeshift cage for the fights while the single lamp hanging overhead illuminated the fighters. Dane had his bullhorn and was egging the crowd on as the sound of their bloodlust filled the room, the shouts and jeers echoing off the high gym ceiling.

Bennett and Noah waited for us at the edge of the mat,

the other students giving them a wide berth. Noah wore Knight-Tech-branded gym sweats—*where did he get those?*—and his hair was wet and smelled like chlorine, which meant he'd done his swim workout this evening. Bennett had just come from crew, so he was in his usual long-sleeve crew team shirt and my favorite little training shorts that revealed his long, powerful legs.

"You're drooling, sweetheart," Noah said into my ear as he pulled me into his side.

I nuzzled into his neck to take a nice sniff of him, sighing at his familiar clean-laundry scent mingled with the chlorine. "Bennett wears those shorts to torture me. He's been doing it since the night last semester when he barged into the weight room and shut off my music because he was being a massive dickhead."

Bennett tore his eyes away from where John Tyler was wiping the floor with some B-Dorm out-of-towner. "I shut off your music because hearing one of my dead best friend's favorite songs made me feel like someone was stabbing me in the fucking chest."

I melted a little bit in Noah's arms, and I gave Bennett a slack, moon-eyed stare. I managed to croak, "Oh."

He returned my gawking with a dark look, like I was in trouble for that moment all over again because yes, I *had* deceived them, and yes, I *had* assumed they'd forgotten me like I'd tried to do to them. I wouldn't apologize for the former, but I'd been wrong on all counts on the latter.

Dane interrupted our little stare-off by shouting into his bullhorn, "Winner, John Tyler Ashmore! I know, I know, big shocker for all you regulars here at Holywell Fight Night." He paused to peruse his clipboard, his eyes widening at whatever he saw slated next. "We have a challenge fight on the books for tonight. You all know what that means—the challenged fighter has to accept the fight or forfeit any and all titles from the past year! So, Chad Hendrickson, step into the ring because *you've. Been. Challeeeeenged*!"

My body vibrated with excitement. I watched Chad march onto the mat with his usual bravado—I knew he wasn't used to losing out here—but there was an air of uneasiness about him.

He'd fucked up, and Zach was about to call him on it.

Dane put his bullhorn to his lips again. "Alright, challenge accepted! Will the challenger please approach?"

I expected Zach to strip and waltz onto the mat. My jaw hit the floor when *Bennett* strode forward, shucking his crew T-shirt as he arrived in his corner.

The entire gym gasped at Bennett's shirtless state, the crowd now taking in his beautifully carved body and the angel wings that stretched across his broad chest, glimmering under the fluorescent bulb that hung above the mat.

"Oh, look at Spencer, publicly declaring how fucking gone he's always been for Jolie Knight," Zach said with a chuckle.

"He's... he's never let anyone see his tattoo?" I asked, my eyes glued to Bennett as he gave Chad the stoniest, most dangerous glare I'd ever seen.

Noah grinned next to me. "Only his tattoo artist, Zach, and I had ever seen it. We aren't sure how he kept it from the crew team, but he always said it was his 'private fucking business.' Now look at him. He's just a lovesick fool, isn't he?"

It was me who was the lovesick fool. The things I felt for Bennett even back when he was being an obstinate ass had been intense enough—now I worried I was going to implode under the weight of it all.

I sniffed, blinking back the tears that threatened to emerge and ruin my reputation completely. "It's still hard to believe," I whispered.

"Believe it, baby girl," Zach replied. "We're *all* that fucking gone for you. Now, watch Spencer give Chad what he deserves for the way he's treated our girl."

And I did. The usually rowdy crowd was almost subdued, watching in horrified awe as Bennett quickly and efficiently beat the ever-loving fuck out of Chad. It was violent, bloody, and gorgeous. It took both Zach and Noah to finally peel Bennett off his sniveling, almost-unrecognizable opponent long after Dane had called the fight.

And then Zach clutched me tight, my back against his chest in a dark, quiet corner of the locker room, as Bennett held my hips in his bruising grip and fucked me mercilessly, still high on the adrenaline of the fight and drunk on our love—on our *obsession*—all while Noah guarded the door and praised me for taking Bennett so fucking good.

That night, I slept like the dead.

CHAPTER ELEVEN
NOAH

"Thanks, Silver. Just keep an eye on him, and I'll let you know if we decide to make any additional moves."

"On it. Stay safe, sir." She signed off, and I locked the screen of my phone before tossing it onto the surface of my desk.

I removed my glasses to pinch my brow like that would stave off the oncoming headache that was dealing with my father. He'd done exactly what I'd known he would the second he realized I'd truly taken everything from him: he cashed out his personal accounts and anything he could still get his hands on at what was left of Hargraves, and he disappeared.

And now I had to decide if that was enough.

But it wasn't really up to me.

"Knock, knock."

Normally, a student arriving in the final thirty minutes of my Friday afternoon office hours would be mildly annoying, but I knew that voice and welcomed the interruption.

Jojo stepped into my office, locking the door behind her.

When I glanced her way, I froze for several long seconds as every blood cell in my body rushed straight to my dick.

"Professor Hargraves?" she said, biting her lush lower lip and giving me a wide-eyed, innocent stare. "I was hoping we could chat for a minute. It's about my... grades."

She slinked forward, and I ran my greedy gaze over her silky white blouse, the black bra I could see through its sheer material, her tiny little navy skirt, her thigh-high white stockings, and her shiny black high heels that I knew had to have been borrowed from Mari. She'd braided her white-blonde hair into two pigtails and painted her lips a glossy pink, which matched the adorable flush in her freckled cheeks.

I needed to pull myself together—because if this was going where I prayed to every version of God ever worshiped by humans it was, all of my fantasies were about to come true.

I schooled my features into something more serious, motioning to the chair in front of my desk. "Have a seat, Miss Knight."

She sat primly, crossing her miles-long legs so that her skirt rode up to the very tops of her silky, toned thighs. She worried at the hem of her skirt, affecting a nervous look, before she said, "I'm just concerned about my grade in Advanced Computer Science, Professor. We're already so far into the semester, and I'm struggling *so* much. It's not that you aren't an *amazing* teacher, but I am really in need of some..." She bit her lip again, giving me a coy glance from under her long lashes. "... *extra credit*."

I leaned back in my chair, steepling my fingers under my chin as I gave her a scrutinizing stare, all the while trying desperately to ignore the raging hard-on I was sporting under my desk. "And what do you propose to do to earn this extra credit, Miss Knight?"

She hummed, now twirling one of her braids around a finger. "Well, I may not be very good with computers"—a ridiculous lie, reminding me I was still sore about her deliberately flopping in my class last semester—"but I do have... *other* skills. Ones I'm trying very hard to improve upon."

At her hopeful, doe-eyed look, I adjusted myself in my slacks before I stood from my chair, then I stalked slowly around to the front of my desk. I crossed my arms over my chest as I leaned back against the desktop, studying her intently.

She blushed, casting her gaze to the floor like she was nervous. I knew she was acting—my girl didn't avert her eyes for *anyone*—but that telltale flush that graced her cheeks was genuine. I realized she might actually be a little nervous to play this part for me, especially for the very first time.

The thought made me even harder.

I leaned forward, grasping her chin between my thumb and forefinger as I forced her eyes back to mine. "Are you going to do whatever I ask you to do here in this office, sweet girl?"

Her pupils dilated, and she nodded slowly.

"Good girl," I rumbled, and I swore her thighs clenched, shooting dopamine straight through my entire body. "As long as you follow my instructions and try very hard—if you give it your *very* best effort—you'll be able to earn your extra credit."

She nodded again, this time eagerly. "Yes, Professor."

I stroked a gentle hand over her cheek, then I said, "On your knees, please, sweetheart."

She lowered gingerly to the ground, her icy blue eyes

never leaving mine, before asking in a breathy voice, "What would you like me to do for you, Professor?"

Fuck me, this was heaven. My beautiful, powerful girl on her knees for me, looking so desperate—so *hungry*—to please me.

Keep it together, Hargraves.

"Unzip my pants," I commanded, keeping my tone gentle but authoritative. She did as I asked, first unbuckling my belt with her nimble fingers before getting my slacks unbuttoned with the singular focus of a woman on a mission. She ran a hand over the bulge in my boxers, and I grabbed her wrist, stilling her. "Do you want my cock, sweet girl?"

She peered up at me, the corner of her lips threatening to tip up into a smirk before she wiped it away, replacing it with a supplicating look. "Yes, please, Professor. I want your cock very much."

"And where do you want it?"

She licked her lips, and I bit back a groan. "In my mouth."

I beamed my biggest smile down at her so she'd know how perfect she was, then I pulled my straining dick from my boxers, giving it a few light pumps for her. "Okay, sweetheart. How much do you want that extra credit? Show me how hard you're willing to work to succeed in my class."

She wrapped her hand around my dick, stroking it lovingly before she licked me from balls to tip like I was an ice cream cone. "Your dick is gorgeous, Professor."

"Then show me how much you want it," I demanded.

And she did. The first time she'd gone down on me when I'd shared her with Zach had been fantastic, but this was transcendent. I had all her focus, as she had mine, and I watched in awe as she swallowed me down. I'd never beheld a more beautiful sight than those wide aquamarine eyes on mine and those pink lips wrapped around my cock as she sucked and bobbed with an easy finesse.

"You're doing so, so good, sweet girl," I rasped, my voice cracking under the strain of holding myself back.

She released me with a low, pleased hum, giving me a few more licks while she stroked me. "Am I? I'm trying *so* hard for you, Professor."

Damn it. I pulled my dick from her grasp before I yanked her to her feet.

"Noah!" she squealed in surprise as I lifted her into the air, cradling her ass in my hands as she wrapped her legs around my waist. I carried her around to the back of my desk, shoving my laptop off to the side before I laid her gently down on the surface. I stood between her legs where they hung off the desk, her ass right at the edge where I wanted it.

I flipped her skirt up, exposing her glistening pussy, then I slapped my palm against her firm ass, the crack of flesh meeting flesh echoing off the walls of my quiet office. "No panties, Miss Knight? That's very naughty."

Her breathing became labored as I began to unbutton her blouse. "I was really hoping to get an A, sir."

I chuckled. "Were you hoping I'd fuck this hungry little pussy too?"

She squeezed her eyes closed and moaned. "Yes, Professor."

I managed to get her blouse open, exposing her perfect tits encased in black lace. I ripped the cups down and wrapped my lips around her beaded nipple, giving it a quick suck and a nibble before I switched breasts. She ran her fingers through my hair, humming appreciatively as I worked, and I loved the feeling so much that I decided not to demand that she keep her hands on the desk—yet.

I ran two fingers through her folds to find her soaking, and I groaned before I released her nipple and began my journey south. "You know, I think I will fuck this perfect pussy, sweetheart," I said, kissing down the taut hollow of her belly. "But I can't resist a taste first. Would you like that?"

"Fuck yes," she replied, her words breathy and eager.

I pulled up my chair and got comfortable, giving her another firm swat on the side of her ass. "Language, Miss Knight."

She snorted, and I suppressed my own laugh. My sweet Jojo now cussed like a sailor—just another way she fit so perfectly with Bennett, Zach, and me.

"I'm sorry, Professor. I'm just so... excited to feel your tongue in my pussy. Sir."

I groaned, issuing one more quick slap to her ass as I muttered, "Playing dirty, I see."

Then I tossed her legs over my shoulders and dove in. I'd watched both Zach and Bennett go down on her in the weeks since that first time she and I had finally made love, and while it had been pretty damn satisfying for me, it was nothing compared to the real thing.

I ran my tongue through her center with some long, slow licks, and she squirmed on my face. I wrapped my hands around her thighs, locking her in place, then I gorged on her like a man possessed, reveling in her sweet taste and even sweeter moans.

"*Noah*," she gasped as I worked her clit the way all three of us knew she loved.

I turned my head to sink my teeth into her inner thigh, and she hissed. "Is that what you call me, sweetheart?"

"No, Professor," she whimpered.

"That's better. I want you to come for me now, sweet girl. Give me one gorgeous orgasm, and then I'll fuck you just like you want me to."

"Yes, yes, yes," she chanted in a strained whisper. "Please."

I sucked her clit back into my mouth, lashing it with my tongue while driving two fingers into her with hard, firm strokes until she contracted around me and screamed.

"Noah!" she cried, and I wasn't going to stop even for a second to admonish her for using my name because my girl screaming it while she came was the greatest sound in the entire world.

I licked her a few more times as she came down, then I rose to my feet to stare down at her—flushed, her bare tits rising and falling with her panting breaths, and those big eyes hooded with satiated lust.

My tenuous hold on my control snapped.

I leaned down to smash my lips to hers, taking one raw, bruising kiss before I gathered her hands in my fist and jerked them over the top of her head. I held her still as I guided my aching cock into her, slamming home in one long, hard thrust, and we both moaned together. Her back arched and her eyes shut, and I held her down beneath me as I pounded into her—so tight, so wet, so *divine*.

And so mine.

"Look at you, sweetheart," I said, my voice low and thick as I fucked her. "Spread out on my desk, taking my cock like you were born to do it. You've been so good for me. So, so good."

"Oh God, Noah," she whined. "Fuck, it's so good. I'm so close."

"Yeah? Am I giving you what you wanted? Did you want

me to put you on my desk, hold you down, and fuck you until you forgot your name? Is that why you pranced into my office in a tiny skirt wearing no panties?"

"Yes!"

"Yes, what?"

"Yes, Professor!"

God, I was going to lose it. This was everything I'd ever wanted, and it was with my Jojo—our angel, the girl we loved and lost who I sometimes still couldn't believe was real.

But she *was* real. I had my hands on her skin and my cock inside her body, and she was tightening under me now in a way that had my head spinning.

"Oh, Noah, I'm coming," she wailed.

"Good girl," I managed to croak as I exploded with her, burying my head in the crook of her neck as I fucked her through her climax, my own hitting me like a Mack truck as I fought to stay standing.

I released her hands, and she went straight to running her fingers through my hair again. I purred like a cat, nuzzling into her neck, and when the feeling returned to my legs, I pulled out of her and made quick work of cleaning her up with the tissues stashed in my top desk drawer.

We righted our clothes, then I pulled her into my lap as I sat down in my chair, cradling her like the priceless treasure she was.

"That," I said, blowing out a breath, "was a dream come true. Wow."

She grinned, her eyes lit up with pride. "Yeah? I took a chance that this kind of thing might be up your alley."

I kissed her. "It was fucking fantastic. Thank you, sweetheart."

She snuggled into me. "I know it's been a while since it was just you and me, Noah. I'm sorry it's been so... busy around here."

"Jojo," I said, squeezing her tight. "Please don't worry about that. I know you must feel pressure to make sure you're giving each of us enough attention, but I promise we're all okay. It's not a competition, and we can all feel how deeply you care for us. Plus...." I paused to waggle my eyebrows at her with a big smile. "I think we've each discovered we are very into *watching*."

She punched me playfully in the bicep. "I've noticed. Pervy voyeurs, all three of you."

We sat in comfortable silence, the clock on the wall ticking down the last few minutes of my scheduled office hours, after which I would officially be on spring break.

"Hey, Noah," she murmured.

"Yes, Jojo?"

"I love you. I have since I was a little girl, and now I love you the way a woman loves a man she knows she can't live without. And I want to make sure you know that just because I said it to Zach and Bennett first doesn't mean I loved them sooner or harder."

I kissed her again, slow and sweet, my heart bursting at the seams. "I love you, too, sweetheart. I might've fallen a little bit in love with you even when you were Joanna Miller, but I think I knew the second your eyes hit mine at the Holiday Ball that I was a goner. Even though we had to... work through a few things to get there."

She chuckled. "You're never going to get over my faking it in your class last semester, are you?"

I growled. "I should've spanked you more."

"I'm sure you'll find another opportunity to punish me for being such a bad girl."

I shivered. "You better believe it." Another minute of easy silence stretched between us, and I knew I needed to have a more serious discussion with her while we had this moment together. I took a breath, then I said, "Sweetheart, I need to talk to you about my dad."

She turned her head to look up at me from where she was curled up in my lap. "Did you find him?"

I nodded. "It wasn't hard. He's in Thailand. Paid cash for a beach mansion and appears to be content to hide away and live on the few millions he was able to abscond with."

"Ah." Her brow furrowed as she contemplated how she felt about that.

I brought my hand to her cheek, staring deep into those mesmerizing eyes. "Listen to me, Jojo. This is your decision. I will keep an eye on him while you and I make what used to be Hargraves great in the name of your parents. Or I will fucking end him."

She stared into my eyes, the intense, calculating woman she was when it came to avenging her parents appearing before me. "Peter participated in my parents' murder. He signed the document sealing their fate, and he forced his twelve-year-old son to watch that depraved act of violence. And yet...." She blew out a breath. "He didn't pull the trigger. I sincerely doubt any of it was his idea, and he probably went along with it to save his own ass."

"I would agree, but I'm his son. I'm biased, in spite of everything."

She leaned forward to give me a quick kiss. "I don't need him to die, Noah. I need to take everything from him, which you've already done for me because you're amazing, and I need to never see his face again. We have bigger fish to fry."

I hated that I felt the tiniest bit of relief at her words, but it was what it was—I was still his son, and he was still my dad.

I despised him for what he did, but it would've been difficult for me to kill him.

The clock struck five. "I love you, Jojo," I said. "Let's get the other two and go home, yeah?"

She beamed at me. "Yes, let's. And I love you too."

CHAPTER TWELVE
JOLIE

"Home" was now my Family's penthouse in Knight Tower, wiped free of any trace of my traitorous uncle and tastefully redecorated in a way that suited the modern young woman and her three live-in boyfriends.

Bennett had ensured the Knight penthouse became a proper home for us as a part of his various projects over the past week, and it was a tough call for me as to whether this extremely thoughtful gesture or his pounding Chad into a bloody purple pulp had turned me on more.

I woke Saturday morning in my new giant bed in the primary bedroom, the space around me where the guys had slept warm but empty.

My feet hit the floor—the carpet of my parents' spacious room had been replaced with dark hardwood in the Anders era. The designer Bennett hired had redecorated the room with soft grays and even softer pinks, and the rug under my feet displayed intricate floral designs in those colors. There was a new white dresser, a matching chest of drawers, and the attached sitting room now sported a brand-new squishy gray couch, a pink armchair, and a moderately sized flat-screen TV mounted over the fireplace.

The en suite bathroom had also changed dramatically from when it had been my parents'—my mom's beige tile and colorful accent borders were now a clean, gleaming white. A clawfoot tub replaced the old jacuzzi, and Bennett's designer had ensured there were towels, rugs, and even shiny new chrome plumbing fixtures that had never been touched by the treasonous hands of my uncle.

After I freshened up and threw on some dark leggings and a cropped long-sleeved shirt, I padded down the hall, past the spare bedrooms that had each been redone and assigned to Zach, Noah, and Bennett. Anything they'd been able to salvage from their rooms at their respective Family homes had made its way here, and Bennett's army of personal shoppers had filled in the gaps. Each of my boys had a tasteful, masculine space to call his own, and I couldn't wait to defile each of their beds on the rare occasion we didn't all pile into mine.

I glanced toward the other end of the hall before I turned to head down the stairs, catching a quick glimpse of my dad's study through the open door. Noah's team had thoroughly searched it for anything else incriminating Anders might have left behind—finding nothing of note—before Bennett's team had cleared the old office furniture and created two mega desks that were built into the side walls, each with two workstations. Now all four of us had a space to study, run the Knight empire, or plot James' and Andrea's ruin.

I trotted down the stairs, and I heard the low murmurs of voices in the kitchen. The renovations done after my parents' deaths had changed the main living area quite a bit, replacing marble tile with hardwood, opening the formal dining room to the new white kitchen with updated appliances and gunmetal gray backsplash. Bennett's team had delivered new furniture for the living room: comfy couches, richly colored rugs and throw pillows, and a giant flat-screen television connected to every kind of gaming console known to man. Gleaming glass doors looked out onto our pool deck where I could see that even the lounge chairs were brand-new.

I loved it all. There were still hints of home here, and I tried very hard to channel that feeling into only the good memories of my parents or the time spent here with the boys growing up. But now it also felt like a fresh space for us to make new memories in as a family.

"Morning, Princess!" Zach called as I trudged sleepily into the kitchen, allowing the smell of fresh coffee to be my guide.

"Hi, guys." I looked around the room and found Zach behind the stove, meticulously pouring pancake batter onto a griddle, shirtless, wearing only an apron and his pajama pants. Noah sat at the dining room table, sipping coffee and typing on his laptop, his blond hair a little rumpled and his eyes focused behind his dark frames. Bennett lounged in a chair next to him, lazily scrolling his phone and drinking something that looked suspiciously like green juice.

"What's up, boss lady?"

I startled, suddenly noticing Rocky sitting at the large kitchen island. He drank his own mug of coffee while doing something on his tablet, his massive shoulders hunched over the counter and his shaved head gleaming under the bright kitchen lights.

"Rocky," I said with a narrow-eyed stare. "Fancy meeting you here."

He grinned at me. "Just stopping by. We're all organized downstairs now, and I'm on the morning 'make sure the boss is alive' rotation."

"Ah-ha," I replied, moseying over to the kitchen after getting a quick good-morning kiss from both Bennett and Noah. "Well, as you can see, I am still kicking. All is quiet in the Knight penthouse."

"For now," he said with a wink. "And my man Ferrero is making some awesome-smelling pancakes."

Zach huffed. "Don't mind him, Princess. He can't take a hint and has invited himself to breakfast."

I kissed Zach's cheek before I poured myself a cup of hot, delicious coffee. "It's fine. I could use a status report, anyway." I shot Rocky a pointed look and waved a hand at him. "Make yourself useful, my friend."

He gave me a brisk little salute, took a sip of his coffee, and began his report. "The three floors below us here in the penthouse are now your security command center, a mix of the Shadows who've decided to officially join the Knight organization and legacy Knight Enforcers who worked for your parents and whom we've thoroughly vetted. We've also picked up a team from Hargraves who apparently had loyalties only to your boy over there."

I glanced at Noah, who just nodded as he continued typing away on his laptop. "They're solid. Silver keeps an eye on them, anyway."

Rocky continued, "And Ferrero here has engaged every independent security firm in the City to fill in the gaps, so we've got them on rotation here, around the Academy, and at Hargraves Tower as it's being remodeled."

"And most importantly," Zach added, "we've prevented them from being hired by James Spencer or my mom."

Rocky nodded. "Yep. And we're essentially paying all

the black-market merc groups just to stay away at the moment. Andrea is having trouble staffing her dirty fights and finding someone willing to take on the runs for whatever she's smuggling these days."

Zach began plating our pancakes. "It's still guns and priceless, stolen artifacts that rich people think need to be on display in their homes and not a museum, as far as I know," he said.

"And everyone's moved in downstairs who wanted a spot?" I asked Rocky.

"Yep. Anyone on the team who wanted an apartment has one in the residence hall two floors below us. The gym and training center are also all set up, and we have a mini command center that links to Silver down on floor twenty-seven. And we, uh… gave the residence hall's corner suite to Frankie Fingers."

I felt my eyebrows hit my hairline. "Frankie lives here?"

Zach slid a plate of pancakes in front of Rocky before glancing at me. "Where else would he live, Princess? He's head of our personal security now."

Rocky shivered. "He's, like, the nicest guy, and yet somehow he also scares the fuck out of me."

"Join the club," Bennett muttered.

I climbed onto the barstool next to Rocky and dove immediately into my own plate of pancakes. Zach delivered plates to Bennett and Noah before hopping up on the stool next to me. I continued to pepper Rocky with questions as we ate.

"How's morale in the big Family businesses?" I asked.

He shrugged. "Low for the ones that are failing, obviously, but everything Knight has been able to snag a controlling piece of is generally in good shape, especially since you guys raised everyone's pay by… a lot."

We were certainly doing what we could to give the working people who were the actual backbone of the City a better life, starting with a living wage, benefits, and access to affordable childcare.

Zach hummed in thought. "I really need to check in on everyone at the Club. It's just been so fucking busy."

Rocky grunted. "Club's fine, man. Andrea would never let her pride and joy fail. And anyway, Knight bought up the shares of the Club sold by all the bailing investors, so everyone's still got a job."

I smiled, nudging Zach with my elbow. "Actually, the Club is now fifty-percent owned by Zach Ferrero."

Zach jerked his head to look at me with wide eyes. "What?"

"I know you care about that place and the people in it," I replied, shoving a bite of pancake into my mouth. "So, Knight gifted you its shares."

That cocky, sexy smile appeared on his face, and he pulled me in for a very syrupy kiss. "You're amazing, baby girl. Thank you."

Rocky finished up his breakfast, drained the last of his coffee from his mug, and hopped to his booted feet. "Alright, team. Back to the grind of holding down this fortress and looking for ways to ruin our evil overlords."

I snorted. "Bye, Rocky. Dom says he wants you down at the gym on your next day off to put the fear of God into his middle-school group."

Rocky gave me a toothy grin as he cracked his knuckles. "Those kids *are* some little mouthy shits. Tell him I'll be there Wednesday."

He ambled out of the kitchen, and a few moments later, the ding of the elevator arriving out in the foyer announced his departure from the penthouse.

Zach watched him go with a furrowed brow. "Those assholes better not think this is a revolving door up here. I will not have one of them just *popping in* while I have Princess bent over the dining room table, screaming my name."

"Only if they want to have their eyeballs torn out of their head," Bennett said.

"Word," Noah added.

So, it seemed we were all still *settling into* Knight Tower.

Later that afternoon, we were lounging together in the living room as we finished up our lingering homework, the boys having traded their pajamas for their daytime sweats. College basketball played on our huge TV with the volume turned low.

I had my head in Noah's lap and my bare feet in Zach's as we sprawled across our huge plush couch. Bennett lazed in the oversized armchair next to us, his long legs crossed as he read a novel for his Lit Seminar.

I'd just finished up my Chem homework when Noah let out a big sigh. "I can't believe we're back here," he said with a quiet reverence. "On Jolie's couch, doing our homework, watching basketball. Just being together like we always were on the weekends. It feels like I'm dreaming."

I reached up to caress his cheek. "I know. If this is a dream, I don't ever want to wake up. And also, this is *our* couch. It belongs to each of you as much as it does to me, just like the whole penthouse does."

Bennett looked up from his novel, his intent stare caressing the length of my body. "Do you like it, Angel? I know it's probably hard to be here again after everything.

If you don't like something, just say the word, and I'll have them up here to change it *today*. I want you to love it."

My heart squeezed, and I rolled off Noah and Zach to climb into Bennett's lap. He grinned, tossing his book to the side as I straddled him, cradling his face in my hands and looking into those beautiful mossy eyes.

"I do love it, Bennett," I whispered. "So much. I don't think I can say thank you enough for turning this place into our home. Change nothing—I love it all because it came from *you*."

I leaned down to press my lips to his, and he wrapped his big hands around my ass, pulling me in tight and deepening the kiss immediately. I groaned as his huge dick began to harden underneath me.

"Oh shit," Zach said, sounding excited. "Are we gonna watch Jojo take that monster again? You better share this time, asshole."

Bennett ignored him, moving one hand from my ass and dragging his rough fingers lightly under my shirt and up my belly, stopping to play at the seam of my flimsy bralette, when the loud ding of the elevator echoed out in the foyer, announcing the arrival of a visitor.

"Attention! Brother entering the house!" Max's deep voice reverberated through the room. "If there is a four-way fuck-fest going on in here, it needs to be *wrapping up!*"

Bennett pulled his lips from mine and buried his face in my shoulder with a frustrated groan.

"That dick," Zach groused as the tromping of Max's boots on the wood floors neared.

Noah also appeared sour. "Does he really *need* full access to the penthouse, sweetheart?"

Bennett flipped me around to cradle me in his lap,

ostensibly for more innocent-looking snuggling, but I was aware that I was also hiding his hard-on from our visitor.

"Hey, team," Max said with a cheeky grin as he breezed into the living room. He wore a tight black Henley, ripped gray jeans, and his dark boots. His hair was tied in its usual messy knot on the back of his head, and he had his backpack that no doubt contained his assortment of weapons and electronics. His dark eyes swept over the large living room, and he whistled. "Damn, this place is killer. Thanks for inviting me to hang out, Jojo."

"Anytime, Maxy," I replied, ignoring the grumbling from my boys. "There's a two-bed, two-bath guest suite down the hall just off the foyer, so that's for you, Dom, and Laura when you want to stay here."

I squeezed Bennett's hand, reminding him that he was the one who had made sure those rooms were ready for just that purpose. He knew I'd want Max to have a place here, and he made it happen, despite the fact that Max had made it his mission in life to annoy the shit out of the guys.

"Sweet," Max replied. "But Mari's my roommate this week, right?"

"Yep." She'd stayed at the Academy last night but would be spending the week here once she finished packing her entire wardrobe. I gave Max a squinty-eyed glare. "Do *not* take her downstairs to the security floors. There are too many young, horny assholes on our new Enforcer team, and they will not care that she isn't into dick. It's Camp Testosterone down there."

He scoffed, waving a dismissive hand at me. "Mari can take care of herself."

Zach leaned forward on the couch, resting his elbows on his knees and spearing me with a dark look. "Speaking from experience, Princess?"

Max chuckled at that. "Like you three dickheads don't know *exactly* how Joanna Miller could turn the heads of just about anyone that crossed her path who's into chicks."

"*Max*," I groaned.

"They know I speak the truth, Jojo. They were *so* confused by their pants-feelings for that unruly scholarship girl from the Southside."

Zach relaxed, Noah's amused smile returned, and even Bennett let out a wry chuckle.

Ah, memories.

"We sure were," Zach admitted with a shrug while Bennett pressed a lingering kiss into the crook of my neck. Zach went on, "Our girl is fucking fire. Good thing she only burns for us."

Max winked at me, his teasing smile softening into one of deep affection.

He was thrilled I'd found them again, and he saw how hard they loved me.

"I'm going exploring," he announced, turning to wander away. "Be back in a little bit!"

After we could no longer hear the stomping of his boots, I turned to the boys. "I love him, but not in even remotely the same way I love you three. Co-exist peacefully, please."

Noah beamed his loving smile my way before he rolled his eyes to the ceiling. "Honestly, what pisses me off the most is that even in spite of everything, he's still so goddamn likable."

I nodded sagely. "That charisma is unmatched."

And then the elevator dinged again.

Zach groaned. "Ugh, what now?"

CHAPTER THIRTEEN
JOLIE

"Honey, I'm home!"

This time it was Mari's voice that floated in from the entryway, the sounds of her suitcase rolling along the wood floor following immediately.

"Does literally everyone we know have access to this place, Princess?" Zach asked. "Not that I mind Mari being here, but security is kind of important given the... position we find ourselves in these days."

I frowned. "Actually, Mari's fingerprint isn't keyed to the penthouse. She was supposed to text me when she got to the lobby."

"This place is amazing!" Mari raved as she waltzed into the living room.

All four of us froze, eyes wide, as we realized Mari had brought a friend with her.

Frankie grinned like a maniac at us. "Love the new digs, Little Knight."

Mari had her hand looped through the crook of Frankie's elbow as he escorted her further into the room, both of them clutching brightly colored drinks speared with fat straws.

"Um, Mari," I began, darting a *what the fuck?* glance over at Zach, who just shrugged helplessly. "What's, uh... what's going on here?"

"Oh, I met Francisco in the lobby when I came by earlier!" she gushed. "We decided to go get our nails done, and then we went for boba tea. You guys didn't tell me Zach had such an adorable *young* uncle."

Frankie preened, waving his drink-holding hand at us, his dark purple nails a stark contrast to the neon orange boba tea. "I hadn't had the chance to make Miss Mari's acquaintance yet, so we decided to get to know each other. I'm responsible for her safety when she's staying here with my other charges, after all."

"Uh-huh," I said, slowly.

"Sorry I didn't text you, but Francisco said he could bring me to the penthouse," Mari went on. "*Joder*, look at the pool!"

She released Frankie's elbow and trotted over to the tall French doors that lead to the pool deck, her flowy pink playsuit swishing around her legs and her espadrilles clomping against the floors as she went.

Noah watched her over his shoulder as she breezed out onto the patio, then he turned back to the rest of us. "So, should we tell her, or...?"

Frankie rolled his eyes, his wide smile never faltering. "You guys act like I can't have friends."

Zach's dark stare turned suspicious. "Since when do you have friends, *Francisco?*"

He shrugged lazily, taking a big swig through his straw. "Sometimes I like to try new things."

Mari returned from her tour of the pool deck, and instead of dropping into the open spot on the couch I'd vacated for Bennett's lap or the other empty armchair, she trotted back over to Frankie's side and clutched his arm again. He offered her a sip of his tea, which she accepted with a gracious smile.

"Just keep calm, Angel," Bennett muttered into my ear. "We don't want to startle either of them."

Right on cue, Max sauntered back into the living room. "Fuck, Jojo, this place is great. Your orgy-sized bed is a nice touch—"

He froze as he noticed our visitors. I watched his dark gaze heat as it landed on Frankie, drinking him in with such enthusiasm that I wrinkled my nose—some things a sister really just didn't need to see *that* up close and personal from her brother—but then his eyes widened in surprise before they *quickly* narrowed as he noticed Mari clinging to Frankie's arm.

"Max, mi amor!" Mari exclaimed. "I didn't know you were already here."

Frankie had also appeared taken aback to run into Max at this exact moment, his big smile morphing into a glower in Max's direction. But the second Max's salacious perusal of Frankie turned into guarded suspicion regarding Mari, a smug little grin crept back onto Frankie's striking face.

"Miss Mari, who's your friend?" he asked lightly, then he eyed Max with a challenging stare as he sucked hard on his straw. "I sure hope you haven't replaced me already."

Max scowled, marching toward them to pluck Mari out of Frankie's clutches, pulling her into a hug that she accepted with enthusiasm. They did the double cheek-kiss thing, and Max stared Frankie down the entire time.

The boys and I just watched this whole thing unfold in uncomfortable silence.

"Maxy, have you met Zach's uncle?" Mari asked brightly, turning in Max's arms to gesture to Frankie. She tossed a really unsubtle elbow into Max's ribs as she stage-whispered, "He's pretty cute, no?"

"Very," Max purred. "But, babe, I'm a little confused as to how you happen to know the bloodiest, most notorious Family Enforcer in the entire City?"

She gasped, turning back to Frankie. She swatted him playfully on the bicep, and the rest of us winced in unison. "Francisco! Is this true?"

Frankie shrugged. "I do have a bit of a reputation. But that's all nasty business—definitely not appropriate conversation for our delightful afternoon together."

Max shook his head, like he wasn't sure he'd heard that right. "Mari, you spent the afternoon with Frankie Fingers?"

"Frankie who?"

We were all saved by the loud buzzing of Frankie's phone. He pulled it from the back pocket of his ridiculously tight acid-washed jeans and put it to his ear. "Yeah?" A slow smirk spread across his face. "Oh, that is excellent news. We will meet you in the workroom."

I slid from Bennett's lap and onto my feet, my back straight and my game face on. "Whose day are we about to ruin?" I asked Frankie as he shoved his phone back into his pocket.

He looked giddy, all the weird bullshit he and Max continued to have between them momentarily forgotten. "The Montgomerys have delivered their rat."

Bennett squeezed my hand. "Are you sure you're okay being back down here, Angel?"

I nodded, feeling resolute. "I know some traumatic things happened to me down here, Bennett, but some amazing things did too. Plus, this is where Knight will be... taking care of certain business. I'm not going to just hang out up in my ivory tower and not get my hands dirty alongside my team."

Frankie tossed an amused smile over his shoulder. "Ah, Little Knight, as much as I'd love to take care of all of these things for you, I do find that position so very respectable. I knew as soon as I caught you on the roof of Spencer Tower that you were something different."

Mari gasped from behind me where she was being led into the lion's den by Max. "Francisco is the one from the Spencer Tower heist?"

She'd insisted on accompanying the group down to Knight Tower's basement "workroom." It was just as well, since Max had pouted when I demanded he stay behind to watch her, and none of my boys were keen on being left out, either, so here we all were, filing into the bleak, cold basement behind Frankie.

Max grunted, answering her question. "Yep."

"Francisco!" Mari barked. "You *shot* at my best friends!"

Frankie turned to give her a guilty little smile. "I wasn't trying to kill them, Miss Mari. If had been, they'd both be dead."

Chilling, but true.

We entered the barren floor of the basement to find Kara and Julie—married couple, two of the most badass ladies I knew, and longstanding members of the Shadows—keeping guard over a lone prisoner. I could tell by the delicate frame of our captive that this was a woman, her spindly arms wrenched tight and bound to the chair behind her. She wore wide-legged denim jeans and a fitted black sweater, and there was barely a smudge on her expensive heeled booties. Her perfectly contoured face was defiant and flushed with rage.

As we stepped into the low light of the single overhead bulb, I realized I recognized her. "That's the fucking makeup artist from the Montgomery Star Media studio," I said, disgusted and just a little pissed off that I'd let this woman touch my face.

"Ah, I see," Kara replied, her defined arms crossed over her chest and her narrow-eyed stare still on the captive. "She's been extremely tight-lipped since they dropped her on our doorstep ten minutes ago." She glanced up at the group of us as we all fanned out around them, and she chuckled. "I see you brought the whole gang, Jojo."

I grinned, shrugging. "Can't let Frankie have all the fun."

"Aw, come on, Little Knight," Frankie said with a playful whine. He began circling the prisoner like a shark, and the determined set of her jaw wavered at his manic smile.

Kara's grim look softened as her eyes landed on Noah. "Hi, Noah. Long time, no see. Sorry we didn't get a chance to chat on our last... op."

Noah returned her smile. "Hey, Kara."

She walked to his side to pull him into a hug. "Look at you, all grown up and so handsome." She ruffled his hair affectionately, and it was entirely too adorable. She went on, "I know I was only your mother's bodyguard for a couple of years, but I remember vividly how close you and the other Heirs were. I'm glad you all have Jojo back with you now."

"Me too," he replied, glancing my way with that

beaming smile full of love that melted me from the inside out. "It's good to see you, too, Kara. How's the shoulder?"

She flexed her left shoulder where she'd taken a bullet from Ramon's gun. "I'll live. Heard from your mom at all?"

His smile vanished. "Not in years."

She scoffed, a disapproving look on her face. "Typical. Peter paid her off long ago, so she's sitting pretty, even after the implosion of Hargraves."

Julie piped up from where she stood next to our prisoner. "Kare, what's the plan here? Our girl already looks a little more open to chatting with us after getting a dose of Frankie's crazy eyes."

Frankie cackled from where he now stood by a table near the wall, sorting through a box of his toys and murmuring sweetly to them.

I stepped closer to Miss Makeup, studying her and finding barely a dark hair out of place. "Did they at least give you a name when they dropped her off?" I asked Julie, keeping my hard stare glued to our petulant captive.

"Emily Hubert," she replied. "Twenty-nine years old, worked at MSM for about a year. She was an administrative assistant at a Spencer wealth advisory firm prior to that."

"She's Elise Proctor's half sister," Bennett said from behind me.

I whirled to gape at him. "Seriously?"

He stood between Zach and Noah, the three of them looming in the shadows with violence in their eyes, like dark princes ready to mete out justice in the name of their kingdom.

"Yes," Bennett replied. "I'd never met her, so I didn't recognize her when she did your makeup. But I know that name, and now I can see the family resemblance."

"Hmm," I said, turning back to Emily. I leaned down to look her right in her flawlessly lined eyes. "That's bad news for you, Emily. Not only are you in trouble for letting Spencer's dogs disrupt my interview with Lucinda and endangering the lives of my boyfriends and my brother, but it turns out the same blood runs through your veins as the despicable cunt who played a vital role in getting my parents killed. It makes me want to bleed you out all over this floor just so I can light it on fire."

"Hot damn, that even gave *me* the chills," Frankie murmured.

Emily's face contorted in anger, no longer the placid, dutiful makeup lady I'd met before. "Fuck you, Knight bitch. You're just a stupid little girl trying to play games with the grownups."

I tutted. "I think you're the one who's stumbled into the *real* grown-up games, Emily. Now I have to make an example of you and make sure your bitch sister and James Spencer get the message. What did they offer you? Money? Power? I hope it was worth it."

She spat at me, and I shifted just in time for the nasty wad to miss my face and land on my shirt instead.

A scandalized gasp sounded behind me, and before I could blink, Mari had darted forward and slapped Emily hard across the face.

"How dare you," she hissed. "You vile bitch. Look at where you are. You got hung out to dry by your own sister, who clearly doesn't give a shit about you. I'd find some manners if I were you, and fast."

I froze, stunned and more than a little bit proud of Mari, and the silence around me said I wasn't the only one.

"Damn, babe," Max said, whistling.

Not to be outdone, Frankie added, "Miss Mari, that was excellent form."

I cleared my throat, squeezing Mari's hand before I looked over at Frankie. "I think it's girls' night tonight. Kara, Julie, and I can take care of this one."

He grinned, giving me an approving nod that filled me with an odd sense of pride.

"I'm staying," Mari announced, her tone daring me to argue with her.

I blew out a breath, remembering Bennett's words about Mari being a big girl who could make her own choices. "Okay. But if it gets to be too much, Max will come back down to get you."

"Fine," she said. "But I think I can handle it. This woman put you and Max in danger. I'd like to see her hurting."

Zach stepped to my side, pulling me in for a quick kiss. "We're sad to miss the fun, but I think this one is definitely more appropriate for you ladies. And Mari will be fine—she's tough."

"Okay," I replied. "Love you. Take care of Max and keep him and Frankie separated, please."

He snickered, while Max moaned, "Jojo, honestly."

After Bennett and Noah had both pecked me on the lips and Frankie had given me a two-fingered salute, the boys filed out of the basement. I could just make out the irreverent tones of Max's hassling the guys as the heavy metal door slammed behind them.

I turned my attention back to Emily, who was still seething in her chair, her nerves now visible—but not nearly enough.

She still hadn't quite grasped how bad this was about to

get for her. Maybe she thought she'd dodged a bullet when I dismissed Frankie Fingers.

She was wrong.

"How far are we taking it?" Kara asked, all business.

"She'll still be breathing when we deliver her to her sister," I replied with ice in my voice. "But only barely." Then I nodded to Julie. "Cut her loose."

Her eyebrows rose, but then she grinned. "How fair of you, boss."

With a flick of her knife, she cut the zip ties binding Emily's legs and arms to the chair. Emily flew from her seat with a scream, running straight at me—the one who was unarmed, dressed in athleisure wear, and looking like an easy target.

"I'll fucking kill you myself, then, bitch," she spat at me.

I launched an uppercut right into her jaw, and she was knocked off her fancy boots in an instant. I followed her to the ground, then I made what Bennett did to Chad look like a fun walk in the park.

Mari, bless her, stood stoically through it all, only growing a little pale at the end.

Kara called it before I went too far—before I'd exorcised every ounce of pent-up rage I had about Emily's role in endangering my boys' lives, about her loyalty to Spencer and the woman who got my parents killed, about every-fucking-thing wrong with the entire goddamn City.

Kara and Julie cleaned up my mess and would later deliver the package to the steps of Spencer Tower.

Frankie reappeared to escort Mari and me back to the penthouse, where Zach helped me wash the blood from my hands and my body in my beautiful new shower. Then he kissed every inch of my skin with reverence before he helped me ride out the last of my adrenaline rush by fucking me into the tile wall while he pulled my hair and I screamed his name until I was hoarse.

That night, Bennett ignored twelve calls from James Spencer.

CHAPTER FOURTEEN
BENNETT

Fate was kind enough to let us enjoy a few days of peace, safely ensconced in our tower fortress away from the bullshit of the Academy, the City, and my father.

It was Tuesday morning, and I was feeling very content as I lay sprawled on the couch with my Angel draped over me like a blanket. I sorted through my email on my phone with one hand while I ran my fingers lazily up and down Jolie's back, reveling in her happy sighs.

I was also reveling in the current quiet of the penthouse. Noah was outside, braving the still-cold pool, intent on swimming laps in his wetsuit under the midmorning clouds. Zach had gone down to the security floors to lift weights and see if he could goad Rocky into a fight. Max had disappeared with Mari on some kind of brunch or shopping date, in what was probably an attempt to ensure his position as best-guy-friend was still solid now that he'd been challenged by Frankie.

The only sounds in the house were the faint sloshing of Noah's strokes out on the pool deck and the low hum of the old Dashboard Confessional song that played through the living room's speaker system.

Bliss.

"Has your father tried to call you again?" Jolie murmured, her cheek still pressed tight to my chest.

I dragged my fingertips through her loose blonde hair. "Not since yesterday morning."

"I wonder what he thinks he'll accomplish by calling you incessantly like that?"

I let out a wry laugh. "Force of habit, Angel. I do something to piss him off, he calls to yell at me."

And I had no doubt he was very pissed off. He certainly wouldn't have given a shit about the welfare of Elise's sister, but Jolie had made a very violent and public example of his mole by tossing her battered body onto the front steps of Spencer Tower. To make matters worse, the Montgomerys published an exposé on the whole thing the next day.

When Jolie had returned from the basement soaked in blood and her knuckles torn all to hell, my heart had broken for her even as my already deep admiration had increased tenfold. My Angel shouldn't have to sink into the brutal violence of this heartless fucking City—she had her three jaded boyfriends to do that for her now. And she had *Frankie*, for fuck's sake.

But she would never allow that. Jolie led by example, and her people respected her first and foremost because she was on the front lines of this fight right alongside them.

Zach had taken one look at her and led her upstairs to get cleaned up, then Noah, Max, and I huddled around the kitchen island and listened to Mari describe every detail of Jolie's brutal and righteous punishment of Elise's rat of a sister.

That woman was also on borrowed time, and I hoped Jolie's message had Elise shaking in her stripper heels.

"Mmm, well," Jolie said as she snuggled deeper into my embrace, "he can't touch you here, Bennett. Not on my watch."

I hummed approvingly, and I marveled at what kind of fucking idiot I'd been, trying to push this perfect woman away from me under the ridiculous pretense of keeping her safe.

The elevator sounded, and Zach waltzed into the living room wearing a stolen Knight-branded gym towel around his neck, a tight tank top, and his joggers. His wet hair hung in disheveled strands across his forehead, and his dark eyes zeroed in on Jolie where she lay—relaxed and very cozy—across my body.

I knew that look. Jolie wore tiny sleep shorts under her oversized sweatshirt this morning, and I'd taken the opportunity to run my hand over the tight curve of her ass several times already. Zach's gaze snagged on that perfect ass and didn't waver as he dropped his gym bag and crawled onto the couch.

"Princess, you look delicious," he purred as he straddled my calves and grabbed two handfuls of her butt. "Has Spencer had you all to himself this morning?"

"Yes, so fuck off," I retorted lazily. "We're relaxing."

He *tsk*'d, shaking his head as he hooked his fingers in Jolie's waistband and dragged her shorts down to her ankles. "It's time for you to learn to share, my friend."

"Zach!" Jolie gasped as he exposed her bare ass to the chilly air of the penthouse. "What are you doing?"

He hiked her hips up high, and her knees came down onto the couch cushion on either side of my thighs as she looped an arm around my neck for balance. I dropped my phone to the floor to hold her steady, and I watched as she shut her eyes tight and pressed her face into my shoulder with a deep moan.

Zach had buried his face in her pussy, taking what looked like slow, deliberate licks up her center as she squirmed in my arms. I was equal parts annoyed at his interrupting our time together and turned way the fuck on by watching my Angel writhe on his face.

"You're not gonna deny our girl this pleasure by being a selfish dick, are you, Spencer?" Zach taunted me, pinning me with a challenging stare as he dipped his tongue back into her folds.

I grasped Jolie's face with two hands, pulling her from my shoulder and forcing her to bring those gorgeous eyes to mine. "Do you like that, Angel? Do you like what Zach's doing to you?"

"Yes," she whispered. "It feels so good."

"Do you want him to keep going? Do you want to take us both right here on this couch?"

"Yes," she hissed, arching her back as Zach spread her ass wide and dove back in. "Share me with him, Bennett. I want you both."

I knew I could never deny my Angel anything she wanted.

My dick was already so hard that I was in physical pain. I knew exactly what Zach was up to, and it wasn't helping. "Where's Zach's tongue, Angel?"

He chuckled, giving her another long lick. "He knows where it is, Princess, but go ahead and tell him anyway."

"My ass," she panted. "He's licking me there."

Fuck. "Do you like that?" I rasped.

"Yes," she moaned. "But I need one of you to give me your cock, like, immediately."

Zach pulled back and sank a finger into what I was certain was a dripping wet pussy. "Just because I am a gentleman and an excellent co-boyfriend, I'll let you take Bennett first, baby girl. Get ready."

He snaked a hand underneath her and yanked on the waistband of my sweats, freeing my cock just as Jolie positioned herself on top of it. She wrapped her little hand around it and guided me to her entrance. Then she sank down, all three of us groaning in unison as she went.

"Fuck, Angel. You're so goddamn tight."

She rocked her hips, bending forward to brace herself on either side of my head. I pulled her lips to mine, kissing her possessively as she rode me.

Suddenly, she gasped, and I felt the intrusion that had caused such a delicious sound. Zach had slipped his slick finger into her ass, letting her rock gently against it as she fucked me.

"Oh damn, I can feel that monster in there, Princess," he cooed. "I bet you're so fucking full right now, baby."

"I am," she cried, moving her hips faster. "Oh fuck, I'm close."

"Feel good, Angel?" I bit out through gritted teeth. "You like us filling both holes like that?"

"Yes, I want to be able to have all of you someday," she purred. "All of my boys. All together."

Fuck me, I might die. Never had I contemplated sharing a woman with the men I called my brothers, but never had I contemplated that the girl we'd all loved since childhood was still alive, walking this earth, and would turn out to be so fucking perfect for each one of us.

Zach caught my eye over Jolie's shoulder, and he winked at me before he commanded, "Switch." He jerked Jolie off my dick by her hips and tipped her back down onto all fours, then he plunged inside of her, fucking her roughly while she hovered over me.

"Bennett," she whimpered as our eyes locked. "I'm going to come."

I stole another filthy kiss. "Yeah? If you come for him, you'll have to come again for me too. It's only fair, Angel."

"Okay," she promised, nodding vigorously. "Just let me come."

"You heard her," I barked at Zach. "No more fucking around."

He rolled his eyes at me, his brutal pace never faltering. "Get her clit, then, man."

I reached between Jolie's legs, finding that bundle of nerves and rubbing it with rough, vigorous strokes. Her eyes rolled back into her head, and I felt her body tense above me as Zach swore viciously.

"That's fucking right, Princess. Choke the life out of my cock. *Fuck*."

She screamed, and I slammed my lips back onto hers to swallow those sweet sounds as she came. Zach let out a pained groan, signaling the end of the road for him.

He slipped out before gently sliding her right back onto my dick, and she took my girth easily this time. She sat up, rocking lazily, her eyes hooded and her grin satisfied as she stared down at me with all the love and affection I craved.

"You want to come inside me, too, Bennett?" she asked. "You want to claim me just like Zach did?"

I growled, "I'm going to fill you so fucking full, Angel. But you have to earn it. You have to come again first."

"His Highness has spoken," Zach teased, kneeling behind her and helping her stay upright as I pumped my hips upward, fucking her from below. "Give us one more, baby girl, and then you can have all the cum you want."

"Yes, yes, yes," she chanted, throwing an arm around Zach's neck as he pressed her back to his chest. "Give it to me, Bennett."

I roared, slamming up into her while she held onto Zach for dear life. He shoved his tongue into her mouth as she cried out, and I knew we'd won as she clamped down hard on my dick, her second climax arriving just in the nick of time.

"Bennett!"

"Oh *fuck*, Angel. Fuck." I let myself go with a low groan, emptying into her as spots danced across my vision.

She sagged, leaning back into Zach's arms as she reached for my hand, threading her fingers through mine. Zach placed a tender kiss into the crook of her neck, and I did the same as I brought the inside of her wrist to my lips.

A throat cleared from the patio doorway, and I quickly moved to sit up on the couch, my softening cock still buried inside my Angel.

Noah stood there with an amused grin on his face, his hair damp and his wetsuit unzipped and hanging down around his hips. "Hi, sweetheart. Have fun?"

She gave him a gorgeous, happy smile. "Hi, Noah. Yes, Zach and I taught Bennett how to share."

"I am not a child. I know how to share," I grumbled.

Noah meandered over to us and leaned over the back of the couch to steal a kiss from Jolie. "Don't listen to Spencer," he whispered. "We'll have to make sure he keeps practicing."

"Often," Zach added.

"Dicks," I muttered, but one look at Jolie's gorgeous, sated face as she smiled down at me and I was certain we would absolutely be doing this often.

Fortunately, when the elevator announced yet another visitor to the Knight penthouse, we were all fully dressed and mercifully free of the evidence of what three of the four of us had just gotten up to on the living room couch.

When Dom, Laura, and my *mother* walked into our kitchen, the sense of how close we'd actually just cut it to having our parents walk in on a fucking threesome was palpable.

"Hi, kids," Laura gushed with a big grin as she took in the kitchen, the living room, and the view of the patio. "Hope we're not interrupting anything? Just wanted to drop by for a quick visit, see the place, check on things. You know, the usual parent stuff."

Jolie coughed into her coffee mug, the pink hitting her cheeks telling me her mind had gone where mine had, before she replied, "Nope, now's a great time for a visit."

I was standing by our espresso machine, so I put another cup on for my mom as she sidled up next to me. "Hey, sweetie. I just wanted to come by to make sure you were... okay."

"I'm great, Mom," I replied, pulling her into a quick hug before stepping back to examine her.

Her blue eyes were bright, and her affectionate smile was big and genuine. She'd pulled her blonde hair into an easy ponytail, and she wore a soft pink sweater and stylish jeans.

She gave me a knowing look, reaching up to run her hand down my cheek. "I'm weaning off my pills, Bennett. I'm ready to be... present in my life now."

I handed her a little cup of espresso, which she took with a gracious smile. "I'm happy to hear that, Mom."

The rest of the group had gathered around the dining room table where Zach had put out the giant cheese board he'd had delivered yesterday, so I led my mom over to an open chair before sliding into another next to Jolie.

"—been chasing Spencer goons out of Olde Town, but that's nothing new," Dom was saying, and my hackles went up immediately.

"Are they looking for my mom?" I asked. "And where's Martinez, anyway, Mom? He's supposed to be watching you."

She waved a dismissive hand at me. "Dominic and Laura are perfectly capable, and I asked them to bring me to see you. John *is* allowed a day off, Bennett."

I narrowed my eyes at that breathy, affectionate utterance of Martinez's first name, then I caught Jolie grinning into her coffee cup.

"Mom, Martinez had better be doing his damn *job,* or I will introduce him to Knight Tower's workroom."

Zach and Noah both tried and failed to smother their amusement at my obvious distress, and Dom was no different. Only Laura kept her face fastidiously neutral, and it was suspicious as fuck.

My mom crossed her arms with a petulant huff. "Bennett James Spencer, that hostility is unnecessary."

"*Anyway*," Dom said. "Bridgette has been... learning a lot now that she's spending time outside Spencer Tower, and she's been worried about you kids."

Mom sighed before turning her clear gaze to me, and the overwhelming relief I felt at seeing her so alert had me kicking myself for not finding a way out for her sooner. "Your father has obviously kept a lot of things from me over the years. I can't say I wasn't aware that Spencer has its hands in some... unsavory things, but I also put a lot of effort into disassociating from it. And from my marriage. I'm so sorry I wasn't more present for you, honey."

Jolie clasped my hand in hers under the table. I never resented my mother for what she'd done just to survive, especially as I'd grown older and seen just how shitty of a husband my father was, but her words did wonders to soothe a wound I'd done my best to ignore for years.

Mom went on, "And now that I see what's really been going on? And what he did to our little Jojo?" She turned her now teary gaze to Jolie. "Sweetie, I'm so sorry. I realize now that you've been very well taken care of, but I also know how much these boys ached without you. I'm so devastated over what my Family has done to yours, I can't even put it into words."

Jolie reached across the table to give my mom's hand a little squeeze. "No apology necessary, Mrs. Spencer. I'm just glad Bennett will be able to provide a better life for you now."

She nodded, wiping her eyes. "It's all thanks to you, sweetie. I'm so happy you're all together again. Even if while you were growing up, we didn't exactly contemplate that you'd be together... like *this*." She shook her head with a tinkling little laugh.

Zach smothered his own laugh with a cough while Noah and I both cleared our throats, all of us doing our best to look really fucking innocent—which was difficult after what we'd just done to Jolie on the couch ten feet away from us.

I gave my mom one last assessing stare. "And you're really not going back to him?"

"No," she said with a sad smile. "Not after what I've learned he did to the Knights. I couldn't stomach being there anymore, anyway, Bennett. He's become much less discreet with his... activities with the staff."

"Fucking Elise," I growled, and Mom winced, the tears flowing freely now, and it made me want to drive to Spencer Tower and bury my fist in father's face *tonight*.

Jolie reached for Mom's hand again. "Mrs. Spencer, listen to me. Elise Proctor is a dead woman walking. I am going to end her life with my bare hands for what she's done to both of us. I promise."

Mom laughed through a sob. "Bennett, please marry this girl."

"Planning on it, Mom," I replied with a cocky grin.

Jolie's jaw dropped the tiniest bit before she snapped it closed, her little smile and pink cheeks satisfying something primal within me. I ignored the grumbling from her other boyfriends.

We'd sort *that* shit out later.

CHAPTER FIFTEEN
JOLIE

After a few minutes, Mrs. Spencer was back to smiling again as she took a delicate bite of cheese from Zach's unnecessarily large charcuterie board. Bennett had wrapped his hand possessively around my thigh under the table, and I tried to decide if I had the brain space to process his casual declaration that we'd be getting married.

"I can't help but be worried for you still, Bennett," Mrs. Spencer said. "Challenging your father like this. Dominic and John tell me that Spencer is... taking some hits, but your father can be so...."

"Vindictive? Soulless? A violent asshole?" Bennett finished drolly.

She let out a humorless laugh. "Yes, exactly."

"Spencer is dying while the Knight empire is thriving and powerful, Mom," Bennett said. "This tower is a fortress. He won't touch us here."

Noah returned to the table after pouring himself a second mug of coffee, and he handed me a fresh mug as well, like the perfect man he was. After a smug smile at the lusty look I gave him *and* my coffee, he looked at Bennett's mom. "Has someone explained the Shadows to you, Mrs. Spencer?"

"John has," she replied, smiling down into her little cup of espresso, and I felt Bennett tense next to me.

Oooh, Martinez was in trouble. But also, *get it, Mrs. Spencer*—Martinez was kind of a Daddy, and I would let Andrea throw me off the roof of Ferrero Tower before I ever said that to Bennett.

Noah smiled warmly at Mrs. Spencer. "Then you know what kind of force has been working against Spencer and the other Families for years now. Jolie's united a lot of connected, talented people, and many of them have a personal stake in seeing the Families fall."

"A lot of us have lost people," Dom added soberly. "We won't let it happen to anyone else."

All three of my boys eyed Dom curiously, and I realized they hadn't heard his story yet. I said, "Dom had a very close friend from his time in the special forces who worked for Ferrero and... didn't make it out."

Zach's eyes widened. "Fuck, did you have someone on that gun run that was ambushed fifteen years ago?"

He nodded. "My best friend from my combat unit—Captain Joseph Turk. He wanted nothing to do with that stuff. He'd been content to work security at the casino, but the powers that be knew his background and wanted his skills on the runs. He refused, but then Andrea's head Enforcer at the time paid a visit to his pregnant girlfriend, and he changed his mind. Seven months later he was dead."

Zach blew out a breath, a pained look marring his handsome face. "I'm sorry, Dom. That incident is still talked about as the worst hit Ferrero ever took—at least before the Shadows blew a hole in my mom's muscle to pull me out of that warehouse. I heard Mom didn't even give restitution to any of the families of the men and women who died."

"That's correct," Dom replied.

"And that's why you joined the Shadows?" Bennett asked him.

He nodded. "I'd heard rumblings about the organization for years. No one on the Southside has any love lost for the Families, but you don't bite the only hand that feeds you, you know? But that incident pushed me over the edge. I couldn't just let Joe die without trying to do something about it."

"And Gemini joining made the mission seem like it could be more than just a dream," I pointed out.

"Gemini?" Noah asked, crunching his brow.

"She's an anonymous benefactor that joined up around the same time I did," Dom replied. "The Shadows really became a power to be reckoned with then, because she brought a *lot* of money with her."

Bennett looked suspicious. "And what's her story?"

I shrugged. "No one really knows. I met her briefly over video once, and she checks in occasionally. Now that Knight is able to fund the Shadows completely, she seems happy to sit back and watch us work."

Mrs. Spencer still appeared uneasy. "And what's the end goal? Will you settle for Peter, James, and Andrea losing their money and power? Or will you keep going until someone is... dead?" Her wide blue eyes went to her son once again. "Will you kill him?"

"If that's what Jolie wants," he replied.

The entire table was silent for a beat before Noah asked me, gently, "What truly was your end goal when you started this, sweetheart?"

I met Dom's and Laura's gazes, both of them warm and understanding, before I formulated my answer. "Honestly? I was going to wreck the City and take everything from Peter, Andrea, and James. I'd destroy their lives—maybe they ended up dead and maybe they didn't, as long as they were fucking *done*, it didn't matter. Then I was going to take my family and get the hell away from this place I thought I hated. I'd leave it to the Shadows to build something better."

My boys watched me closely. "But...?" Noah prompted.

"But...." I blew out a breath before I met Noah and Zach's eyes, and I squeezed Bennett's hand where it remained wrapped around my thigh. "I think a big part of that was the idea of living in the City without you guys—on opposite sides of everything, with you knowing I was alive and hating me for what I was going to do to your Families—it was too much for me. I wanted to run away. But now that I have you? Now that we have a home together and are all working to take everything from your parents and use the power of Knight to make some real changes for the City?"

Zach's smile was so wide, so full of love, that I almost stopped breathing. "Now staying here doesn't seem so bad, does it, Princess?"

I felt the flush hit my cheeks, which only made all three of my boys chuckle. "I think I'll stick around," I replied with a nonchalant shrug of my shoulder. "I know Dom didn't really want to sell the gym and run off to the Virgin Islands with me, anyway."

Everyone laughed, and the mood lightened considerably for a few seconds until Dom said, "You'll get your happily ever after, Jojo, but first we have to keep you alive. We know Ferrero and Spencer don't have the resources now to attack the behemoth that Knight has become, so they'll continue to target you personally like they did at Montgomery. Everyone needs to stay alert until we can end this thing."

Bennett pulled his hand from my thigh and threw his arm around my shoulders instead, pulling me tight to his side. He looked at Dom. "Always. Nothing touches her."

Zach and Noah nodded, resolute as he was, but I knew the score. I was going to bear the brunt of the Families' anger and frustration as they attempted to cling to power and relevance in the City—and tried to take their Heirs back by force.

I just had to be ready.

The rest of the break flew by, and the four of us never left the lovely little cocoon we'd created in the Knight penthouse except to pop down to the security floors on occasion to train or bullshit with the team.

Max and Mari were more adventurous, coming and going from Knight Tower as they pleased, Max keeping Mari safe while Mari enjoyed showing Max her favorite spots in the City he'd rarely visited as a born-and-bred Southsider.

On Friday morning, Max, the boys, and I spent our usual couple of hours in the gym. Zach and Max had gone several rounds in the cage while I ran on the treadmill next to Noah. While I ran, I kept one eye on the two idiots beating the shit out of each other and the other on Bennett's ass while he squatted an ungodly amount of weight.

We returned to the penthouse sweaty and in good spirits, and even Max and Zach's bickering in the elevator over who actually won their fight couldn't put a dent in my relaxed mood.

As we exited the elevator, Mari's soothing voice sounded out in the living room. "And now reach forward, rooting your energy into your feet as we move into warrior two."

We padded quietly into the kitchen, and there in front of our huge couch was Mari, hair braided back, wearing a sparkly purple sports bra with matching high-waisted leggings, and holding the warrior two pose on her mat. A shirtless Frankie was next to her, mirroring her pose.

"Alright, well—now I've seen everything," Zach muttered. "Frankie's wearing yoga pants and happily engaged in an activity that doesn't involve maiming anyone."

I grabbed Max by his shorts and physically sat him down on the barstool furthest from the living room. I didn't have to even look at him to know his eyes were now glued to Frankie's lean, tattooed torso and those extremely low-slung, tight pants.

"Jojo, what the fuck!"

"Lock it up, Max," I said, pointing a finger in his face. "No eye-fucking Frankie, and no weird posturing with him over Mari's friendship. I am in a fantastic mood, and I don't feel like dealing with your weird bullshit with him *that you still refuse to tell me about.*"

I wasn't pouting, no sir.

He smirked at me. "Stop pouting, sis."

"Hi, guys!" Mari called, waving. "We're almost finished."

Frankie ignored us, bending over into a perfect downward dog that made me want to slap my hand across Max's eyes.

Zach's phone buzzed. "What's up, Marcus?" he asked as he lifted it to his ear, stepping away from where he, Noah, and Bennett had been setting out food for lunch and very purposefully ignoring the Frankie situation in the living room. "Oh, really? They just showed up without an appointment? Bold move." He listened for a few seconds. "Let me run it by the boss. I'll text you."

He hung up, and I raised an eyebrow at him. "What are we running by me?"

"Actually," he replied with an amused grin, "I meant Mari. Her parents are here unannounced, and they request a meeting with the head of Knight."

"What!" Mari shouted from where she now lay flat on her yoga mat.

"Shh, Miss Mari," Frankie cooed. "We're doing *savasana*—relax your body and your mind."

I sighed. Back to business, then.

Mari regarded her parents coolly from across the conference room table. "And you two thought you'd just show up here at Knight Tower and demand to see Jolie Knight, without a prior appointment, on a random Friday morning?"

"Mija, this is ridiculous," Mrs. Anzaldua replied, bristling. "We were in the neighborhood and popped by. You act like we're doing something so *terrible*—your own parents."

Mari didn't respond, instead continuing to stare at her mom and dad with an air of superiority that had just the right amount of annoyance mixed in, and it made me very proud. She looked the part too. While she still wore her French braid from her yoga session with Frankie, she'd changed into a baby pink wool skirt suit, silky cream-colored blouse, and some towering no-bullshit nude heels.

Her mother, who had a similar classic sense of style as her daughter, wore a periwinkle blue skirt suit, and her chocolate brown hair was pulled into a low chignon. She'd turned her nose up at being received by her own daughter in a way that did not have me wanting to grant the Anzalduas any sort of favors.

But it wasn't up to me.

Mari's dad's pursed lips said that he, too, was irritated, and he reached over to rub his wife's back gently. "Ah, Ana María, our daughter is enjoying playing the part of the boss while her friend indulges her. I am sure she does not mean to insult us."

I flicked a look over at Zach, who lounged next to me where we'd taken up the corner of the long table. I wore a silky red blouse, cropped dress pants, and chunky heels that I'd thrown on before we came down to the tenth floor to receive our guests, but Zach had decided ripped black jeans and a very tight long-sleeved shirt sporting Dom's gym's logo were his corporate attire for the day.

It was going to take some effort to ignore how delicious his pecs looked in that shirt to focus solely on supporting Mari, but I'd suffered through worse in my life.

Zach looked just as unimpressed as I was with Mari's parents, despite the few respectful looks they'd tossed his way since they'd sat down. He was here as Knight's liaison for all things Ferrero, and the giant luxury hotel chain run by the Anzalduas was solidly linked to Andrea's crumbling hospitality and entertainment empire.

"Yes, well," Mrs. Anzaldua continued, shaking her head at her daughter. "That's quite enough, mija. We are here to meet with Miss Knight so that we may discuss a... strategic alliance."

"Unfortunately for you," Mari said, arching a perfectly microbladed brow, "the person you'll be discussing that *strategic alliance* with is me. I am the new head of Knight Hotels and Resorts, Inc., after all."

Their mouths dropped open in unison, and Mari's resulting triumphant grin had me feeling the warm fuzzies.

Mr. Anzaldua looked at me. "Surely this isn't true? Mari is a college sophomore, por amor del Dios."

"And I'm a college freshman," I replied. "Yet you two were ready to negotiate with me like an equal. I suggest you try a little harder with your daughter because *I'm* not inclined to give you anything you want. I know how you've treated her since she returned to the City to attend Holywell."

Mr. Anzaldua blanched, turning a scandalized look on Mari. "Mija, that is a *family* matter. It has no business being brought into this conference room."

"That's too bad," she snapped. "I make the rules in this room, Papa. And I know that you two are here because our family's association with Ferrero is costing us business, am I correct? Our out-of-town hotel guests have heard all about the crimes of the Four Families and are deciding they'd rather stay elsewhere?"

They stared at her for a beat before Mari's mother gave her a curt nod.

Mari continued. "And Ferrero is, of course, not currently in a place to invest further in their allies either. Isn't that right?"

Another nod.

"So, you're here not only looking to glom onto the Knight name to improve our reputation, but you're also begging for a handout, yes?"

"Mija, this is *your* legacy," Mr. Anzaldua pressed. "If you are the one truly tasked with this decision, you must remember that."

Mari hummed, looking casually down at her pale pink fingernails. "Actually, I'm creating a new legacy for myself here." She looked up, now letting all of the hurt and anger I knew she'd been nursing since the day she'd been forced to leave Carmen behind bleed into her cold stare. "And here at Knight, I can be vocally and enthusiastically queer and receive nothing but love and support from everyone in this *entire* tower, from top to bottom. So, I'm just not sure that the regressive values of Anzaldua are a good fit for us."

"*Marisol*," her mother barked, banging her own pink manicured fist on the table. "You will stop that talk at once. We have told you that your private life is your own, but it should remain *private*. This is *business*, mija."

Zach shook his head, muttering, "Jesus, read the room."

Mari stood up, crossing her arms over her chest and glaring down her nose at her incredulous parents. "This meeting is over. Knight does not feel that it is in our best interest to ally with or invest in Anzaldua at this time."

"Marisol!" her father all but shouted. "You are making a huge mistake."

Mari stood her ground, but I caught the echo of a tremble through her petite frame. Zach saw it, too, and he was on his feet and marching around to the Anzaldua's side of the table.

"She said the meeting is over," he rumbled.

They were both out of their chairs the moment they realized Zach was stalking straight toward them. Mrs.

Anzaldua slung her large designer purse over her shoulder as they backed slowly toward the door. Zach stepped into the space they'd vacated, leaning casually up against the table and blocking their view of Mari.

"Mr. Ferrero, surely *you* can see the large financial benefit for Knight that a partnership with our family would offer," Mari's father said, still managing to remain haughty in the face of a scowling Heir.

"I only see what your daughter sees," he replied, flippant. "Same as Jolie does. See yourselves out before I call security up here."

They sputtered in protest, but one more dangerous look from Zach had them turning to hurry from the room without another backward glance.

I rose from my chair and made my way to Mari's side, clasping her hand in mine as we watched her parents slink toward the elevator through the glass walls of the conference room.

"You okay?" I whispered.

"Yes," she replied quietly. "That felt good. They're still my parents, and I won't be cutting them out of my life, but I'm going to enjoy living on my own, away from their expectations. I'll probably make sure our hotels do survive, but they need to learn their lesson first."

"Good. It's all your call."

She nodded, standing straighter. "I'm going with Francisco to the spa this afternoon. I think I've earned it."

Zach snorted, and I could only shake my head.

I was going to miss the weird shit that went on in Knight Tower when we went back to the Academy this weekend, but then again, weird shit tended to follow me wherever I went.

CHAPTER SIXTEEN
JOLIE

It was an odd feeling, remembering that it was only about six months ago that I sat where our classmates did, watching with something like awe—or trepidation—as the Heirs entered the dining hall for the first time, striding down the aisle between the long tables like the royalty they were in this City.

Despite the massive shift in the City at large since then, not much had changed in this hall, and those awed eyes were now on me just as much as my boys as we entered, ready to grab breakfast and get back in the swing of school after our blissful week locked away in my tower.

"Still getting used to it, Princess?" Zach murmured from next to me, his fingers threaded lazily through mine as we walked. "Hate to break it to you, but eyes were on you like this even when you were pretending to be a mouthy brat from the Southside."

I elbowed him. "I was not a brat."

Bennett tossed me a hard look over his shoulder. "You were and still are."

Noah chuckled from beside him. "She behaves for me."

We reached our table at the front, the seats on the end near the aisle left vacant for us as usual. We sat, and Bennett's dark look in my direction intensified before he shot a skeptical glare at Noah. "Seriously?"

Noah shrugged, a smug grin now on his lush lips. "I ask her nicely."

Mari was already in her usual spot, and a few friendly faces were with her. "Ugh, chica, make them stop. We all get it, you kinky jerks. Be considerate—some of us are in a dry spell."

I felt the color hit my cheeks, which only put cocky smiles on the faces of all three of my boyfriends. I glanced across the aisle and found Harper nestled among her remaining diehard Family-worshiping friends and staring at me with a look of such profound hatred that I almost shivered.

Almost—because Harper Jansen didn't fucking scare me.

"That deluded bitch is still wearing her ring," I muttered to Bennett, who had just returned to the table with a plate of bacon and eggs that he slid in front of me.

His jaw tensed, but he didn't spare Harper a look. "My father has probably promised the Jansens that I'll return to the fold well ahead of the actual wedding date set in the contract. He thinks I'm having some kind of temper tantrum."

I cocked a brow at him. "I believe you accused me of the same thing at the beginning of the semester."

He grinned—a little sheepish, at least—before reaching for my hand and lifting it to his lips to press a sweet kiss there. "I remember, and I was wrong, Angel."

I was about to request that he please repeat that statement while I recorded it for posterity when we were interrupted.

"Spencer!" a happy, deep voice boomed, then Hatcher Robicheaux bounded up to our table, his twin brother Hans in tow.

Bennett rolled his eyes almost affectionately at two of the only guys on the men's crew team that he seemed to actually like as they swarmed his spot at the head of the table.

"Dude, the lacrosse team has challenged the crew team to a paintball battle," Hatcher said, punching Bennett playfully in the shoulder while the rest of our table tried not to look mildly horrified by that. "Those little bitches have been talking a lot of shit, and we need you to play. Hans says he heard you're a fucking crack shot."

"It is what they say," Hans agreed with a cheeky grin.

"I'm alright," Bennett replied with a casual shrug. "I'm not as good as Noah, though."

Hatcher pouted. "It's crew team only, man. Hargraves is out."

"Bummer," Noah muttered as he sipped his coffee, not sounding bummed in the slightest.

"But," Bennett went on, a slow, evil smile spreading across his handsome face. "You know who's almost as sharp as Noah? Jolie Knight—and she happens to be on the crew team."

"*Bennett*," I grumbled. "Paintball? Really?"

Hatcher's dial had already been cranked back up to exuberant. "Jolieeeee! Come on, we need you. It's gonna be super fun, and Spencer will play if you will—I know it. Pleeeeease."

Bennett was really grinning now. "Come on, Angel. Live a little. A pretend gun battle—how *exciting*."

I glared at him over Zach and Noah's snickers, but now Hatcher and Hans were both giving me some serious puppy-dog eyes.

"Sure," I said, capitulating after about five seconds. "Let's go spray the lacrosse idiots with paint pellets. I'm so pumped."

I stared across the wide expanse of the farmland that made up Rodney Blaze's Paintball Park. It was nearly dusk, but the waning light of the clear spring day afforded me enough visibility to take in the course before the stadium lighting that bordered the field would be switched on.

It looked like someone had raided a junkyard and scattered every item across the field that could conceivably be used to shield a human body. There were rusty metal feed troughs, several canoes, numerous pieces of metal siding out of which a bunch of huts had been constructed, and even a hollowed-out school bus painted in brown camouflage like it would somehow blend into the trampled, dying grass. The course extended through the tall trees that bordered the field, and the soft bubbling of the nearby creek was just perceptible over the symphony of insect noises playing us into the evening.

Once the men's crew team had agreed to meet the lacrosse team's challenge, one of those entitled assholes had pulled strings to clear out Rodney's facility a mere forty-eight hours later, so here we were, in the middle of a fucking school week, standing in a field five miles north of the City while a bunch of testosterone-drunk boys got hyped to shoot at each other with pretend guns.

"Don't look so excited, sweetheart," Noah called from where he lounged on a hay bale at the entrance to the course. "It'll all be over in an hour, and then we can get you your fancy dinner sandwich."

I scowled. "Don't remind me that I'm hangry, Noah."

Zach laughed from where he reclined next to Noah. "I fear for the lacrosse team, Princess. Remember your briefing: no headshots allowed."

Those two, here for guard duty, were enjoying the hell out of this. Bennett smirked down at me, his goggles sitting on top of his black beanie just as mine were, while we watched Rodney, the grizzled old owner of the place, bark instructions at the rest of our group.

"Damn, you guys must be desperate if you're recruiting from the girl's team," one of the lacrosse guys commented to Hans before he shot me a patronizing look. "We'll go easy on her, though. No one wants to be responsible for bruising the delicate skin of the Knight Heir."

I bared my teeth at the douche, who was the team captain, I was pretty sure. "Why don't you ask Cameron over there how *delicate* I am in a fight?"

All eyes slid to Cameron Murphy, the mullet-headed asshole whose knee I fucked up when he and Chad attacked me after the A Dorm party last semester. He wore a titanium knee brace over his black fatigues, and his face reddened at the attention as he looked anywhere but at me.

The death stare Bennett now aimed at him would've had anyone pissing their pants. He let Cameron squirm for a few seconds before turning those intense green eyes on me. "Angel, did he fucking touch you?"

"Not really. I broke his knee and knocked him out cold before he could do much besides call me slum trash."

Everyone stared at me in wary silence for a beat, then the lacrosse captain spat, "Un-fucking-believable, Murphy. Now Spencer's going to take your head off in the first thirty seconds. You're fucking useless to us."

"Alright!" Rodney shouted at us. "Green team, move out through the trees to the second half of the course. Blue team will start on this side. Remember, if a paint pellet is broken anywhere on your body, you're out. Exit the course through any gate in the perimeter fence and return to this spot. If you get lost out there, I'm not coming to fucking find you."

Fair enough, Rodney.

The lacrosse team—wearing dark green vests over their matching black fatigues—dispersed out into the field and disappeared into the trees. Our team wore navy vests over our own black clothes, and I watched in amusement as they all became very serious as they combed over the junkyard to find the best places to hide.

"Ready, Angel?" Bennett asked, pulling his goggles down over his eyes. "If you manage more kills than me tonight, I'll reward you by letting you put my cock in your mouth."

Noah laughed. "So generous, Spencer."

I gave Bennett a savage grin as I pulled my own goggles down and adjusted my beanie. "And in the unlikely event you beat my kill count, I'll reward you by sitting on your face *while* I suck your cock."

Bennett let out a pained groan, adjusting himself in his fatigues as the other two howled.

"Did that backfire on you, Spencer?" Zach called.

Rodney sounded the starting bell before Bennett could

respond. With one last wave at Zach and Noah, I bolted for the trees, intent on taking out all of our opponents before the hour was up so that I could return to the Academy to finish my homework, eat my sandwich, and snuggle up naked with any or all of my boys.

Sometime later, I stalked quietly through the trees, headed into green team territory like the silent, deadly predator I was. Bennett and I were in a dead-even heat on kills, and I knew there were at least three more lacrosse assholes hiding in the woods, because I'd seen them flee this way like a bunch of babies after I'd taken out four of their group from behind an old tractor parked at the tree line.

Bennett had indeed eliminated Cameron from the game within the first minute by nailing him with a clean shot right to the base of the throat, causing him to collapse to the ground and gasp for air like he was dying until one of his teammates dragged him across the field to dump him unceremoniously by the fence line. Then Bennett and I had stuck together for a bit—an unstoppable and frankly unfair force, the two of us—but he'd just peeled off to chase a few stragglers back into blue team territory.

I knew he wanted to beat me, and I welcomed the challenge. I was maybe *kind of* actually having fun out here, putting my skills to use in a non-life-threatening situation for once.

Later, I'd kick myself for having those sorts of thoughts, because it just wasn't the life I'd chosen to live.

The snapping of a branch caught my ear, and I whirled just in time to catch a green-vested body duck behind a boulder that sat in a small clearing. I advanced, creeping from tree to tree and working my way around to the side to see if I could get a clear shot.

When I finally darted out from my chosen tree, ready to fire, my opponent did the same, his weapon raised high and aimed right at my head.

That is not a fucking paintball gun.

CHAPTER SEVENTEEN
JOLIE

The thought registered a split second before he squeezed the trigger, and I felt the *real fucking bullet* graze my shoulder as I dove back behind my tree.

I dropped my useless fake gun immediately, digging a gloved hand under my long sleeve to depress the panic button on the dainty rose-gold Rolex the boys had gifted me over the break.

Then I yanked *my* real gun from the pocket of my cargo pants.

"Motherfucker," I growled under my breath as I flicked the safety off and checked the magazine. "I was enjoying a little *frivolous fucking fun* with my teammates." I leaned around the tree and fired a quick shot at the asshole, who had jumped back behind his boulder. "But noooo. No, can't have that, can we?"

The skin at the top of my left shoulder stung, and I could feel the cool breeze of the evening air hitting the exposed wound where the bullet had torn my shirt. It was just a graze, and I was really fucking lucky it wasn't more serious.

The sound of heavy boots crunching the dead grass and not even trying to be stealthy kicked my heart up into my throat. Reinforcements were arriving now that I'd been located—alone and vulnerable.

"Orders are to eliminate target on site!" someone shouted.

"She's behind that tree, but she's armed," boulder guy announced.

I yanked my goggles from my face and chucked them behind a nearby tree. The sound of them thumping to the ground pulled their focus away from my tree for a split second, and I used it to lean around the trunk to fire into the group.

There were half a dozen or so of them, and I witnessed my bullet burying itself in one guy's thigh before I shielded myself again.

As he roared in pain, the one who was apparently the leader shouted, "Advance! Secure her now!"

Adrenaline pumped at a furious pace through my veins. I readied myself to take another shot and make it fucking count, but I knew I couldn't take six attackers alone.

It was a good thing I wasn't alone.

Gunshots sounded from the trees surrounding us, and two men dropped to the forest floor with little more than pained grunts.

"Take cover!" the leader roared.

Another shot from the trees. Another body dropped.

Bennett stalked into my line of sight, his goggles on his forehead and his Glock raised high.

And he looked really fucking mad.

"Hey, Princess. Save some for us?" Zach whispered as he appeared from behind a dense group of shrubs nearby, sneaking toward me with both of his guns drawn. His smirk died when he saw my shoulder. "Baby, you're bleeding," he said, alarmed.

"It's just a graze, Zach," I replied under my breath. "I'm okay. I promise."

Another shot—another cry of pain before the thud of a body dropping.

Zach nodded, momentarily satisfied, then he motioned for me to get moving. I rolled to my feet and crept out from behind my tree. Bennett advanced on the boulder where the remaining attackers hid, and we joined him, fanning out around it, our weapons raised.

"Where's Noah?" I asked Zach under my breath.

He jerked his head toward the hill that rose beyond the clearing. "Finding the high ground."

"Good," I said. "Let's smoke them out."

We converged on the boulder. Some haphazard shots flew in our direction, then the leader shouted, "Retreat!"

Two bulky black-clad bodies bolted from behind the huge rock. They took off through the clearing and up the small hill, and we gave chase, firing round after round as we all weaved through the trees.

"Fuck, I'm out of ammo," I huffed.

"Me too," Bennett said as I heard the telltale click of his gun.

Zach had holstered one of his pistols already, and he waved his remaining gun. "I have a few left in this one. They've got to be getting low too."

A shot sounded from up ahead, and one of our targets went down. The remaining man dove behind a fallen tree trunk, swearing viciously, then he fired several rounds up into the branches of a nearby tree.

Then his gun clicked.

"Take him alive!" I called to Zach as he ran at top speed toward the log with a feral smile. I heard the sounds of flesh hitting flesh as he tackled the man to the ground.

"Noah?" I called out, looking up into the trees. The shots that felled the last few men had come from somewhere.

"Here, Jojo," he rasped.

I turned to find him gingerly dropping from a low branch of the big, stately maple tree to my right. His sneakered feet hit the ground, and he collapsed like his legs couldn't hold him.

Then I saw the blood.

"Noah!" I screamed, my heart in my throat, icy dread shooting through my entire body, the breath snatched violently from my chest as the world spun because *my Noah was hurt.*

I ran to him with Bennett hot on my heels, my own legs giving out as I reached him.

"Oh, Noah," I cried. "No, no, no."

He'd taken a bullet to the outside of his thigh, the wound bleeding heavily as Noah sucked in deep breaths and winced as he shifted on the ground.

"I think it's okay, sweetheart," he said, forcing a smile. "It missed the femoral artery. I'll live. I'll live."

Tears streamed from my eyes as I yanked the black bandana from around my neck, and with shaking hands, I shredded a long, thick strip from its edge.

"I've got it, Angel," Bennett said softly, taking the strip from me and helping Noah tie it tightly above his injury. He took the rest of the fabric and padded the wound in a rough patch job that would have to last until we could get Noah to the hospital.

"Hey," Noah said, already sounding calmer as he cupped my tear-streaked cheeks in his hands. "Sweetheart, I'm going to be okay. I promise. It was a lucky fucking shot. They're all in much worse shape."

It was only then I belatedly noticed there were four more bodies strewn about the forest floor.

"I wasn't able to get back here in time to catch the first group after we got your distress call, but I got the second one as they snuck through the back gate of the property," he said with a little grin.

I forced a smile. "You're amazing, Noah."

"I know," he replied, his grin widening and almost convincing me he wasn't in serious pain.

Zach's voice rang out from over by the log. "Everything okay over there?"

"Help me up," Noah demanded.

Bennett pulled him to standing, and I ducked under his arm to support his left side while Bennett got his right. I was still shaking, the gut-wrenching panic I'd felt now bleeding into the familiar feeling of violent, simmering rage.

They hurt my Noah.

They would pay.

Zach's face paled as we approached with Noah limping along between us. "Oh, shit, man. They got you?"

"They got me. I'll live, I swear."

We lowered Noah to sit on the log, then I took the opportunity to kick Zach's captive hard in the ribs.

"What the fuck, you bitch," he hissed, struggling

against the restraints binding his hands and feet that Zach must have procured from one of the bodies.

Zach buried his fist in the guy's face, and the crunch of his nose breaking echoed through the trees. "Do *not* speak to her like that, Anderson. You're already in so much fucking trouble, and I am happy to make it even worse for you if you even *look* at my girl."

"You know this guy?" I asked, glaring down at the asshole.

"Oh yeah," Zach replied. "Daniel Anderson, previously one of Ferrero's top Enforcers until he must have run like a little bitch from the tiny skirmish we had at the Industrial City warehouse." He crouched next to Anderson, who glared at him as blood gushed from his nose, running over his mouth and dripping down his chin. "Ballsy of you, my friend, to show your face in the City after that. Did you promise to deliver the Knight Heir to my mom on a silver platter in exchange for her not putting you on one of her cargo ships and having your pathetic ass dumped into the river?"

Of course, Anderson said nothing, and Zach stood from his crouch to look at me, his face heavy with regret. "This was a Ferrero hit, baby girl. I'm so sorry we weren't more careful."

I shook my head. He had nothing to apologize to me for.

I sat down next to Noah on his log, my own legs in danger of giving out on me as I fought the fury, the adrenaline crash, the soul-deep panic that Noah wasn't as okay as he pretended to be. I gripped his hand, breathing through my nose as I tried to steady myself.

I looked at Bennett, then at Zach, and I said, "We have to end this."

They both nodded, their faces grim, but determination shone in their eyes.

My phone buzzed from its spot in one of the pockets of my cargo pants. I fumbled for it, and I saw Max's name on the screen.

"Hey," I said, ignoring the loud grunts from our captive as Zach kicked the shit out of him.

"Can you stay out of trouble for, like, five fucking minutes, Jojo?"

I sighed. "It's what I get for thinking I could go and have normal college student fun."

The loud clanging of weights in the background told me Max was at Dom's gym tonight. I heard a deep voice muttering, then Max said, "Rocky says to tell you he's pissed you went and did this on his day off."

I didn't have it in me to come up with a snarky retort.

"Max," I whispered, unable to keep the anguish from my voice. "Noah's hurt."

"I know, babe," he said, his tone softening considerably. "Spencer called it in. Kara and Julie already cleared the park and are on their way to you now."

"It was Andrea," I said gruffly. "We have her Enforcer bagged and ready. He's not talking much."

Max snorted. "That's gonna suck for him later."

The sound of motorized vehicles approaching caught my attention, which meant it was time to get Noah out of here. "Tell Dom and Laura I'm completely unharmed," I said. "Then call Zepp and tell him Andrea's time is up."

"Will do. Love you."

"Love you too."

I hung up just in time to see two ATVs crest the small hill and zoom in our direction. They came to a stop a few feet away from where we'd gathered, and Julie dismounted from one while Kara sat on the other, taking in the scene. She'd apparently brought a passenger, his long, bare arms looped tightly around her middle from his seat behind her.

"I cannot believe you all have summoned me into the fucking *woods*," Frankie griped, climbing down from the ATV and looking around the forest, his lip curling in disgust. "If a *bug* touches me, I swear to God...."

I could only stare blankly at him. He did look a bit out of his element here in... nature.

Zach rolled his eyes. "Stop bitching. I have a present for you." He motioned to Anderson, who now appeared appropriately terrified.

Good.

Frankie perked up at that. "For me?" He stomped toward us, pausing to glare at a root that caught his ratty Converse sneaker, then his usual manic grin returned. "Oh, hey there, Anderson. So nice to see you again. Looks like you and I will be going on a date—are you excited?"

"Fuck you, you fucking freak," Anderson managed to sputter like a man with a death wish, and Frankie giggled.

He *giggled*, and then he stepped casually forward, placing his shoe squarely on Anderson's crotch and leaning his weight onto it. Anderson squealed while Frankie ignored him, crossing his arms and surveying the rest of us with mild interest as he stood on Anderson's dick. He said, "Everyone doing okay? That doesn't look too good, there, Hargraves."

Noah let out a wry chuckle, motioning to our captive while Kara fretted over him in a motherly way that relaxed me the tiniest bit. "This one got off a lucky shot. Make sure he pays for that—it upset Jojo."

Frankie ground his heel down, and Anderson screamed again. "Oh, that is cardinal sin number one in this City, my friend," Frankie cooed, then he nodded at Zach and Bennett. "Help me load him up, then I'll sit on him while Miss Julie drives us out of here."

They went to work, dragging a flailing Anderson to Julie's ATV, and I helped Kara carefully load Noah onto hers.

"I'll get him to our hospital, Jojo," she told me. "They'll patch him up good as new. You guys are safe to hike out of here—I had the rest of my team clear the area." She revved the engine and then flicked on the headlight, as the night had finally settled around us. "And don't let Rodney give you any shit about the ATVs—he wasn't in the mood to be helpful, so we weren't in the mood to ask his permission to use them."

I scoffed. "Rodney's going to have worse problems if I find out he had anything to do with letting Andrea sneak fucking mercs onto his property."

Kara chuckled. "I didn't get the sense that he did, but we'll see what Frankie can get out of our guest."

I leaned over to kiss Noah, who was now pouting about being carted out of here while he clung to Kara like a child. "I'll be right behind you," I whispered. "I love you. Please don't die."

He pressed his lips to mine again. "I'm not going anywhere, sweetheart. See you soon."

I watched them drive away, dread settling in my gut like a lead weight. Bennett stepped in front of me, and he pulled me into his arms. "It'll be okay, Angel. Noah's tough."

I sniffed, the tears welling again. "It's because of me," I said in a pained whisper. "I'm the reason he's hurt."

Zach snuggled up to my back, sandwiching me between the two of them, and he ran a soothing hand down my spine. "You're the reason he *lives*, Princess. Same for the two of us. We'll do anything to keep you safe, because there's no us without you. We're not doing that again—not ever."

I could only nod into Bennett's shoulder. I took one moment to let two of the three men I loved hold me while I broke in the dark, quiet woods, then I pulled myself together and marched out of there next to them, Noah's recovery the only thing on my mind.

But Andrea's demise would be next in line.

CHAPTER EIGHTEEN
NOAH

I scowled at Kara from the cushy hospital bed I'd been confined to since last night. She was unmoved by my ire, her arms crossed over her chest as she stood at the foot of my bed, daring me to try to sneak out of here before I was discharged.

"They said twenty-four hours, Noah," she reminded me. "Twenty-four hours of observation, then you can go home. And Jojo would send me straight to Frankie's workroom if I let you walk out of here before you're ready."

I sighed dramatically, falling back onto my pillow. "Fine," I said. While Jojo would do no such thing to Kara, she would have my balls if she thought I was doing anything to compromise my healing. "I'll behave."

"Thank you," she replied with a grin. "And settle in. I have Frankie's report for you."

That pepped me up a bit. Anderson would not be enjoying his stay in Knight Tower, and I suspected Frankie—who was developing a soft spot for his lovely boss, Jolie Knight—made sure Anderson paid for what he'd put Jojo through in his desperate attempt to earn back a shred of credibility from Andrea Ferrero.

As I'd suspected, my gunshot wound, while it'd hurt like a bitch, hadn't been life threatening, so the doctors working in the emergency clinic in the new and improved Hargraves Tower had been able to patch me up without too much fuss. Jolie, Bennett, and Zach had camped out in my room until I sent them all home to sleep comfortably in an actual bed, and I made them all swear to go to class this morning too.

"So, was Frankie able to confirm this was Andrea's doing?" I asked Kara.

She nodded. "Yes. The sense we're getting is that while Andrea and James Spencer are technically still aligned and claiming to be united as the sole representatives for the Four Families, they're butting heads, and this was Andrea's attempt to claim she succeeded eliminating Jolie where Spencer failed."

The pain that lanced my chest at her words was so familiar. I'd already been forced to watch my small, fragile best friend die right in front of me once, and the thought of losing Jolie again—for good—was a nightmare I couldn't fathom.

My mood darkened. "Who the fuck tipped them off to the paintball match?"

"Our guest did not actually have that information," she replied. "And Frankie assures us that he was very thorough in checking the veracity of that claim."

And Frankie was nothing if not thorough.

I crossed my legs and shifted to sit up higher against my pillows, thankful I'd been allowed to change into my worn Holywell Crew long-sleeved T-shirt and track shorts instead of continuing to look ridiculous in a hospital gown.

I pulled my phone from the table next to the bed and went straight to my secure chat with Silver to see if she had any news.

"Really, it wasn't a secret that Jolie was going to participate in that ridiculous dick-measuring contest between men's crew and men's lacrosse," I said as I hammered out a text to Silver. "Hatcher Robicheaux practically shouted it across the dining hall. Any one of the students from families who remain loyal to Spencer or Ferrero could've squealed."

Kara's no-nonsense face softened as she looked me over, her understanding gaze taking in my bandaged leg before moving to the troubled look I wore. "I know you boys are worried for her—we all are—but she's so strong, and she's surrounded herself with capable, loyal people. And—" She paused to shoot me a wink. "—let her worry over you a little bit too. I've known the grown-up Jolie Knight for a few years now, and frankly, it's good to see her acting like a normal teenager in love and not an emotionless robot."

My mind flashed to the *vast* array of emotions I'd been able to elicit from my girl since she'd literally parachuted back into my life. She was hardly emotionless around me, not even when she'd been masquerading as Joanna. I was saved from having to adjust myself in my shorts in front of Kara by a knock on the door. She turned away from me, back in bodyguard mode, and strode over to answer it.

"What are *you* doing here?"

I sat up straighter. I wasn't expecting a visitor who wasn't Jolie or the guys, and the venom that had dripped from Kara's words was alarming—Kara was tough and took no shit, but she was generally pretty chill.

"Kara, oh my gosh," a familiar voice gasped, and my

stomach sank. "Are you back with Hargraves after all these years? Are you working for my son?"

"What do you want, Celine?"

"Goodness, what is with that attitude? Is that how you're supposed to address your superiors, Kara?"

Well, that was enough.

"*Mom*," I barked. "Do not speak to Kara like that."

There was a beat of silence before my mom said, "Oh, Noah, what on earth—"

"Do you want me to let her in?" Kara asked me, looking back over her shoulder.

I sighed. "She can come say whatever she thinks she needs to say to me."

Kara shot me a concerned look before stepping out of the way so that my mother could enter the room. "I'll be just outside," she told me before slipping out and shutting the door behind her.

My wayward mother, Celine Hargraves, now stood in the middle of my hospital room in the state-of-the-art emergency clinic that I owned—the clinic that was in the heart of Hargraves Tower, which I also owned with Jolie. She wore a peach-colored sundress, strappy high heels, and the giant diamond pendant necklace that had been her Christmas present from my dad when I was six. Her honey-brown hair fell in perfectly styled waves over her bare shoulders, and her tanned body was still the lithe one of a woman who subsisted on yoga, Pilates, and whatever cleanse was the most popular amongst her coastal California friends at the moment.

She took in the dressing wrapped around my exposed thigh with wide eyes, bringing her manicured hand to her chest with a scandalized little gasp. "Noah, I just cannot believe all of this. I keep hearing about all of this nonsense going on in the City, and I finally called your father, only to find out that our own son has disowned the Family name and given all of our hard work to the *Knights*?"

"Why do you care, Mom?" I asked with a tired sigh.

She ignored me. "And then I come home to *our* tower only to find the penthouse vacant and basically falling into disrepair. Buckley informed me he was let go, and now I discover my son is in the hospital for reasons no one will tell me about. Noah, this is just insanity."

I stared at her. I hadn't seen my mom since my high school graduation, and she'd only flown in for the ceremony before flying right back out again. She'd moved away permanently when I was ten years old, leaving with the nine-figure check from my dad and not looking back. I hadn't revoked her clearance to this tower because frankly, I hadn't thought about her at all, much less anticipated she might decide to show up here now, of all times.

"Mom," I said, infusing as much patience into my tone as I could muster, "why are you here? You have no remaining interest in Hargraves, so the state of the Family empire means nothing to you. You don't actually give a shit about Dad, so my tossing him out of the City on his ass also means nothing to you. My graduation from Holywell is not for another two years. You have no reason to be in this City or in *my* tower right now."

She huffed, drumming her long pink fingernails on her diamond pendant as she stuck her nose in the air. "I am still a *Hargraves*, Noah. I am still married to your father, and I am still your mother. Our name has always carried the highest clout all over the country, and this mess you've been making here is *ruining* it."

There it was. My mother still valued the Hargraves name, and news of the Families' fall from grace was setting her back with the other rich housewives she ran around with, even all the way on the West Coast.

"Does it bother you even a little bit, Mom," I asked, reclining against my pillows again, "that Dad conspired with James and Andrea to murder the Knights in cold blood just so they could steal a priceless technology from them?"

She waved a dismissive hand. "I do not meddle in your father's business, Noah. I presume he did what he thought he must to protect Hargraves. And now I'm hearing that not only have you allowed that trampy Knight girl to take everything from us, you're *sleeping* with her? I will not allow it, Noah. I am still your mother."

I wondered if I'd done something to deserve being shot in the leg and then subjected to this. I felt a cold, quiet rage creep through my body—a foreign emotion when it came to my mother because I'd stopped caring about her existence long ago. "Mom, *I* am Hargraves now, and what I do with it is absolutely none of your business. And if you insult the girl I love in front of me ever again, I will find a way to take everything from you just like I did from Dad. Am I clear?"

"Noah! How could you speak to me like that—"

"What's going on in here?"

Jolie slipped past a furious Kara, appearing in the doorway like a glorious mirage. She'd taken advantage of the warm spring day and changed into denim shorts that showed off her long, gorgeous legs, which she'd paired with a flimsy long-sleeved T-shirt from Dom's gym. She carried a plastic to-go container from the dining hall in one hand and a cup of coffee in the other, and she assessed my mom with a silent intensity that spelled trouble.

I tore my glare from my mom, dismissing her, and I only

had a warm smile full of love for my girl. "Hey, sweetheart. Missed you."

She meandered further into the room, still watching my mom like a predator that had sighted her prey, and she set what looked like my lunch on the table next to my bed before handing me the warm cup of coffee she'd brought me because she was a goddess among mortals.

"Hi," she murmured, now looking at me with the same worry on her face she'd worn since I'd fallen out of that tree last night. She leaned down to kiss me softly, and I cupped the back of her head to deepen the kiss, drinking in her tiny moan like I needed it to live. After a second, she pulled away, assessing me again. "How are you? Are you in any pain? Kara said you were trying to leave early. Noah, you have to do what the doctors say or you'll hurt yourself again, and I just can't—"

I kissed her again, ignoring the dramatic huff from my mom. "I'm okay, sweet girl. I was okay last night, and I'm still okay now."

My mom cleared her throat. "Noah."

"You promise you'll stay here until the doctor clears you? I can skip crew practice this afternoon and hang out with you—"

"*Noah.*"

"I wouldn't complain if you stayed with me for a little while," I replied. "I'll share that sandwich you brought me, and then we can take a nap."

"Noah! I am not finished speaking to you. You will stop carrying on with that traitorous little skank and help your father reunite Hargraves with the Families!" She stomped a high-heeled foot like a toddler.

Jolie went rigid, standing up from the side of my bed and turning to face my mom. "I'm sorry, Mrs. Hargraves," she said, her voice ice cold. She paused to look down at me, stage-whispering, "Are we still calling her that?"

I snorted. "They are still carrying on with their farce of a marriage."

She nodded, turning back to my mom. "Mrs. Hargraves, do you know who put a bullet in your son's leg last night?"

"Whatever happened, I am certain it was due to his involvement with *you*."

"It was a *Family* Enforcer. He could have *died*. But you don't give a shit, do you? You're ambushing him here *in his hospital bed* to whine about—what? Your fake husband no longer being the fake ruler of the City? Did someone make a snide comment during Pilates class and hurt your feelings?"

I shifted uncomfortably in my bed. My mom needed to get the *fuck* out of here so I could put my hands on my girl.

"Noah, I cannot believe you're letting her speak to your mother like that!"

I shrugged. "I don't see a mother in this room. Do you, Jojo?"

"Noah!"

Jolie's beast was out now, and she stalked slowly forward, and whatever my mom saw in her face caused her to take an alarmed step backward.

"Leave," Jolie said in a low voice. "You're nothing to Noah, just as you've shown he's been nothing to you since he was ten years old. I remember what it did to him when he realized you really weren't coming back. He might've forgiven and forgotten a long time ago, but I haven't. If I see you in my City again, I'll break your face so badly that your plastic surgeon will have a hell of a fucking time fixing his hard work."

She gaped at Jolie, her cheeks flushed red as she sputtered, "Noah, she threatened me! I cannot believe you're carrying on with this crass... *pretender*!"

"Get the fuck out, Mom," I said gruffly. "I'd like to spend time with my real family now."

Kara appeared at the right moment to grasp Mom around her scrawny bicep and march her toward the door. "Let's go, Celine. Your access to Hargraves Tower has been revoked."

Mom's whines and protests faded into the background as Jojo's ethereal eyes met mine, shining with fury on my behalf and so full of love for me that I felt like I could fucking fly, bum leg and pain meds be damned.

"Come here, sweetheart," I demanded. "In this bed with me. Now."

She slinked back to my bedside, a coy smile now gracing her lips. I kicked the covers down, waiting until she'd crawled in with me before pulling them back up and over the both of us.

As she melted into my arms, she whispered, "Yes, sir."

And my mom was forgotten.

CHAPTER NINETEEN
JOLIE

I vaguely registered the sound of Kara unlocking the door before Zach's amused voice said, "Oh, what's going on in here?"

He slipped quietly into the room with Bennett right behind him. I'd left them both out in the lobby earlier to take care of their assigned tasks while I went to Noah: Zach had been on the phone with Marcus, and Bennett had tracked down Noah's doctor like a bloodhound to get the latest on Noah's condition.

By the time they joined us, I was snuggled up under the covers with Noah, tucked solidly into the little spoon position while he moved his dick leisurely inside of me, a gentle but firm hand wrapped around my throat.

Zach flopped into one of the cushy chairs near the bed, his dark eyes pinned on my face. "Princess, did you let the invalid sweet-talk you into putting out? Did Hargraves charm his way right into those sexy shorts you had on?"

"Mmm," I hummed, closing my eyes and biting my lip as Noah slipped his free hand between my legs. "He's hurt,

Zach. And his fucking *mom* was just in here. I'm taking care of him."

"She is," Noah rumbled, his hot breath right next to my ear.

Bennett loomed at the end of the bed, arms crossed, disapproving look on his face, but those mossy eyes were heated as he watched Noah slowly wind me tighter and tighter. After a second, my words registered, and he barked, "Celine was here?"

"Don't wanna talk about it," Noah huffed, his long fingers strumming my clit as he ground into me. "She came to whine, and Jojo and Kara tossed her out."

"Good," Bennett rasped. "Hurry up and make Jolie come. We have shit to discuss."

"Fuck," I whimpered. Noah had already brought me so close, and now that Bennett and Zach were here watching me with those eager, almost *desperate* eyes, I was about to implode in Noah's arms.

Noah groaned. "You feel so fucking good, sweetheart. So good for me."

"Goddamn, Princess, you're the sexiest thing I've ever seen," Zach purred.

"Give it to us, Angel. Now," Bennett demanded.

Pleasure pulled me under, and I screamed into the pillow as Noah found his own release behind me with a long, satisfied groan into my shoulder.

Five minutes later, I was cleaned up, fully dressed, and curled up next to Noah as I ran my hands through his wavy golden hair. Bennett had given me a stern look while adjusting himself in his pants, then took a seat next to Zach. With all three of them here, I felt centered for the first time since the start of the paintball fiasco.

"Noah's doctor will release him tonight around

dinnertime," Bennett told us. "We'll go to class tomorrow morning as usual, and then we'll move to Knight Tower for the weekend. I took the liberty of cancelling your office hours tomorrow afternoon," he added, glancing at Noah.

"Much appreciated," he murmured as he lazed in my lap, enjoying his head rub.

I looked at Zach. "And Marcus thinks we'll be able to just waltz into Ferrero Tower on Saturday night?"

"Well, I don't know about *waltz*," he replied with an amused grin, "but a Ferrero gala with about half the security usually required for that type of event is as good a time as any to pay my mom a visit."

I sighed. Frankie's sessions with Anderson had proved invaluable to our efforts in constructing our final move against Andrea, but I hated that Noah had to take a bullet for us to get there.

"You guys should go back to class," Noah said halfheartedly. "I know you have crew practice today, sweetheart."

I laughed. "Bennett and I are barely even on the team right now. We're not going to regattas while people are trying to kill me, and I no longer need the scholarship. My coach knows she'll see me when she sees me."

"My coach knows not to say a goddamn thing to me about anything," Bennett added like the entitled ass he was.

Zach shot me a cocky grin. "The TA of my bio lab has a major crush on me, so I can get away with skipping this afternoon."

I rolled my eyes. "Of course she does. Make sure she knows I'll break her fingers if she touches you."

"Who said my TA was a chick?" Zach countered, wagging his eyebrows at me.

"And stop talking like that unless you want to be bent over the bed, Angel," Bennett added gruffly.

And the afternoon passed just like that. We all stayed with Noah, planning, laughing, and eating the snacks that Zach had delivered to the room. Every hour or so, one of my boyfriends threatened to fuck me on Noah's bed regardless of who could walk in at any given moment. Dom dropped by to check on his favorite shooting buddy, and Silver called with her report right before the doctor arrived to discharge Noah.

By the time we arrived back at the Academy, I could tell everyone was looking forward to one day of normalcy before it was ripped away from us once again. As I clung to Noah in my bed that night, my thoughts were a confusing whirl of righteous anger and unrelenting dread.

The Families were never going to touch anyone I loved ever again. I'd make sure of it.

"So," Mari said as the four of us slipped into our seats at breakfast. "I presume you all have a solid story concocted for what happened on Wednesday?" She eyed the crutch Noah was using to take some weight off his injured leg. "Because the rumor mill is working at top speed."

Since I *had* actually learned my lesson, I'd updated Mari as soon as I'd had a moment to breathe at the hospital Wednesday night, including gently reminding her that her new best friend Frankie was likely removing a man's appendages in the name of Knight at that very moment. She'd just hummed like that was mildly interesting before scolding me for thinking it was a good idea to be creeping around the woods alone for any goddamned reason.

I shrugged. "Kara and Julie cleared the farm by telling everyone there was a gas leak. Noah heroically ran out into the forest to find me and... pulled his hamstring?"

Hannah Langford eyed us all dubiously. "Sure thing," she said after a second, taking a dainty sip of her chai and tossing her dark red hair over her shoulder. "I presume the real story is not something I need to be aware of as a Knight Tech board member?"

"Definitely not," Noah replied.

"Great," she replied with a bright smile. "So, is everyone caught up on our Finance homework then? If you guys aren't because of..." She waved her hand in Noah's general direction. "... all of that, I'm sure I could help smooth things over with Professor Roberts. She's in my mom's book club."

Zach grinned. "Yeah, that would be great, actually. This week has been... busier than we'd have liked."

Mari gave Hannah an approving nod, and I agreed. Influence was influence, no matter how small, and we'd use whatever we could to stay ahead.

After breakfast, Bennett left the group for his Lit Seminar, but only after he'd cupped my chin in his rough grasp and laid a possessive kiss on me in the middle of Holywell Hall. Mari snickered at my flushed face—sometimes I hated being pale—before the rest of us made our way up to the third floor for Finance class.

By the time we'd made it to our usual seats in the back of the auditorium-style lecture hall, Noah's happy smile was nowhere to be found as he griped endlessly over my babying him all the way up the stairs.

"Dude, just let it happen," Zach told him from his spot on my other side. "We're lucky that's all she's doing in response to you getting *shot*. Do you remember what happened when Alastia's goons gave Bennett a booboo on his face? Would you prefer she march into Ferrero Tower alone so she can claw my mom's eyes out? Because I had to talk her out of that about five times after we left your hospital room the first night."

I crossed my arms and sank lower in my seat, pouting. "I'm still mad about that."

"I know you are, Princess," Zach cooed at me like I was a fussy child. "But you feel better now that we have a solid plan, yes?"

I huffed. "Maybe. A little."

Noah threaded his fingers through mine as Professor Roberts entered the hall and began writing on the whiteboard. "I'm sorry for being a butthead, sweetheart. I just don't like being the weak link. We all have to be at our best to keep you safe."

"We're keeping *each other* safe, Noah," I reminded him.

Mari, who'd been engrossed in her phone even more than normal this morning, chimed in. "Sí, this is a group effort, and I have been working for the last two days on assisting in this little endeavor—*not* that any of you have asked." She sniffed primly, but the devious smile that *just* graced her blood-red lips said she wasn't actually angry with us.

Zach raised an inquisitive brow. "Oh? Whatcha got for us, *Miss* Mari?"

She hummed, that smile growing. "We will see."

It was hard to focus on the lecture after that—though I'd had the same problem when Noah made us go to class yesterday—but when the professor finally dismissed us, I felt like I'd retained at least enough to pull a B on the upcoming test.

The cluster of Family loyalists rose in front of us, and Chad sneered in my direction as usual.

"Nice face, Hendrickson," I called down to him, giving him my middle finger just like old times. He'd had to convalesce for a week after Bennett beat the shit out of him, but he was back in class now and pissier than ever. The swelling in his broken nose was only just starting to go down, and his black-and-blue face had turned a putrid shade of yellow green.

"Fuck you, bitch," he said through gritted teeth.

Zach snapped his head in Chad's direction like a demonic Doberman. "What was that, Hendrickson?"

"Nothing," he mumbled, turning to hurry down the stairs with his groupies in tow.

Before any of the students had made it to the door, it was thrown open, and Dean Jansen marched in with two uniformed campus security officers following close behind her.

"Bettina Gomez?" the dean called, her shrewd, pinched gaze scanning the classroom.

A squeak came from the gaggle of girls surrounding Chad. "What?"

"You'll need to come with us."

She cast a harried, confused glance around at her friends, but, fair-weather as they were, they all looked away, some of them even taking a physical step to separate themselves from her.

I loved to see it. Bettina was on my crew team, and she happened to be one of the bitches who'd helped Harper dump me in the river last semester.

As I watched her gallows march to the door, her shoulders slumped in her tight suit dress, a realization hit me, and I felt my eyes narrow in suspicion.

Bettina's family was in the bar and strip club business, and they were one of the few families still clinging to

Andrea's skirts as they tried to weather the storm Knight had brought onto the City.

Mari sidled up next to me, watching with an extremely smug smile as the door shut behind Bettina and the dean. "Bettina has been a naughty girl," she said in a low voice. "It didn't take much asking around for me to ferret out who'd decided to pass the information along to Andrea Ferrero that Jolie Knight would be at a paintball park on Wednesday night. I called Marcus, and he helped me set up a nice little present for her."

All three of us gaped wordlessly at her.

She stuck her nose in the air with a little huff. "Honestly, your astonishment wounds me."

Zach shook it off first. "Did you get her expelled?"

She grinned, and it was evil enough to give me a little shiver. "Her family is no longer able to pay her Academy tuition, so she will be packing her dorm before being escorted from campus, I presume."

"Girl," I said, blowing out a breath. "What did you do to the Gomezes?"

She examined her fingernails casually. "Really, they should have known better than to put so much of their worth—and their investors' money—in cryptocurrency. Marcus and I just nudged their crypto exchange of choice off the ledge it was already teetering on anyway."

Noah barked out a very loud laugh. "You two crashed CryptoCity? And you didn't tell us? *Unreal.* Oh, Silver is going to be so pissed Marcus hid this from her."

Zach snorted. "Those two need to just fuck and get it over with. I'll make sure Marcus gets a raise for this, because *damn.*"

"You know, Spencer actually had a pretty sizable stake in CryptoCity too," Noah added.

"Did they?" Mari asked, still with the tone of complete nonchalance. "How unfortunate for them."

I smiled so wide my cheeks hurt. "I bow down to you, girl. Fuck me, this is amazing."

"Yes, I *am* amazing," she replied. "Obviously. Now, I'm off to my next class, but if all of you would please try to refrain from making any more messes I'll need to clean up, that would be great."

CHAPTER TWENTY
JOLIE

"Mr. Ferrero," the doorman sputtered at Zach, "we, uh... we weren't expecting you."

Zach's cocky grin conveyed exactly how much he didn't give a fuck. "Well, I certainly couldn't miss a gala in honor of Ferrero's favorite charities *and* my mom's fiftieth birthday, now could I?"

The poor asshole checking IDs at the entrance to Ferrero Tower's largest and most opulent ballroom was now sweating in his ill-fitting tuxedo. He stared at Zach again in confusion, his eyes bouncing over to me and widening in actual terror before he finally lifted his walkie-talkie to his face. "Um, I have the Ferrero Heir and his...."

"Girlfriend," Zach prompted.

"... girlfriend here requesting entrance to the gala."

I nodded to his walkie. "Inform the head of security we're unarmed."

"But that we are happy to make a giant scene in front of the small sliver of the City's elite still willing to associate with Ferrero by being here tonight if we're made to wait much longer," Zach added lightly.

The man did as he was told, and we were instructed to await a more "thorough inspection."

Zach looked devilishly sexy tonight in his all-black tuxedo, while I'd donned a flowy mauve chiffon gown with a sweetheart neckline that dipped low across my modest cleavage. I swatted Zach's wandering hand away from the high slit in my skirt as we waited to be frisked by whoever had the unfortunate designation of heading up the paltry security Andrea was able to throw together for this event.

Noah's voice sounded in the microscopic earpieces we both wore. "Knight Three and Knight Four are about to drop. Do you think you'll have problems at the door?"

"Nah," Zach replied. "My mom will want to see me, despite everything, and she would *detest* a public scene."

"Let me know when the guys hit the roof, please," I whispered, attempting to keep my emotions in check. I was focused on playing my part here—I was the distraction—but it didn't change the fact that Bennett and Max were about to drop from a moving helicopter onto the tower's roof. That unnerved me *just* a bit.

Max's voice came through next. "Five minutes. Stow that worry I heard in your voice, Jojo. Big Man and I have this in the bag."

I heard Bennett grunt before Noah muttered, "I'm still pissed you guys left me in Silver's command center.... Hey, you two, stop fucking bickering.... Silver, you know we put Marcus on lead tonight because it's a Ferrero job.... Oh my God, what am I, your mom? Quit tattling to me. Lock it up, both of you."

I smothered a laugh as Zach and I watched a fresh-faced Ferrero Enforcer approach the door from inside the ballroom. I whispered, "And I thought Zepp was a pain in my ass."

The nervous doorman moved aside, and the Enforcer stepped into the lobby where we waited. He eyed Zach and me with extreme distrust.

"Mrs. Ferrero has graciously agreed to allow her Heir and his date to attend this evening, but you'll have to be searched."

Zach shot him an innocent smile. "I'm happy to receive a pat down, but if you put one slimy hand on my girl, I'll break it."

"Mr. Ferrero—"

I stepped forward and did a little twirl. "See? Nowhere to hide any weapons in this flimsy dress." I giggled like an airhead, though I doubted he bought it.

The Enforcer glared at me before approaching Zach and frisking him from head to toe. Finding nothing, he straightened and looked me over. His scrutinizing gaze lingered a little too long on my boobs before Zach growled menacingly at him. "You done, man? I'd like to get a drink in my hand before I'm fucking thirty."

The Enforcer motioned to the door. "We'll have eyes on both of you all night. Don't try anything."

"Thanks!" I said brightly, then I grabbed Zach's hand and flounced into the ballroom like I didn't have a care in the world.

Something I did have, however, was a tiny knife in the bra cup of my dress. I could never go anywhere truly unarmed, and it was my security blanket.

"Knight Three and Knight Four have landed," Noah said softly.

Bennett's deep voice added, "Roof is clear. We'll check in when we access the elevator."

"Mmm, can't wait to be working that *shaft* with you, Big Man," Max purred.

"Max, for fuck's sake," I hissed.

"Can someone please remind me why my assigned partner in this heist is an eighteen-year-old high school senior and not one of the many seasoned military veterans we have working for us?" Bennett griped in his monotone.

"Unfortunately," Noah said, his tone belying his deepest empathy at Bennett's plight, "he's the best lockpick we have, and that somehow includes breaking open elevator doors with a drop key."

Max chuckled. "I am very skilled with my hands, what can I say?"

"Jesus Christ," Zach muttered.

"Can you all fucking focus?" I said through the gritted teeth of my fake smile. "Knight One and Knight Two are in. We have eyes on Andrea."

She was easy to spot, floating around the cavernous ballroom amongst the white-linen-covered tables on the arm of whatever opportunist had replaced Ramon as her head bodyguard. Her magenta mermaid gown fit her ample curves like a glove, and her black hair had been swept into a classic up-do. Her dark eyes—so achingly familiar to the ones I loved—scanned the room, calculating and cold.

A chamber orchestra performed Vivaldi's "Four Seasons" from the small stage erected at the back of the room, the classical vibe of the music striking me as at odds with the almost gaudy theme of the room. Atop every table was a floral arrangement that stood at least four feet high, all the flowers a shade of magenta similar to Andrea's dress. Large neon-blue chandeliers hung from the black ceiling, each draped with endless strings of lights and hovering over the tables like gargantuan jellyfish floating above our heads. As we drifted past an empty table, I noted that the flatware had actual *diamonds* inlaid in the handles.

"Fake," Zach said with a chuckle, noticing where my gaze had strayed. "No way my mom forked out that kind of cash given her dire financial straits. She's only putting on this show to convince anyone who's looking that everything is just fine."

And we were here to put the final nail in her coffin.

"We're in position," Bennett said in my earpiece.

"Preparing to cut power," Noah replied. "You'll have ten seconds to pop the elevator doors open before it turns back on."

"I'll only need eight seconds," Max said with a scoff. "Then Big Man and I will be shimmying down that *shaft* together. I can't wait to watch him work it."

"Keep running your mouth and I'll leave you on the fucking roof," Bennett retorted.

"Bennett, you will do no such thing," I said under my breath. "Play nice, both of you."

Grumbling sounded through my earpiece, and I tuned it out to focus on the task at hand. Andrea watched us now, her deep suspicion about our presence here written all over her face, but she couldn't hide the little hint of longing—of *possessiveness*—that flashed every time her eyes landed on her son.

And while she was down here in the ballroom, wooing potential new investors, pretending to give a shit about charity, and acting like the fact that she was turning fifty didn't make her die a little inside, we would be taking from her the last leg she had to stand on.

Frankie's sessions with Anderson—one of the only long-tenured high-level Ferrero Enforcers still breathing—had yielded some helpful, but also disturbing, information. We'd already known that soon after Zach and Frankie had officially defected from Ferrero, Andrea had removed her most sensitive records from her basement office at the Euphoria Club. Zach thought their new home was most likely somewhere in Ferrero Tower, and Frankie was able to *persuade* Anderson to confirm the exact location was Andrea's hidden safe in her penthouse office.

Ferrero had always made a substantial portion of its fortune in illegal fights, running guns, and smuggling priceless art and other antiquities. With Andrea's legitimate businesses either gobbled up by Knight or flagging as investors abandoned the sinking ship, she had to lean heavily into the illegitimate side of her enterprise. The records for these endeavors were kept old school—on paper ledgers locked away in a cabinet to which only Andrea had the key. If we could put our hands on those records, we would have detailed instructions for wiping Ferrero off the map for good.

And there was more riding on our success tonight than just my burning desire for retribution and the City's need to be washed clean of its filth—Anderson let it slip that in her desperation for cash, Andrea had finally decided to throw her hat into the ring with the lowest of the low when it came to smuggling.

Sex trafficking.

Andrea had always prided herself on her *legal* prostitution operation at the Club, where the escorts were there of their own free will, their clients were strictly vetted, and they were paid handsomely for their services. But apparently, she was desperate enough now to deal in illegal, unwilling skin, and we needed to put our hands on the details of her first shipment—imminent, per Frankie—and we needed to do it before those poor men and women were harmed further.

With any luck, Andrea would be on the fast track to

prison after tonight.

The lights flickered, and the crowd let out a collective gasp as the room was plunged into darkness.

"Power's off," Noah barked. "You're on, Max."

"Got it. Thanks, Nehemiah," Max replied.

Noah's long-suffering sigh was audible. "Eight seconds."

I heard the slow grind of metal on metal through my earpiece, and after five seconds that felt like five hours, Bennett announced, "We're in."

The lights flickered again, and the neon jellyfish burst back to life. The orchestra resumed the music, the bartenders resumed serving drinks, and the partygoers returned to their shameless attempts to vie for Andrea's attention.

But Andrea only had eyes for her son as she floated closer, her dark pink talons wrapped around a crystal champagne glass and her haughty smile intact.

Zach and I had each grabbed our own drinks from a passing waiter, mostly for show, and he snuggled me tighter into his side as we watched Andrea approach us like she was the predator and we were her prey when, really, it was the other way around.

All the while, I tried not to think too hard about Max and Bennett *Ocean's Eleven*ing their way down the penthouse elevator shaft right about now.

"Zachary," Andrea purred as she and her bodyguard came to a stop in front of us. "This is unexpected. I was hoping you were finished with your little rebellion, but seeing as how you have that traitorous bitch on your arm, I am not optimistic."

The fake charm Zach usually displayed for his mother was nowhere to be found. "Disappointed your little hit job failed, Mom?" he spat. "Jojo and I are both getting tired of putting down your shitty mercs and subpar Enforcers."

Andrea's bodyguard frowned like he was greatly offended by that, but Andrea's cold smile only grew as she remained focused on her son, ignoring me completely. "Is that why you dropped by, Zachary? To gloat? You shouldn't bother—I can't help but be proud of the capable, ruthless man you've become. I just wish you weren't using everything *I* gave you for the wrong things, baby."

I gave Zach a little squeeze where my arm was wrapped around his waist. I knew he wouldn't let anything his mother said bother him, but none of this was fun for him. My boys had all lost one or both of their parents—not in the same way I had, certainly—but it didn't mean the loss wasn't meaningful.

It didn't mean it didn't hurt just the same.

Zach made a show of tossing back a huge swig of his drink, then he said, "We're here because we heard you were trying to lure some of Ferrero's old allies back onto this sinking ship. As the Ferrero liaison for Knight, I thought I'd check on my interests. See if anyone was having second thoughts."

Andrea sneered. "It breaks your mother's heart to hear you talk about *your* legacy like that, Zachary. This is not a sinking ship, and this is a *charity* gala. You're just so determined to make me out to be a monster, baby, when I have done nothing but protect our Family and give you the lavish life a Ferrero Heir deserves. You've let that *whore* poison your mind."

"Not another word about her, Mom," Zach snapped. "Not another *sound* out of your mouth about the girl who you tried to *murder* when she was eleven-fucking-years old. Just like a *monster* would."

Andrea blew out a frustrated breath, her smile strained as her burly blonde bodyguard ran his hand down her back to soothe her. She took a dainty sip of her champagne, and with a little shake of her head like she was clearing out the anger, her chilly poise was back.

She finally turned to face me. "Leave—you're not welcome in Ferrero Tower. I don't care how entranced you've made my son. This war you've started only ends one way, and it's with you at the bottom of the Obsidian where you belong and order restored to this City."

I smiled back, snuggling deeper into Zach's side as he vibrated with tension next to me. "It's over for you now, Andrea. We're really just here to say goodbye."

She scoffed, turning and giving me her back as she began to walk away. Then she paused, looking back over her shoulder at Zach to say, "I'm out of patience, Zachary. Return to where you belong before you end up at the bottom of the river too."

We watched her stalk angrily away, dragging her bodyguard along, and they disappeared from the ballroom and down a hall that led to bathrooms and the kitchens.

"You okay?" I whispered.

"Yeah, baby girl," he replied, sounding tired. "I just... don't ever want to see her again."

I could only nod, and we stood there in silence for several minutes.

Until that silence was shattered by Max's urgent voice cutting into our ears. "Fuck, fuck, fuck. We're locked in. Andrea's office was outfitted with some kind of panic-room alarm, and we're fucking locked in here."

Zach and I looked at each other in wide-eyed alarm, then we sprinted out the ballroom doors.

CHAPTER TWENTY-ONE
ZACH

"What the fuck is going on, Noah?" Jolie barked as we raced to the elevator.

"Some kind of electronic lock engaged when Max and Bennett breached Andrea's safe," he replied. I could hear his rapid typing in the background. "Silver and Marcus are trying to access it, but, as you know, the Shadows have tried for years and haven't been able to hack Spencer or Ferrero at their highest levels like this."

Marcus' voice popped online. "Ferrero, if you can get your phone close to the lock, I can get in that way."

"What the fuck kind of shit have you put on my phone, man?" I asked as I jammed my finger into the button to call the elevator. We were headed to the highest floor we could reach without a top-level security card, and then we'd take the fire stairs.

"We'll talk about it later," Marcus replied, the evasive fuck. "Just fucking get up there. We don't know who this alarm notifies and how fast they'll be able to get to the office."

"Cool, cool, cool," I chanted as we stepped into the

elevator. "Seeing as how we only have the one small knife in Princess's bra between the two of us."

"We'll improvise," Jojo said, her face now eerily calm as she focused solely on saving Bennett and her brother.

Bennett was also cool as a cucumber as he said, "We're fine. We're both armed and can handle whatever they throw at us. Angel, do *not* put yourself in unnecessary danger."

"Fat chance," Noah, Max, and I muttered all at once.

Jojo scowled at me, and I just pulled her closer to press a little kiss to her shoulder.

"I'll gut Anderson for failing to inform us of this new little enhancement to Andrea's security," she declared. "I'll do things to him that make Frankie look like a fucking lovable Care Bear."

Fuck me, now was not the time for an erection.

"Oh, Spencer looks turned on now," Max said, chuckling. "Gross, I do not need to be on the line for your phone sex, sis."

The elevator dinged, stopping us at the sixtieth floor and saving all of us from a tongue lashing from the Princess. She bolted out the doors, moving impressively quickly in those sexy stiletto heels I'd spent the evening imagining digging into my ass as I buried my dick in her, and I raced after her.

The door to the emergency stairwell just off the elevator bank was never locked—safety first, people—and in a few quick, arduous minutes, we'd run up six flights of stairs to the locked door that accessed the first floor of the place I no longer called my home.

"Hold your phone to the keypad, Ferrero," Marcus instructed.

I did, and within seconds, the loud beep announced the door unlocking.

"You know," Jolie muttered, breathing hard. "This would've been nice to have back when I was breaking and entering into Family towers."

"No fucking shit," Max said in our ears.

"It's in beta," Marcus replied, nonchalantly.

Noah added, "And apparently it doesn't mask the entry—it'll still appear to security like foreign access, so it's only for emergencies, such as the one we find ourselves in now."

"You don't need to remind us," I griped, grabbing Jolie's hand and leading us through the entryway toward the kitchen, to find the main level dark and completely devoid of life. "So far the house is clear."

"Still clear here," Bennett added. "Get a fucking move on."

"We are on the way, Your Highness," I drawled.

Mom's office was located just off the kitchen down a short hallway. We raced that way, the light clicking of Jojo's heels against the marble tiles the only discernible noise in the eerily quiet penthouse. When we arrived at the locked door, I swore viciously.

"What in the ever-loving fuck is this?"

Mom rarely kept her home office locked, presumably because the penthouse security as a whole was tight, and also because until very recently, she'd kept her most sensitive items locked away in the basement at the Club. But now I was staring at some kind of electronic deadbolt—not a Knight brand, either—that had been remotely activated to lock the occupant inside.

"Just hold your phone up to it, dude," Marcus barked in my ears.

I did, and the seconds ticked by as we all listened to

Marcus' rapid typing. Bennett, the impatient fuck, grumbled, "Why isn't this extremely useful tech on anyone else's phone?"

"I said it was in *beta*," Marcus growled. "I didn't anticipate you lot getting yourselves trapped in a fucking Family penthouse."

Finally, a bright green light flashed, and the whir of the locking mechanism disengaging was music to our ears.

We heard Noah chuckle. "Oh, don't look so impressed, Silver."

Jojo, not in the mood to fuck around, shoved the door open and darted inside. I followed on her heels, ready to lay my eyes on our brothers to ensure they were unharmed and then get the fuck out of here with the documents we'd come for.

The office was dark, the City lights outside the large window giving us just enough light to make out the shapes and features of the room. Max and Bennett had both parked themselves on the front of Mom's large desk, their booted feet swinging and their boredom evident even under their face coverings.

Jojo threw herself into Bennett's arms while Max mumbled something about being chopped liver, and I took a moment to scan the office for anything else I might want to abscond with before we bailed.

"All good?" Noah asked. "Get moving. There's no way that alarm didn't dispatch the security team. Jojo, can you shimmy up the elevator shaft in your dress?"

Princess scoffed, sounding offended. "Noah, I fucking scaled the side of Hargraves Tower in one of those stupid little skirts the Holywell bitches love to wear."

"You did *what*?" Bennett growled.

Silver cut in, apparently having wrestled control from

Marcus because he was a little bitch. "Focus, please, everyone. Get to the roof. The helicopter will meet you—"

The creaking hinges of a door being opened at the back of the office *where there was not actually a door* sent a jolt of fear and adrenaline through me as though it was the sound of a gunshot.

Bennett and Max whirled, pistols raised and aimed toward the sound. Bennett shoved Jojo behind him while Max stepped in front of me like the upstanding dude he actually was despite how much he liked to annoy the shit out of me.

"Well, well, well." I knew that silky feminine voice so very well. "Zachary, it appears you lied to me."

We were staring at a secret fucking doorway. A secret fucking passage into this office, hidden behind a bookshelf, that I had no idea about, and I'd lived in this fucking penthouse for eighteen years of my life.

Mom stepped into the room, still wearing her ridiculous pink dress, her new bodyguard at her side. Both of them had their handguns raised and pointed at us, so it was two guns to two.

Stalemate.

"Oh, Zachary, stop looking so shocked," she said, flicking on a lamp that sat atop a nearby side table while keeping her dark eyes pinned on me. "I've made some sensible upgrades to this office since you decided to *abandon* your Family. I do know a thing or two about being prepared."

The fact that this actually wasn't something she'd hidden from me for years only made me feel marginally like less of an idiot.

"Rocky's team was on standby, and we're sending them

in," Noah said, his voice soft in our ears. "But it is going to take some time."

I would stall, then.

"Mom, I have to say I'm extremely disappointed in you," I began, stepping out from behind Max. "Or, I should say, I'm even more disappointed than I already was, given what you've done to me and the woman I love. I'm *ashamed*, even. Human trafficking? You said things were going just fine here at Ferrero, but it seems you're more desperate than even I thought."

Her brow no longer had the ability to furrow, but I could still make out her pout in the soft yellow light of the lamp. "That's hurtful, Zachary. Ferrero has always been in the business of procuring rare, pretty things for those with the proper funds. This is *your* legacy, baby. Now," she went on, pausing to smooth her dress with her free hand. "I am willing to let you, Mr. Spencer, and even this little Southside street rat you've brought into my house walk out of here—after you've returned what you've taken from my safe, of course. Then I'd like to have a... *private conversation* with Miss Knight."

"No fucking way," came from me, Bennett, Max, and Noah all at once.

Jojo tried to muscle her way between Bennett and Max but did not get very far. "I like that idea, Andrea," she said with a feral smile. "Send your bodyguard-slash-fuckbuddy out with your weapon, and you and I can settle this like women."

My mom barked out a laugh. "Nice try, you little bitch. I suggest you do as I say—it's your only chance to save your *brother* before the rest of my team arrives. I'll make sure he dies first—while you watch. And I can't really guarantee the safety of Mr. Spencer, either."

Jojo struggled against Bennett and Max, but those two were unmovable, thank God. "Fuck you," she spat at my mom.

Noah's quiet voice cut in again. "ETA ten minutes for Rocky's team. We can't find her Enforcers, so they must be coming via the secret entrance we had no fucking idea about. Be ready, and *please* be careful."

We were running out of time here. I knew I was going to jump in front of our entire group if I had to—ultimately, my mom didn't want me dead. Hopefully, that would buy them enough time to lay down some cover fire and get the fuck out of this office.

I would *never* let my mom hurt Jojo again. I would take fifty bullets from her shitty Enforcer team if it meant my Princess—the love of my life, the other half of my soul, the missing piece who had finally made my brothers and me whole again—walked out of here alive.

"Zach, I know what you're thinking," Jojo whispered from behind me. The wobble in her soft, husky voice cut me down to my core. "Don't do it. We will fight *together*."

The sound of footsteps echoing in the dark, empty space behind the bookshelf sank my stomach to my feet.

"Uh-oh," Mom cooed. "Looks like you're out of time. Last chance to save your best friend and the thug, Zachary."

I moved fast, shoving Max behind me next to Jojo. "Get her the fuck out of here," I hissed.

"Zach, no!" Jojo cried.

"Go!" I shouted. "Please, baby girl. *Please*."

"Stop it, Max. *Zach!*"

And then Frankie emerged from the secret doorway.

He raised his handgun and fired one clean shot into the back of Mom's bodyguard's head. Gore splattered the bookshelves, and the guy dropped to the floor, just another expendable Ferrero soldier after all.

"Oh, are we having a party?" Frankie asked as he crept into the office, his gun now trained on the back of Mom's head. "Sorry I'm late, but it took me just a minute to find this very neat new set of stairs off floor fifty-nine. I'm almost impressed, sister."

My mom had frozen, her gun now limp in her grip as she raised her hands slowly in the air. "The ways you've betrayed me, little brother," she said through gritted teeth. "After everything I've done for you. Everything I've given you."

Frankie smirked. He looked like he'd been busy—his black tank top was so blood spattered, I could barely make out the image of Che Guevara on the front. His dark hair stuck to his sweaty forehead, and he had a nasty-looking gash on his bicep.

"What the fuck is going on?" Noah hissed in our ears.

"The cavalry is here," Jojo whispered back. "I don't think Andrea's team will be joining us."

"Indeed," Frankie said to my mom as he prowled around her, gun still leveled at her head. He came to a stop as he reached her front, and his warm brown eyes clashed with her dark ones—the loathing palpable between them. "You *have* given me so much, dear sister. Lots of interesting work. A paltry salary that kept me fed until I received access to the guilt trust our father left me. The Ferrero name. The constant reminder that I'm lucky you didn't drown me in the bathtub when I was a baby."

"Bitch," Max rasped under his breath, the single word soaked with ire on Frankie's behalf.

Those two were cute. Jojo did not know I was on this ship, and I had no plans to tell her.

"So," Frankie went on, "I have actually brought *you* a present, sister. To repay you for everything you've done for me. I'm excited for a little family reunion, as it were."

What the fuck...?

Another body emerged from the secret doorway—a woman, vaguely familiar to me, dressed in a billowing black evening gown as if she'd just come from the gala downstairs.

I studied her features as she stepped into the low light. Blonde hair swept into an elegant, low ponytail. Brown eyes. Slight wrinkles at the corners of her eyes that said she was close to my mom's age but had allowed herself to age a bit more gracefully than Mom had.

The woman wore a wide smile that set off flashes in my memory. Bits and pieces of another blond whose smiling face had faded away over all of these years.

"Aunt... Aunt Gemma?" I sputtered.

Mom whirled with a gasp. "What the hell is this, Gemma?"

I could only stare, struck dumb. I hadn't seen my aunt since I was five years old. Sensing my need for her, Jojo snuck into my arms. She whispered, "I didn't realize it, Zach. I've only met her once, over secure video. That's Gemini."

The original benefactor of the Shadows. My dad's sister. The absent family member I never thought about because she lived in Switzerland and hadn't come back to the City after my father's death.

Gemma didn't wither under my mom's challenging stare. "This is about the fact that I never once believed that my brother died in his sleep of natural causes," she said, her calm, resolute words slightly accented. "It was too convenient that he just happened to pass away so suddenly—so tragically—a mere three days after he'd called to tell me he'd decided to leave his cold, morally bankrupt wife. So soon after he'd decided he was going to run away with his son and never look back."

Cold leached into my veins. My ears began to ring. I clung to Jojo to remain standing. Bennett pressed into my other side.

"You're delusional, Gemma," Mom spat.

Gemma grinned again—her familiar smile making my chest ache. "You forget, Andrea, that the von Rotz family is not without resources. Just because we don't hail from one of your top Tier *City* families doesn't mean we don't have connections. And lots and lots of money."

My dad was Christian von Rotz, and he came from old Swiss money. He and my mom met on vacation in the Alps back when they were both in college. I was told I'd been to Switzerland once when I was two, but I didn't remember it at all.

Gemma went on, "I had his body exhumed, Andrea. Right under your nose."

Mom paled, and I knew without a doubt it was all true.

"Fentanyl. Enough to kill a horse," Gemma spat. "How nice to have the medical examiner on the Family payroll."

I clutched Jojo tightly as she gaped at my aunt before she turned to whisper into my ear, "I didn't know, Zach. Gemini never told us who she was or why she joined the Shadows—only that she'd lost someone close to her to the Families. I promise I would've told you if I'd known."

I pressed a kiss to her hair. "I know, baby girl. It's okay."

Nothing was okay, but the fact that Jojo had been allied with my aunt—who had been hiding this huge fucking secret—without knowing it was not the issue.

Frankie tutted. "Terrible, sister. Murder is so run-of-the-mill around here, but your own husband? The father of your precious son and Heir?"

"He was going to *embarrass* me," Mom said, seething. "He threatened to take Zachary from me. I did what I had to do to protect this Family *like I always do*."

Gemma glared at her, her lip curling with disgust. "And everything I've done since I figured out what you did has led to this moment. I put my fortune into the very organization that's now brought you to your knees, led by the brave girl you tried to *murder* when she was eleven years old."

My mom shook her head, like she refused to accept any of this. She finally turned those cold, lifeless eyes to me. "Zachary, I only ever wanted to protect you. You are a Ferrero. You can't listen to anyone that isn't *our* Family. I am your *mother*."

I threaded my fingers through Jojo's as I met my mom's imperious stare. "Not a monster, huh? Fuck you, Mom. Every single person standing in this room is more my family than you have ever been. You took my dad from me. You tried to take my girl from me. You can *rot. In. Hell.*"

Frankie beamed at me, pride in his wild eyes, and he nodded his approval at what we both knew I was going to do next.

I went to grab Bennett's gun from his hand. I *had* to end this.

She had to pay.

But Gemma beat me to it.

She pulled the tiniest pistol I'd ever seen from the pocket of her dress, and she fired one shot into my mom's temple.

I shut my eyes. My mom deserved to die for everything she'd done, but I didn't need to see her skull blown apart—

even if I had been about to be the one to do that very thing to her.

She was still my fucking mom.

Princess pulled me closer, pressing my face into the crook of her neck, and I breathed her in. She smelled nice—like vanilla—and her warm skin and slow, measured breaths soothed me. "It's over, Zach," she whispered. "She's gone."

"Is he okay?" Noah asked quietly.

"I'm fine," I croaked. "I will be. I promise."

I felt a hand squeeze my arm, and I lifted my head from Jojo's shoulder to meet Frankie's eerily subdued stare. "This was the best way," he said quietly. "I'll just be going now."

I could only nod as he slipped quietly back out the secret entrance, disappearing into the night, like he did.

"Zach?" Gemma asked tentatively.

I turned her way, studying her and ignoring my mother's body strewn at her feet. The apology was clear on Gemma's face as she said, "I know I took that away from you just now, but ultimately, I thought it was the least I could do for you—so you weren't... burdened with it forever." She stepped around the bodies on the floor, moving closer to where I still stood, holding Jolie in my arms. "And I'm so sorry I haven't been there for you all these years. I... I didn't know that you hadn't become just like your mother. I'd thought you were probably a lost cause."

I shrugged, finding I didn't have it in me to be offended by that. "There's nothing more you could've done for me, Aunt Gemma. You did what you could—supported the Shadows, who saved my girl and brought her back to me. You got justice for my dad and for Jolie." I released Jojo, and I walked over to Gemma and pulled her into a hug. "Thank you," I whispered.

"You're welcome, honey," she whispered back. "I'd... I'd like to come around more. Get to know you, if that's okay? You look so much like a dark-haired Christian. It's uncanny."

"Sure," I replied. "I'll set you up with a suite in Knight Tower. I'm thinking I'll gut this one."

Her smile was grateful. "That sounds perfect."

Then the door behind us—the office's actual door—burst open.

Rocky stood there, weapons raised in both hands and a whole group of tactical-geared Shadows behind him. "Everything good in here?" he asked, lowering his guns as he took in the scene. "Oh, hey, Gemini. What, uh... what are you doing here?"

I sighed as everyone let out an awkward chuckle. "Fuck this night. I hate it here—let's go home."

"You got it," Jojo said, grasping my hand again. "I love you, Zach. I'm sorry it came to this."

"I'm not," I said. "I love you too, Princess. You weren't going to be safe until she was gone."

She nodded solemnly, squeezing my hand as she led me away from the scene, and I felt lighter with every step I took.

CHAPTER TWENTY-TWO
JOLIE

Somehow, Zach slept like the dead last night. It was now a few hours after sunrise on Sunday morning, and I lay next to him in my giant bed, watching him sleep peacefully, like I was worried he would shatter at any moment.

The woman who murdered my mother was dead. One more piece of my soul was now at rest. I'd always known it might come to this—violence was the foundation upon which the Families had built their ivory towers, after all—but last night I'd been prepared to send Andrea on her way to prison where she could rot, watching as I took everything from her in the name of my parents, including her Heir.

I wasn't sorry in the slightest that the night had ended with a bullet in Andrea's head, but she was still Zach's mom. None of this was easy for him.

Noah and Bennett had crawled out of bed about an hour ago, and they'd both kissed me on the cheek before heading down to the gym a few floors below our home. Noah—still put out about being left behind last night—

was itching to do some light working out to strengthen his injured leg, and Bennett had sworn on pain of no sex for a month that he would ensure Noah didn't overdo it.

I suspected they also wanted to give Zach some alone time with me, and I loved them very much for taking such wonderful care of their brother.

"Stop looking at me like that, Princess," Zach mumbled, his gruff voice heavy with sleep.

"Like what?"

"Like you think I'm about to fall apart."

He cracked an eye open to spear me with a *look*, but it took a lot more than an adorable, sleepy-eyed glare to intimidate me. "Zach," I said softly, "we killed your mom last night. You found out some truly fucking terrible things about what happened to your dad. Your estranged aunt showed up, and we discovered she was the Shadow's first major benefactor and has been scheming against Ferrero for a decade and a half. It's okay to need a minute."

He groaned, pulling me closer. I pressed my face into his chest as he wrapped his strong arms around me. "Baby girl, you need to understand something," he whispered into my hair. "The moment your gorgeous eyes met mine at the Holiday Ball last semester—the moment I realized my Jojo had survived and come back to me—I knew my mom wasn't long for this world. She was always going to be a danger to you, and there was no way I was losing you again." He shifted us, tilting my face up to look him in those bottomless dark pools. "I'd thought it'd be you, or me, or even Frankie that did it, and I can't say I'm not a little relieved that I wasn't forced to commit matricide, but I'm not sorry she's gone. She was a vile, soulless person. She hadn't been my mom for a long time."

I ran my fingers through his messy black hair. "And your dad?"

He sighed. "I think that'll take a while to sink in. I'll never know him—she took that from me. But, if I'm being honest, I'm not sorry I didn't grow up hidden away in Switzerland, because I'd have lost you, Bennett, and Noah—the three most important people in my life."

"But she wouldn't have been able to hurt you," I whispered. The thought of little Zach being tortured on the orders of his mother made me want to raise Andrea from the dead just so I could kill her again myself.

"Princess, I'd have let Ramon and his cronies break my ribs every damn day if it meant I ended up right where I am—holding you in my arms, in *our* home, so, *so* close to being free of the Families forever."

I brought my lips to his, pouring every ounce of my love into my kiss. I nibbled on his lip ring, and he growled before he rolled me onto my back and slotted his trim hips between my legs. We made out, lazy and unhurried, while Zach ground his very aroused dick into the apex of my thighs with only his tight boxers and my little sleep shorts separating our heated flesh. I raked my nails up and down his back and reveled in the feel of his taut muscles under my fingertips.

"If you're trying to distract me, baby girl," he said as he ran his lips down the slope of my neck, "it's working. I approve of this plan."

"Can't I just want to fuck my boyfriend without an ulterior motive?" I asked, gasping as he yanked the straps of my silky tank top down to expose my breasts to the cool air.

He made himself at home there, sucking and licking with great enthusiasm. "Princess, you can fuck me with or without an ulterior motive, anytime, anywhere."

I rolled us, as much as it pained me to remove him from his diligent ministrations on my tits, and I straddled him, locking his muscular thighs between mine and threading my fingers through his.

I did want to distract him. I wanted him to feel free and loved and cherished. I wanted to show him in some small way what he meant to me, how much I knew he'd given to me by choosing me over his Family.

"You know," I said with a sly smile I hoped was extremely sexy, "it's odd that for some reason, *Noah's* the only one of my boyfriends who's had my mouth. Multiple times, even."

"Fuck," he groaned. "Don't remind me, Princess. I still dream about watching you suck him off while I fucked you. And don't think for a second Noah didn't brag to Bennett and me about your hot little student-teacher fuck in *excruciating* detail."

I flushed, the reminiscing adding fuel to the fire Zach had already stoked within me. I slid further down his thighs, peeling his tight gray boxers down until his thick dick sprang free. "So, how 'bout it, Ferrero?" I ran my palm lightly up and down his hard length, teasing him.

"Baby girl, I am so ready. Just stop torturing me."

I ducked down and got to work. Zach was thicker than Noah but not quite as long, but I gave his dick the methodical focus I gave most tasks, and after a few minutes he was groaning as he gripped my hair and fucked up into my mouth with shallow, frantic thrusts.

"Fuck, Princess. *Fuck*," he panted, yanking me off of his cock. "That was fucking phenomenal. We gotta slow it down because I've decided I want to hit another milestone with you this morning."

"What—"

Suddenly, I was on my stomach, my shorts ripped from my body and tossed across the room and Zach's hulking, nearly naked body looming over me. He hiked my hips into the air, palmed the globes of my ass with his big hands, then spread me wide as he buried his face there.

"*Zach*," I whimpered as he laved his tongue over my tight hole. "Ugh, why does that feel so good?"

"Because I'm so good *at* it, Princess," he purred. He slipped a finger into my pussy, pumping lightly through the slickness. "You want to see if you can take me in this perfect ass? Only if you're feeling up to it, baby girl. We have forever to explore the limits of this body."

He slid his slick finger slowly into my ass, and I moaned as he began moving with slow, careful thrusts. "Do I ever back down from a challenge, Zach?" I asked, throwing a defiant glare over my shoulder only to be confronted with the image of my gorgeous, tattooed boyfriend kneeling behind me, his obsidian eyes hungry and filled with wonder as he watched his finger slide in and out of my ass.

It almost undid me on the spot.

"Oh, baby," he said as he finally tore his eyes from my ass. "This perfect ass is going to take my cock so fucking good."

He added a second finger, gently working me open, the bite of pain only driving me higher, and I trembled with the anticipation and the *need* for him to have me like this.

"Zach," I moaned. "I can do it. I can take it."

"Of course you can, baby girl." He pulled away, flopping onto his back and relaxing against my mountain of pillows. I watched as he leaned over to dig in the top drawer of my nightstand before returning to his pillow throne with a little plastic bottle of lube. With a sexy wink, he kicked his boxers all the way off, then he proceeded to slather his still very erect cock with the lube, pumping his fist up and down as he held my greedy stare.

"C'mere, Princess," he said, motioning to his lap. "Come take this cock."

I did my best to sexy-crawl my way into his arms. When I reached him, he wrapped his non-lubed hand around my neck and pulled me in for a searing kiss that gave me everything—his love, his pride, his own need for me in this moment. Then he flipped me around, pressing my back to his hot, hard chest before he positioned my ass over his dick.

Slowly, I sank down. I pushed past the burn and, with determined effort, took him all the way to the hilt. He held me tight to his chest, whispering curse-laden praise into my ear. "Holy shit, Princess, this is fucking heaven. You're such a fucking dream come true. Fuck me, I'm going to die like this. Right here, holding you in my arms, your ass clenched around my dick. *Fuck*."

"Mmm," I moaned, rocking my hips gently in his lap, exploring this erotic, foreign sensation. "Don't die, Zach. Stay with me. Just like this. Fuck me just like this."

His warm lips—and his cool lip ring—found my neck again. "Slow down, Princess. I don't want to hurt you. We're easing into this."

"Easing into what?"

The bedroom door creaked open, and Noah ambled in, his limp barely noticeable as he toweled his wet hair from his post-workout shower. He wore some tight gray sweatpants and a white V-neck tee that molded to his sculpted chest.

His eyes landed on me, naked from the waist down, tits free of my tank top, reclining in Zach's lap and impaled on his cock, and those baby blues went comically wide behind his glasses before an eager, sexy smile spread across his face.

"Oh, sweetheart, look at you," he purred, dropping his towel and creeping onto the bed. "What has Ferrero gotten you into now?"

Zach chuckled in my ear. "Don't be jealous, Hargraves. Aren't you proud of our Princess?" He hooked his arms under my thighs and lifted, spreading me wider for Noah's viewing.

"So proud," he agreed as he crawled over the two of us. He leaned in, dropping a sweet kiss on my lips before he pulled away to study me. "How are you feeling, sweet girl? You're taking that cock in your ass so well. Such a good girl."

I preened under his heated perusal. "I feel amazing, Noah. But Zach seems to think I'm breakable."

Noah tutted. "Of course not, sweetheart. You're the toughest."

"The strongest," Zach agreed.

"Ugh, then fuck me," I whined. I was so wound up—so turned on, *needing* to come—I had no qualms about begging.

Noah grinned, scooting back to straddle Zach's legs and position himself between my thighs. "Fuck me, look at this pussy. So needy. Has Zach been neglecting you?"

"*Noah.*" I was whining again, and I didn't care.

"I've got you, sweetheart." He dropped his head between my legs and shoved his tongue inside me.

"Oh fuck, oh my God," I whimpered as Noah licked long stripes through my soaking folds, paying no mind at all to Zach's dick buried in my ass.

"Excellent idea, man," Zach said. "Let's get Princess nice and relaxed."

Noah hummed happily as he ate me out with enthusiasm. "Give us one, sweet girl. Then you can have my cock too. Would you like that?"

"Yes," I hissed. "Noah, *please*."

He groaned. "Fuck, I love it when you beg me. So good." Then, finally, *mercifully*, he wrapped his lush lips around my clit and sucked hard, sinking two fingers into my pussy and driving them into me with fast, hard strokes until a wave of ecstasy melted me from the inside out.

"Oh fuck," Zach groaned as I threw my head back onto his shoulder and screamed. "She's fucking strangling my cock, man. I'm not gonna make it."

After a quick kiss to my inner thigh, Noah sat back and speared Zach with a reproachful look. "Keep it together, Ferrero. We're not done here." He shucked his shirt, revealing his tanned, sculpted torso, and his sweatpants followed.

"Noah," I said with a gasp as my eyes landed on the gauze wrapped tightly around his injured thigh, jolting my brain back online. "Your leg! No—*no*—don't pout at me. You can't fuck me like this. You'll hurt yourself."

Noah, now completely naked, wrapped his long fingers around my ankle—which was still held aloft by Zach's vice grip around my thighs—and he pressed a kiss to my calf. "If I didn't know any better, I'd say that sounded like you were giving me orders in bed, sweetheart."

"Oooh," Zach said. "Bad girl."

I elbowed him, and he grunted before retaliating with a nip to my ear.

Noah just cocked a blond eyebrow at me before he crawled to the edge of the bed and opened the same drawer from which Zach had produced the lube. He rummaged around for a few seconds before he pulled out a handheld vibrator with a long handle and a blunt, round head. Then he returned to his spot between my legs.

He waved the toy at me with a triumphant grin. "I'll just employ a little extra assistance. Won't have to overexert myself to make you cream all over my cock and choke the life out of Zach's again. Will that be satisfactory, sweetheart?"

I gaped at him. "When the hell did you guys find the time to stash all these sex toys in my nightstand?"

Zach snickered in my ear. "Spencer thought of everything, baby girl. Let's have Noah snap a picture of you taking both of our cocks, and I'll have it made into a thank you card for him."

Noah laughed, now leisurely running his dick through the slippery mess between my thighs. "How about it, Jojo?" He dipped the tip in, teasing me. "Show us you can take us both. Own us both just like you already do, mind, body, and fucking soul."

I met those hungry blue eyes one more time just as I felt Zach's soft, reverent kiss behind my ear. "Yes," I said with a little moan. "Do it, Noah."

He sank all the way into me, and all three of us groaned in unison, the sound so loud, it echoed off the tiles of my en suite bathroom. Noah began to rock his hips, grinding his dick deep inside me as Zach held me tight, pulsing his own dick upward in gentle thrusts.

"Fuck me, that is a trip," Zach rasped. "I can feel him inside you, Princess."

Noah pressed the now vibrating toy to my clit, picking up his pace. "How's it feel, sweetheart?"

"So fucking good," I moaned. I was bordering on incoherent. I was so full, the pressure an exquisite torture and the vibration on my clit sending my inner walls into a mind-melting spasm. "Oh shit, oh shit, oh shit," I chanted. "I'm so close. So close."

And then the bedroom door burst open once again.

Noah tossed a look over his shoulder. "Perfect timing, Spencer," he called between labored breaths, then he turned those heated blue eyes back to me. "Bennett's here, sweet girl. Now you can come for all of us."

I gasped as Bennett slammed the door and stalked to the side of the bed just as Noah and Zach both upped their pace once again.

"Holy fuck, Angel," Bennett rasped, his mossy eyes hooded with lust as he raked them over my trembling body. "Are you taking both these assholes' cocks? You're so fucking hot right now, baby. Jesus Christ."

"Bennett, touch yourself," I demanded. Or was I begging again?

His nostrils flared, and he pulled his huge, already half-hard dick from his track pants. He began to stroke it with long, angry pulls as he watched his best friends fuck me within an inch of my life. I kept my eyes on Bennett and my mind on the two cocks moving in sync inside me.

Within a minute, I was gone.

I felt my body clench around them as I shrieked at the ceiling, a chorus of deep, guttural groans following me over the edge.

When I came back to earth, Zach and Noah still held me tight, both panting hard, and Bennett loomed over me, kneeling at my side as he admired the mess he'd made on my stomach.

"That was beautiful, sweetheart," Noah said with a happy, satiated smile. "Bennett and I made the right call leaving you and Zach to some alone time this morning if this is what you two are going to get up to while we're gone."

"Princess takes such good care of me," Zach purred in my ear. "She loves me."

"I do," I said with a big sleepy sigh. "I love all of you."

Bennett ripped his shirt over his head and wiped me clean while I stretched languidly in Zach's arms, and I took the opportunity to ogle Bennett's broad tattooed chest and those gorgeous angel wings as he worked. When he finished, he tossed the shirt onto the floor and reached down to caress my cheek with his big hand. "I hope you know what you've gotten yourself into now, Angel. We're going to own every piece of you. You're *ours*."

"Mm-hmm," I hummed in agreement before turning to snuggle into Zach's shoulder. "Always have been."

And now we were so close to finally being *free*.

CHAPTER TWENTY-THREE
JOLIE

"Drink this, baby girl," Zach said as he handed me a steaming mug of coffee. "You need to recharge."

"I am perfectly fine," I retorted as I accepted the mug. I was on the living room couch with Bennett, snuggled tightly into his side, while the other two had just finished puttering around the kitchen to throw together some breakfast. We were all clean and dressed in our Sunday loungewear, and Zach had snapped at each of us at least once for giving him "pity eyes."

"Sure you are, Princess," Zach replied, smirking at me as he flopped onto the couch next to me. "Thoroughly used, but perfectly fine."

Noah slid a tray of bagels onto the table before dropping into one of our cushy armchairs. He smiled fondly at me as he sipped on his own coffee. "Boy am I glad I left Bennett downstairs to bother Kara while I came back to check on you two."

Bennett scowled, though he was currently rubbing sweet little circles on my thigh with his thumb. "Yes, at least one of us was doing something productive while the three of you were *fucking*. A lot of shit went down last night, and we have to be on top of it."

"You saying Noah and I fucking our girl through two orgasms together wasn't productive?" Zach quipped.

Bennett normally would've shot him a withering glare for that, but instead he only glanced at Zach over the top of my head with a patient sort of look.

Zach huffed, losing his cocky smirk to glare back at Bennett. "I said to cut that shit out. I'm not that fucking breakable. I'm *happy* my mom's dead because now Princess is that much safer. And I've had fifteen years to mourn my dad. I'm *fine*."

I reached for his hand and tucked it into mine, then I redirected Bennett before he could argue. "What did you find out from Kara? They made it in time to the ship carrying the trafficking victims, right?"

"They did," Bennett replied. "Max and I downloaded the details we were able to find in Andrea's records while we were locked in the office, and Kara got on the road with her team immediately. They apparently also called the Coast Guard, so the shitty merc team Andrea had meeting the boat in Port Santo Carlo didn't stand a chance."

I breathed a sigh of relief. I'd known before we went to bed last night that our team had likely left with enough time to catch the boat before it was unloaded and those poor people disappeared into a nightmare, but I'd wanted to hear confirmation that everything went according to plan. "And everyone they rescued from the boat is okay?"

Bennett cleared his throat. "Twenty-nine girls and four boys, all between the ages of fifteen and nineteen. Scared, malnourished, and a little roughed up, but yes, everyone is okay. Kara and Julie had the foresight to bring a mostly female team, and apparently that went a long way toward making the victims feel safer."

I whipped out my phone and typed out a text to Zepp. "I'm going to make sure Knight is funding anything and everything they need. Housing, school, jobs, travel back home if they have a safe family to return to...."

Noah's affectionate smile appeared over the top of his coffee cup. "It's being taken care of, sweetheart, but a message from the boss never hurts to make sure things are moving along... efficiently."

Bennett squeezed my thigh and pressed a soft kiss to the top of my head, then he continued, "Silver and Marcus stayed up last night to sort through the rest of the documents we dropped off with them. They've contacted the Feds and the European authorities with the names of Andrea's most prolific buyers of stolen artifacts."

Zach hummed. "Good. I suppose cutting off that supply of cash to Ferrero no longer really matters, but I enjoy knowing those greedy bastards are all probably about to get raided. That'll ruin someone's Sunday golf game."

"Unfortunately, Andrea didn't have the names of the buyers for this latest shipment," Bennett added. "She used a 'broker' with a codename, but Kara tells me that Julie managed to get a real first name and the contact information of the broker out of the guy in charge of the merc team receiving the boat." He shuddered against me. "She says Julie's been spending a little too much time with Frankie lately."

I wrinkled my nose and saw Noah do the same, while Zach just chuckled. "Frankie is an excellent teacher, believe it or not."

"I believe it," I muttered, remembering Zach's skill with a scalpel. "So do Donavan's balls."

Zach grinned, shooting me a sexy wink that told me he, too, was probably reminiscing about our first time together, before he looked at Bennett. "Did we call in the skin broker or are we sending our own team?"

"Kara said it's up to the boss but that the team would very much like to take this one in house."

"In house it is," I said, grabbing my phone to add that to my instructions to Zepp.

"One last thing, Angel," Bennett said. I pulled my gaze from my phone and looked up into his intense mossy green eyes. "Andrea hadn't taken a weapons shipment since the day we blew apart her Enforcer team, but apparently, she'd finally assembled enough of one to schedule another run. Dom's going to take that one."

My smile was grim. "Yeah. That'll be cathartic for him, I suppose."

I leaned back into the couch cushions, my hands on Bennett and Zach and my eyes on Noah as we sat in silence for a few minutes, each of us contemplating the true end of the Ferrero empire.

Now there was only one Family remaining that stood against me, and it had always been the toughest nut to crack.

My phone buzzed in my lap, and I swiped to answer on speakerphone when I saw it was Zepp calling.

"Hey, boss lady," he drawled before the crack of a soda can sounded. "I've got some news for your boy Ferrero."

"Oh yeah?" I replied. "Where's Marcus?"

Zepp snorted. "The little fucker's taking a nap. You lot kept him super busy last night, and Silver threw him out of the command center for the day anyway. She's pissed at him for keeping some very handy tech from the rest of the team."

Noah chuckled. "Those two are still... working out the kinks."

"What's the news for Zach?" I asked.

The clicking of his keyboard sounded through the phone, then Zepp said, "The office of the Ferrero liaison was contacted this morning."

"That means Marcus got an email," Zach supplied.

"Right," Zepp said. "The email was from your mom's lawyer, Ferrero. It appears you were still her Heir, so what's left of the Ferrero Family jewels is now yours."

Zach's eyes widened before he blew out a breath, sagging back into the couch. "I guess I'm not surprised. She thought I'd come back eventually."

"And so, we await your instructions, oh Head of Ferrero," Zepp said, and I could envision the mocking flourish of his hand.

Zach looked at me, a dark brow raised in question. "What do you think, baby girl?"

"It's up to you, Zach," I said gently. "Sell what you don't want. Keep what you do."

He was thoughtful. "Zepp, have it all moved under the Ferrero arm of Knight for now. And have all the shitty people who are current tenants of Ferrero Tower notified that they have thirty days to get the fuck out. I want to do something useful with that thing, like Noah's doing with his."

"I will leave detailed instructions for Marcus when he wakes up," Zepp replied with a devious chuckle, his fingers flying over the keys again. "He'll be so thrilled with his to-do list."

"Tell him I'll give him another raise if he can manage to do it without bitching," Zach said. "And everything's cleaned up in the Ferrero penthouse and the press release is ready to go tomorrow?"

He paused his loud typing. "It is. Your cleanup crew is the most professional I've ever seen, and Jojo's lawyers got on top of the statement to both the law enforcement and the public when Silver woke them up this morning at about four a.m."

I winced, making a mental note that pretty much everyone on my team deserved a muffin basket and a raise after this weekend.

"And Zepp?" Bennett rumbled next to me.

"Yes, Spencer?"

"Has there been any further progress on our project?"

He sighed. "No. Your dad's tech team is good. I'm starting to think we should just try to buy them off instead of attempting to slip in the way we are."

"Won't work," Bennett said in his unaffected monotone. "I'm sure there are threats to their lives or their families hanging over their heads that aren't worth any amount of money to them."

"We'll figure it out, Bennett," I said with a comforting squeeze of his hand.

"That's the spirit, team," Zepp said with faux exuberance. "Alright, I'm out. Don't bother me this afternoon unless it's an emergency—the Knicks are playing."

He signed off before any of us could comment on his shitty taste in basketball teams.

It only took about sixty seconds from the moment our press release went live at eight o'clock Monday morning for the student phones in the Academy's dining hall to start lighting up.

One by one they looked at their screens, then eyes widened, jaws dropped, and their wary stares hit our table, where the boys and I sat with Mari and the rest of our friends, casually enjoying our breakfast like it was just the beginning of another stimulating week at Holywell.

"Ah, I see the news is out," Mari said lightly. She picked up her own phone and began to scroll. "Let's just see what the great minds at Knight have come up with for this latest little incident, shall we?"

Mari was up-to-date on the gory details and had apparently taken *Francisco* to the spa again yesterday afternoon to distract him from any "weird feelings he may have about the death of his shitty sister." Zach did try to assure her that Frankie didn't have feelings in the traditional sense of the word, but she'd waved him off like he didn't know what he was talking about.

"Andrea Ferrero had a heart attack?" Hannah Langford asked, shooting a very dubious look down the table in our direction.

"Stress," Zach replied with a shrug. "Things hadn't been going particularly well for her since Jolie Knight returned from the grave."

"Uh-huh," Hannah said slowly. Her shrewd emerald gaze darted around the table to look at the others—John Tyler, Devin, Raiford, and her friend Nick Ruiz, whose Tier Two family's boutique fitness empire was now majority owned by Noah's arm of Knight. Not a one of them looked up from their plates, uninterested in asking any further questions. Hannah's stare returned to Zach. "Well, then—my condolences, Ferrero."

"Appreciated but not necessary, Langford."

Mari hummed in amusement. "'Zachary Ferrero, the new head of the Ferrero Family, requests privacy at this time. A *closed* service will be held for Mrs. Ferrero that will be limited to friends and relatives only.' Que listos, my friends."

The chatter throughout the hall began to intensify to its normal level. From the equal mix of shocked, pitying looks that were being sent Zach's way and the terrified ones being sent at me, it appeared the student body was about evenly split on whether they believed the story, or they thought I'd finally killed the bitch.

I kept an easy smile affixed to my face—a thing that came much easier to me these days now that I had all three pieces of my heart back with me. My classmates could speculate all they wanted about my murderous tendencies.

That thought made me chuckle, and I turned to the table across the way to glance at Harper, Chad, and their dwindling group of cronies, letting a touch of psycho slip into my smile. Chad was furiously texting someone, his square jaw grinding in irritation, while Harper did her best to sneer in my direction.

But even she couldn't keep the tremble out of her hand, her healing wrist now wrapped in a soft splint.

That's right, Jansen. Fuck around and find out.

Again.

"I see that, Angel," Bennett said, his chiding tone more amused than serious. "Stop making crazy eyes at the sheep. If they still don't know not to fuck with you, then they'll deserve what they get."

His voice was loud enough to carry across the way, and Harper's scandalized gasp at being called "the sheep" by her beloved was the cherry on top of my already stellar mood after vanquishing my enemy and being lovingly double teamed by two of my sexy boyfriends.

"Change of subject," Zach announced. "I don't think we should let all of the... stuff we have going on distract us from the fact that we are coming up on a couple of important birthdays."

I caught Noah's blue-eyed stare from across the table, and my whole body warmed at the memories I now welcomed with open arms instead of trying to smother because they once brought me so much pain. I smiled from ear to ear as I whispered, "Hey, birthday twin."

"Hey yourself, birthday twin," he replied, his own sunshine smile lighting up the entire damn room. "Wanna have a joint party, for old time's sake?"

Noah's birthday was March 31st; mine was April 1st—this coming Friday and Saturday, respectively. When we were growing up, sometimes our parents—or our nannies—would split the labor and throw us a single birthday party.

I'd never minded sharing the spotlight, and neither had Noah—even when I'd insisted on picking the theme.

He'd always let me.

"Only if you'll dress up as Kristoff again so I can be Elsa," I replied, teasing him.

His grin only grew wider, but I saw the emotion hit him suddenly. He wiped his misty eyes under his glasses. "Our last party together. God, you made us watch *Frozen* so many times that year."

Bennett gave me such a warm, fond smile that even I had to blink back tears. Zach clapped Noah on the shoulder, giving us both an excited grin. "Excellent. I think we can throw together a little something by this weekend. Mari?"

She tittered excitedly. "Sí, not a problem at all. I presume budget is not an issue?"

I frowned. "I mean, no, but you don't need to do anything big deal."

Everyone at the table laughed like I'd told a funny joke. "You've been living on the Southside too long, chica," Mari said. "You are the richest person in this City! Luckily Max knows how to dream bigger. I've already texted him, and he has suggested a yacht."

"What?" *Max, what the fuck....*

"Who here has a yacht we can use?" she inquired around the table.

Five hands went up, including Noah's.

"Really, though?" I asked. "That is not a *little* something—"

"Not another word out of you, chica. Noah, you're with me, yes?"

His smile for me was extremely smug and a little naughty before he turned to Mari. "I'm with you, Mari. I'll procure us a birthday boat."

CHAPTER TWENTY-FOUR
NOAH

"Marcus, I don't care that it's Tuesday morning and I have class in half an hour. I will drive my Ferrari down to the tower and punch you in your annoyingly fucking punchable face if you do not stop calling me for every little goddamn thing and acting like we don't have people for this. Bother Rocky, for fuck's sake."

I suppressed my amused smile at Zach's tirade. I knew firsthand the stressors of assuming an entire Family empire, but I'd laid the groundwork and had made small moves for years before Jolie returned to steal my heart and the rest of Hargraves for me. Zach had it all dropped in his lap forty-eight hours ago, and it appeared Marcus was enjoying ruffling his feathers about all the big *important* decisions that needed to be made by the new head of the Ferrero Family.

Zach hung up his phone with an annoyed jab of his finger before glancing at me where I lounged on our leather couch, lazily scrolling through my own messages. "Oh, I'm glad you think this is funny," he groused as he shoved his tablet into his messenger bag. Apparently, I hadn't hidden my amusement after all. "Running the Family is just sooo easy for you."

I shrugged. "Purge the shitty people and keep the good ones. It mostly runs itself. You've only got the dregs to sift through anyway. Our girl sorted the rest for you already."

"True," he said with a wistful grin, no doubt thinking of our avenging angel. "She's the best."

Bennett strode into the room, his brown hair perfectly styled and his suit pressed to perfection, as usual. "She is," he agreed. "And she will have our balls if we're not downstairs to get her from her dorm in time for a full breakfast."

A loud buzzing sounded from his pocket, and his jaw tensed.

"How many is that?" I asked.

"Eleven," he replied tersely, clearly at his wit's end. "And five from that bitch Elise, like he thought I'd somehow take her call but not his."

Zach dropped onto the couch next to me, throwing his head back onto the cushion and pinching his brow as he muttered, "Let's just satisfy his burning curiosity. Then he can sit and think about the writing on his own wall."

I nodded at Bennett. "Might as well. You up for it?"

He bristled. "I'm not afraid of my fucking father. I just no longer care to speak to him about anything, ever." His phone began vibrating in his hand again, and he rolled his eyes to the vaulted ceiling of our dorm living room. "Fine," he grumbled before answering the phone with a furious swipe of his thumb.

"Bennett Spencer!" the voice of James Spencer barked through the phone's speaker.

"Father," Bennett drawled, bored.

"I don't know what you and that little *bitch* think you're playing at. Andrea Ferrero did not just *happen* to drop dead of a heart attack on the same night the Knight whore was spotted at her fucking gala!"

"It is an interesting coincidence, isn't it, Father? You know, Zach's right here, if you want me to pass along your condolences."

He sputtered, "You—you *children* cannot just go around murdering the heads of the Four Families!"

"Scared, Father?" Bennett asked smoothly, a tiny smile quirking at his lips.

"Is that a *threat*, son?" James spat.

"It's a promise, Father. It was you who taught me that we should do *anything* to protect our Family, the murder of members of the other Families expressly included."

"*Bennett—*"

"And Jolie Knight is the center of my Family, Father. It no longer includes you, and if you're a threat to *my* Family, I will remove you from the board. Stop fucking calling me."

He hung up the phone. Zach and I watched warily as he slid it gingerly into the pocket of his suit jacket before straightening his spine and rolling his shoulders with a calming breath. Then he glanced down at us, a relaxed, almost placid look on his face. "What are you two getting Angel for her birthday? Her birthstone is diamond, and I'm thinking of returning a nice little chunk of Alastia to her as a necklace."

I couldn't help the huge grin that spread across my face. Bennett had finally freed himself from his intrinsic need to please his father, and I was so damn proud of him.

For a few days, we were able to just be college students again.

College students who were now running three of the Four Families and very behind on our homework.

Zach was able to transition the bulk of Ferrero into the capable hands we already had within Knight, and after Frankie assisted in running off the most unsavory people still attached to businesses he wanted to keep, everything began to hum right along. Zach even talked Rocky into overseeing security at the Euphoria Club, and he'd promptly booted the slimiest clientele off the list and hand-picked a crop of new bouncers.

My dad attempted to call me twice after the news of Andrea's death broke, and unlike Bennett, I didn't feel the need to clue him in about our role in it. He was still in Thailand, and Silver dropped me a note midweek, informing me that he'd actually called my *mom* and asked her for a loan.

She undoubtedly laughed in his face and then yelled at him for losing his entire empire to his son and Jolie Knight.

Our Jojo seemed mostly content. Getting back into the grind of class, homework, and crew practice was always good for her, as was getting thoroughly fucked by whichever one of us was lucky enough to end up in her bed on a particular night and brave enough to be subjected to Mari's scathing annoyance regarding the "shrieking sex noises" the next morning. But as the end of the week approached, I could tell that her begrudging excitement for our birthday party had been infected by her growing frustration that we'd still made no progress on crippling Spencer once and for all.

Bennett was starting to get moody about it, too, but we were used to his shit.

Spencer was flagging but remained stubbornly resilient, the white-collar conglomerate of banks, hedge funds, private equity, and venture capital groups able to hold strong, diversify, and bring on outside money that was insulated from City politics and still unaware of how terrified they should be of Jolie Knight.

Silver, Zepp, Marcus, and their entire team had prepared a nice package for James Spencer, but we needed a way to deliver it.

But now it was Saturday night, and we were all going to put aside our schoolwork, work-work, and nefarious plans to have some goddamn fun for my twentieth and Jojo's nineteenth birthday.

"This is not a *little* something!" Jolie barked at the three of us as she gestured wildly at the three-hundred-foot, three-story superyacht currently parked at the docks of the Academy's boathouse.

"What do you mean, sweetheart?" I asked innocently as I dragged her along the dock by our intertwined hands. "You don't like the Contessa? She was always my dad's favorite."

"Didn't we take this one on vacation once in like, fourth grade?" Zach asked as he and Bennett trailed along behind us.

I chuckled. "No, that was the Silver Lion. Dad only took his favorite yacht out for his stable of mistresses, and we were not invited on those trips."

"Lovely," Jojo muttered as she craned her neck to take in the full breadth of the Contessa. "I'm thrilled we're having our birthday party on Peter's fuckboat, Noah."

"I had it thoroughly sanitized," I replied, before I said, with a little more bite, "Relax and enjoy the night for me, please, sweet girl."

She let out a tiny moan and relaxed against my side, which got a knowing snicker out of Zach and a scoff from Bennett.

"Ahoy, mateys!"

Our attention was pulled to the top of the boarding ladder at the entrance to the Contessa, where a line of students waiting to board had formed as they went through our security—comprised tonight of some of the younger members of the Shadows or the Knight Enforcer squad.

Max waved excitedly at us, and I narrowed my eyes in his direction. "What the fuck is he wearing?"

The asshole had on what looked like a sailor outfit, complete with tiny shorts, a navy scarf, and a ridiculous white hat. He also had several handguns strapped to his body and was twirling a knife through his fingers.

Jojo elbowed me before she waved back at him. "It's very nautical, Noah. You and Zach tried to get me to wear a fucking *bikini* to this thing."

We had. The spring night air was warmer than usual, and we wanted to stare at that tight body all night long, but Jojo had rolled her eyes at us, then Bennett had put his big possessive foot down, anyway.

She compromised with her little denim shorts that showed off her long legs and a cropped T-shirt that revealed the top of her toned stomach. The three of us were in designer jeans and dress shirts, or a too-tight white V-neck if your name was Zach Ferrero.

We left our shoes along the dock with the dozens of others already abandoned there, and I led us past the line to board—obviously, since this was *my* fucking boat—before we all clambered onto the main deck.

Max smirked at me, clapping me on the shoulder like we were good buddies because *ugh*, we fucking *were* now. "This thing is *sick*, Nigel. Martinez already gave me the tour. It'd be so killer if I could use this for my graduation party. Bruce would totally let us park it at the Boathouse."

Jojo gave him a fond smile, hugging him as she cooed, "Anything you want, Maxy." She tossed a look at me over her shoulder. "Right, Noah?"

Zach snorted, and I returned her look with my most charming smile. "Of course, sweetheart."

Max could have the Silver Lion.

"I can't believe you guys talked Martinez into captaining the yacht for this ridiculous party," Jojo gushed as she looked around the expansive deck. It was packed with our classmates already, drinks in hands as they spread out around the various tables and lounging areas. We'd been diplomatic about the invitations, opening it to the entire student body on a first-come basis until the yacht was at capacity.

"Oh, he is so fucking excited about it," Max replied. "He was in the Navy, but they sure as shit weren't sailing one of these babies. We're going on our little voyage down the river as soon as everyone's loaded."

Bennett eyed Max. "My mom is with your parents?"

Max grinned. "Relax, Big Man. Dad's cooking for the ladies tonight."

Bennett smiled contentedly at that, and I caught Jojo's rough swallow like her mouth had just gone dry as she stared at his serene face. He said, "I doubt she's ever had a man cook for her. That's really nice."

It was. Those three were the only parents we all had left, and I was glad they were safe and happy.

I held my elbow out to my birthday twin. "Shall we? Mari made sure we had a little VIP area reserved for us up front."

We made our way around to the bow, but not before we took a pass through the grand ballroom, where the DJ already had quite the party going, and the yacht's bar, where Zach helped himself to three bottles of expensive champagne.

The sundeck out on the bow of the ship was crowded, but the largest white couch had been roped off. Mari and Hannah Langford sat primly in the center, drinking champagne and giggling. Max flung himself onto a cushion next to Mari, and Bennett and Zach veered toward the additional bar located on this deck.

"Finally!" Mari shouted, motioning for us to sit. "Chica! What do you think? Your boyfriends have such fun toys."

"It's great, Mari," Jojo replied with a genuine smile, tugging me down to sit next to her on the couch. "Thank you for putting this together." She turned to look at me with those mesmerizing aquamarines, so soft with her love for me now and such a stark contrast to how sharp and cold they'd been when she first came back to us. "And thank you, birthday twin."

"Love you, sweetheart," I murmured, stealing a kiss that quickly turned heated. I sipped her little moans like they were the glass of champagne that had been shoved into my hand, and I thought this was the best fucking birthday I'd ever had.

"Hey, you two," Max hollered from the other side of the couch. "Get one of the many rooms below deck if you're going to paw at each other. That's my *sister*, Neal."

I groaned against Jojo's lips, and I felt her smile against mine before she pulled away and tucked herself under my arm. That settled me, and I took a moment to sip my actual champagne and take in the view of the City lights and the clear night stars as they reflected back at me in the glassy black surface of the river.

After a few peaceful minutes, Jojo stiffened under my arm.

"What is it, sweetheart?"

Her eyes had narrowed dangerously as she scowled in the direction of the bar. I followed her glare to where Bennett remained chatting with the Robicheaux twins while Zach had just turned to head this way with his hands full of drinks. An unfamiliar girl—who was, in fact, in a purple bikini—slinked along behind him and wore a very determined look on her face.

"Who's that bitch?" Jojo asked, her light, causal tone fooling no one.

Hannah's evil grin did not improve the situation. "I believe that is one of the Robicheaux twins' cousins. Definitely not from here, just visiting, has no idea she's two seconds away from a knife to the throat."

"Don't encourage her, Langford," I admonished, then I had to glare at Max because his giddy fucking smile was also not helping.

Zach made it to us, his lazy smirk indicating he was oblivious to the impending danger, and he unloaded his drinks onto the table with a flourish and a wink at Jojo.

"Hey there," bikini girl purred as she reached Zach's side, and she slithered a hand up his bicep. "I'm Nikki, and I couldn't let another second go by without talking to you. You are the hottest guy I've ever seen, and I'd love to get to know you. *All* of you," she added, licking her lips as she looked him up and down.

Zach was certainly an expert at having women throw themselves at him, but even he couldn't help the flash of alarm that crossed his face before he smoothly removed Nikki's claws from his arm. "I'm flattered," he replied as he pasted on the cocky smirk of the Ferrero Heir. "But I'm not looking for new friends at the moment."

I rubbed Jojo's back as she watched this with a cool detachment that scared the shit out of me.

Nikki only moved a little closer, fluttering her lashes and waving her rather large boobs at him. "Oh, but I wasn't suggesting we be *friends*, baby. I will be anything you fucking want."

Jolie cleared her throat. "Read the room, Nikki. Zach wants you to fuck off."

She gasped, whipping her scandalized stare to where Jojo sat, tense but calm, and still snuggled into my side. "No one asked you, bitch," she sneered.

"Oh fuck," Max said with a cackle.

"Uh-oh," Mari hummed at the same time.

But Jojo just smiled at her. "You probably *should* ask me, Nikki. That's my boyfriend you're pawing at."

She let out a derisive laugh. "Sure he is. I saw you making out with the blond hottie you're sitting next to. But go on."

I shot Zach a pointed look that invited him to step in at any moment here, but he'd crossed his arms lazily over his chest, his eyes ping-ponging between the two women like it was the final match at Wimbledon.

Jojo calmly set her drink down on the low table in front of us before she stood up and smoothed her shorts.

"Sweetheart, be reasonable," I said, the warning clear in my tone.

She turned to give me an innocent smile before pressing a sweet kiss to my cheek, then she stepped around the coffee table to where Zach stood next to Nikki. Her lip curled in utter contempt as Jojo melted into Zach's arms.

He beamed at our girl, pulling her into a deep kiss before releasing her and wisely exiting the arena to flop onto the couch next to me.

Nikki rolled her eyes. "Cute. Are you fucking both of them? Good for you. But it's not like *Zach* will want to limit himself to just *you*. I'll show him a better time, and I won't be pumped full of another guy's cum while I do it."

"Oh shit," Zach murmured.

I glared at him. "Oh, now you're catching on?"

Jolie moved with her cat-like speed, shoving Nikki backward until she was trapped against the side of the boat right next to our couch. She squealed and clutched at the railing behind her, and Jojo eyed her with complete disdain as she wrapped her hand around Nikki's thin neck and squeezed.

"Listen up, you dense bitch," Jojo said, her voice low. "Zach Ferrero is my boyfriend. The blond hottie, Noah Hargraves, is also my boyfriend. And that big guy over there"—she jerked her head at Bennett, who had just wandered over from the bar and stood watching this with raised brows—"is Bennett Spencer. Wanna guess what he is to me?"

"You," Nikki wheezed, "are a crazy whore."

"Fine, I'll tell you," Jojo said with a dramatic sigh. "Bennett's my boyfriend too. Those three belong to me and *only* me for the rest of fucking time. I'll give you a pass, since you're not from around here and you don't have a goddamn clue who you've just tried to tangle with, but I suggest you turn that skinny ass around and keep your eyes off my boys for the rest of the night."

Nikki's face had flushed an angry red, and she struggled against Jolie's hold on her, but she was no match for our warrior queen.

"You're... fucking... kidding yourself," she spat. "Men... like them... would never. Settle for... *sharing*."

Jolie's smile was evil. "They have and they do." Then

she leaned in as if to whisper conspiratorially. "And you're right, Nikki—they *love* pumping me full of their cum. It's a competition, and the winner is always me."

Hot arousal shot through me, and Zach and I both groaned. So did Max—for different reasons.

"Damn, get it, Knight," Hannah said with a whistle.

Nikki screeched, swiping at Jojo. "Fuck you. I don't know who the fuck you think you are, but you're a deluded, disgusting *slut*."

"This is *my* party, you dumb cunt," Jojo said evenly. "And you're no longer on the guest list."

Then she dumped Nikki over the side of the boat and into the brisk waters of the Obsidian below.

Yep, best fucking birthday I've ever had.

CHAPTER TWENTY-FIVE
JOLIE

I leaned against the railing of the Contessa as we sailed south on the river. The warm breeze tickled at the strands of hair that had come loose from my ponytail, and I breathed a contented sigh as my gaze landed on the soft yellow streetlights of Olde Town and the hulking log cabin structure that was Bruce's Boathouse.

Noah was entertaining well-wishers a few yards away at the bar while Zach lounged on the couch like the lazy prince he was, chatting amiably with Mari and John Tyler. Max had attracted a gaggle of girls and was enjoying himself nearby, his keen dark eyes popping up to check on me at regular intervals out of longstanding habit.

Bennett stood next to me, his back against the railing, sipping his bourbon and watching me intently as he always had ever since I'd stormed out of the dining hall on that very first day of school.

"Gonna scold me, Bennett?" I asked, looking up at him with a wry smile.

He tried to keep a serious face, but the corner of his lip quirked up as he said, "I know better than that, Angel. That girl's lucky she only took a bath in the river instead of having her entire trust fund wiped away before she did a stint in jail or something."

Very true. Poor Nikki had only had to swim about ten feet to the dock, where her unfortunate cousin Hans—who'd bolted off the boat at the first sound of her scream—had yanked her out of the water and dragged her off to the locker rooms in an angry huff. Hatcher had rushed over to apologize profusely to me for his cousin's rude behavior, then he went right back to enjoying himself again somewhere on the dance floor inside the yacht's grand ballroom. I could feel the thump of the music rattling the deck under my bare feet.

"Mmm," I replied, turning back to the water. "She *touched* Zach, Bennett. And she called me a slut a few times, though I guess if I threw anyone who's ever called me a slut off this yacht, about half our classmates would be in the river right now."

He chuckled, all low and sexy. "It was unnecessary, Angel, but it was also hot as fuck. Zach just texted Noah and me to inform us he still has a hard-on."

I snorted. My boys were so fucking horny. "You know, if Joanna Miller had thrown a rich girl off a boat, you would've had her kicked out of school."

"Probably, but I'd have still thought it was hot as fuck."

He moved up behind me, then I felt something heavy and cold settle along my collarbone before his warm hands brushed the back of my neck. He leaned down to lay a kiss behind my ear. "Happy birthday, Angel."

I lifted the necklace with a finger to take a look, and I was met with a chain consisting entirely of tiny cherry blossoms woven together to create a vine, each flower inlaid with a large round diamond set in rose gold.

"Bennett Spencer!" I gasped. "You did not. This had to have cost hundreds of thousands of dollars."

His grin was smug. "You're worth so much more than that, Angel, but I knew you'd throw a fit if I went into the seven figures for your present."

"You've already spent so much on the penthouse, you ridiculous man. And you wouldn't let me pay you back."

He spun me around to face him, crowding me up against the railing. "You pay me back every single day, Angel," he rasped. "By coming back to me. By being mine. And I just want to be worthy of you."

I grasped his face and pulled him into a fierce kiss, which he returned with hungry fervor. "Of course you're worthy of me," I murmured against his lips. "I love you. You're a part of me, Bennett. We've been over this."

He smiled, so free and so happy that it made my heart soar, and I pressed my entire body into his as he kissed me again.

"Ahem." Mari's voice sounded from behind Bennett. "I'd say take this below deck to whichever room you four have reserved that hasn't already been defiled by the horde of deviants on this boat, but I have had *no* time with the birthday girl. Hand her over, Spencer."

He growled, squeezing me tighter and continuing to stroke my tongue languidly with his, and I melted into him and became one with him for a few more blissful seconds before I extricated myself in the name of friendship.

"Sorry, girl," I said to Mari. "Wanna get fresh drinks and go exploring?"

She marched forward to grab my hand, her wide-legged, navy-blue playsuit swishing in the soft breeze as she went. "Yes! Tell your biggest, broodiest boyfriend goodbye."

Bennett huffed, rolling his eyes, but he popped one more kiss on the top of my head before Mari dragged me away. "Have fun, Angel."

Twenty minutes later, I had something fizzy in my hand that smelled like ginger and rum and had finally escaped the dance floor where the exuberant crowd had trapped me like a riptide until I'd managed to work my way out.

I'd left Max at the main bar to bask in the attention of the hot bartender, and Mari and I were now nosing around the much quieter aft deck at the back of the yacht. There were a few low cushioned seating areas, but apparently no one wanted to hang out back here, since it was so far from the bars.

"Do you need to take a load off?" Mari asked me with a teasing grin. "Carrying around all those diamonds you've got around your neck must be *so* taxing."

"It really is," I lamented, dropping onto a cushion. "As is destroying my enemies and keeping three sexy men satisfied. I'm very tired, Mari."

"I know, chica. The struggles we must bear."

We laughed, but before either of us could make ourselves comfortable, the sounds of a struggle hit my ears.

I bolted to my bare feet and pushed through the nearby sliding door that led to a small empty lounge.

A shriek sounded through a closed door at the bottom of a narrow staircase just inside the entrance.

"Stop fighting me, you redheaded bitch."

"Fuck you! Get off me!"

A wave of panic shot through my veins. I knew both of those voices.

I hurried down the stairs and yanked hard on the door, finding it locked.

"Is that... Chad? And *Hannah*?" Mari asked in a horrified whisper. "What do we do?"

I jerked my head at the little designer backpack Mari'd insisted I wear to this thing instead of my trusty black one. "Can you get my lockpick kit?"

She jumped behind me and unzipped the bag in a rush, all the while more grunts and shrieks sounded from behind the door.

Chad's gruff voice sounded again. "If you would just fucking behave, I'd make this really fucking good for you. I want a taste of what I'd been promised before the Knight bitch fucked everything up!"

"Shit shit shit," I whispered as I jammed my tension wrench into the lock.

"We never had an actual marriage contract, Chad!" Hannah screeched, and I was relieved to hear her sounding angry and generally unharmed. "You've lost your fucking mind!"

"I'll take her and run," Mari whispered. "I don't want to leave you here, but I also know that's what you're going to tell me to do."

I nodded as I slid my rake into the lock above the wrench and wiggled until I felt the pins catch. "Go get the guys or Max. I'll be fine."

I turned the lock and barreled into the room without a second thought.

Chad had Hannah trapped on the small bed in the room —the cramped space and sparse furnishings indicating it was a bedroom meant for the crew. He'd thrown his big body on top of hers as she thrashed valiantly under him. The strap of her sapphire blue dress was torn, and she had what looked like a busted lip, but she was thankfully still fully clothed and spitting mad.

"Shit!" Chad barked as I flew at him.

I rammed my shoulder into his substantial gut, knocking him off Hannah, and we both tumbled to the floor as Chad bellowed in rage.

"Hannah, get the fuck out of here!" I yelled. "Go with Mari!"

Hannah scrambled off the bed and stumbled to the door where Mari waited. Hannah cried, "We can't just leave her with him!"

Chad tossed me off him, and I rolled to my feet, readying for his attack.

Mari just shook her head before she grabbed a wide-eyed Hannah's hand, and they bolted out the door.

"Well, if it isn't the Southside trash, here to ruin my fun once again," Chad drawled as he got to his feet. He cracked his thick neck and rolled his shoulders as his beady eyes took me in with a hunger I did not like. "Your timing is inconvenient because I was really looking forward to sampling the goods I'd been *promised* before Langford switched fucking teams. But I had planned for us to have a little chat tonight at some point. Might as well be now."

He slipped his phone from the pocket of his dumb fucking khaki shorts and scrolled, now looking smug. His wide body was blocking my way to the door, but if he thought I was going to just stand here and "chat" with him, he was truly an idiot.

"I don't allow rapist bullies at my birthday party, Chaddy," I said, taking a small step forward. "So unless you want my knife stuck into another one of your appendages, you're going to follow me to the bridge. I think Captain Martinez will be happy to drop you off as we pass Industrial City on our return trip. You can walk your fat ass back to the City from there."

He laughed—because he was stupid and hubristic and still just a fucking *man* underestimating a woman once again. "Fuck that. We're going to stay right here."

"Are you fucking dumb?" I spat. "I know you still haven't gotten it through your thick skull that I can handle you, but did you forget all three of my deadly boyfriends and my equally deadly brother are on this boat? I *know* you haven't forgotten what Bennett did to your face, Chad. Your nose didn't quite go back to the way it was, did it?"

"Shut up, you filthy fucking whore!" he barked.

"Move," I demanded.

"Fuck you."

I leapt at him. We collided, and he had to fling me off him before his back hit the ground, since he didn't want me to have the upper hand—just like I'd known he would. He launched me over his head, and I landed lightly on the staircase outside the door. He rolled over, and I bolted up the stairs as he scrambled to follow me.

I crested the stairs in the small lounge with Chad right on my heels. I felt him snag the straps of my little backpack, and I whirled on him. I blocked the meaty fist he launched at my face, and I sank my knee into his stomach. He released my backpack, then tossed a follow-up punch at me that just clipped my ear. It stung like a bitch, but I didn't have time to fret about it because Chad was coming again, determined to keep me in this room for whatever reason, while I was slowly but surely backing us toward the door to the aft deck with vague plans to chase him in the direction of the bridge—or let him chase me there—until one or all of the bloodthirsty men in my life showed up for an assist.

This time I took the brunt of our collision, taking us to

the ground and rolling Chad off me. I flipped, getting my feet under me and ready to sprint the last five feet to the door, when Chad's hand closed around my ankle and dragged me backward.

It was all so eerily familiar, and unfortunately, this time I didn't have my knife in my hand. Chad would avoid having his hand impaled, but he would not avoid having my bare foot jammed right into his barely healed nose.

"Fuck!" he shouted, rearing back and bringing his hand to his nose, the blood immediately seeping through his fingers.

I turned again, jumping to my feet.

"Oh no, you fucking don't!" he bellowed, lurching to stand up and still surprisingly nimble for someone so wide and also gushing blood from his nose.

I ran for the door.

Come on, Chaddy. Come get me.

He slammed into me again, and we went careening out onto the aft deck, still quiet and deserted with only Chad's grunts and the distant laughs, shouts, and thumping of the music filling the night air.

I bounced off the railing, shoving him away from me, and I'd just turned and readied myself to hurdle the loveseat we'd upended on our way out the door when I froze.

The barrel of the tiniest little handgun imaginable was pointed right at my head as Harper held it aloft in a shaky hand. She crept along the narrow walkway that bordered the yacht's spacious main cabin until she was standing a few feet in front of me, just out of my reach.

"Fucking took you long enough, Jansen," Chad spat. He grasped my forearms roughly and wrenched them behind my back, keeping me locked in place.

It was a hold I knew I could break out of without much sweat, but I didn't trust Jansen and her trembling hand on that fucking gun.

"Yes, well, I'm here now," she barked at Chad. "I had to make sure I wasn't seen coming back here, *obviously*."

I'd be having a discussion later with my security about letting this bitch sneak a gun into my party, but I suspected she'd stashed that little thing in her bra—Harper was wearing a suspiciously ample amount of clothing for someone who would have jumped at the opportunity to run around in a bikini in front of Bennett or any other man on this boat.

"Hurry up and fucking do it," Chad hissed. "We can't fuck this up."

That didn't sound good. My mind whirled, and my mouth started running.

"Are you two on a secret mission?" I asked. "What's in this for you, Jansen? Seeing as how you'd be going down for murder if you pull that trigger, it must be something pretty spectacular."

She scoffed. "I will not be going down for anything. Spencer still runs this City, and I'll be taken care of once you're gone."

I gave her a pitying look. "And you think Bennett is just going to fall right back into your engagement if you off me?"

"We have a binding contract!" she screeched, her hand shaking even more. "If you would just *die*, we could put everything back the way it was."

Chad yanked on my arms, and sharp pain shot through my shoulders. "Shut the fuck up, bitch. Jansen, she's trying to distract you. Fucking *do it*."

"I dunno, Chad," I said, trying to calm my thundering

heart. I had to watch Harper so, *so* carefully or else I really would be fucked. "That's her bad wrist, and that hand looks pretty wobbly. I'd say it's fifty-fifty whether it's you or me who gets the bullet."

"Chad! Make her stop talking!"

"What's in this for you, Chad?" I went on. "An *attaboy* from James Spencer himself?"

"Try a fucking Heirship," he growled behind me. "Hendrickson elevated to Four Families status. Knight fucking wiped from the City completely. You at the bottom of the fucking river where you belong. Everything I could ever want."

James Spencer sure did love dangling a seat at the table of the fabled Four Families to entice people to kill me.

I was getting so fucking tired of it.

"Chad, she needs to be still!" Harper snapped.

"Come on, Jansen, for fuck's sake!" Chad screamed back at her.

The moment I clocked the twitch of her finger—the same moment that thundering footsteps sounded along the walkway behind her—I moved.

I dropped like a rock, startling Chad as he lurched forward to hang onto my arms. The blast of the gunshot sounded, and an excruciating pain ripped through my right shoulder.

Zach's panicked shout came next. "Jojo!"

Blood splattered all over me. I felt it wash over my head, my neck, dripping down my back as I hit the deck hard.

Harper screamed. Bennett tackled her to the ground, her gun clattering to the teak floor where Noah scooped it up and flicked the safety on, stashing it in his pocket before pivoting to run to me.

I rolled, turning to face the back of the boat. Strong

arms banded around me while I watched with detached fascination as Chad stumbled backward, his fleshy hands now clamped around his own neck. Harper's bullet had hit him there, and he was helpless to stop the bleeding or the momentum of his stocky form as he slammed into the railing and flipped right over the side. No scream, just a loud splash.

And then fucking Chad Hendrickson—asshole of the highest order, idiot bully, and confirmed sexual predator—was gone.

CHAPTER TWENTY-SIX
JOLIE

"Princess, fuck, are you okay?" Zach breathed into my ear as he held me.

I groaned. "Yeah. The blood is all Chad's, but I'm pretty sure I dislocated my fucking shoulder."

Noah skidded to a stop next to us and dropped to his knees, totally unconcerned with his lingering injury or the puddle of blood that was now soaking through his fancy chinos. He reached out to cup my face in gentle hands. "Oh, Jojo. Shit. I'm so sorry we weren't here. I'm so fucking sorry."

I gave him a rueful smile. "Noah, it all happened really fucking fast. I made the decision not to wait for backup because Chad was hurting Hannah. You came as quickly as you could. I know you did."

Harper screeched from nearby. Bennett loomed over her with an enraged look on his face as Max had her pinned to the floor, straddling her as he zip-tied her hands behind her back.

"Get your dirty Southside hands off me! Bennett!" she wailed.

He ignored her, glancing over to look at me instead. His stoic face broke as he took me in, disheveled and covered in blood. "Angel. *Fuck*."

"I'm fine, Bennett," I croaked. "But someone tell Martinez to divert us to the Boathouse because I need Dom to put my shoulder back in place."

Max stood up, keeping a booted foot on Harper's back. "I already texted Dad, Jojo. No doubt he's calling Martinez as we speak to demand he turn this boat around immediately."

On cue, the yacht began to list. We were already on the cruise back north toward the Academy, but Martinez was now taking us west toward Olde Town.

Bennett left Harper with Max and strode over to me. He scooped me gingerly into his arms before sitting us on the low couch nearby. He cradled me, and I could feel the slight tremble of his body beneath me.

I leaned into him with my good shoulder, burying my face in his chest. "Shh, Bennett. I'm okay. None of this blood is mine. It's not like last time."

"I know, Angel. I just... I can't look at you like this. It hurts."

Zach joined us, sliding my legs into his lap before clapping Bennett on the shoulder, an understanding look in those dark eyes. "I think from now on, you're not allowed out of our sight, Princess. None of us are going to handle this well. We almost just lost you again." He swallowed, and a tiny tear leaked from his eye.

I sucked in a breath and reached for his hand, wincing as pain shot through my shoulder. "Zach. I know. Please don't cry. Please. I would never leave you again."

Noah sat down on the coffee table in front of us, his blood-soaked knees almost knocking into Bennett's. He hung his head in his hands. "We need to call this in and get it cleaned up. I can't believe we just... let those two on the yacht without asking questions. It almost fucking cost us *everything*."

I met Max's concerned stare. He was rattled, too, but he knew how triggering this was for the guys and was going to let them have their time with me. "I've got it, Hargraves," he said, whipping out his phone. "Silver's got access to all the onboard cameras, right?"

"Yeah," Noah muttered, not lifting his head.

"We'll make sure the evidence of Tier One Barbie's crimes makes it into the right hands. I say we toss her to the cops in Olde Town and let them deal with her parents."

I nodded. It was still unlikely that Harper would actually go down for whatever had happened here—accidental homicide, attempted murder—but the Jansens were going to have to spin their wheels for a while to clean this up.

"Have Silver send the tape to Montgomery Star Media," I added.

That was the thing that made Harper gasp and start shrieking again. "Bennett! You're going to regret this. Our parents have been making these plans for us for *years*, and I'm not going to let you ruin our future because you're blinded by this crass, trashy bitch!"

Bennett acted like she wasn't even here. "Angel, we're going to get you fixed up, and then I'm going to tie you to the fucking bed and never let you leave," he growled in my ear.

"Amen," Zach added.

I huffed. "Stop that."

"Three against one," Noah said with a small smile. "We'll just fuck you until you're too sated and exhausted to even think about ever leaving the bed."

Max sighed audibly as he put his phone to his ear. "Can we table the gang-bang discussion until I've had more to fucking drink, Nelson?"

"SONUVABITCH!" I shouted as Dom shoved my shoulder back where it belonged with a lot of force and no finesse.

"That was so good, sweetheart," Noah cooed. He stood next to me where I sat on a barstool at the counter of our little kitchen because he'd won the roshambo to be the one whose hand I crushed into dust as Dom fixed me.

"Honey, honestly, this is not what I wanted to give you on your birthday," Dom said with a big sigh. He popped a kiss on the top of my head, hopefully avoiding the dried blood caked into my hair. "But thank God you're okay. I'm having a meeting tomorrow with the security team we put on that boat because this is extremely unacceptable."

"Don't be too hard on them," I said as I rubbed at my shoulder. "We didn't expressly forbid any Holywell student from the party."

"We got cocky," Bennett muttered. He sat at our little dining table next to his mother, whose enjoyable night with Dom and Laura had been rudely interrupted by our trudging into the apartment covered in varying amounts of blood. Martinez sat with them, looking tired but also pleased to be excused from babysitting a bunch of drunk college students and back with his... charge.

Bruce had not exactly been thrilled to be receiving a superyacht full of entitled students at his dock, but those students had been even less thrilled when Martinez announced that the ride stopped here and everyone could put their fucking asses on the train back to the City.

The Olde Town cops had been almost bewildered that we'd called them at all, and then had passed a crying, thrashing Harper into their custody before leaving them with the murder weapon and a statement that was generally the truth. We didn't have to hide what had happened to Chad Hendrickson—Harper shot him, he fell overboard, and we'd have the security camera video proving this to them shortly.

The cops could deal with Edward Jansen, and then Edward Jansen could deal with Benedict Hendrickson, whose son was now lost to the black depths of the Obsidian because of Edward's daughter.

A little Tier One civil war was always entertaining.

"Here, sweetie," Laura said, appearing in front of me to hand me an ice pack. I took it from her, then she started rubbing at my face and neck with a wet towel, scrubbing the blood away like she would the streaks on the windows of her bookstore. "I'm sorry your birthday party was ruined. As much as I've worried over the years about how trained for violence Dom and the Shadows have made a grieving girl, tonight I'm thankful for it."

"You can say that again," Zach said, shooting me a strained but sexy smile from his spot on our couch. He and Max—with whom he'd had an armistice for a while now—were collegially cleaning their handguns together at the coffee table.

It was pretty much a Rockwell painting in here.

As Dom moseyed into the kitchen to finish doing the dishes from their earlier dinner, Martinez blew out a frustrated breath. "Of course we couldn't get through my first yacht voyage without someone being killed on my ship. Not that I'm sorry that little bastard's gone," he added, nodding at me.

I wasn't either. Chad had crossed the line and onto the kill-if-convenient list the moment he laid a hand on Hannah, and he'd only solidified his spot by becoming James Spencer's hitman.

Mari had shooed us off to Dom's with the promise that she'd see Hannah safely back to the Academy and watch over her there. Before we parted, I'd made sure to tell Mari what a capable lieutenant she'd become—because she'd done everything exactly right from the moment we first heard Chad's disgusting grunts. Hannah seemed shaken but otherwise just generally pissed off that she'd been taken unaware by Chad when she'd wandered to a quiet part of the boat to film a video for her social media.

"Oh, Bennett," Mrs. Spencer said suddenly, perking up. "Laura and I made a cake for your lovely girlfriend. And for Noah," she added, sending Noah a little wink. "Why don't we end this night on a higher note?"

Bennett squeezed her hand. "Sounds great, Mom." Then he narrowed his eyes at Martinez, whose soft, smitten stare at Bridgette was... not subtle.

And so, after I'd taken a quick shower and the boys had changed out of their blood-smeared clothes, we all stood around our little kitchen as Laura produced a three-tiered monstrosity of a chocolate cake topped with a mountain of sprinkles. She'd just begun to light the candles when the doors to our small balcony patio opened, and Frankie breezed into the living room.

We all just stared at him.

"Oh, are we having cake?" he asked casually, strolling into the kitchen and side-eyeing Max oh-so-quickly. He hopped onto an open barstool and dabbed the sweat from his brow using the hem of his blue tank top—this one had "Reel Big Fish" scrawled across the front—exposing his leanly muscled, tattooed torso. He glanced around the room again and said, "At least I didn't miss *all* the fun tonight."

Laura—of all people—was the first to respond. "Frankie, honey, we've talked about using the front door."

My boyfriends, Max, and I slowly shifted our stares to Laura.

"Mom," Max said slowly. "You've been having Frankie Fingers over here?"

Frankie grinned as he accepted the can of strawberry sparkling water Dom handed him without comment. "I like books," he said with a shrug.

I coughed. Clearly he was doing this while Max was at school or the gym, and I did not know what the fuck kind of game those two were playing with each other but would be getting to the bottom of it in short order.

"That's true," Zach said. "Frankie's partial to smutty shit with, like, vampires and demons."

"And dicks," Frankie added, wagging his pierced eyebrows and determinedly *not* looking at Max, whose dark stare was boring a hole in the side of Frankie's face.

Zach rolled his eyes at his uncle before he gave him a stern look. "Where the fuck have you been, man?"

"I was at the Snake Pit, if you must know," he replied with a withering look. "I can't chase you four around at all hours of the day. I do occasionally have other business to attend to."

I raised my hand.

"Yes, Little Knight?"

"The Snake Pit's still going, even after the demise of Ferrero?" I asked, confused. That was Andrea's main underground fighting club. A lot of dirty money, no rules, illegal gambling, the works.

Zach cleared his throat. "Yeah, I gave that to Frankie. He likes to blow off steam down there, and it's still a good place for Enforcer recruitment."

I shrugged. "Cool."

It was probably good for Frankie to have hobbies.

Bennett's mom clapped her hands. "Well, then. Let's all have some cake, shall we?"

Laura finally lit the candles, and after a rousing round of "Happy Birthday to You," I inhaled a very large slice of my yellow cake with chocolate frosting and sprinkles—that combo a thing that Noah and I had always agreed on.

I leaned into him, our chairs smashed together at the table in the place of honor.

"Happy birthday, sweetheart," he whispered in my ear while the rest of the group laughed and chatted.

"Happy birthday, Noah," I murmured back, then I gave him a chocolatey kiss. "Even with the, you know, murder plots and bloody deaths and whatnot, this is still the best birthday I've had since our *Frozen* party."

"Me too," he replied, pulling me in for another kiss. "Because we're together again."

That night I snuggled up to my birthday twin in my little bunk bed. Max collapsed into his bed below us after growling at Noah to keep it in his pants. Bennett and Zach took Mrs. Spencer home to her cute townhouse a few blocks away and stayed the night there, sending Martinez home in a huff.

Frankie disappeared to who knew where, and Dom and Laura stayed up and cuddled on the couch while watching whatever rom-com Laura had chosen for the night that Dom would gripe about but secretly enjoy.

My heart was full, and I tried to take a moment to bask in the warm feelings of the end of the night, when I had all of my people around me—minus Mari, who I missed a whole lot—and we just had a *normal* time like a normal family would.

It was time to rid the City of its last cancer—James Spencer and those who continued to prop him up, but it would have to wait another day.

I was at peace with that fact as I fell quickly to sleep in Noah's arms.

CHAPTER TWENTY-SEVEN
BENNETT

My posture was rigid, reminiscent of my father, as I sat behind the desk in Andrea's old office at the Euphoria Club, awaiting my scheduled meeting. My navy suit was pressed to perfection, my shoes shined, and my hair freshly cut and styled by Rocky's barber next-door.

I took a sip of the glass of scotch that sat on a golden coaster on the ostentatious desk, then I adjusted my cufflinks as I cast my critical stare around the room. Zach had officially taken full control of the Club after Andrea's death, but erasing her presence from this place would take longer than the two weeks he'd had. The gaudy trinkets and the worst of the artwork had been removed, but the furniture was still frilly and way too fucking French.

It was Friday night, and it was also John Tyler's birthday. Having learned a hard lesson last weekend about throwing giant, ridiculous birthday parties, Zach suggested an intimate gathering at the Club so that he could swing by and check on things. Our small circle of friends was out on the floor at the VIP table, enjoying the music, the drinks, and the show.

For the past week, Zach, Noah, and I had watched Jolie like a trio of jumpy, obsessive stalkers, which she'd fucking hated but also kind of loved. If I didn't know exactly where she was at this very moment, I'd have struggled to keep the placid, calm demeanor I desired for this meeting.

My phone buzzed against the top of the lily-white desk.

Zach: I offered JT a night upstairs for his birthday present but he declined

Angel: he has a thing for Devin, how have you not noticed?

Noah: oh no wonder he looked so awkward

Zach: ha shit, my bad

Zach: excited for your meeting, Spencer?

Me: I'm beside myself with joy.

Sarcasm aside, I was actually looking forward to crossing another thing off our list. Harper was finished—released into the custody of her parents but expelled from Holywell. Chad's parents were frothing at the mouth to press charges against her, and the infighting between the two Spencer Tier One giants had already rattled my father's few remaining staunch allies. I suspected Benedict Hendrickson was itching for some new way to throw his weight around because he'd been on house arrest ever since Jolie sent the feds to his door and those of every other member of his little child porn club.

Only a few more dominoes left to fall.

A knock sounded.

"Come in."

The Club's new head bouncer, a hulking man named Demetrius who I knew from Dom's gym, stuck his head in the door.

"I have your ten o'clock appointment to see you, Mr. Spencer."

I waved a hand. "Send her in. Thanks, D."

He disappeared, and the door creaked open further to reveal the reason I was in a meeting on a fucking Friday night instead of enjoying time with our friends.

Elise Proctor.

She prowled into the office, her smile sly as she ran her ravenous gaze from my face down my body and to where my hands lay clasped on the desk. She'd changed out of her usual sexy-secretary-themed work attire and instead wore something more suited for a night at the Club—a slinky red dress that dipped low between her large breasts and clung to every curve of her body. Her strappy heels added four inches to her stature, bringing her to just about Jolie's height in bare feet.

"I'm so pleased you agreed to see me, Bennett," she said, her voice breathy and excited. She helped herself to one of the chairs in front of the desk, making sure she crossed her legs slowly and deliberately, letting the hem of her dress ride up her thighs. "You certainly look like you belong behind that desk. The desk of the leader of the Four Families."

I didn't respond, instead just taking a sip of my scotch as I eyed her, detached and bored.

After my father's last plan to take my Angel from me failed miserably and got the son of one of his closest associates killed, he hadn't called me. Spencer Tower had been suspiciously quiet, but Elise had reached out to me two nights ago.

And she'd done it via a burner phone, which was how we knew she had finally abandoned hope that my father was her ticket to a life of power and luxury.

Her coy smile didn't falter. "I'm sure you're curious as to why I've requested a meeting."

"I can guess, Elise."

Her smile grew. "Of course. You're an intelligent, capable man, Bennett. It's clear to me that it should be *you* at the helm of Spencer. I'm ready to assist you... in *any* way you need."

I leaned back in my chair, steepling my fingers under my chin just as my father would have, and I pretended to consider her. "I have certainly learned some things about you, Elise," I said quietly. "It appears you played a crucial role in a plot that almost made my father richer than anyone else on the planet."

She chuckled, her grin smug. "It takes a woman to get things done, Bennett. Men are... simple creatures. Present company excluded, of course."

"Of course," I agreed. "I suppose it took very little effort to play Anders like a fiddle."

"Oh, I wouldn't go that far, sweetie," she replied with a tinkling laugh, looking me up and down again. "Anders very much enjoyed my *efforts*. It wasn't the most fun I've ever had, but it was all for Spencer."

I lifted a brow. She apparently thought I'd find her admitting she'd whored herself out for the Family attractive. "And yet, your *efforts* were for naught, weren't they? Jeffrey Knight's discovery is now in the hands of a charitable foundation and twenty research universities around the world."

She bristled. "Trust a man to screw it up in the end. Anders was useless after all, unfortunately." She uncrossed and recrossed her legs, then her sultry smile was back. "But I hear you're the one who rid the City of his whining once and for all. James was in a rage about it all, but I have to say I found the thought rather... stimulating."

Christ.

"And yet here you are, abandoning Spencer," I said, tutting. "The disloyalty to my father, Elise."

"*You* are Spencer, Bennett," she replied, leaning forward now so I had a clear view down the front of her dress. "I've known it for a while now. I am ready to serve you. To see to your *every* need."

I resisted the urge to pinch my brow. "You mean you're ready to fuck me, Elise. Stop playing coy."

She sat back, unruffled, that persistent smile remaining on her painted red lips. "I would show you things you could never have *dreamed* of while you've only been with little girls and hookers, Bennett. It's time you had a real *woman* by your side."

I sighed. This charade had gone on long enough.

"So, let me get this straight," I began, finally letting some of the venom I felt for this reprehensible woman seep into my voice. "You saw the writing on the wall as each one of the remaining Families fell under the sword of Jolie Knight. Attempt after attempt on her life has failed. Peter Hargraves is long gone. Andrea Ferrero is dead. Spencer is on its last legs. And instead of going down with the ship—instead of staying loyal to the man you've literally destroyed *lives* for over these past eight years, the man you're *fucking*—you thought you could waltz into this office, hop onto my dick, and I'd shove everything aside to make you the queen of my new kingdom?"

Her seductive grin had faltered as I went on, her eyes widening in true shock as I laid the truth right at her feet.

"Bennett—"

"No," I snapped. "I've heard enough out of you to last

me five lifetimes, Elise. Listen carefully: I wouldn't touch you if you were the last woman on earth. *You* are the reason I lost the love of my life for seven long, brutal fucking years. *You* are the reason her parents were senselessly murdered right in front of her. *You* are the reason my mother can no longer stand to be in her own home. You are a despicable, conniving cunt, and your time is up."

She stood abruptly, smoothing her dress, her simpering smile strained. "Well, I can see I have wasted my time and yours, Bennett. I'm just sad you've been led this far astray from who you were born to be. I'll see myself out."

"Oh, I don't think so, you evil fucking bitch."

Jolie stood in front of the closed office door, casually twirling her knife through her fingers and looking like a fallen angel ready to burn down the world. Her skin-tight purple top, short black skirt, fishnet tights, and chunky black combat boots were a striking contrast to the soft, ethereal waves of her white-blonde hair that framed her face and the sweet dusting of freckles on her cheeks.

The hints of the little girl who'd been my best friend melded seamlessly into the gorgeous phoenix risen from the ashes of what the Families had wrought.

And I was so in love with her, my whole body ached at the sight.

Elise stopped cold, unaware that my Angel had been sitting quietly in a recessed corner of the office just inside the entrance where Andrea had kept her fully stocked bar cart. Elise's lips pursed, and her nose went into the air. "Jolie Knight. We meet at last."

Jolie's answering smile was slow. Eager. "Indeed. I did have the opportunity to get acquainted with your sister, but I've been looking forward to our introduction for some time now."

Elise flushed at the mention of her sister, who was still bedridden in her mother's apartment in Baltimore, last we checked. "Yes, the entire City is aware of your penchant for using your fists to get what you want like the ghetto-raised deviant you are."

Jolie's blonde brow quirked. "Ah, yes, instead of using my pussy like high-class ladies such as yourself."

Elise scoffed. "Stones and glass houses, Miss Knight. You're screwing all three Heirs of the Families, and look what it got you."

Jolie advanced, causing Elise to take a startled step back. "First of all, two of my boyfriends are the *heads* of their Families now, and the third will be the same imminently—you just said so yourself. Second, everything I have I got without opening my fucking legs. I planned, I earned the loyalty of my people, and I *took* back what was mine. And then I buried the people responsible for killing my Family and stealing from me."

Elise's backside hit the chair she'd been sitting in earlier as Jolie crept toward her, the blade of her knife glinting under the office's harsh fluorescent lighting. I kept my blank, bored stare even as my dick was growing hard under the desk.

"How does it feel, Elise?" Jolie murmured, stopping to run her icy eyes over Elise's stiff form, her lip curling with disgust. "How does it feel to know all that dick you've ridden over the years in hopes of becoming queen of the City has only led you here? Staring into the eyes of the little girl you were ready to see executed next to her parents to please your master?"

Elise was seething. "You really are just a little girl playing at being a queen. Your parents are dead because they were *weak*, and this precarious little kingdom you've built by stealing from the *real* leaders of this City is going to crumble around you." She straightened, standing tall and sneering at her like Jolie was her equal and not a predator that had cornered her prey. "And you'll *never* be able to please Bennett like I could."

With a movement so fast I almost missed it, Jolie ceased the lazy twirling of her knife, grasped the hilt, and buried the blade in Elise's stomach.

Elise gasped, then she shrieked in pain as Jolie jerked the knife free. She lifted her heavy boot and kicked Elise to the floor, and she crumpled in a heap of red satin and blood. She coughed and screeched as Jolie jumped on top of her, pinning her flailing arms with her knees. I watched in awe and utter fascination as Jolie leaned down until the two of them were almost nose-to-nose, her face hardening into the cold, focused killer I knew she harbored inside of her.

"Fuck you, Elise Proctor," she growled. "You will never destroy another family, and you will never, *ever* have Bennett Spencer. He. Is. *Mine*."

She slit Elise's throat with a flash of her blade, and then as fast as it had happened, she was on her feet. She kicked the body away from her before turning to face me, breathing hard and saying nothing.

I jumped to my feet and strode quickly around the desk, and I stopped just a few feet in front of her, holding her fiery stare with mine, looking desperately for a sign that my Angel was still with me—that she was okay.

She tossed her knife to the floor without a second glance, then she threw herself into my arms, wrapped her legs around my hips, and plastered her mouth to mine.

I groaned against her lips. *There's my Angel*.

CHAPTER TWENTY-EIGHT
JOLIE

"Bennett," I moaned. "Oh fuck."

He stared up at me from between my thighs with those heated moss-green eyes, his wicked tongue working my clit relentlessly. I was slumped in Andrea's white leather desk chair with my legs tossed over Bennett's shoulders as I rode the adrenaline high of ridding the world of that duplicitous bitch with my own two hands.

My body had begun to shake as what I'd just done hit me, but Bennett had held me tight and consumed me with his kiss before he dumped me in the chair, knelt at my feet like I was his queen and he was my servant, then ripped through the crotch of my tights like they were made of tissue paper.

Now I trembled for a different reason.

Bennett wrapped his lips around my clit and sucked hard, driving two thick fingers into me without warning. I squirmed, my muscles tightening, the ball of pleasure building in my core with every thrust of his fingers before it burst.

He growled against my pussy as I came hard, and I had

no doubt the entire Club would've heard my scream if Andrea's office hadn't been soundproofed years ago.

As I came down, I met his eyes again, the intensity of his stare never wavering as he ran his tongue slowly through my folds. "Why are we always fucking in front of the bodies of people we've killed, Bennett?" I asked with a soft sigh.

He hummed against my sensitive flesh before he rumbled, "Because nothing gets me hotter than the destruction of anyone who's ever hurt you, Angel."

If I hadn't already been a boneless heap from Bennett's masterful mouth between my legs, his beautiful words would've had me docile as a baby lamb.

For a minute, anyway.

I gazed fondly down at him—my broody, serious, perfect love. I ran my fingers through his chocolate-brown hair, mussing it just the way I liked, before my hazy little bubble was broken.

Bennett stood abruptly, yanking me to my feet as he went. He wrapped a firm hand around my neck and pulled me in for a filthy, possessive kiss, and I moaned into his mouth as I bunched the lapels of his suit tight in my greedy little fists.

Before I'd gotten my fill of his kiss, I found myself thrown facedown onto the surface of the desk, Bennett's glass of scotch and some loose papers flying off the side. A big hand pinned me down as another flipped my skirt up to expose my ass to the beast behind me.

"*Bennett*," I growled as I bucked under him. "I want to watch you fuck me."

"That's too bad, Angel," he said lightly as he gathered my wrists behind my back, somehow still mindful of my sore shoulder even as he forced my limbs to move exactly where he wanted them. He leaned down, pressing his cheek to mine as he growled into my ear. "Because I want to fuck you just like this. I want you under me, submitting to me, screaming my fucking name. I'm going to own your body here in this office because you get to own my *soul* the rest of the time." I felt the soft silk of his tie loop around my wrists, and I groaned as I felt my pussy clench around nothing. He went on, "So, you're going to lie here and take my cock, and you're going to fucking love it."

I was—I knew I was. I always wanted to fight Bennett tooth and nail at every turn, to prove I was powerful, his equal in every way, to show him what I was made of.

But Bennett knew what I was made of. He knew I was a force to be reckoned with and that I would do *anything* for the people I loved, including slitting the throat of the woman whose scheming had killed my parents and torn apart his mother's home.

And *fuck* it felt good to be dominated by this powerful, wonderful man.

Still, I yanked on the tie binding my wrists behind my back and hissed, "Fine. Show me, then, Spencer. Fuck me like you *mean it*."

I heard the sound of his zipper one second before he plunged that giant dick into me so hard, I shrieked. He held me steady, one hand pressing me into the desk while the other gripped my hip, and he pounded into me ruthlessly because he knew I could take it.

He knew how much I wanted it, craved it, *needed* it after the events of the night.

"Bennett, oh fuck, oh fuck, oh fuck," I chanted as I felt my climax begin to crest again.

"Fuck yes, Angel. You look so fucking pretty with my tie around your wrists and my dick driving into your pussy. I'm going to truss you up like a fucking feast and keep you underneath me forever. Maybe I'll even feed you my cock—I know how much you're fucking craving it."

I moaned, then I gasped as he increased his already brutal pace. "*Yes*," I hissed. "Yes, oh—oh God, Bennett!"

I fell over the edge, and he let out a hoarse shout as he fell with me. Even the soft click of the door opening and closing couldn't derail the train I was on. I was lost to Bennett, and he to me, until a throaty chuckle finally tore me from the clouds.

"Goddamn, Spencer," Zach said as he stepped over the body on the floor without so much as a second glance. "Are you giving our Princess a reward for her hard work?"

"That looks like he's giving himself a reward," Noah mused, eyeing Elise with a wrinkled nose and a curled lip before he turned to us and gave me his big, beaming smile. "Hi, sweetheart. I see you got Bennett's tie—were you not behaving?"

I grinned lazily at him. "I only behave for you, Noah. You know that."

Bennett scoffed. He'd eased out of me and was busy untying my hands. Then he rubbed my wrists gently before he flipped my skirt back down and pulled me down into his lap where he sat in Andrea's chair. He pressed a kiss into the crook of my neck before he retorted at Noah, "We negotiated. I got what I wanted."

"Mmm, well," Noah said as he ran his deep blue gaze over the two of us. "You're both a little gross. I think you should take Jojo upstairs to the shower while Zach's cleanup crew fixes this mess."

I nodded. I'd certainly made a mess earlier, but I was only just now noticing how much of it I was wearing. I looked at Zach. "Do you guys still have a special courier like you used for Silverman? I think we should send her head to James Spencer."

His eyebrows jumped, and Noah also gave me a confused look. Bennett snorted like he wasn't even surprised.

"Do I even want to know how you know about that?" Zach asked as he brought his phone to his ear.

I shrugged, pasting a nonchalant look on my face. "You're aware I broke into the Club's basement last semester. It just happened to be on a... busy night for you guys."

Zach rolled his eyes. "Of course you were there that night. Of course you were."

Noah shook his head with an amused smile. "Still full of surprises, sweetheart. It's hard to believe we ever thought you were just a troublemaking scholarship student with a hot body and a smart mouth."

"When in actual fact you're a troublemaking *heiress* with a hot body and a smart mouth," Bennett added.

I elbowed him. "You love me."

"I do."

Zach hung up his phone, then he moved to stand over the body on the floor. "Did she have a purse? The crew chief reminded me to search her for anything we wanted to keep."

I motioned to the little black clutch that had landed a few feet away. "There. Get her phone at least."

Noah trotted over to grab it, looking thankful the purse was relatively free of gore. "I'll get this to Silver. Go get clean, you two. We'll inform our friends that you guys are having some alone time after Bennett's meeting in which nothing weird or violent happened whatsoever."

I awoke the next morning in a pile of limbs in my bed in Knight Tower, the urgent buzzing of Noah's phone on the nightstand pulling me from a lovely dream about being eight years old and building a snowman with the guys during one of the rare times it had snowed in the City.

"Damn it, Hargraves," Zach croaked sleepily. "Answer that."

Noah groaned, then he rolled onto his side and fumbled for the phone. "Yeah?"

"Sir." I could hear Silver's no-nonsense voice. "We've got it. You guys should get down here as soon as possible."

I bolted upright, turning to stare down at Noah with wide eyes. "They got what they needed from Elise's phone?"

Noah gave me a quick nod as he said to Silver, "Give us ten."

It only took us nine to jostle Bennett awake, throw on clothes, and pile into the elevator. We exited twenty-odd floors below our home and barreled through Knight's IT floor like a herd of anxious elephants. Noah let us into Silver's command center with a press of his thumb to the scanner by the door, and we found Silver and Marcus alone in the dark room, both of them seated in front of a panel of half a dozen large screens.

"Boss lady!" Zepp crowed from one of the screens as we entered.

Well, everyone was here, then—Zepp had deigned to make an actual video appearance. His thin face was partially obscured by his low baseball cap, and his dark gray hoodie definitely had donut dust on it. He had his long auburn hair pulled into its usual low ponytail at the nape of his neck.

Silver glanced our way, still looking every bit the professional she always did—dark-framed glasses, fitted blouse, cropped black pants and sensible flats. If it weren't for her shocking pink hair, I'd have thought she was one of my lawyers.

"Right on time," she said, motioning us over. Noah slid into an open seat at the computers and logged right in.

Zach and I dropped onto the small couch nearby, and Zach's big hand fastened around my thigh immediately. Bennett remained standing, looming and rigid as he prepared to watch us finally land the killing blow on Spencer.

Marcus spun in his chair, looking disheveled and irritated about being here on a Saturday morning—which he really shouldn't have been, since he and Silver both had extremely nice apartments one floor above us. He was shorter than Zach but just as muscular, and he had even more tattoos. There wasn't a bare patch of skin on his arms or hands, and even his neck sported creeping vines that disappeared into his dark hair.

He eyed me warily as he said, "Silver informs me that I don't want to know the details of how you came to possess Elise Proctor's cell phone."

I shrugged. "She waltzed into a meeting with Bennett and basically handed it over."

Zach laughed at Marcus. "You cut your teeth in the Snake Pit and you're afraid to hear about our Princess's... *abilities* with a knife?"

He shivered. "There's a reason I'm tucked safely in here and not on your security floor, Ferrero."

"Marcus," Silver snapped, and he rolled his eyes before

he swiveled back to his screens. "Focus and prepare to deploy the package."

Bennett vibrated with tension. "You're sure this will work?"

"Yep," Zepp replied. "You were right in guessing that Proctor would have the same access to all of Spencer and anything it touches as your father does. We were able to pull the cypher from what we could access on her phone. The whole Spencer system is about to get fucked in the ass."

Silver glared up at Zepp, irritated but surely not surprised at his lack of professionalism. "Yes, we're confident we'll get in this time, Mr. Spencer."

Bennett could only give her a sharp nod, his eyes glued to the screens like any of the code and other gibberish that was up there made much sense to any of us besides Noah.

Silver began the countdown. "In three, two, one... package deployed." She hit one last key, then they all sat back in unison to stare up at the screens.

After a minute that felt like an hour, Noah slammed his hands on the tabletop. "Fuck yes!"

The middle screen went black, and a gorgeous design of a white horse appeared. Scrawled across the bottom in big, looping letters was the word: Checkmate.

I jumped to my feet, Zach and Noah followed, and we all converged on Bennett, who remained still as a statue, almost in shock. The guys clapped him on the back as I pulled him into a deep kiss, which he returned immediately.

"It's done, Bennett," I whispered.

He nodded. "He deserves it."

James Spencer, and all of those who still stood by him, did deserve it. We'd just locked them out of every system we could infect, paralyzing the banks, hedge funds, private equity groups, and other white-collar businesses in the Spencer empire.

And unlike similar ransomware attacks, we wouldn't be unlocking them, no matter how much money they offered us. It would take even the most skilled computer genius at Spencer weeks to dig them out of this, and by that time it would be too late.

"She's a beauty, isn't she?" Zepp asked, motioning to the white horse. "Congrats, Jojo. Nearly to the finish line."

Marcus produced a bottle of champagne from who knew where and made sure to pop the cork right next to Silver's ear, and she hissed at him before swatting him on his large bicep.

I sank back into the couch and watched as everyone celebrated the culmination of years of work from Zepp and several long, hard months for Silver and Marcus. After Noah reiterated to Silver for the third time that yes, it was okay for her to have a glass of champagne on the job, she finally took a sip as her eyes met mine.

"*Thank you*," I mouthed.

She flushed, gracing me with a small smile and a respectful dip of her head.

Maybe someday when things calmed down, we'd see if we could get Silver to loosen up a bit.

But for now, we would wait.

CHAPTER TWENTY-NINE
JOLIE

"*We can confirm that companies within the Spencer Family's vast portfolio have all experienced the same mysterious computer virus that has completely prevented them from functioning. Many of Spencer's affiliates and allies in the City's Tier One families are seeing the same issue. Stock is tanking and investors are panicking.*"

I took a giant bite of my panini as I watched Montgomery Star Media's evening news coverage of the implosion of Spencer. Zach, a saint and a king, had swung by the dining hall after his workout to grab our dinners so that we could catch the Monday evening news cycle on the guys' stupid-huge TV. I sat on the floor with my back propped up against the couch, Noah's long legs splayed on either side of my body as he was distracted by his phone.

"*Consumers have likewise been spooked, and we've received reports of what is essentially a run on the bank for many of the affected companies. Oddly enough, allowing bank customers and outside investors with the various funds and wealth management firms to withdraw money from their accounts is the only function currently operating as normal at any of these companies."*

Zach snorted from where he was sprawled out in the corner of the couch. "That was a nice touch. Whose idea was it again?"

"Silver's," Noah replied. "Unlike Zepp and Marcus, who are self-taught and do not believe in higher education, she went to business school. She started at Hargraves in hospital administration before I plucked her out and put her on my tech team."

"It is likely that bankruptcy filings are imminent for many of these companies. We here at MSM's business desk are predicting this as the death knell for Spencer, following in the wake of Hargraves and Ferrero that have both met a similar fate recently."

Bennett let out a big sigh, like he was maybe, finally, releasing the last of the tension he'd been holding... for forever. His big body was pressed up against mine as he sat next to me on the floor, his hair still wet from his shower after crew practice.

I nudged him with my elbow. "You okay? I know you wanted this, but I imagine it's still hard to watch it all fall apart after being raised to believe Spencer was your entire purpose in life."

He threaded his fingers through mine. "My purpose in life is sitting next to me, Angel."

I was melting again, both into Bennett's side and under Noah's long fingers, which he was now running absently through my hair. Happiness fizzed in my body like a drug, but somewhere in the back of my mind, dark thoughts remained.

James Spencer had been quiet—he hadn't called Bennett even once—and I didn't know if that was a sign of his true defeat, or if he'd do something stupid to try and take everyone down with him before he was branded a failure and laughed out of the City.

Zach, wearing a pair of black sweatpants and nothing else, rolled off the couch and bounced to his feet, the muscles of his tattooed chest and cut abdomen rippling deliciously as he clapped his hands. "This calls for a celebration. Fuck homework."

"Zach!" I squealed as I found myself pulled to my feet then scooped into his arms, bridal style. He marched us determinedly toward his bedroom, a feral smile on his face. "I can walk, you caveman!"

Zach cackled. "You won't be able to walk when we're through with you, Princess."

Noah and Bennett launched to their feet and scurried after us.

We reached Zach's bedroom—a homey, masculine space that perfectly suited him. The exposed brick of the back wall framed his California King bed like a pretty picture—its comforter a deep, serene blue that invited us to wreck it. He set me gingerly on my feet near the foot of the bed, and he leaned in for a deceptively sweet kiss as he began to undress me.

The door slammed as Bennett and Noah jostled their way into the room. Noah made it to my back first, his lips landing on my neck as he joined Zach in his task. Zach unlatched his lips from mine just long enough to pull my crew team T-shirt over my head, and Noah kissed down my spine while he dragged my soft shorts and panties down to the floor in one swift tug.

"I'll just be over here then," Bennett grumbled, settling himself on the end of the bed to watch the guys strip me with his fiery green gaze.

Noah unhooked my flimsy bralette, and Zach peeled it away and tossed it in the pile accumulating at Bennett's feet. Zach ducked down to pull my nipple into his mouth, and I arched my back to give him better access, my head landing on Noah's shoulder.

"What would you like first, sweetheart?" Noah rasped in my ear as he held me. "After Zach's had his fill of those perfect tits, do you want him on his knees with his tongue in your pussy?"

I moaned as Zach switched nipples. Yes, I wanted that.

"Or," Noah went on after a lingering kiss to the crook of my neck, "do you want Bennett's cock in your mouth? Want to show him who's the boss of him with that wicked tongue of yours?"

Oh, I wanted that too.

I cast a glance over at Bennett, who remained perched on the edge of the bed, his enormous dick in his hand as he stroked it slowly. A smile teased the corners of his lips as he held my stare, the challenge evident in his.

I moaned again as I nodded vigorously.

"Greedy girl," Noah purred. "She wants it all. Let's have Zach warm you up just a little bit, and then we'll finally show Bennett how well you suck cock."

"*Noah*," I groaned. "Your filthy mouth gets me so hot."

I felt him grin up against my neck. "The things we're going to do to you, sweetheart."

Zach dropped to his knees and tossed my leg over his shoulder, wasting no time before his tongue was buried inside of me, licking and sucking, his happy growls a heavenly vibration on my heated, aching flesh. Noah held me steady, his hot breath teasing my neck as he whispered praise in my ear, reminding me what a good girl I was and how delicious he knew I tasted for Zach.

All the while Bennett watched, and I sucked in a little gasp when my gaze floated his way again and took in his now naked body, his crew joggers and tight T-shirt in a heap at his feet next to my own discarded clothes. His forearm flexed as his big hand pumped lazily over his dick, and when he caught my desperate stare again, he grinned, taunting me. "I'm waiting, Angel."

Zach chuckled against my pussy before he finally put me out of my misery, sucking my clit into his mouth and driving two thick fingers into me like a jackhammer, and I fell apart in Noah's arms.

"Mmm, fuck yes," Zach rumbled as he stood, sucking his fingers into his mouth before giving me a quick kiss. "Delectable as ever. Now go get him, baby girl."

He swatted my bare ass as I turned to slink the last few feet to where Bennett sat on the bed, my body still buzzing from coming so hard on Zach's tongue. I fell to my knees and crawled right between his powerful thighs, and I gave him my biggest doe-eyed stare, like I was a little flower and he was the sun.

His cocky smirk fell away, his nostrils flaring and his eyes hooding as he bit back a moan.

"Not looking good for you already, Spencer," Noah quipped from behind me.

"I know, man," Zach added. "There is no greater sight on God's green earth than our Princess when she's begging for your cock, but keep it together."

Bennett blew out a breath before reaching down to gently cup my cheek. "Ignore them, Angel. It's just you and me right now."

I let out a pleased hum, then I smacked his hand away from his dick because it was *mine*. I licked him from base to tip, taking great pains to move oh so slowly, teasing him until I finally wrapped my lips around his head and sucked.

"Angel," he growled, his hips starting to buck as I licked a little circle around his tip.

"I know what you want, Bennett," I said in a low husk. "Do it. I can take it."

I was going to fucking try anyway. This was a massive cock, so I would be leveling up from my previous blow job experience, but I never could back down from a challenge—especially not from Bennett Spencer.

He threaded his fingers into my hair, pulling it loose from my ponytail, and he gripped it just tight enough to take me to the edge of pain before tilting my head to look up at him. "You want me to fuck your face, Angel?"

"Oh, shit," Zach groaned. In my periphery I could see he'd lost his pants, and he was standing just off to my right, stroking his very hard cock as he looked on.

Noah was on my other side in the same state—gloriously naked, mouthwateringly erect, and looking almost pained at the idea of watching Bennett take my mouth. "You can do it, sweetheart. Open wide."

I brought my hungry gaze back to Bennett. Then, with great determination, I swallowed as much of that monster as I could, opening my throat and digging my nails into Bennett's thighs, ceding control.

"*Fuck*," he swore, his grip on my hair tightening. He pumped his hips, gently at first, then he let his own beast take over, thrusting hard and fast into my mouth. "Perfect," he rasped after a minute. "So fucking perfect. This mouth is mine, Angel, do you hear me?"

I nodded, tears beginning to leak from my eyes, but he never gave me more than I could handle.

And then it was over too soon.

"Enough," he barked, yanking me from the floor and right into his lap. I straddled him as he kissed me, ravenous and wild. We made out like eager teenagers while Zach and Noah chuckled knowingly.

"Good effort, Spencer, but I think she won that one," Noah said.

Bennett ignored him, shifting to toss me on the bed behind us without warning.

"Bennett!" My back hit the comforter, and he crawled on top of me, moving to pin me to the mattress with his big body.

I rolled us before he could settle on top of me like I would have if we were in the cage. Now I pinned him down, and I tutted at him as he bucked his hips in an effort to throw me off. "Easy, Bennett," I purred. "You're acting like you don't want me to ride this dick until I'm choking it."

He bared his teeth at me, but his eyes were so glazed with lust he almost looked high. "Such a fucking brat, Angel. Behave, and I'll let you fuck me."

Noah had crawled onto the bed behind me, and Zach made himself comfortable on his pillow throne at the headboard next to us. I felt Noah's hands wrap around my hips, and he moved me so that I was hovering over Bennett's huge erection. "Resistance is futile, Spencer. Let our girl have her ride." Then he gently lowered me onto Bennett's dick.

I gasped at the stretch, and Bennett's guttural groan signaled his surrender as I sank down until he was fully seated inside me.

Noah's hands came up to cup my breasts, and Zach's dark gaze drank me in as he fisted his dick, moving his hand in time with the tentative rocking of my hips as I adjusted to Bennett's girth. Soon that pinch of pain gave way to pleasure, and I began to ride Bennett with gusto, chasing my release and wanting so desperately to pull Bennett's orgasm from him too.

I was vaguely aware of Zach and Noah shuffling around on the bed as I lost myself in Bennett, but it wasn't until I registered the telltale *snick* of the lube cap that it dawned on me what they were up to.

Noah's low voice sounded against my ear. "Fuck, you're a goddess. Bennett's never seen a more beautiful sight in all his life than you riding his cock. Right, Spencer?"

I slowed as Noah's slick finger began to tease at my tight hole, and Bennett groaned in frustration, his brow pinched as he pumped his hips upward. "No," he grunted. "There's nothing better than this."

Noah ran a hand along my spine before gently pushing me forward. I collapsed onto Bennett's chest, now nose-to-nose with him as I continued the slow rock of my hips.

"Bennett," I whispered as Noah kept up his ministrations. "I think Noah's going to fuck my ass while you're still inside me."

He shut his eyes and ground his jaw like he was in real pain, then we both groaned as Noah slid his slick finger into my ass. I dropped down for a kiss, and I busied myself there administering sweet kisses to Bennett and continuing to move my hips, taking the slow-building pleasure as Noah stretched and readied me.

"Fuck me, Princess," Zach said, still watching us avidly. "Hargraves has more patience than I did, that's for sure. But Spencer looks like he's about to die."

Noah chose that moment to begin to push into me, and I buried my face in Bennett's chest to let out a rasping moan.

"Oh fuck," Noah bit out. "Oh, sweet girl, this is so tight. You're doing so well."

Bennett had sucked in an agonized breath at Noah's invasion, but he quickly put his game face back on. He swept my wild hair away from my face and cupped my cheeks with his big hands. "Okay, Angel? We're about to utterly fucking ruin you, but only if you're ready."

I was so full, sandwiched between the hard bodies of two of the three pieces of my heart, any sense of where I ended and they began quickly slipping away. I wanted to get lost. I wanted nothing to exist except me and them, here in Zach's bed.

Wait.

"I'm almost ready," I breathed. I pushed up on Bennett's chest and met Zach's hot, dark stare. Expecting a cocky smirk, all I saw was complete and utter devotion. "*Zach.* I need you."

He was on his knees immediately, shuffling to close the distance between us. He stroked his dick as he looked me over, and I somehow still had the presence of mind to admire the flexing of his defined Adonis belt as he moved. He rumbled, "Princess, are you gonna take all three of us?"

Bennett and Noah started moving inside me, spurring us on. I nodded. "Yes. I can do it, Zach."

"I know you can, baby girl. Never doubted you."

"You've got this, sweetheart," Noah said, his voice strained. "We'll hold onto you."

And they did. Bennett and Noah were a seamless team, keeping me propped at the right height even as they began to fuck me mercilessly, while Zach fed me his weeping cock and began his shallow thrusts in time with the others. He caressed my cheek reverently with one hand even as his grip on my hair with the other was rough and possessive. I screamed around him, and Bennett and Noah quickly threw me into a body-shattering climax.

"Oh, fuck *yes*, Angel," Bennett growled as I clamped around him.

"Good girl," Noah panted. "Such a good fucking girl."

Zach tensed. "Fuck, baby girl. Fuck, get ready for me."

I managed a nod, then I swallowed around Zach as he followed the three of us over the edge with a hoarse shout.

We fell into a pile of limbs, and the boys took care to move my boneless body into Zach's waiting embrace.

Bennett had rolled next to us, and I reached for him, linking our hands together. Noah disappeared to the bathroom and returned with wet washcloths for everyone.

I dozed in Zach's arms, happy and content to listen to the low murmurs of the guys as they chatted, easy and free and apparently not caring in the slightest that we were all still naked.

"Love you all," I whispered.

Zach kissed my temple. "We love you too, Princess."

CHAPTER THIRTY
BENNETT

My phone vibrated on Zach's nightstand, pulling me from the deep sleep I'd slipped into after we'd all finally cleaned up and thrown on some semblance of clothing. I'd roused Jolie, who was drowsy and adorable after I'd fucked her into a coma with a little help from her other boyfriends, and put her into the bathtub. Zach, Noah, and I had taken a quick shower, then we'd tucked Jolie in for the night and piled in around her like we so often did.

The clock on my phone read 11:30 p.m. The annoyance at being called at this hour on a Monday night was quickly wiped away by the alarm that jolted me all the way awake when I registered who was calling.

Why was Jolie's dad calling me?

"Dom?" I barked into the phone. "What's wrong?"

"Bennett," he said, and his grave tone knocked my heart into my throat. "I need you to remain calm."

Jolie's hand snaked into mine, and I held on like my life depended on it. "Where's my mother, Dom?"

He sighed. I could hear him pacing, the background buzzing with activity. "He's taken her, Bennett."

"*What?*" I shouted.

Everyone was awake around me now, my brain muddling their hushed, urgent whispers as I struggled to grasp what Dom was saying.

"They ambushed Martinez and your mother a few hours ago when they were walking home together from... an outing."

A fucking date, he means.

"Did they hurt her?" I croaked.

"Not physically, no. But they shot Martinez."

I was real fucking pissed at Martinez, but shit, I didn't want him dead.

Jolie gasped next to me. "Did they kill him?"

Dom heard her. "No, he's in the hospital. They left him for dead in an alley in Olde Town, but he managed to get a call out to us. Kara and I are here with him."

Deep breaths. "He's taken her for ransom," I said dully.

"Likely," Dom replied. "I've put out an all-call to the Shadows, and Zepp's woken up your team, but listen to me, son"—my heart lifted momentarily at the sound of the man who saved my Angel and for whom I'd developed a deep, sincere respect calling me *son*—"Do not go running off to Spencer Tower right now. I don't think he'll hurt your mother. By all accounts, he does care about her."

"He thinks she's his possession and nothing more," I spat.

"Be that as it may, we need time to plan. Zepp reports that every last remaining member of Spencer's security has been called back to guard the tower. It's a fortress now."

"Fuck," I muttered, hanging my head in my hand. "I'm

going to see what he wants, then I want everyone at Knight Tower first thing in the morning."

"Already done," he replied. "Tread lightly with your father, Bennett. This is a desperate move from a desperate man."

"I know." I paused, then I said, "And... tell Martinez that I hope he pulls through so I can beat his ass."

Dom chuckled. "He's known he's had that coming for a while, don't you worry."

I hung up and dropped my phone onto the bed as the familiar numbness crept into my body. My fucking father was hurting my mother yet again, but this time it was to get at me.

Noah had flicked on the light sometime during my call, and I turned to take in the concerned faces of my brothers and my love.

Jolie took my hand again, her stoic silence a sign that she was descending into the same place I was. Noah appeared concerned; Zach just looked pissed.

"I hate it, but you're right," Noah said. "You have to call him."

I picked my phone up again. No sense in delaying the inevitable.

I wasn't scared of my fucking father.

He answered the call immediately. "Hello, son."

"Father."

"To what do I owe the pleasure of your deigning to speak to me?" He sounded almost giddy, and it was fucking weird.

"You know why I'm calling," I snapped. "Your megalomania won't allow you to accept that you're fucking finished in this City, so you've kidnapped Mom to get my attention. You have it now—don't fucking waste it."

He *tsked*. "I don't like that tone, Bennett. That's no way to enter a negotiation—I know I've taught you better than that. Perhaps I was just missing my *wife* and wanted her back home where she belongs."

I scoffed. "You couldn't have given two shits if Mom was home or not except when you needed her on your arm for appearances. What's the matter, Father? Are you missing your simpering fuckbuddy of a private secretary? We did preserve her head when we sent it over, so you should be able to visit her whenever you're feeling nostalgic."

I could feel his anger bubbling through the phone. "That was beneath you, Bennett—wholly unnecessary and *grotesque*. Even if that traitorous bitch is probably the reason you were able to pull this neat little *trick*."

"No tricks, Father. It's truly the end of the road for you. Release Mom or I'll be coming to retrieve her."

"No!" he shouted, and I heard the distinct sound of glass shattering against the wall. "You will release the Spencer companies from this bullshit cyberattack. Once you do that, I will offer you a trade." He paused, and my pulse spiked. "Jolie Knight for your mother, Bennett. The longer you wait, the less patient I'll become, and I might start taking my anger out on your mom."

I trembled in rage. My father had been a shitty husband and certainly emotionally abusive, but he'd never hit my mother or physically harmed her. "Fuck you," I bit out. "I will fucking kill you, you son of a bitch."

"Time's ticking, son."

Then he hung up.

I sat there, vibrating, numb, oblivious to my surroundings. It was only when Zach and Noah's alarmed shouts penetrated my brain that I snapped back into the present.

"No fucking way, Princess."

"You'll have to go through us, sweetheart."

Jolie was in a standoff with Zach and Noah, who were shoulder to shoulder in the doorway of the bedroom. She glared at the two of them, still dressed in just her tiny sleep shorts and silky tank top.

But she did have her knife in her hand.

"Jolie," I growled. "*No.*"

She whirled to face me, and she pointed at me with her knife. "I heard him, Bennett. He's going to hurt your mom if I don't go over there! I'll go, he'll release her, then you guys can extract me. The Shadows have had these kinds of contingency plans in place since I started this whole thing!"

I gaped at her. "Are you insane? He will kill you. And then Dom will kill me for letting you do it, and I would fucking let him because *I will not live without you!*"

I'd bellowed that last part, and I sucked in a big, shaky breath as I tried to tamp down the soul-sucking despair at the thought of my father murdering the love of my life *again*. She held my pleading gaze, and finally, the panic and anger melted from her face.

She turned to look at Zach and Noah, who were wearing similar somber, desperate looks, and she sighed. "I'm sorry," she whispered. "I just... I can't let Bennett's mom suffer because of me. This is *all* because of me."

"No, sweetheart," Noah said softly. "This is all because of *them*. Our parents. Not you."

I opened my arms in invitation, and she trudged back to the bed and crawled into them. I held her close as Zach and Noah climbed back in bed with us. We knew she'd settle easier if we were all there. "Angel, you're not doing this alone anymore. I'm worried for my mom, too, but I agree with Dom that we need to be prepared. This is my father's last stand, and I will not let him take you down with him. Or anyone else."

"Okay," she whispered. "I'll feel better when we have a plan."

I kissed her forehead, and Zach pressed his lips to her shoulder as he curled in behind her. I murmured, "Love you, Angel."

As she drifted off to sleep, I glanced over the top of her head to meet Zach's and Noah's stares in the low light. They were both wound as tight as I was, but I could feel our collective tension releasing now that we had our girl contained and not running off headfirst into certain death.

"We'll get through this," Noah whispered.

"Just like we always do," added Zach.

We're the Heirs, I thought reflexively, even though that wasn't true anymore.

"We're *the* Family," I said instead. "The entire City is about to learn once again what happens when you fuck with us."

"*Max*," Jolie hissed into her earpiece. "I will march back down there and beat your ass if you don't hold this crane still."

I couldn't help my satisfied smirk, and one glance at Noah and Zach said they were feeling the same. We'd all grown *begrudgingly* fond of Max in the annoying little brother kind of way, but it didn't change the fact that he was a shit, and it was very satisfying for us when Jolie was the one to snap at him.

"I'm just *adjusting* it, Jojo," he replied with a chuckle.

"We want a straight shot onto that balcony for you guys when it's go time."

It was sometime in the middle of the chaotic meeting of the top minds within Knight and the Shadows this morning that the idiotic suggestion was made for our main extraction team to enter Spencer Tower via a large balcony off the fortieth floor—and that we access it via the tower crane conveniently parked next-door.

That main extraction team consisted of Jolie, Noah, Zach, and me, and we were now crouched on the narrow walkway of the crane's horizontal arm while someone had let Max Miller, eighteen-year-old high school senior, man the controls in the cramped glass cab.

"Hold steady, Max," Dom's deep voice said into our ears. "The ground team is getting into position."

Dom was posted up on the roof of the Serpentis Casino one block over with a couple of other members of the Shadows who had sniper experience. They'd wanted Noah, too, but now that his leg wasn't giving him grief, he refused to be separated from us.

After a few minutes of silence, Jolie asked, "Any word on Martinez?"

"Yeah, he's awake," Dom replied, "and... unhappy that Bridgette was taken. He tried to leave the hospital until we sent Julie down there. I think she's holding a gun on him so he'll stay in bed."

Zach chuckled, nudging me with his elbow. "Sounds like you've got a new daddy now."

He received my stoniest glare, the ambient light of the City's night life giving us just enough visibility that I knew he did not miss it.

Rocky's voice crackled online. "North Team is in position and ready."

Kara was next. "South Team is also in position and ready."

"Extraction Team will be ready to move at the signal," Jolie announced.

"And we've got the roof covered," Dom finished. "Currently half a dozen Enforcers guarding the roof entrance."

"We're looking at another two dozen at the North entrance and about thirty at the South," Zepp said over the clicking of his computer keys. "We don't have eyes in the penthouse, as usual, but prepare for Enforcer presence there, Team Jojo."

"Got it," Jolie replied, giving me a knowing nod.

We knew my father would put as many "expendable" hired guns between himself and us as he could get his hands on as Spencer flailed. His vast kingdom had disintegrated and was now slipping through his fingers like sand. He'd played his last card.

But all he'd really done was piss me off and then paint himself into a corner. This was only going to end one way, and I was at peace with it because I'd known somewhere deep within me that we'd find ourselves here, one way or another, the moment I'd realized my Angel had come back to me.

"On my signal," Dom boomed through our ears. "All teams—*go!*"

The arm of the crane began to move. "Max, slow it down," Noah barked. He stood at the front of our group, ready to direct us to the balcony. "You're going to miss."

"I've got it, Nikolai," he replied smoothly. "Don't worry your adorable little blond head."

We held on for dear life then as Max swung the crane arm toward the fortieth floor of Spencer Tower. The sound of shouting and rapid-fire gunshots echoed into the night air from the ground below us, where our teams had been tasked with distracting and eliminating as much of the tower's main security force as possible while we would sneak in from the middle.

I was pretty sure they were letting Frankie loose in the tower somewhere, too, but he was never on comms, so who the fuck knew.

"Fuck, I think we're gonna make it," Zach said, blowing out a breath as Max settled us just over our target entrance.

"Ye of little faith," Max retorted in our ears. "Hop off, team, because I need to swing this thing back around so it doesn't look too suspicious."

"Thanks, Maxy," Jojo chirped, and she hustled forward to join Noah at the end of the arm. "Be safe, please."

"Back at you, Jojo. *All* of you."

One by one, we climbed over the end of the crane arm and dropped down onto the balcony. I adjusted my gear, then I did a quick sweep of Jolie's kit, reassuring myself she was fully armed and her helmet was on tight.

She caught my anxious perusal, and she smiled softly before she pulled me in for a quick kiss. "I'm ready. We're all ready, Bennett. Let's go get your mom."

And let's go put an end to my father.

Then my Angel would be safe, and I would be free.

CHAPTER THIRTY-ONE
JOLIE

I flicked open the app that Marcus had installed on my phone this morning, then I pressed its face up against the security scanner outside the balcony doors.

"This better fucking work, Marcus," Zach growled into his earpiece. "I am not crawling back onto that crane."

"Of course it'll work," Marcus retorted in our ears. "What? Oh, don't fucking look at me like that, Silver. If you could build a better program, you would've done it already."

"Children," Noah snapped. "Focus."

"Sorry, sir," Silver muttered.

"You two need to fuck already," Zepp chimed in.

"Zepp!" Silver hissed, sounding scandalized.

The scanner beeped with a flash of green light, so we were in and moving on from the bickering of our brilliant tech professionals. Bennett yanked open the heavy glass door, and we followed him into the dark, deserted office that had been James Spencer's base of operations in his law firm.

"Looks like someone had a tantrum," Zach mused,

eyeing the sleek computer monitor that was in pieces in the middle of the floor.

"Typical," Bennett grunted. He held up a gloved hand as we reached the office door, and we all paused to listen for anything that could indicate we weren't alone up here. We could make out the faint sounds of the battle raging outside, spilling into the streets from the lobby on both sides of the building, but the middle floors were silent. Bennett lowered his hand and said in a quiet voice, "Let's move. There's an elevator on this floor that has penthouse access."

We exited the office and treaded silently down the marble-tiled hall, our boots occasionally rustling a paper or file that had been tossed haphazardly on the ground. It appeared that the employees of James B. Spencer and Associates had dropped what they were doing the instant we'd shut it all down and just... left.

When we reached the elevator bank, Bennett jammed his gloved finger angrily into the button. For a moment, the four of us just stood there, milling about, checking our watches or our phones as we waited for the elevator like it was the most normal fucking thing in the world while we ignored the muffled shouting and popping of gunshots in the distance.

The elevator arrived, and we climbed aboard. I raised my phone to the security sensor once again as Bennett smashed the button for the penthouse. The flash of green light said we were a go, and up we went.

"Weapons ready," I whispered to my boys. "We should have the element of surprise, since they won't have clocked any of our team leaving the ground floor."

They all nodded, raising their pistols as the elevator finally came to a stop.

The ding announced our arrival.

"Extraction Team is going in," I announced into my earpiece.

And then it was on.

We moved quickly, a seamless team, striking at the three Enforcers stationed in the lobby only seconds after they comprehended they were being attacked. Shouts rang out from the living room, and the four guards who rushed into the foyer met the same end.

"Foyer and living room clear," Bennett barked.

Zach hissed from behind me. "Motherfucker, that stings."

I whirled, the panic rising into my throat and nearly suffocating me. "Zach! Are you hurt?"

"Bullet just grazed the vest, baby girl," he replied with a wink that had no business being sexy at this moment. "Totally fine."

The sound of boots stomping sounded from the floor above us. "We need to move," Noah said. "They'll have put out the call to downstairs, so we should expect more Enforcers to try to make their way up here."

Bennett was already darting toward the stairs, and we quickly fell in behind him. At the first appearance of an Enforcer on the stairs, Noah fired and did not miss. He took down two more before we'd crested the stairs.

"Second floor is clear," I announced, then I turned to Bennett. "You think he has her upstairs in their bedroom?"

"Likely."

Dom buzzed into our ears. "Extraction Team, Spencer's helicopter is landing on the roof as we speak."

"Shit," Zach swore.

Bennett was already running for the stairs to the third

floor. "Dom, are there still Enforcers on the roof?" he barked.

"We took out all of them but one who's cowering behind a cement pylon. If anyone exits that helicopter and moves into our line of sight, we'll get them too."

Our boots pounded on the stairs, all attempts at stealth abandoned the second we stepped off the elevator with guns blazing.

"He's making a run for it. I'll fucking kill him," Bennett growled as he came to a stop on the third-floor landing—the same place Frankie had pulled me back down the stairs and wrestled my pack away from me just a few short months ago.

Being back here again, invading Spencer Tower with my boys at my side, the four of us united in the common goal of eliminating James Spencer once and for all, was a fantastical dream I could never have *dared* to hope for the last time I stood on these steps.

Bennett raced for the main bedroom, and we darted after him. "Where the fuck is that bastard?"

"Here, son."

James Spencer stepped into the shadows at the doorway to his bedroom. His suit was wrinkled, his tie askew, and his dark hair—so similar to Bennett's except for the graying at his temples—looked as though he'd yanked it in four different directions.

He also held a trembling Bridgette Spencer in front of him like a shield, his small black handgun pressed to her head.

The four of us froze. No one lowered their weapon, but not even Noah was confident enough to take a shot at Bennett's dad while he hid behind Bridgette.

"Let her go," Bennett snarled. "Your fight is with me, Father."

"I don't think so," he snapped. "I'm not an idiot, Bennett. You've broken into our home, and you've brought your little girlfriend here to finish me off. She's spun you this noble tale of justice while you've had your dick inside her, and now you've destroyed *everything*."

Bridgette struggled, but he only clamped down harder with the arm he had wound around her neck. Her eyes were puffy and red-rimmed, and I wanted to tear her away from that evil fucking man this instant.

"Is John alive?" she croaked at Bennett.

"Shut up," James hissed into her ear. He jerked her into the hallway and began backing around the corner, still holding her in front of his body as he headed straight for the stairs to the roof.

"Martinez is okay, Mrs. Spencer," I said softly, catching her eyes. "He's awake and missing you."

She let out a shaky sigh, giving me the tiniest of nods.

James scoffed, still taking slow steps backward as the four of us inched forward, following them. "You approve of your sweet, innocent mother fucking her bodyguard, son?"

We all knew Bennett did not *exactly* approve of that, but he gave no indication he'd even heard that question as he held his father's glare with the same cold fury he had since the second he stepped out of his shadow. "What's your plan here, Father?" he asked, just the edge of a taunt in his voice. "Despite the fact that you have a gun to my mother's head, I have no intention of handing Jolie over to you, and I have *every* intention of letting your failing business empire stagnate and rot. This little outburst has accomplished nothing."

"It would have if all of these meatheads I pay to guard

this tower weren't so fucking worthless!" he bellowed, making Bridgette flinch in his arms. "You'd think that fifty trained guards would at least manage to eliminate the Knight bitch, if not her *and* your traitorous Heir friends. Then you'd have seen it, son—you'd have seen what a monumental fuckup this whole *thing* was for you." He began to climb the stairs, taking careful steps backward, his gun never leaving Bridgette's head and his hard brown eyes never leaving his son. "We could've left here as a Family, started over with your trust fund and my personal accounts. Maybe someday you would've proved to me that you were truly my son and worthy of the Spencer name."

Rocky's voice sounded in our ears. "Hey, Extraction Team, you've got incoming. We have it mostly contained down here, but we lost four or five of them when they got the distress call from the penthouse. I've sent a group after them, but you guys need to be ready."

"Fuck," Zach muttered. He nodded at Noah, understanding passing between them. "We'll be back, Princess," he said softly.

Noah gave my hip an affectionate squeeze, and they turned to run back down the stairs.

I refused to let my brain touch even for a second on the worry that I might not see them again.

James and Bridgette were at the top of the stairs now, while Bennett and I stood shoulder to shoulder on the bottom step, both of us stalking our prey with singular focus.

"I don't want your fucking name," Bennett growled at his father, taking one more step forward. "You're a craven, murdering narcissist. You're a shitty husband and a prick of a father. Let Mom go, and I'll give you a ten second head start to run to your helicopter like the sniveling fucking coward you are."

James just shook his head like he was disappointed in his son before he moved with some of the stunning catlike speed Bennett possessed. He shouldered the heavy door open and yanked a struggling Bridgette through, shoving her forward and disappearing out of our line of sight.

"Shit!" I yelled. "Dom! Hold your fire. Spencer and Bridgette are on the roof, and we're coming out."

Bennett and I sprinted up the stairs, barreling onto the roof in hot pursuit. The rooftop was brightly lit by both security lights and the cool blue glow of the obnoxious Spencer trident that jutted from the top of the tower.

Bennett's father continued to shove his mother toward the waiting helicopter, digging one bruising hand into her bicep and the other still holding a gun to her head.

The lone Enforcer left on the roof chose that moment to make a last showing for his boss, popping out from his hiding spot and taking a shot at Bennett and me. We both dropped to the ground, rolling away from each other, and it was all Dom needed for a clear shot.

Dom's gun cracked, the Enforcer dropped, and I jumped to my feet again just in time to see one of the guards that had been hiding in the helicopter open its door to receive a struggling, shrieking Bridgette.

She kicked and flailed, and I fired a haphazard shot at the door of the helicopter, high enough so that I was sure to miss Bridgette. It clanged against the metal, and it startled the guard enough to drop her.

Bennett was also on his feet, sprinting toward them. I continued to fire shots at the side of the helicopter, trying to keep the guards inside at bay.

"Worthless!" James roared at the helicopter. "All of you!"

With one last mighty yell, Bridgette tore her arm from James's grasp and slapped the gun out of his hand. It clattered to the ground at the same moment that Bennett reached them.

Time slowed. My breath hitched and my stomach dropped as Bennett shoved his mom clear of his father and tackled James to the ground. Bennett's bigger body slammed into James's strong but smaller form, and they skidded across the concrete until they crashed into the railing that bordered the tower's roof.

It took every ounce of willpower I possessed not to run to them; instead, I continued to fire shots at the helicopter to keep the guards from exiting and snatching Bennett's mom or hurting Bennett to retrieve his father.

I screamed, "Bridgette! Get behind me!"

My shouts were barely audible over the deafening whirl of the helicopter's blades, but she didn't need to be told twice. She ran for me, and I tucked her safely in between my back and the railing.

"We've got the penthouse cleared!" Noah called into my ears. "Zach and I are on the way back up."

"Rocky's team is staying on the penthouse entrance inside in case more Enforcers make their way up from the ground," Zach added.

At the sound of their voices, I released one tiny fraction of the tension I was holding, even as Bennett and his father grappled on the ground like wild animals.

"We've still got at least three guards in the helicopter!" I shouted. "Dom doesn't have a clear shot, and I'm running low."

Suddenly Max came online. "Delivering you a package, Jojo. Hang tight."

"What?" I shouted again over the noise.

Just as Zach and Noah burst from the penthouse door, the end of the long metal arm of the tower crane appeared, just peeking over the edge of the roof.

Frankie vaulted from it like fucking Spiderman, his tank top a streak of neon yellow soaring through the sky before he landed on light feet and disappeared behind the helicopter. Within thirty seconds, three bodies were tossed unceremoniously out the bay door, and Frankie's lithe form appeared in the cockpit.

"Did you know he could fly a helicopter?" I asked Zach as he skidded to a stop beside me.

Zach could only look on with well-worn resignation. "He can't, as far as I know."

Frankie tossed us a jaunty salute from the cabin's window, then I watched, momentarily struck dumb, as the helicopter rose from the roof and disappeared into the night.

Silence settled over the rooftop—until Bennett's angry roar pierced the air, jerking us back to reality.

CHAPTER THIRTY-TWO
JOLIE

"Penthouse is clear," a voice from Rocky's team announced in our ears.

Kara came on next. "Ground is clear. All Spencer forces have either been taken out or subdued."

"Roof is clear," Dom announced.

"Almost," I clarified in a hushed whisper.

Bennett and his father were on their feet now, circling each other near the railing opposite us. Zach, Noah, and I holstered our weapons, and with Bridgette clinging tightly to Noah's arm, the four of us walked slowly toward them.

We came to a stop a few feet away, and we watched in solemn silence as Bennett exorcised the last of the demons he harbored for his father—and for Spencer.

James' face was bruised and bloody, and he limped a bit as he moved, eyeing Bennett now with open loathing. My beast quieted as I registered that Bennett had only one purpling bruise on his jaw, and his powerful body moved with no signs of serious injury.

"You," James spat, bloody saliva flying from his lips, "are such a disappointment."

Bennett smiled, and he was so *beautiful* like that. "I'm everything you're not, Father, and I'm so fucking proud of that. It's over."

James nodded, and he stilled, suddenly standing tall and adjusting his ruined suit in a way that reminded me so much of his son. "I suppose it is. You've taken everything from me, Bennett. But before we part, I'd like to return the favor."

Bennett frowned.

Then his father moved.

With a shocking speed he must've pulled from the deepest, most desperate place inside of him, he lunged for Bennett. Bennett braced for the attack, but not before his father reached for the gun strapped to Bennett's belt, yanking it free and taking aim right at me.

Shouts rang out. Noah shoved Bridgette behind him and dove for me. Zach jumped from my other side, both of them so fucking brave and so fucking *infuriating* as they tried to take a bullet for me.

I loved them so much, I thought my heart would burst from my chest.

"NO!" Bennett screamed.

His father squeezed the trigger just as Bennett's big body plowed into him again, knocking his arm to the side. The bullet ricocheted off a concrete pylon and buried itself in the giant Spencer trident, which sparked in anger.

I'd dived on top of my valiant boys, dragging Bridgette down with us. I landed with a thud, sprawled over Zach's back, and at the sound of one last guttural roar from Bennett, I lifted my head.

Bennett had shoved his father over the side of the railing, taking his gun back in the process. James had caught himself, clinging to the top rail, his feet dangling as he fought to pull himself back up. Bennett stood there, breathing hard, holding the reclaimed gun and aiming it one more time at James Spencer's head.

"Bennett," he rasped. "I am your *father*. You wouldn't."

"Don't worry, Father," Bennett replied, his tone suddenly eerily calm. "Unlike you, I can be a *little* merciful."

The terror on James' face was replaced with a smug grin. "I knew you didn't have it in you."

Bennett's answering smile was cold, but his eyes were almost exuberant—the look of a man who knew this was the last time he'd ever have to listen to his own father belittle him. He pulled the trigger just as the blue light of the giant trident flickered and went dark.

His aim was true, and then James Spencer was gone.

Dead *before* he fell the sixty-plus stories to the unforgiving City streets below.

A small mercy, indeed.

Bennett turned back to us. His shoulders sagged, years of tension leaking from his body in a striking, visceral way.

I climbed to my feet, and Zach, Noah, and Bennett's mom followed.

I opened my arms, and Bennett came to me immediately. He buried his face in the crook of my neck, and I held him tight as the others pressed in around us.

"Let's go home, Angel."

"The City feels quiet tonight," Noah said, his voice soft and almost distracted as we both leaned against the railing that bordered our pool deck at the penthouse.

"Mmm," I replied, snuggling closer to him. "I like it."

Maybe it was because it was Wednesday, or maybe the

extra humidity in the air was keeping more of the City's residents indoors. Personally, I thought the quiet was more in the look of it—Spencer Tower was now a blackened husk against the backdrop of the starlit river, and Ferrero Tower was the same, save the low red glow of the serpent affixed to its side. There were a few lights on at Hargraves, but most of them would go out, too, when the last of Noah's hired construction crew went home for the evening.

It might have been the first time in seven and a half years that I gazed upon the City's skyline without feeling the echoes of terror and the burning anger I'd nursed all those years.

Zach joined us, giving me a quick kiss before handing me a glass of champagne. He dropped his elbows onto the railing and pressed into my other side. "Feels weird, doesn't it?"

"Yeah," I murmured. "It's ours now, huh?"

"You bet, Princess. If we want it to be."

A laugh sounded behind us. I glanced over my shoulder to where Mari sat, lounging in her bikini and gauzy sarong and gripping her champagne glass between delicate fingers as she and Frankie giggled together. Frankie's pool party attire was his usual—ripped jeans, scuffed Converse, and a white tank top with arm holes cut so big, I could make out almost every detail of the serpent tattoo that wound its way up his torso.

Dom and Laura had commandeered one of the outdoor couches, while Julie and Kara occupied the other one. Max was actually in the pool, sprawled lazily on an inner tube, his tiny swim trunks hiding nothing and his keen gaze rarely leaving Mari and Frankie.

Rocky manned the grill, and Martinez was propped on a pool lounger nearby. Rocky and Dom had schlepped him all the way to Knight Tower earlier this evening so that we could all see with our own eyes that he was alive and well. Bennett may or may not have silently acquiesced to his spending the night in our guest wing with Bridgette, who sat daintily on the end of Martinez's lounger, fawning over him. For his part, Martinez looked much more like a cat who'd gotten the cream than a man who'd been shot in the stomach forty-eight hours ago.

Zach chuckled as I turned back to gaze out at my City. "You think we should expect to be invited to more of these impromptu barbecues at our own pool?"

"Yes," I replied, feeling the wide smile creep across my face. "It feels... right."

Noah reached for my hand. "We can have these people at our pool every day if it makes you smile like that, sweetheart."

"Well, not *every* day, Noah," I replied, squeezing his hand. "And they do need to stop showing up out of nowhere. Zach had only barely cleaned up the mess he'd made between my thighs when my *parents* waltzed into the living room."

Zach shot me an indignant look. "Excuse you, that was not a *mess*. That was my *love* for you."

I snorted, but before I could retort, a big, possessive hand wrapped around my neck.

Bennett turned my head so that he could steal a searing kiss over my shoulder, and I whimpered against his lips. My other boyfriends groaned at the sound, then Bennett released me, pressing his big hard body up against my back.

"Are you happy, Angel?" he rumbled in my ear.

"I am, Bennett." I sighed contentedly. "My favorite place in the entire world is being pressed in between the three of you, after all."

They all groaned again. Bennett leaned down to whisper in my ear, "Don't talk like that unless you want us to haul you back to bed. I'll do it in front of our family—I don't give a fuck."

Happy tingles raced through my body at Bennett's declaration that all of these people were our *family*, then I had to smother the other tingles that hit me between my legs at the thought of going back to bed with them—which was where we'd spent most of the day today. We'd needed to be together after the events of last night, and my boys had loved me hard until I was wrung out and deliciously sore.

Noah gave me a knowing grin before he turned back to the City's skyline. "I can't believe that after all of this, we have to go back to school tomorrow. Like nothing's changed."

But of course, everything had changed.

What I'd set out to do the day I'd finally pulled myself out of Max's bed and vowed to end the Families—that was finished. But instead of leaving the City in burning ruins like I'd intended, I'd simply cut off its gangrenous limbs. The heart of it remained intact, and now I had something I could make... great.

And I'd do it with my team, my family, and the loves of my life at my side every step of the way.

I could only hope that it would someday look like my mom and dad might have wanted when they envisioned a City where the Families could actually do *good*.

"I *am* looking forward to being a normal college student for a while," I said to the boys, and they all grunted in agreement. "Though, now that I don't have any ex-best friends to dupe or evil, murderous oligarchs to destroy, I'm not exactly sure what I'm going to do with myself."

Noah shot me a dark look full of promises—the reminder of my behavior last semester probably earning me some punishment later, and I shivered at the thought. Then his face softened as he said, "You're going to heal, sweetheart."

"We all will," Zach added.

"Exactly," Bennett finished. "Together."

Together.

EPILOGUE
JOLIE - ABOUT TWO YEARS LATER

"That's it, Princess," Zach rasped into my ear, his rough cheek scraping along the side of my neck. "Fucking come for me."

"Zach, ugh, shit," I whimpered as he thrust furiously between my thighs, my leg hiked up over his hip and my back smashed against the door in Noah's office. "You're going to be late for the lineup."

He chuckled. "Like they'd start graduation without four of the Academy's trustees."

On cue, a fist pounded on the office door. "Hurry the fuck up in there, you two," Bennett growled. "Do not mess up Angel's dress, you fucking animal. Or her hair."

Noah's muttering was barely audible over Zach's heavy breathing in my ear. "Losing battle, dude. Let's not act like we weren't already running late because you decided to ambush Jojo in the shower earlier."

The memory of Bennett slipping into my shower this morning, then bending me over and fucking me into the wall pushed me over the edge, and I screamed Zach's name for the entire administrative wing of Holywell Hall to hear as my climax rocked through my body.

"Yeah, that's fucking right, baby girl," he said with a groan.

He slowed as he finished, all the while taking my lips in a sweet, gentle kiss.

"Finally," Bennett huffed from outside.

I snickered. Zach's decision to drag me into Noah's office and fuck me up against the door ten minutes before graduation began was not that surprising, though it was going to put us even further behind than we already were. Noah had only wanted to swing by his office to grab his favorite tie, but the quiet hallway, locked door, and my flimsy dress had apparently been too big a temptation for my rules-breaking-est boyfriend.

After cleaning me up like a gentleman, Zach righted my dress and zipped his graduation robe back into place. He picked his cap up off the floor and stuck it back on his head, and he still somehow made it look lazy and disheveled. He smirked at my perusal of him as he adjusted his tassel.

We opened the door and stepped into the hall, and we found Bennett and Noah both looking very dapper in their caps and gowns. Noah shot me a knowing smile, while Bennett rolled his eyes.

"Nice going, Ferrero," Bennett groused. "She's got that just-been-fucked flush, and your beard burn is clear as day on her neck."

I snuck into Bennett's arms and pulled him in for a kiss, and he melted into me without any more fussing. "Relax, Bennett," I said with a big smile. I fluffed my hair around my shoulders to hide the aftermath of Zach's rough cheek against my pale skin. "See? Good as new. Now we need to move, unless Noah also needs his graduation present before you guys walk that stage?" I tossed Noah a coy smile.

He grinned. "Absolutely not. I want mine later. In your bed. For several hours. These idiots need to learn some patience."

None of my boyfriends were really *that* patient, but Noah certainly had the most... discipline.

The other two grumbled while I smoothed my pale pink dress. I was feeling very girly and emotional today, so my dress color suited my mood.

I turned to beam at the three of them. "Let's go get you boys graduated."

I waved at Mari from my seat at the front of the dining hall, which had been cleared of its banquet tables and instead filled with rows of folding chairs facing a small stage at the front of the room. Mari, as an "A" last name, was first in line on the little stairs to the side.

"I'm gonna miss her and Carmen being on campus all the time," Max pouted from his seat next to me.

I elbowed him. "You still have *me*, your loving sister."

He grinned. "You mean my loving *roommate*."

I rolled my eyes, but I couldn't help the little grin that tugged at my lips. Max would move in with me next year for my senior year—his junior—at Holywell. I'd stayed true to Mari and remained her roommate for three glorious years. But with my boyfriends finally graduating and clearing out of the A Dorm penthouse, I was taking it over, and Max would join me. It wasn't quite our shared bunk room back at our apartment over the bookstore, but I was actually looking forward to living with my brother again.

Though we were going to need to have a discussion about the *entertaining* I was certain he'd be doing in his room.

"I hope you're excited for me to be all in your business about keeping your grades up," I added.

"Ugh, why?" he moaned. "You basically run this place. You'd never keep my degree from me."

That was not exactly true, but as a trustee, I did have a lot of sway over the things that went on at Holywell, including the expansion of the scholarship program, the overhaul of the admissions criteria to move beyond a student's last name and how much money their family had, and, of course, the hiring of the new dean.

I watched as Dean Foley toddled up to the stage to begin his opening remarks. He was a tiny man with a hunched back, wispy white hair, and a mind as sharp as his smile. He was not from the City, so he didn't give one iota of a fuck about anyone's family name. Our previous dean, Harper's mom, had gotten the boot at the end of my freshman year due to the many scandals plaguing the Jansen family. They left the City shortly after the fall of Spencer, and the last I'd heard, they'd run off to New York to beg for a role in Edward Jansen's second-cousin's investment firm. They'd also stuck Harper in some small, isolated women's college upstate to finish her degree.

Dom nudged me from my other side where he sat with Laura. "I can't believe in one short year, I'll be watching you cross that stage."

"Don't get all sentimental on me, old man," I whispered.

He laughed. "I mean, I'm not sure I was convinced either of my children would graduate college back when we'd planned to ditch the City with your inheritance. Our days were going to be surf lessons and seafood."

I hummed. "Are you disappointed they aren't?"

"No, honey," he replied, reaching over to squeeze my hand. "You've made this place something great, and you have the loves of your life. In my wildest dreams, I couldn't have imagined you so happy."

I felt a tear well up, but I blinked it away. Too early in the ceremony for that shit.

"And we're just overrun with sons!" Laura added, leaning around Dom to smile at me and Max. "It's good for Dom. It keeps him young."

Dom grumbled something about getting enough testosterone at the gym already, then the dean began to announce the names of our graduates.

Mari stepped across the stage first, moving effortlessly in her towering Mary Jane heels. She waved at us as she received her diploma, then turned to look back over at the line of students waiting to graduate. She blew a kiss at Carmen, who beamed and waved excitedly.

As Mari exited the stage, she sent a polite nod to the chairs somewhere behind us, where I presumed her parents had found seats.

Mari's relationship with her parents was on the mend, but they still had a long road ahead. As Knight flourished in the months following the end of the rule of the Four Families, she did decide to bring the Anzaldua hotel empire into our fold. She'd stepped into the role of co-CEO with her mother, and they had a polite and functional business relationship. Unfortunately, Mari's parents still couldn't manage to completely hide their disapproval of Mari's public relationship with Carmen, so for now, polite and functional was all it would be.

I'd made it my mission for Carmen to start her junior year of college at Holywell instead of continuing at her Spanish university. It only took a partial scholarship and a personal phone call from yours truly to her parents, but I would've flown across the ocean and kidnapped her myself if I'd had to. Zach had even offered to plan it all out, the psycho.

The two of them were still very much in love and would be moving into Mari's apartment in Knight Tower after graduation. Mari would continue her work in our hospitality group, and Carmen would be starting her job on Silver's team after interning with her last summer.

I loved having all my people close.

Max and I waved enthusiastically at Carmen as she trotted across the stage a few minutes later, and then it was time for the first former Heir of the City's Four Families to cross the stage.

Zach Ferrero received his diploma to a rousing round of applause. His dark eyes found mine, and he winked at me. There was so much love in that cocky smile that overwhelmed me in that moment, and I blinked back tears again.

"Ugh, tell Ferrero we didn't *all* need to see his bedroom eyes," Max complained, but he squeezed my thigh affectionately as he said it. He knew Zach was a part of my heart, and the two of them were pretty much besties even if neither would ever admit it out loud. Max and Zach's love language was beating the fuck out of each other in the cage.

After some time spent getting his sea legs, Zach was now running what was the successor to the Ferrero Family empire like he was born to do it—because he was. He'd taken a page from Noah's book and turned Ferrero Tower into his own personal project to better the City, and it now housed a boarding school for at-risk youth and the offices of several community-based organizations.

His pet project, though, was his gym. Andrea had demolished the last of the public housing in the City to build a parking garage for the Club, so Zach decided to give that back to the City—in a way, at least—by using that space to open a gym similar to Dom's. It catered to the struggling teens raised in the violent underbelly of the City that used to end up in the Snake Pit, trying to make a buck. He hired Rocky to run it, and it was truly an amazing place.

As Zach exited the stage, he nodded at Gemma, who sat in the row behind us. Zach's estranged aunt had slowly tiptoed her way back into Zach's life, calling occasionally and visiting the City twice more since she'd pulled the trigger ending the life of the vile woman who'd murdered both my mother and Zach's father. We were looking forward to visiting her chalet in Switzerland over the holidays this year, and Max had already spent a fortune on snowboarding gear in anticipation.

Zach stopped along the wall of the hall to shake hands with Frankie, who definitely hadn't been there thirty seconds ago. I darted a glance at Max, whose heated gaze was now squarely aimed in that direction, a knowing smirk on his face.

Only a few graduates separated Zach from the next former Heir to ascend the stage. Noah Hargraves lit up the room with his lovely smile, his big blue eyes shining behind the dark brown frames he wore today. He accepted his diploma, then those eyes searched for me in my spot on the front row.

I beamed at him, and he blew me a kiss. The pride I felt at watching *my* Noah graduate at the top of his class had me bursting, and I thanked all the deities of the world that he would still be around campus next year, taking graduate classes and teaching.

It meant I'd get to pay him some more visits in his office to request extra credit.

"God, the way Nick looks at you is going to get *me* pregnant—ow, fuck," Max groused as I elbowed him for the tenth time. Then he muttered, "I hope he's at least going to start putting a tie on his office door or something when you guys are fucking in there. I don't need to be scarred for life when I need help with my fucking advanced computer science homework—*ow*."

I rolled my eyes, though I couldn't help my smile. Noah was both proud and annoyed by Max's increased presence in his orbit because of Max's computer science major, and it was yet another bromance that neither of them would ever cop to but was one hundred percent a thing.

Noah planned to keep his Academy obligations part-time so he could run his healthcare empire the rest of the time. His hospital and clinic serving low-income citizens in Hargraves Tower flourished, and he enjoyed his positions on the boards of several up-and-coming businesses in the healthcare tech space.

He also enjoyed tying me to the bed and edging me until I begged him for mercy while Zach and Bennett watched. Noah was a man of diverse interests and hobbies.

He was so happy, so focused, that he often forgot about his father. Peter hadn't left Thailand, but he'd had to pay off a fair few of his more unsavory creditors over the years and had only narrowly avoided a stint in Thai prison.

And his numerous calls to Noah, presumably to beg for money, always went unanswered.

When Bennett finally strode across the stage, his presence commanded the attention of the entire hall. He towered over every person around him, and his broad chest and wide shoulders were prominent even in his gown. He accepted his diploma from the dean with the same intense, serious energy he gave to most tasks, and I could sense every eye in the room was glued to him as he marched off the stage with a purpose.

He was, after all, the former Spencer Heir, the son of the deceased king of the City, James Spencer, whose tragic fall from the roof of Spencer Tower had been splashed across every news site in the country.

Bennett's heavy stare landed on me as he turned to walk back to his chair. Only he could strip me bare with a mere glance, and I felt myself flush from my cheeks to my chest as those eyes burned into me before he shifted his gaze down the row to his mother.

His face softened for her, and a tiny smile graced his lips at her exuberant waving in his direction. Brigette was now as happy and healthy as Bennett could have ever wanted, and he'd even finally come around on Martinez, who was head over heels for Bridgette and pretty much attached to her hip.

Though anyone who suggested Bennett call Martinez his daddy received a look that could flay flesh from bones.

Unlike my other two loves, Bennett had washed his hands completely of what was left of the Spencer empire. He'd tossed out anyone who'd ever floated even remotely close to James Spencer's inner circle, then he sold everything off to buyers we'd thoroughly vetted. It wasn't what he wanted to do with his life—"Fuck banking and finance," he'd said—so now the man who was once my most rigid, strait-laced, corporate-world-bound best friend had no concrete plans after graduation.

And he liked it.

Bennett was richer than sin and wouldn't need to work a day in his life, but I'd insisted he find something to busy himself with that wasn't his preferred activity—watching me. I assigned him a spot on the board of the Knight Foundation because if there was one thing Bennett knew how to do, it was spend money. The Foundation had more funds to give away than it knew what to do with from even the small fraction of a stake it had retained in my dad's miraculene research, and Bennett seemed excited to start giving it all away to charities and causes that struck his fancy.

And maybe, on the days he wasn't doing that, or working out at Dom's, or stalking me around the Academy, he might visit our park.

Bennett had ordered Spencer Tower demolished as soon as it had been cleared of its occupants. He'd wanted that blight removed from the City's skyline, ridding us of the reminder of the man who'd orchestrated the murder of my parents and countless other atrocities. In its place stood a riverside park—a gorgeous green space surrounded by cherry trees and containing flower-lined sidewalks, benches, and a small playground.

He'd named it Angel Park.

I turned into an emotional wreck almost every time we visited. Bennett's love for me—and mine for him—was something so profound, something so powerful and deeply ingrained within our souls, that I marveled over how I'd ever thought I could live without him.

At long last, the dean wrapped up the ceremony, congratulated our Class of 2025, and then caps flew into the air to cheers and applause.

My boys converged on me, and I managed to steal a kiss from each of them before pulling them in close. They surrounded me, their hands on my body as I tried to find purchase on each of them, and the boisterous noise of the room fell away as we stood together, my boys and me, quietly absorbing it all.

It was the end of our time together as Holywell students. Our journey back to each other began right here in this dining hall less than three years ago. I came here to deceive my old best friends, to steal from them, to begin my quest to destroy their Families in the name of the parents that had been stolen from me.

And I'd done it. *We'd* done it. None of it had brought my parents back, but the emptiness I'd expected to feel for the rest of my life once I'd gotten my revenge had been filled with *them*.

I was whole, because this journey brought me back to Zach, Noah, and Bennett. We had each other, and we had our City.

"I love you guys," I said with only the slightest crack in my voice from inside our huddle. "I'm so proud of you."

"We love you, too, sweetheart," Noah replied, his long fingers threading through mine.

"Forever and always, baby girl," Zach said.

Bennett's stare burned into me one more time as he tilted his head down to press his forehead to mine. He whispered, "Ours."

BENNETT

I stared at my reflection in Jolie's bathroom mirror, finally loosening my tie after the end of a long fucking day.

We'd graduated. Once upon a time, this day was supposed to come with the tiniest hint of freedom for my brothers and me—access to our trust funds, a little more power, and a lot more responsibility within the Families. I'd looked forward to it with equal parts excitement and dread.

Then my Angel returned to me, rid the City of the cancer that was the Four Families, and changed the course of my life forever.

Now it was only her.

So instead, this day had come with a huge party thrown at our penthouse pool with our loving family members and true friends. I now had a bright future that was mine to do whatever the fuck I pleased with it.

First, I would be finally taking off this suit and curling my body around Jolie while I slept for twelve straight hours.

I'd just begun unbuttoning my shirt when I heard, "Oh, holy *fuck*, Princess," from the bedroom.

Curious, I wandered out of the bathroom and froze.

Joanna Miller stood in the bedroom doorway, her smile wicked as she passed that violet gaze over the three of us. She'd dyed her hair and eyebrows the same dark brown from her first semester at Holywell, and she wore ripped jeans, a purple tank top, and her ratty sneakers that I'd tried to get her to throw away for years now with no luck.

I could only gape at the mirage of the girl who'd stirred up so much fucking trouble that semester while she snuck around behind our backs.

"What's this, sweetheart?" Noah asked cautiously from his seat on the bed.

She took a few slow steps forward. "It's a graduation present, Noah. I thought you guys might like to fuck Joanna Miller, since all three of you apparently harbored that dirty fantasy back when I first came to Holywell."

I swallowed as I felt my dick wake all the way up. "You

mean we wanted to fuck some goddamn sense and manners into her," I growled.

Those purple eyes met mine in an achingly familiar challenge. "Come and get it, then, Spencer."

I tossed my shirt from my shoulders and ran for her. Zach and Noah were quick to follow.

We didn't let Jolie rest until the early hours of the morning. My Angel never did learn sense or manners, but she had my heart forever, anyway.

THE END

Do you want a sneak peek of the *spicy* prologue of Max & Frankie's novella coming later this year? Sign up for my newsletter!

ACKNOWLEDGMENTS

I have been staring at this blank page for some time now, as I quite honestly don't have the words for how humbled and appreciative I am of you, reader, and everyone who has come along on this wild ride with me in my first foray in both contemporary and Why Choose romance.

I love these characters, and just as it was with Mave, Ben, and all the Blackstone Academy team, I am so sad to be letting them go. Writing a true trilogy—with *three* love interests—has challenged me in ways I hadn't yet experienced since I first scribbled a book idea on a legal pad in late 2020. I'm tired, y'all!

BUT! I'm not really letting them all go quite yet, because if you know me, you know I cannot resist an unplanned spin-off for a side character or three, so to answer what I know is a burning question for many of you: *yes, Frankie and Max are getting their own story.* Probably a novella, probably mid-2023. Follow me on social media or sign up for my newsletter for all the details (especially if you want that sneak peek of their spicy prologue).

Keep an eye out also for bonus scenes and the like that may end up in the boxed set of this series—which I will definitely make happen if there is enough demand!

Thank you as always to my core team: my PA, Steph, my Alpha readers Morgan, David, and Delaney, and my beta team (sorry this one came in under the wire, you guys). Massive thanks to McKinley and Jamee at Hot Tree for their thoughtful editing for this entire series, to Cherie, of course, for the artistic genius of the covers, and to Corina and Morgan for proofreading.

A special thank you to all of the bloggers and bookstagrammers who have shouted this series from the rooftops. I've never had quite the reception for a book or series that I've had for this one, and every post, comment, and review has meant so much to me.

Thank you to the foremost purveyor of angel smut, Merri Bright, for the support, the friendship, and the love for this series you've helped to spread far and wide out of the kindness of your heart.

To my husband, as always—thank you for supporting me in this crazy journey.

And in case anyone was wondering, I am a San Antonio Spurs fan.

ALSO BY ELIZABETH DEAR

Blackstone Academy

New Adult, Paranormal Romance

Mave Fortune: A Rejected Mates Story *(M/F)*

Ben Fortune: A Shifter Love Story *(M/M)*

Knox: An Alpha's Redemption Story *(M/F)*

Asher's Story: A Blackstone Academy Novella *(M/M)*

Harriet's Story: A Blackstone Academy Novella (2023) *(M/F)*

A Knight's Revenge

New Adult, Dark Contemporary Why Choose

Storm the Gates

Seize the Castle

Kill the King

Max & Frankie: A Knight's Revenge Novella (2023) *(M/M)*

ABOUT THE AUTHOR

Elizabeth Dear is the super-secret alter ego of a chick who just wants a little romance and adventure in her life every now and then. She's writing the books she would want to read as an indie romance fanatic and voracious reader and is developing her brand of smart-mouthed heroines, sexy supportive men, and strong family bonds. She loves ALL the tropes and only hopes you enjoyed the ride. Please follow her at the links below to keep up with the latest news.

Sign up for my newsletter!
Join my reader group on Facebook!
Merch: www.elizabethdearmerch.com

Made in United States
Troutdale, OR
07/06/2023

11015900R00212